MARTYRS' SHRINE
The Story of the Reform Movement of 1898 in China

Martyrs' Shrine
The Story of the Reform Movement of 1898 in China

By Lee Ao

Translated by Leo Ding,
Tony Wen, and Wu-wu Young

OXFORD
UNIVERSITY PRESS

OXFORD
UNIVERSITY PRESS

Oxford University Press is a department of the University of Oxford.
It furthers the University's objective of excellence in research, scholarship,
and education by publishing worldwide in

Oxford New York

Athens Auckland Bangkok Bogotá Buenos Aires Calcutta
Cape Town Chennai Dar es Salaam Delhi Florence Hong Kong Istanbul
Karachi Kuala Lumpur Madrid Melbourne Mexico City Mumbai
Nairobi Paris São Paulo Singapore Taipei Tokyo Toronto Warsaw

with associated companies in Berlin Ibadan

Oxford is a registered trade mark of Oxford University Press

Published in the United States
by Oxford University Press Inc., New York

Chinese text originally published as
The Fayuan Temple in Beijing
by Lee Ao Publising Inc.
PO Box 26–35, Taipei, Taiwan
June 1991 © Lee Ao

Translated from Chinese by
Leo Ding

© Oxford University Press 2000

First published 2000
This impression (lowest digit)
1 3 5 7 9 10 8 6 4 2

British Library Cataloguing in Publication Data
available

Library of Congress Cataloging-in-Publication Data
available

ISBN 0-19-592438-X

Printed in Hong Kong
Published by Oxford University Press (China) Ltd
18th Floor, Warwick House East, Taikoo Place, 979 King's Road, Quarry Bay
Hong Kong

Preface

I decided to use *Martyrs' Shrine* as the name of my book seventeen years ago when I was jailed for the first time as a political prisoner by the Kuomintang (KMT). I have been jailed twice by the KMT regime since 1971. The first time I was jailed for exactly five years and eight months, and the second time for exactly six months. Added to the fourteen months I have been under house arrest, this makes for a grand total of seven years and four months.

I have been jailed in seven different rooms, including an unlit cell, the stinking Cell 11 of the Military Detention Center, a bungalow at the Unit of Benevolent Education, and Cell 32 of Taipei Prison. Cell 8 of the Military Detention Center is where I spent the longest period; I spent two and a half years alone in there. Cell 8 was less than two *ping* (or 0.6 square metre) in size. If one allows for the toilet and water tank, which occupied one quarter of the space, and the 'desk' which I made out of a broken door and which occupied another quarter of the room, there was not much space left. All my activities throughout the day, including eating, drinking, pissing, shitting, and sleeping, were confined to this small space. However, there was no shortage of life in the room; there were plenty of termites, cockroaches, geckos, spiders, and centipedes. None of them were restricted by the boundaries of the door and windows; they came and went as they wished. As human beings, we were worse than the dog and pig, and could only admire them.

Communication between Cell 8 and the outside world relied on a small rectangular hole at the foot of the wall, about 30 by 15 centimetres. The three meals of the day were pushed in through this small hole, along with drinking water contained in a five-litre plastic pail. Everything came in through this small hole, including any daily supplies one had purchased, a borrowed needle and thread or nail clippers, and everything went out through it, including letters and garbage. Even a cotton quilt sent in from outside was stuffed through this small hole after it had been inspected and rolled into a long cylinder. Although there was a door in this cell, it was extremely difficult to open, and was always kept closed. The windows high above could be opened, but the view outside seen through the grating was an expanse of grey wall and a deathly silence, which made you feel gloomy even when the sun was shining. During those gloomy days, year after year, I thought up several novels; one of them was *Martyrs' Shrine*.

As writing was prohibited in jail, I was only able to work out the rough plot of the novel so that I could follow up and write it after I was released. I was released from jail in 1976 and started, after I had settled some personal affairs, to work on the first few chapters on and off. In 1979 I started writing in earnest again and have been writing other things for twelve years. I have had one hundred and twenty books published; ninety-six of these titles have been banned by the government, and 117,600 copies were confiscated. During these twelve years all my efforts were dedicated to the writing of other works; as a result, the writing of *Martyrs' Shrine* was delayed. Only a little more than ten thousand words were produced in twelve years—I could never manage to get it finished.

The delay was not entirely due to lack of time, but also because I wanted to do the best job on it possible. Voltaire said: 'The best is the enemy of the good.' It was precisely because I wanted to make it my best novel that I took so long to write it.

After the ban on the establishment of new newspapers was lifted (which had been in force for thirty-seven years), I decided to establish the newspaper *Truth*. My aim in doing so was on the one hand to combat the corrupt KMT regime, to defeat it and bury it, and on the other hand to use the medium of the newspaper to start a trend that could be implanted deep inside the heart of the people, to help create the future of China.

I knew full well that as soon as publication of the newspaper began, I would be trapped by time, and that the completion of *Martyrs' Shrine* would be further away than ever. So I spent two hours or more every day working on it, and it took me just over a month to finally complete it at the end of last year. Evelyn Waugh said that it took him six weeks to finish the first draft of a novel; that was exactly how long this book of mine took to write. As it is only one of my epic novels, naturally I did not try to cover all possible topics; therefore it covers less than four hundred sub-topics, already an impressively high figure.

Martyrs' Shrine uses the concrete presence of an ancient temple (that is still in existence today) as the vertical line, and the historical people and events of the vanished dynasty as the horizontal line. All major topics, such as life and death, God and the Devil, monk and citizen, in and out, work and retirement, government and people, home and nation, emperor and courtier, patriot and traitor, barbarian and Chinese, domestic and overseas, strong and weak, group and self, collective and individual, public and private, emotion and reason, common and varied, leaving and staying, cause and result, and rule and aid, are included within the scope of my discussion. This novel has strongly expressed ideas and is unusual in the richness of its content.

Why is it unusual? Because *Martyrs' Shrine* is a historical novel. The typical historical novel is full of romantic nonsense, such as details about the imperial concubine bathing, or the washing of the Empress Dowager's feet: *Martyrs' Shrine* is completely different in style. The emphasis is on heroes. This is a masculine work, with only one woman (and an evil woman at that) appearing in the book. The content relates to the thoughts and activities of the men. It depicts male chivalry, loyalty, and determination, yet does not look down on women, a fact reflected in the sorrow of the Pearl Concubine of the Guangxu Emperor and Tan Sitong's parting from his wife. Nevertheless, the subject matter is not limited to the emotional relationship between man and woman.

The historical people and events described in *Martyrs' Shrine* have all been checked for accuracy, resulting in a much higher level of fidelity to historical fact than that of the professors of history. (For example, when Zhang Hao wrote *The Spirit of the Martyr and the Sense of Judgement*, the author appeared to be an expert on Tan Sitong. It states in the first few pages of the book that Tan Sitong lived for thirty-six years, but actually Tan Sitong was born in 1865 and died in 1898; where did he get the figure of thirty-six years from?) Having undertaken this historical verification, I tried to eliminate as far as possible all unreliable testimony (such as the *Xiaohong Anthology*, by Wang Zhao; the *Collections of Sight and Hearing in the Year of Wuxu* [the year of 1898], by Tang Caozi; and it would have been impossible for Tan Sitong to write letters to Kang Youwei and Liang Qichao while in jail), and to stick to the truth.

However, in order to meet the demands of the novel, I retained elements of crucial significance at key points even when there is doubt about their historical accuracy, such as the poetry written by Tan Sitong in jail: 'live or die, just be faithful and brave like the soaring Kunlun Mountains', which I have already investigated and verified in my book *History and Portraits*. But this comes under the scope of history, not of novels. In a novel, I have to treat these elements differently, even leave something in when I know it to be historically inaccurate. For instance, when Tan Xucong, the grandson of Tan Sitong, wrote the chronology of Mr Tan Fusen of the Qing Dynasty, he mentioned 'visiting the Martyrs' Shrine in person to see Yuan', but according to *The Diary of Wuxu* by Yuan Shikai, the place where he was staying was Fahua Temple. In order to enhance the dramatic effect of *Martyrs' Shrine*, I have followed the account given in the chronology without correcting it.

Generally speaking, the historical events in my book are faithful to historical fact to a very high degree. Besides history, a lot of what happens in the novel against the authentic historical background is of course fictional. However, the fiction is often heavily based on historical events. For example, in the novel 'a long row of square wooden window-frames' is seen by Tan Sitong in the Japanese legation. This 'long row of square wooden window-frames' is based on a photograph of the Japanese Embassy taken in the year 1900, which I used as a blueprint in my imagination. Moreover, the Martyrs' Shrine as it is today was photographed and drawn for me by Xu Yiqi in Beijing; the information about the tomb of Yuan Chonghuan was obtained for me by Li Rongsheng of the Association of Beijing Writers, through the good offices of Pan Junmi; and the present condition of the former residences of Kang Youwei and Tan Sitong was investigated for me by Chen Zhaoji. Qing Dynasty historians talked about 'the effort in the lines that can't be revealed', and 'the adjustment in the lines that nobody is aware of'. Generally speaking, this is also the case with this work.

Besides historical events, I have also attempted to remain faithful to history with respect to the characters. In terms of characters that actually existed and events that are known for certain to have occurred, I have conformed to historical fact as closely as possible. There are also a number of fictional characters in the novel. Even here though, I have tried to find some historical basis for them. For example, the monk Pu Jing is a combination of three historical characters. Insofar as he has participated in two revolutions, he is Dong Biwu; insofar as he has a detailed knowledge of Buddhist doctrine, he is Song Shili; and insofar as he has sacrificed himself heroically for the Communist Party, he is Li Dazhao. It is for this reason that I named him Li Shili, and included his name last on the list of twenty prisoners, including Li Dazhao, who are hanged. Another example is General Stilwell of the American Legion, who has a conversation with Kang Youwei. Stilwell did in fact speak good Chinese and was friendly to China. I have him come to China earlier and become friendly with Kang Youwei. There are a lot of adjustments like this in my book.

In general, during the writing of historical novels one faces the problem of having to express two kinds of truth, namely literal truth and artistic truth. There has been a great deal of discussion of this problem in the theory of novel-writing. In theoretical terms, *Martyrs' Shrine* is sometimes intentionally different. Sometimes, it ignores the conventional theories of novel-writing, both of the past and the present. It seeks neither to be a nonsense novel like *The Secret History of the Royal Court of the Qing Dynasty,* nor a modern technical novel. Therefore, it describes what other novels omit, and omits what others describe; save your words when you have to pass the bridge quickly, and explain in detail when necessary, ignoring the possibility that it may be subjected to the same kind of criticism levelled at George Bernard Shaw, which was that his plays were nothing more than extended speeches.

The conventional novel originated in the eighteenth century and flourished in the nineteenth century. It is already too late for the novelist of the twentieth century to develop it further. T. S. Eliot was convinced that there was not much more that could be done to improve the novel after Flaubert and Henry James, and he said that seventy years ago. If Eliot had lived to see the challenge presented by film and television seventy years on, he would have been amazed at how much novels have come to lack visual effect, and at how poorly they have fared compared to other media.

It is precisely because of this that I believe the novel will have little future, unless it can be made to concentrate on those ideas that can only be expressed by novels. Those who try to use the novel to tell a story and those who emphasize form are likely to prove equally ineffective in rescuing the novel from oblivion.

In comparison with the typical novel that has nobodies as its characters, I am glad that *Martyrs' Shrine* has heroes as the leading characters. What a wonderful thing it is to describe a hero and to inspire yourself and others. Tan Sitong, one of the heroes in this book, sacrifices his life for truth. As Zhang Taiyan describes him, he is 'among those who dare to die'; Xiong Shili calls him 'the only true man the Qing Dynasty has produced'. The goals to which he devotes his life are encapsulated in his book, *Benevolence.* At the end of the book, he is affected by the recent loss of Taiwan to Japan, and on the cover of the book proclaims it to be written by 'a Taiwanese' instead of giving his own name, to remind his countrymen of the loss.

Now I live in Taiwan, and have written *Martyrs' Shrine*. After one hundred years of silence, once again this is 'a book written by a Taiwanese'. I have been absent from my homeland for forty years. Publishing this book is a homecoming for me. In my transient existence, I cannot forget that I came from mainland China.

LEE AO
12 June 1991

The above is a translation of the afterword in the original Chinese edition.

Contents

A Brief Chronology of Chinese Dynasties

Xia	Approximately 16–21 centuries BC
Shang	Approximately 11–16 centuries BC
Zhou	
Western Zhou	Approximately 11 centuries to 771 BC
Eastern Zhou	770–256 BC
Spring and Autumn Period	770–476 BC
Warring States	475–221 BC
Qin	221–207 BC
Han	
Western Han	206 BC – 8 AD
Eastern Han	AD 25–220
Three Kingdoms	
Wei	AD 220–265
Shu Han	AD 221–263
Wu	AD 222–280
Western Jin	AD 265–316
Eastern Jin	AD 317–420
Southern Dynasties	
Song	AD 420–479
Qi	AD 479–502
Liang	AD 502–557
Chen	AD 557–589
Northern Dynasties	
Northern Wei	AD 386–534
Eastern Wei	AD 534–550
Northern Qi	AD 530–577
Western Wei	AD 535–556
Northern Zhou	AD 557–581
Sui	AD 581–618

Tang	AD 618–907
Five Dynasties	
Later Liang	AD 907–923
Later Tang	AD 923–936
Later Jin	AD 936–946
Later Han	AD 947–950
Later Zhou	AD 951–960
Song	
Northern Song	AD 960–1127
Southern Song	AD 1127–1279
Liao	AD 916–1125
Jin	AD 1115–1234
Yuan	AD 1271–1368
Ming	AD 1368–1644
Qing	AD 1644–1911
Republic of China	AD 1912–
People's Republic of China	AD 1949–

A Mysterious Coffin

Following a discussion of the funeral customs of Beijing, the stage is set for the story to unfold. We observe a man dressed in black, furtively and in the dark of night retrieving, or rather stealing, a corpse left, dismembered, and mutilated on the execution ground. Carried through the streets in a burlap bag, the corpse is finally placed in a plain coffin, which is then carried to a temple. We are not told the identity of the corpse but we do discern that the man in black is surnamed She. After leaving the coffin at the temple, one of the pallbearers who asks the name of the temple is told it is 'Minzhong Temple' (later renamed Fayuan Temple).

—◦◦◦◦◦◦—

The Milky Way is like a ribbon, running directly north to south across the sky. People in Beijing have a saying, 'The Cowherd is to the east of the Milky Way, the Weaving Maid is to the west. They can see each other for one day in the seventh lunar month this year, then they have to wait until the seventh day of the seventh lunar month next year.'

After the seventh day of the seventh lunar month, the Milky Way changes direction. There is another saying for this, 'A corner of the Milky Way has dropped off! A corner of the Milky Way has dropped off! Padded cotton trousers and padded cotton jackets!' That is to say, it's going to start getting cold soon. The next important date in the year is the fifteenth day of the seventh lunar month, the Ghost Festival. On this day, every household 'offers cloth-wrapped bundles'. 'Offering cloth-wrapped bundles' means going to the paper shop to buy gold leaves, piling them up into a small round tower, attaching wads of spirit money to them, and then putting them all inside a paper bag. The paper bag is specially made for the purpose; woodblock printing is used to print a decorative pattern on the front.

The living members of the family write the names of their deceased relatives on the bag, hang it outside the front door, and then burn it. When the bag is burned, two sheets of spirit-money have to be put to one side to be burned separately, to serve as 'postage'. In this way, the living 'remit' money to the dead by burning it.

Having taken care of the dead on the fifteenth day of the seventh lunar month, the fifteenth day of the eighth lunar month is the day for taking care of the living. The fifteenth day of the eighth lunar month is the Mid-Autumn Festival, when every family prepares reunion cakes. The cake is two centimetres thick and has six or seven layers. The ingredients include grapes, longans, watermelon seeds, rose petals, osmanthus, brown sugar, white sugar, 'black hair', 'red hair', peach stones, almonds, and flour. Only one cake is made in each steamer. The cake is cut the day after the Mid-Autumn Festival, and it is cut into the same number of pieces as members of the family, to symbolize the fact that the family has been reunited. So with reunion cake, everyone has a piece—not to eat it implies that you are not reunited with your family.

In this way, the Mid-Autumn Festival comes round again every year in Beijing. As one year follows the next, the various festivals and customs are repeated again and again. Getting together, getting together, getting together again. How many Chinese have dreamt of this while enduring hardship or exile, dreamt of this and wept? Eventually, the act of being united with one's family comes to be divided into many parts, just as the reunion cake is divided into many parts. And in the end, everything comes to nothing; except for the misery and the tears, it all comes to naught. All that is left is the coffin.

———— ⊃○⊹○⊂ ————

The application of lacquer to the coffin is an important event for people in Beijing. The finer the coffin, the more important it is that it have lacquer applied to it; in some cases, a fresh coat is applied every year. Only poor people are buried in an unlacquered coffin. Chinese place great emphasis both on how one lives and on how one dies; if anything, there is more fuss made over the process of death. Death is a more complex business in Beijing than in any other city. The most striking thing about funerary arrangements in Beijing is the practice of *gongfang*. The *gong* are round pieces of wood of varying thickness, which are stacked up one on top another crosswise and carried by *gong*-carriers, with the coffin on top. There can be either forty-eight or sixty-four *gong*; the more there are, the more prestigious and stable the coffin is. In fact, it can be so stable that a bowl of water can be placed on top of the coffin while it is being carried on the *gong* and not a single drop will spill out. The reason for this is that each *gong*-carrier walks without bending his knees, like a zombie. The man who directs them is known as the 'fragrant rod-beater'. He controls their movements like someone hurrying along a group of zombies, without saying a word; he issues his commands by beating a red sandalwood ruler thirty-eight centimetres long and 7.6 centimetres wide. All instructions, whether to lift up the coffin or put it down, speed up or slow down, turn a corner, change positions or shift the *gong* to the other shoulder, are issued by beating the ruler. Another characteristic feature of funerals in Beijing is the money-thrower. The money-thrower is a professional spirit-money scatterer. He wears a white sash around his waist to symbolize respect for the dead. Once the funeral procession gets underway, whenever it reaches an intersection, government office, or temple, the money-thrower comes forward and throws up into the air several pieces of white spirit-money with a hole in the middle, about the size of a rice bowl. When the spirit-money is thrown up in the air, it rises into the air about nine or ten metres like a white chain, and then flutters back to earth like a flock of white doves. The effect is so impressive that passers-by often stop to applaud.

All these practices symbolize the importance that is attached to death in Beijing. The living cannot make do with half measures when it comes to death.

⟨∘✦∘⟩

On the evening of the sixteenth day of the eighth lunar month (the first day after the Mid-Autumn Festival), a well built man dressed in black walked cautiously towards the Xisiganshi Bridge on the western side of the city of Beijing. As he came near to the grassy open space under the memorial arch, he ran over to a wooden pillar while removing a large hempen sack from his back. Under the moonlight, he placed a body that was lying beneath the pillar into the sack. He glanced quickly around the open space, then picked up some objects scattered on the ground and put them in the sack too. He then tied up the sack, threw it over his back and ran off.

After running one block he turned around, confirmed that there was nobody watching, and then turned off into a side street. Late in the night when the watchman beat the drum for the third time, he had already succeeded in leaving behind the Inner City of Beijing.

The Inner City had nine gates, popularly known as the 'Inner Nine'. The Outer City, lying to the south of the Inner City, had seven gates, known as the 'Outer Seven'. The three gates linking the Inner City with the Outer City were Zhengyang Gate (Lizheng Gate) in the centre, Chongwen Gate (Wenming Gate) to the east, and Xuanwu Gate (Shuncheng Gate) to the west. Carrying his hempen sack, the man in black bribed the guards to let him through Xuanwu Gate, and then turned left into an alley. He turned into another alley, then another, and finally into a cul-de-sac. There stood an empty house in the dead end alley with a small courtyard in front of it, where two men were waiting for him. A coffin had been placed in a hole in the ground, with the lid left open. On seeing him, the two men took the hempen sack from him, opened it up and placed the corpse inside the coffin. The man in black took the other pieces from inside the sack, examined them carefully, and placed them in the coffin too. He took a handkerchief from his waistband and wiped the face of the dead man.

The face had been cut with knives so badly that it was covered with blood, but the profile could still be made out. It was an imposing face, starkly clear under the moonlight. The dead man was naked, and his whole body had been sliced with knives so that there was not a single patch of skin left whole, and all his limbs had been broken. He had been executed by the 'lingering death'.

The 'lingering death', an agonizingly slow process of death by dismembering the body before beheading, was a method of execution developed in China around the time of the Liao and Song dynasties. It was designed to cause the victim as much suffering as possible before their death, and was used on traitors or other people who had committed a similarly heinous crime. The 'lingering death' was popularly known as 'scraping', or cutting off the flesh from the bones. The victim was tied to a wooden pillar, and the executioner then began to make tiny cuts with a knife, a process known as 'descaling the fish'. The knife used was twenty centimetres long with a wooden handle on which was carved the head of a demon; the knife's blade was extremely sharp. The Chinese expression 'May you die of a thousand cuts,' originated from this form of punishment.

After cleaning the corpse's face, the man in black arranged its limbs and then covered it with a thin quilt. He placed the lid on the coffin and then hammered in the wooden nails. The man lit an incense stick, placed it at the head of the coffin, and kowtowed three times before it. He then threw himself onto the coffin, wailing, 'Oh master, what a terrible death! Terrible!' It was as though all the tension of the last few hours was released in the flow of his tears.

The other two men were busy attaching ropes to the two ends of the coffin, which in turn were attached to a wooden *gong*, or a pole. This coffin did not have sixty-four *gong* or even forty-eight, just a single *gong* carried by two men. The coffin was an unlacquered one of the cheapest kind and the wood was very thin.

One at each end, the two men picked up the coffin. The man in black dried his eyes, picked up the incense stick, and walked ahead of them. As the watchman beat the drum for the fourth time—a signal that it was very early in the morning—it was already quite cold in Beijing.

<hr/>

Walking quickly, they came to a high red wall. The top of the wall was covered with grey tiles, while the lower part was coated with grey cement. They followed the wall until they came to three great gates. The gate in the centre was the largest, with a stone lion on each side. A monk stood in the middle, and waved to them to come in. Inside the gate on the right was a room with two long benches. The coffin was placed on these benches.

'Is everything ready?' asked the man in black.

'Yes,' replied the monk. 'We can start the funerary rites right away.'

'The sooner the better. We came here tonight to release the spirit.'

'Where are you planning to bury him?'

'We'll bury him on the east side of Wofosi Street by Guangju Gate. It won't attract attention there; nobody's likely to notice.'

'Good, good,' said the monk, placing his hands together. 'It's very good of you to do this, Mr She. To have the courage to go and collect the body when it's forbidden to touch it, this demands great virtue and great bravery. We are all filled with admiration.'

'You are too kind,' replied the man in black. 'What's really admirable is that you should agree to perform the funerary rites in secret to help his spirit escape to the afterlife.' The man in black made an obeisance, and then said, 'I leave the funerary rites in your hands. I have to go out again to prepare for the funeral.'

'By all means. Rest assured, we will take care of everything.'

Once again, the man in black made an obeisance, and then walked through the temple gate with the two other men. As they passed under the gate, one of the other two asked the man in black, 'What is the name of this temple?'

The man in black turned around and pointed to the name written above the gate in large characters—Minzhong Temple.

CHAPTER ONE

Minzhong Temple

Now our history lesson begins in earnest. The origins of Fayuan Temple begin with an emperor's defeat. In AD 645, Tang Taizong, the second emperor of the Tang Dynasty, returns to the capital, defeated in his attempt to subjugate a neighbouring kingdom to the north. Sorrowful for the lives of his soldiers lost in vain, he erects a temple and shrine in their memory, named Minzhong Temple, or 'Sorrow for Loyalty' Temple, as a martyrs' shrine. The tall shrine eventually falls into ruin, but the temple remains intact. The boundaries of Beijing change with the construction and reconstruction of the city walls and the rise and fall of dynasties, so that the temple is at times inside and at times outside the city wall. However, the temple remains squarely outside the political and cultural mainstream, and is the site of various tragedies throughout history, several of which are recounted here. A thousand years after its construction, the temple draws the attention of the Qing Dynasty emperors, one of whom renames the temple Fayuan or 'Source of Law Temple'.

In AD 644, China was ruled by the second emperor of the Tang Dynasty, Tang Taizong. After forcing himself to wait for many years, he finally made the decision to personally lead a campaign against the kingdom of Koryu in the north-east. At that time, Koryu dominated not only the Korean peninsula but also the Liao River valley in what is now north-east China. Thirsting for military glory, Tang Taizong could not stand this. Thirty years before, the campaign launched by the Sui Dynasty against Koryu had bled the country white and sparked a rebellion. It was this that had given Tang Taizong the opportunity to overthrow the Sui and establish the Tang Dynasty. Now, thirty years on, in planning his own attack on Koryu he had to be very careful.

Tang Taizong's plan was to conduct a lightning offensive using a small force of under 200,000 men. When he explained this plan to an old soldier who had participated in the attack on Koryu thirty years before, the old soldier told him that the Liaodong region was too far away, that it would be difficult to keep the army supplied, that the Koryu troops would put up a stubborn resistance, and it would be very difficult to bring the campaign to a speedy conclusion. However, Tang Taizong would not listen to the old warrior, and after Wei Zheng, the last of his ministers who was able to dissuade him, died, he decided to launch the attack.

By the third month of AD 645 he was ready to set out. The son who he left in command in his absence was worried, and wept for many days. When Tang Taizong finally set out, he pointed to his own clothes and told his son, 'I will not change this robe until we see each other again.' If he was not going to change his clothes, that meant he was confident of securing victory before winter came.

By the fifth month, the Tang army had fought their way to the gates of Liaodong, today's Liaoyang city in the north-east. After a bloody battle, the city fell. By the sixth month, they had advanced as far as An (located in the north-east corner of Gaiping County, Liaoning Province). Koryu had mobilized an army of 150,000 men, and a fierce struggle ensued. Finally, the Koryu army was forced to retreat. They adopted a scorched earth strategy, devastating the country for hundreds of miles around, so that the Tang army had no means of securing supplies. And so the war dragged on.

Summer came. Tang Taizong was still wearing the same robe, and refused to change it. The seventh month came and went; the eighth month came and went. The army was starting to run out of food, and the weather was beginning to turn cold. Tang Taizong's robe was torn and tattered, but when a new robe was brought to him, he refused to put it on. He said, 'My soldiers' clothing is falling apart; how can I be the only one to put on new clothes?' In the end, he was forced to withdraw. It took the army two whole months to get back to where they had started from; they did not reach Youzhou until the eleventh month. When they reached Youzhou, only one-fifth of their horses were still alive. Today, Youzhou is the city known as Beijing.

Tang Taizong was devastated. He took off his old robe, but he could not remove the emotional scars. He kept thinking to himself, 'If only Wei Zheng were still alive. If Wei Zheng were still alive, he would have convinced me not to undertake this campaign.' The Emperor sent men to Wei Zheng's tomb to erect a memorial stele; he also sent for Wei Zheng's wife and son to express his condolences to them, and to tell them how much he missed Wei Zheng.

The Emperor built a temple in Youzhou to commemorate the soldiers who had died during his campaign in the north-east. As he saw it, they had died far from home out of loyalty to the state. Their death was tragic, and their fate pitiable. He wanted the temple's name to express these ideas. The Emperor finally decided that it should be called Minzhong (Sorrow for Loyalty) Temple.

A huge hall called the Minzhong Pavilion was constructed within the temple. Placed within the pavilion were the memorial tablets of the dead soldiers, both the known and the unknown. The pavilion was so tall that a saying became current, 'The Minzhong Pavilion is so tall that you can touch heaven from its roof.'

This was the precursor to today's Martyrs' Shrine.

One thousand years passed. After one thousand years of war and strife, the high Minzhong Pavilion had already fallen into ruins, but Minzhong Temple still survived in all its stark grandeur.

The old city of Beijing, as it had stood at the time when Minzhong Temple was first built, had long since disappeared. No historical monuments survived that would have made it possible to trace the boundaries of the old city: the earliest surviving records were from the Liao Dynasty in the tenth century. The Liao built a new city at Beijing and Minzhong Temple lay within the confines of the new city, in the eastern part. In the twelfth century the Jin defeated the Liao, and rebuilt Beijing on a larger scale. A new city wall four times longer than the old Liao wall was built around the city. Minzhong Temple now found itself located in the south-eastern corner of the city.

In the thirteenth century, the Jin were in turn destroyed by the Yuan, and the city of Beijing was once again rebuilt. The whole city was moved north, so that only part of the north-eastern corner of the Jin city fell within the walls of the Yuan city. Minzhong Temple now found itself lying outside the city walls to the south-west. In the fourteenth century the Ming Dynasty drove out the Yuan, and rebuilt the city again further south. The city was constructed as a square, incorporating two-thirds of the old Yuan city. At this time, Minzhong Temple still lay outside the city walls to the south-west, but closer to the city than it had been one hundred years before.

In the sixteenth century, a high-ranking government official informed the eleventh Ming emperor that there were twice as many people living outside the city walls as inside, and that something should be done to protect them. As a result, in 1550 the Emperor instructed one of his ministers, Yan Song, to direct the construction of a new outer wall to the south of the city. The new wall was longer than the old city wall from east to west, but only half as long from north to south. The form of the old city remained unchanged from that time on, for more than four hundred and thirty years.

When the outer wall was completed in 1550, Minzhong Temple found itself within the walls of the city of Beijing. After ninety-four years, the Ming Dynasty was succeeded by the Qing, and the Manchus from the Liao River valley took control of China. Another eighty-seven years passed. In the ninth year of his reign (1731), the third Qing emperor, Yongzheng, remembered the existence of this 'martyrs' shrine', and had it renamed Fayuan Temple (Source of Law Temple). Forty-nine years later, the fourth Qing emperor, Qianlong, visited the temple and bestowed on it a memorial plaque bearing the inscription 'The True Source of Law', which was hung in the temple.

Another hundred and sixty years elapsed. There were now more people living in the vicinity of the temple, and unattended new cemeteries had been established in the vast area of donated land to the south of the temple. Many people from other parts of the country who had died in Beijing and could not be taken home for burial were interred here. Cremation was not popular at this time, and when someone died, in theory the body and coffin should be taken home for burial, which was no easy task. People who had been unable to return home while they were alive and who were buried there after death wanted to retain some connection with their home region, so the cemeteries were divided up into sections. People from Jiangsu were buried in the Jiangsu cemetery; people from Jiangxi were buried in the Jiangxi cemetery; people from Henan were buried in the Henan cemetery. There were also cemeteries for those who did not belong in any of the other cemeteries. Where it was intended that the deceased should be transported back to their home for burial, the coffin would be stored temporarily in the temple, placed on a long wooden bench in an empty room. Sometimes the coffin was left there for a long time; sometimes no one ever came back to enquire about it. If the coffin was badly made and the body started to decompose and produce a foul odour, all the monks at the temple could do was try to block up the holes in the coffin with a thick coat of lacquer. If the lacquer would not stay on, they would dispose of the coffin themselves by burying it in the cemetery for unwanted corpses.

In this way, the temples of Beijing came to take on a special function in the transition between life and death. Besides seeking their own salvation, the temples' monks had another important responsibility—to deal with matters of the spirit on others' behalf during life, and to deal with the spirits of the dead after death.

This was just as true for Source of Law Temple and its monks as for any other temple in Beijing.

What was different about Source of Law Temple was that it had a particularly melancholy atmosphere about it. With most of the other temples in Beijing, the reasons for their construction were relatively straightforward. For example, Longfu Temple and Fahua Temple were built by Ming emperors at the request of their eunuchs to glorify Buddhism; Huguo Temple and Pudu Temple were built on the sites of the former residences of Yuan Dynasty Prime Minister Tuogetou and Qing Dynasty Prince Regent Dorgon.

The situation with Source of Law Temple was completely different. Construction of Source of Law Temple began four years before the death of Tang Taizong, and the purpose of its construction was to commemorate martyrs who died for China. The temple's tragic atmosphere was present right from the start in its original name of Minzhong Temple. None of Beijing's other temples (such as Bolin Temple, Xianliang Temple, Puji Temple, Guanghua Temple, Baochan Temple, Miaoying Temple, Guangji Temple, Chongxiao Temple, Longshu Temple, and Longquan Temple) have names with tragic connotations. In some cases, the names are actually quite cheerful, such as Songzhu Temple, Ruiying Temple, Daqingshou Temple, and Yanshou Temple. Only Minzhong Temple has been gloomy and sombre right from the start.

The temple's subsequent history has reflected this atmosphere. Four hundred and eighty years after the temple was first built, a deposed emperor was imprisoned there—Qinzong, the last emperor of the Northern Song Dynasty. Qinzong had a pathetic existence. His father, Huizong, was a far better artist than he was an emperor. After letting the empire go to wrack and ruin for twenty-five years, Huizong passed it on to his son, who ruled for only one year before the dynasty fell, after which he spent thirty years as a prisoner. He must have spent a miserable time in Minzhong Temple, thinking back on his lost kingdom.

In the thirteenth century, the Southern Song also fell. Xie Fangde, a Presented Scholar from Jiangxi, was defeated in the resistance to the Mongol armies, and his wife and children were taken prisoner.

Xie changed his name, and supported himself by working as a fortune-teller. He refused to accept coins minted by the Yuan Dynasty, insisting that he be paid in kind. If people tried to give him money, he would fly into a rage, and hurl it to the ground. After his identity was revealed, he fled to the Wuyi Mountains of Fujian. Once the Yuan Dynasty gained control of the whole of China, in order to win over the Chinese they sought out former partisans of the Song Dynasty in the Jiangnan region to try to get them to serve the new regime. A list of thirty names was drawn up, including Xie Fangde. An ambitious local official located him and forced him to go north to the Yuan capital. On arrival in Beijing, he was installed in Minzhong Temple. While there, he saw the Cao E stele, and thought about this fourteen-year-old Han Dynasty girl who committed suicide while searching for her father's body. Deeply moved, he exclaimed, 'If a little girl is capable of doing this much, I can do no less!' He then proceeded to starve himself to death inside the temple. He was sixty-four at the time of his death.

Minzhong Temple had just this kind of melancholy history. In the fourteenth century Zhang Zhu, who was born in the reign of the first Yuan emperor and died in the reign of the dynasty's last emperor, wrote the following sad poem about the temple:

> One hundred steep staircases rise backward toward the blue heavens,
> Leaning against the rail, I face the overwhelmingly vast sky;
> Way up in the sky, there stand the Gold and Silver Palaces;
> Down below, the beautiful old country lies.
> Gone are the past and the old dynasty, and now I have become old;
> There has been so much change; I can only hope to be a hero in the next life.
> Pity those former dignitaries that used to reside at the south end of the city;
> Now, they still harbour the desire to re-establish the old dynasty.

It is in the temple's latter days that our story begins.

CHAPTER TWO

Decrepitude

Now we turn again to our story as we meet Kang Youwei, a visitor to Fayuan Temple in the year 1888. He encounters the abbot of the temple, surnamed She. The two engage in conversation, covering a wide range of topics, including certain aspects of Buddhism, the notion of good deeds, the history of the temple, and whether or not it should be counted as a good deed for the Tang emperor to have built the temple. They discuss various heroes and patriots of Chinese history. They discuss their own origins and we discover the identity of the corpse we encountered in the prologue, and its connection to Abbot She. Kang Youwei identifies himself as a political reformer with the goal of saving the country. He discusses the weaknesses of the traditional Chinese education he received, which only required him to read ancient texts and taught him no modern or practical material whatsoever—the sole purpose was to enable one to pass the civil service exam. He plans to petition the emperor through a formal petition process, to propose political change. The two men acknowledge the difficulty of effecting political reform against the strong forces of self-interest and the status quo. Abbot She invites Kang Youwei to lunch with him at the temple.

——◦◦◦◦◦——

In the afternoon of the second day of the first lunar month in 1888 and the fourteenth year of the reign of Emperor Guangxu, the ninth Qing emperor, a young man approaching his thirtieth birthday, walked slowly towards Minzhong Temple. The young man had large, piercing eyes, and walked with his mouth tightly closed. He was dark-skinned, and was easily recognizable as being Cantonese. His hair bound up in a queue, he wore a long, grey gown, a black jacket, and fur boots to ward off the cold. It was already one hundred and fifty-seven years since Minzhong Temple's name was changed to Source of Law Temple. The temple was located in the Xizhuan Alley just outside the Xuanwu Gate. Viewing the temple from afar, one could see the row of three great gates, each with two doors. Above the doors the gates were constructed in the heavy style of palace architecture; the walls running between the gates were topped with blue tiles. The first impression one received when looking at the gates was one of solidity; it was as though every part of the gates was weighed down by a thick, heavy hat, solemnly awaiting your arrival. The central gate was the largest and the most imposing, with a stone lion on either side. The central gate was open, but gave off a cold, empty feeling; no one was visible inside the gate.

Although it was the second day of the first lunar month and the whole city was bustling with the Chinese New Year celebrations, few people would come to visit a temple like Source of Law Temple. The most popular temple among Beijing inhabitants at this time was Dongyu Temple outside Chaoyang Gate. This was a Taoist temple dedicated to the Dongyu Emperor. The temple contained life-sized replicas of the seventy-two courts of hell. These were terrifying to look on; tradition had it that they were made by the noted Yuan Dynasty sculptor Liu Yuan. Some of the scenes of hell had mechanical operations, but these were halted after one visitor died of a heart attack. As can be imagined, the general tone of this temple was not very high. Dongyu Temple was visited by huge crowds of worshippers every Chinese New Year. From daybreak on, large numbers of men and women came to the temple to burn incense. In the rear courtyard of the temple there was a bronze ass, as high as a man and very finely cast. According to legend, this ass had special powers. If a sick person touched a certain spot on the ass's body, that part of their own body would be cured; if someone who wasn't sick touched a particular spot, they would never get sick in that part of their body. Touching the ass had to be performed at New Year, as this was when its spiritual powers were at their height. As a result, when New Year came around the ass was touched so many times that it took on a brilliant sheen. No one dared to openly touch its genitals, but it was noticeable that they were also extremely shiny. According to one of the temple priests, large numbers of people used to come to touch this part of the ass's body in the dead of night, most of them suffering from venereal disease.

Besides the bronze ass, Yuexia Laoren Temple was also very popular with worshippers. Hung up in this temple was a beautifully written couplet. The top line read, 'May all lovers under heaven be united in marriage,' while the bottom line read, 'Who you spend this life with is determined in a previous existence; make sure that you are married to the one you are fated to be with.' These two lines were taken from the *Tale of the Western Chamber* and *Story of the Lute* respectively. The exquisite way in which they were put together helped bring great fame to the little temple. All of the people who came to burn incense there were old women who brought their daughters with them. Sometimes when the daughters realized who the temple was dedicated to they were embarrassed and refused to bow down in obeisance, in which case the old woman would force her down, and the daughter would then go off in a huff. Others didn't realize who it was dedicated to, and made their obeisance in a haze of confusion. By the end of the day, the floor was covered with the ash from the incense sticks.

After praying for health and longevity at Dongyu Temple and praying for a happy marriage at Yuexia Laoren Temple, one still had the problem of money to deal with. Both men and women flooded into Temple of the God of Wealth outside the Guangan Gate. Temple of the God of Wealth had a huge incense burner in which large numbers of people came to burn incense. As soon as an incense stick was placed in the burner, the priest in charge would pull it out and throw it into the pool of water underneath. Those people who wanted their sticks to be left in to burn for a little longer would beg the priest to leave theirs in, but there was nothing the priest could do, unless the incense stick had been purchased at the temple, in which case it could be left in for a little longer. The temple also produced large quantities of paper ingots. These were not for sale, which would have been sacrilegious, but if worshippers were prepared to make a large enough offering the deity might be prepared to give them some. In this way, the one who really got rich from the worship at Temple of the God of Wealth was the God of Wealth himself.

Compared to all this, Source of Law Temple was a quiet place.

The main hall of Source of Law Temple was not high; the main entrance could be reached by climbing up only eight steps. There were four doors in the middle of the entrance, but only the central two opened. Couplets were hung on either side of the main entrance, with a latticed window above. Above the window was a board bearing the inscription 'Daxiong Precious Hall' or 'The Treasure Hall named Great Hero'. By the side of the steps leading up to the main entrance were some old steles, as the temple had been built over a thousand years before, there were many ancient monuments of this kind. Some of the steles were supported on a stone platform in the shape of a giant turtle. These turtles, known as *guidie*, first began to appear in the Tang Dynasty. The turtles' heads were raised upwards at an angle, as though they could hardly bear the great weight of history on their backs.

The young man stood in front of the first stele besides the steps and carefully scrutinized the inscription. He then squatted down to look at the *guidie*; he seemed more interested in the *guidie* than in the inscription. In China, the turtle is a symbol of fate. Far back in antiquity the Chinese developed the practice of roasting tortoise shells to read the future from the cracks that appeared in the shell. As the Chinese see it, the long-lived turtle has accumulated enough experience to be able to warn people of what the future will bring. Unfortunately, turtles cannot speak, so the only thing to do is to 'torture' them with fire to get them to 'confess'. The cracks that appear in the shell can be interpreted to find out what the omen is.

When Tang Taizong was preparing to kill his brothers to seize power, those around him urged him to act quickly, before his brothers killed him. Nevertheless, he hesitated, and finally ordered a tortoise shell brought so that he could consult the omens. Zhang Gongjin, a confidant, walked up, picked up the turtle shell, and threw it to the ground, saying, 'What is the sense in consulting the omens before making your decision? You already know that you have to act; if the omens say you should not do this, are you really going to go along with that?' So Tang Taizong did not consult the omens.

Prior to the overthrow of the Shang Dynasty by the Zhou, the omens were consulted, and it turned out that they were unfavourable. Everyone was afraid, but Jiang Taigong, a sage of the Zhou Dynasty when Wen Wang reigned, hurled the turtle shell on the ground and stamped on it with his feet, saying: 'What do dead bones know about the auspicious and the inauspicious?' So King Wu of Zhou went ahead and attacked the Shang after all. Nevertheless, with the exception of a few outstanding heroic figures like these, nobody in Chinese history has ever dared to fly in the face of this traditional belief.

The young man was lost in his contemplation of the *guidie*, and did not notice that a monk was standing behind him. The monk watched the young man with curiosity, scrutinizing the young man just as the young man was scrutinizing the *guidie*. Eventually the young man stood up, stretched, and walked around behind the *guidie*. It was at this point that he noticed the monk.

The monk did not look like a monk; he had a hard, decisive look about him, and was tall and well built. He was in his early forties and ruddy faced, with a pair of bright, piercing eyes below his thick eyebrows. The monk was smiling, and his thick eyebrows and piercing eyes radiated compassion. He didn't quite have the look of a bodhissatva, but neither did he have the fierce gaze of one of the Buddha's warrior attendants; it was as though both had been rolled into one. The monk's appearance startled the young man.

Looking at the young man, the monk also was startled. It was clear that this was no ordinary youth. The monk had met many people in his forty-odd years, but none with the special quality that this young man exuded.

The young man returned the monk's smile. The monk joined his hands in greeting, and the young man did the same. Neither spoke.

After a short time, the young man picked up a piece of stone and began to rub it. He spoke:

'Master, which of this temple's names do you think has the better ring to it, Fayuan Temple or Minzhong Temple?'

The monk showed no surprise at this sudden question. He answered straight away:

'For the living, Fayuan Temple is better; for the dead, Minzhong Temple is better; for a monk, both are equally good.'

The young man smiled knowingly, and the monk smiled with him.

'I think Minzhong Temple sounds better, because everyone has to die sooner or later.'

'Temples don't only exist to provide funerary rites for the dead, they also have the function of enlightening the living.'

'But when Minzhong Temple was first built, it was built in order to conduct the rites for the dead.'

'Conducting funerary rites is something which is done not only for the dead, but also for the living. When Tang Taizong buried two thousand of the men who had died all together and built Minzhong Temple to appease the spirits of the dead, this was partly so that it could be witnessed by the living.'

'Talking about Tang Taizong, Tang Taizong killed his younger brother Yuan Ji and seized his brother's wife, a woman surnamed Yang. Later on, he had his dead brother enfeoffed as King of Chaoci, and made the woman Princess of Chaoci. Even more remarkably, he made the son who had been borne to him by his sister-in-law the successor to his dead brother, whereas his brother's own five sons had all been killed by him. Would this also be, as you put it, appeasing the spirits of the dead so that it could be witnessed by the living?'

'I suppose you'd have to say that it would,' the monk replied, unfazed. 'Among all the past rulers of China, few had as many strengths as Tang Taizong. There are many respects in which he was unsurpassed, but he also had many weaknesses in which he was unsurpassed. The way he acted towards his father and brothers was unpardonable. In some cases he had no choice but to act in the way he did, in other cases he did have a choice. After he had acted, his good side came to the surface again, and he tried to make up for what he had done. I think he did a very good job of making up for it. The fact that he built this Minzhong Temple is evidence of that. From our point of view as monks, the fact that he was willing to build this Minzhong Temple was a good intention.'

'Might it not have been a form of hypocrisy?'

'In judging whether or not something is truly good, you have to look at what effect it produced. If what came out of it was good, then we can say that that was a good act. If the person didn't actually do it, but only thought about doing it, then that doesn't count. I think that the fact that Tang Taizong actually built the temple, whether it was out of remorse, regret, because of all the women he had left widows, or because he wanted to rebuild his popularity among the people, whatever the reason was, he did it. You can't say that this was hypocrisy; the most you can say is that his motivation was complex, that his motives weren't sufficiently pure.'

'My understanding of good is not the same as yours. If you want to decide whether someone is a good person or not, you have to look at their underlying intent, at whether or not, deep down, they are being hypocritical. It can only count as good if your basic motivation is good. Even if the end result is bad, that doesn't cancel out the good deed. By contrast, if the ultimate motivation is evil, then the deed is evil too; even if good comes out of it, you can't say that it was a genuinely good deed. In fact, this is true not only where the ultimate motivation was evil. Even if there was no desire to do evil, but also no desire to do good, and if good came out of it, you can't say that that was a good deed. To push the argument a stage further, if there was no underlying motivation to do good or evil, but rather a calculating desire to do good, then even if good came out of it you cannot say that it was a praiseworthy act. This is why they say, "If you are trying self-consciously to be good, then there should be no reward for your deed; if there is no desire to do evil, then even if the results are evil there should be no punishment."

The key point is whether or not the person is fundamentally good. Good should make itself felt naturally, rather than in a calculating desire to do good. Deliberately attempting to do good is too self-interested, it goes against the essence of good. The essence of good has no ulterior motive, the only goal lies in the good itself. As for doing good even without the intention of doing good, that's even more inconsequential; it just so happens that something good comes out of what you do. Of course, that's still better than when someone deliberately tries to do evil but something good comes out of it. There is nothing more ludicrous than when someone attempts to do evil but actually ends up doing good. The would-be evildoer finds himself being eulogized for his action—that's just too unfair! So as I see it, Tang Taizong's action was hypocritical.

As I just said, when judging whether or not a good deed is authentic, you have to look at what the person actually did, and not what they wanted to do. To use this standard may not seem very idealistic, but it has the merit of being objective. You are asking too much if you think you can determine a person's original intent. People are such complex animals, and their souls are so complex. The human soul isn't a simple thing; there's no clear-cut division between good and evil. The soul is actually a mixture of good and evil: it contains the good, the bad, the bright, the dark, the high, the low, the altruistic, and the egoistic. And these different elements aren't necessarily in conflict with one another, they are all mixed up together in an amorphous mass, so that even the person himself can't unravel them. Given that the soul is so unknowable, how can you use this kind of standard to judge whether someone is trying to do good, trying neither to do good nor evil, trying to do evil, or self-consciously trying to do good? The soul is a mess; neither the individual nor anyone else can understand it.

So I turn the whole thing upside down. I base my judgement on what was actually done. Perhaps my criteria are too all-embracing. They are wide enough to embrace all of the categories you just mentioned except self-consciously trying to do good—in other words, trying to do neither good nor evil, trying to do good, and even trying to do evil. As long as some good comes out of them, no matter whether it was intentional or not, and no matter whether the person was trying to do good or evil, as long as a good deed occurred, I view that as being praiseworthy. That's why I say that Tang Taizong's building of this temple was done with a good intention.'

'You're too kind-hearted, preferring to think the best of people. Your definition of a good deed is too all-embracing.'

'That may be true, but I do make distinctions. That's why I say that for Tang Taizong to build this temple was a good intention rather than a good deed.'

'By this standard, if building a huge temple like this only counts as a good intention, then what would he have had to do for it to count as a good deed?'

'It depends who we're talking about. If Person A has only one *liang* (1 *liang* = 0.04 kilogram) or tael of gold and contributes nine-tenths of it to the building of a temple, then even if that money is only enough to pay for a few bricks and tiles, it is still a good deed. If Person B has one hundred thousand *liang* of gold and contributes one thousand *liang* of it to the building of a temple, then that is more like a good intention; you can't really call it a good deed.'

'So Tang Taizong's building of this temple counts only as a good intention?'

'Tang Taizong was an emperor. Of course he had far more wealth than just one hundred thousand *liang*. So his building of Minzhong Temple can't be classed as a good deed. This is even more true when you consider that he was in a position to have prevented the events that led to the building of the temple from occurring in the first place. No one forced him to attack Koryu. If he hadn't gone to war against Koryu then all those people wouldn't have died, and there would have been no reason to build Minzhong Temple. If TangTaizong had of stopped himself from attacking Koryu, that would have been a good deed.'

'But if you follow this standard of weighing up actions according to the individual, then you end up being even more judgemental than me. Tang Taizong was surrounded by enemies on all sides; if he hadn't attacked them, one of them would have been sure to attack him. You are using the Buddhist code of behaviour, with its prohibitions against war and killing, to measure the actions of a man who rose up in revolt at the age of nineteen, defeated his enemies at the age of twenty-four, and established himself as emperor at the age of twenty-nine. Surely you are expecting too much.'

'There's some truth in that; perhaps I am being too judgemental. But when a person of importance makes a mistake, it's always a big one. If Tang Taizong hadn't been such an important person, I would not be so demanding. Because if you study the history of that era, you will find that at that time Koryu was no threat to the Tang

Dynasty. Although Koryu was oppressing its neighbour to the south, Silla, it had accepted tributary status from the Tang and was paying tribute regularly to the Tang court. After Tang Taizong launched his unsuccessful attack on Koryu and after he built Minzhong Temple, two years later Koryu sent ambassadors to apologize for their actions. They also sent Tang Taizong two Korean beauties as a tribute. Their actions show that at least as far as Koryu was concerned, Tang Taizong had no reason to fear that if he did not attack Koryu first, they would attack him. I think the main reason Tang Taizong attacked Koryu was because he wanted to establish himself as a universal ruler; you certainly can't call him a lover of peace. But I admit that you can't really expect someone like Tang Taizong not to want to go around attacking people.'

'So you feel his actions were praiseworthy?'

'Of course. When anyone performs a good deed, I am in favour of it. You can't ignore the good deed just because you don't approve of the person who did it. What doesn't count is if you just think about or talk about doing a good deed, but don't actually go ahead and do it. The good and the action are two different things; if you don't actually put it into practice, it doesn't count as a good deed.'

'Your emphasis on action, on performance, this goes completely against the thinking of every philosopher from Mencius to Wang Yangming.'

'That's true. Mencius believed that good lay in good thoughts. As he put it, "If the intention is there, it can be considered to be a good deed". Wang Yangming believed that goodness was what existed in the soul: "Goodness lies in the purity of what is in the soul". I do not agree with these abstract standards of goodness. Goodness has to be put into action, it is not enough merely to have it in your heart.'

'That seems a strange attitude to take. It's not sufficiently idealistic. Buddhism is an idealistic religion.' The young man seemed to be half-mocking.

The monk seemed slightly put out. He thought for a minute, and then said: 'True idealism has to do with overcoming the ego. When Sakyamuni was debating with the Harassan yogis, he said, "True enlightenment is to break away from subjectivity, to abandon everything". If a good deed is not put into practice, if you take the subjective view that merely wanting to do good counts as goodness, then this is a perverted form of idealism, not true idealism. The true path of idealism is to break away from this view that thinking and saying is enough. True idealism lies in telling people what the limits of idealism are, and what cannot be accomplished by relying on idealism. Take eating, for example: you have to physically perform the action of eating. It's not enough to want to eat or to say that you are going to eat; there has to be the physical action of eating. The same is true with goodness. There has to be action; without action there is no goodness, only "false goodness".'

'I'm impressed. But it still seems strange to me that you, a monk, a Buddhist, should take this attitude. I don't mean that as a criticism—please don't take offence.'

The monk smiled, and once again brought his hands together in the sign of greeting. He then stretched out his right hand, and pointed to the temple gate.

'It's the second day after the Lunar New Year; outside everybody is celebrating. For a young man like you to come here on your own to a forlorn old temple like this to look at the steles and *guidie* shows clearly you are no ordinary person.'

The young man laughed. Someone let off a firecracker nearby, and an echo could be heard a long way off.

'Judging from your accent, you must be from Guangdong?'

The young man's smile faded. He had heard the saying, poking fun at Cantonese too many times: 'There is nothing more fearful in heaven or earth than the sound of a Cantonese speaking Mandarin'. His poor pronunciation was even more marked here in Beijing.

'I come from Nanhai, in Guangdong. And you, Master?'

'Can't you tell from my accent?'

'This is my first time in the north; I can't recognize the different regional accents yet. I just know that you speak Mandarin very well.'

'You won't believe me when I tell you, but I also am Cantonese.'

'You too?'

'Yes, I'm Cantonese. From Dongguan.'

'That makes us near neighbours. But you don't speak with a Cantonese accent; how is it you speak Mandarin so well? Can we speak in Cantonese?'

'I'm afraid I can't speak Cantonese very well. I was born in Beijing, and I've always lived here.'

'Did your father always live in Beijing, too?'

'My branch of the family has been living in Beijing for over two hundred and fifty years now.'

'That long?'

The monk nodded.

'For a Cantonese to have come all the way to Beijing two hundred and fifty years ago, he must have come here to serve as a government official.'

'Actually, no. My ancestor came here as the retinue of an official. The official was executed by the emperor, my ancestor stole the body, buried it in Beijing, and remained by the graveside until he died. Since then, our branch of the family has always lived in Beijing—we have never gone back to Guangdong.'

'You said the official was executed by the emperor . . . was he from Dongguan too?'

The monk nodded, with an anticipatory look on his face.

'It was Yuan Chonghuan! Governor General Yuan Chonghuan!'

The monk smiled. 'I told you I could see at a glance that you were no ordinary man. I was right. To have such wide-reaching knowledge at such a young age, I'm impressed. Yes, you're right; it was Governor General Yuan Chonghuan.'

'Then I know your surname, too. Is it She?'

'Amazing. You really do have an amazing store of knowledge. How did you know my surname is She?'

'I heard years ago that when Governor General Yuan was executed on false charges, his body was dumped by the Xisiganshi Bridge, and that no one dared to retrieve it, except his servant, a man named She, who came in the dead of night and stole the body away. After burying it, he stayed by the tomb until his death; after he died, he was buried next to his master's grave. The She family kept watch over the tomb for generation after generation. How fortunate I am, to have run into not only a fellow countryman, but also the descendant of an honourable man.'

'You are correct in every particular. Governor General Yuan's tomb is in Beijing, in the Guangdong cemetery by Guangju Gate, to the east of the Outer Wall.'

'I've been there.'

'You've been there? I'm amazed.'

'Governor General Yuan was the first Cantonese to play a significant role in national politics. If the Ming authorities had not killed him, the Manchus would have been unable to invade China, and the whole course of Chinese history would have been changed. If the strategy that Governor General Yuan recommended had been adopted, the Ming would not have wasted so much money on the defence of Liaodong, the people would not have become impoverished, the rebellion led by Li Zicheng would not have occurred, and Beijing would not have fallen. Governor General Yuan was a figure of great importance.'

'Governor General Yuan was a great man; he was widely admired.'

'For your ancestor to remain by Governor General Yuan's tomb until his death, he must have been an admirable man himself.'

'He acted as he did because Governor General Yuan's character was so admirable.'

'Generally speaking, admiration for another's character has its limits. The fact that your ancestor dared to risk death by taking away the corpse and stayed by the tomb until he died demonstrates remarkable loyalty and moral rectitude.'

'You are too kind. But there was an even more remarkable example of moral rectitude. After Governor General Yuan was put in prison, a scholar named Cheng Benzhi appealed repeatedly for clemency for the Governor General, until the Chongzhen Emperor ordered that he too be executed. His body also was buried by my ancestor, by the side of Governor General Yuan's tomb.'

'I remember. Someone wrote ten characters on his tombstone: "Both of them crazy; both of them brave as lions." Isn't that right?'

'Yes, that's right. You really do have an incredible memory. Not only had this Mr Cheng not been a particular friend of Governor General Yuan, there had actually been some unpleasantness between them. Mr Cheng called on Governor General Yuan three times, and on every occasion the Governor General refused to see him. After the Governor General was arrested, he repeatedly begged for clemency for him, and in the end was sentenced to death himself. His dying words were, "I'm dying not because of a personal friendship, but for justice." My ancestor had been Governor General Yuan's servant for many years; what he did was motivated largely by private emotion. What Mr Cheng did was solely motivated by a desire for justice. When the emperor ordered the Governor General to be killed in a fit of temper, Mr Cheng spoke up for him. He was a man of great strength of character. Unfortunately, he was only a scholar; he had no special status, and was not well known. What Mr Cheng did shows what a great man Governor General Yuan was— the fact that he was able to move someone to do something like that. I can still remember a few sentences from the petition that Mr Cheng submitted. He wrote: "Among the great mass of sophisticates, Governor General Yuan stands out as a crazy man. His craziness lies in the fact that everyone else loves money, but he does not; everyone else fears death, but he does not. He is willing to take on the tasks that no one else dares to attempt, and he does not avoid that which everyone else most wishes to avoid." This is the origin of the words you saw: "Both of them crazy; both of them brave as lions".'

'Amazing.'

'Cheng Benzhi's description of Governor General Yuan as a "crazy man" was spot on.'

'You think so?'

'By the standards of the time, of course it was. The Ming Dynasty was corrupt, no distinction was made between right and wrong, and the eunuchs had amassed great power. Xiong Tingbi, the great general who had been successfully defending the northeast, had just been executed on a trumped-up charge; his head was paraded round the empire, his property was confiscated, and his family sold into slavery. Despite this, Governor General Yuan knowingly risked the same fate. He not only refused to grovel before the evil ministers at court, he had Mao Wenlong killed, depriving the corrupt ministers of their main source of funds. Who but a fool would act in this way? Ever since the death of Governor General Yuan, no Cantonese has ever played such an important role in government, and no one has been willing to act as crazily as he.'

'In the last few centuries in China it has been difficult for those wishing to achieve something significant in government; the forces of conservatism and the forces of self-interest are too strong. These two forces are so obviously powerful that anyone who wants to do something meaningful for the nation can guess in advance how they are going to end up. Since you know in advance what the end result is going to be, if you don't let the fear of death put you off, and go ahead and do it anyway, what is that if not madness? Anyone who takes action in this way can expect to come to a bad end.'

'Are there no exceptions?'

'Exceptions? In recent history, very few. Some people have managed to overthrow the forces of conservatism and achieve something meaningful, but they have had to appease the other party, the party of self-interest, to do so. Look at Zhang Juzheng, the senior grand secretary in the Ming Dynasty. He wouldn't have been able to achieve anything if he had not appeased the forces of self-interest. But having done so, what good did it do him? What became of all the great deeds he had accomplished? Immediately after his death, the legal system he had introduced was overthrown, his property was confiscated, and his eldest son committed suicide under torture. The gate of his house was blocked up so that no one could get out, and a dozen members of his family starved to death inside. Those who survived were conscripted into the army and transported to the frontier district. A tragic end.'

'Your knowledge of Chinese history astounds me. And I'm surprised your study of the subject leads you to take such a pessimistic view.'

'You are too kind. It's true that I am pessimistic. It was because of my pessimism that I became a monk; it was only after I became a monk that I discovered just how pessimistic one needs to be in this world. Ha ha ha.'

At this point, a young monk walked up to them. He could only have been around fifteen years old; fresh-faced, but with an air of courage about him. He joined his hands together in greeting to the monk, and said: 'Master, Master Fahai of Wanshou Temple is here. Their temple is performing the funerary rites for the mother of Chamberlain Li, and they want you to attend. I told them that you are busy on the fifth, as we have funerary services of our own to perform.'

'You answered well.'

'But he still insists on seeing you.'

'Tell him I have a guest, and cannot see him.'

The young man hurriedly waved a hand at the monk. 'Master, don't mind me. I was just passing by.' He made the sign for the monk to leave if he wished to. He extended his right hand with his palm upturned, and gestured to the monk.

'Don't worry,' said the monk to the young man, raising his right hand. 'I don't particularly want to see him anyway.' He turned around. 'Pu Jing, you answered him very well. Keep going along those lines, and get rid of him.'

'But he insists on seeing you.'

'Pu Jing, I'm sure you can think of something. Off you go.'

The young monk smiled, made a sign of greeting to the young man, turned and left. The monk watched him go, and smiled appreciatively.

'That young novice's parents starved to death in the Henan famine. His elder brother brought him here when he was eight years old; they had had a terrible journey to get here to Beijing. When they reached this temple, his brother told him to wait here, and said that he would be back soon. His brother said, "If you get hungry, eat the cornbread in this wrapper." He said, "There's only one piece. I'll wait until you get back and then we can eat it together." He sat and waited outside the temple until it was nearly dark; his brother still hadn't returned. He started to get worried, and began to cry. I saw him, and asked him what he was doing here. All he knew was that they had fled to Beijing to escape the famine; he didn't know if they had any relatives here. When I opened the wrapper and looked inside, I saw that there was a letter his brother had written, addressed to the temple. He said that he was not capable of looking after his brother, and asked the temple to take him in.

So you could say that he was accepted as a novice at someone's request. I felt I had no choice but to let him stay. I must say he was very obedient and never got in anybody's way; he helped to move the tables about and sweep the floor without waiting to be told, as though he wanted to earn his keep. But at night he would cry furtively, and sometimes I saw him staring at the temple entrance as though he were waiting for his brother to return for him; but his brother never came back. He has spent the last eight years studying here. He has progressed very well in his studies; he's quite bright.'

'I thought when I saw him just now that he looked an intelligent boy.'

'Just now he came to tell me that a monk from Wanshou Temple was here to see me. Do you know Wanshou Temple? It's that big temple just outside Xizhi Gate.'

'I haven't been there, but I've heard of it.'

'It's far more popular with worshippers than our little temple. They have several thousand Buddhist images in their One-Thousand Buddha Pavilion. You can imagine what the rest of the place is like. He said they were performing the funerary rites for Chamberlain Li's mother; have you heard of him?'

'Would that be Li Lianying?'

'That's him. He is the most powerful man in China at the moment. The Dowager Empress trusts him, and follows his advice in everything she does. He asked Wanshou Temple to perform the funerary rites for his mother, and Wanshou Temple is trying to get monks from every temple in Beijing to attend. We can't allow ourselves to participate in flattery of this kind; that's why I refused to see him.'

'I'm impressed.'

'Monks should have no interest in the trappings of worldly success. I don't know whether it's because they are too close to the seat of power, but many monks in Beijing curry favour with the officials. They show one face to high government officials and another face to the common people. But then that's nothing new.'

'This is probably the reason why government officials have always been helpful to the growth of Buddhism in China.'

'You're quite right. Did you hear the joke about the poor scholar who sees an old monk fawning upon a high government official in the temple? When the monk then proceeds to treat him in a disrespectful manner, he asks him, why the discrepancy? The old monk says, "You've got it all wrong. In Zen Buddhism, showing respect really means not showing respect, and not showing respect really means to show respect." The scholar slapped the monk in the face, and said, "Among us scholars, not slapping means slapping, and slapping means not to slap." Ha ha.'

'Ha ha.'

'That reminds me. I should ask whether you are a poor scholar yourself.'

'More or less.'

'Then this is my lucky day. I haven't been slapped yet.'

'Ha ha.'

'I forgot to ask your name.'

'Kang Youwei. The Kang is the Kang in 'kang ji xiao min' in the *Book of History*. The Youwei is the Youwei in 'yang qi shen yi wei you wei' in the *Book of Rites*.'

The monk nodded. 'What a fine name. It says in *Mencius*, "There are things that one should not do if one is to achieve great things in the future." If this applies to you, then I have to congratulate you. There are so few people who can live up to that requirement these days.'

'In difficult times such as these, it is hard enough just to refrain from doing the things one ought not to. For example, for you to refuse to attend the funerary services for Chamberlain Li's mother, this is no easy thing to do.'

'I have to say that's true; I dread to think how much inconvenience my decision will cause the temple. Some of the other monks disapprove of my attitude. In times such as these, even passive refusal to become involved in improper acts is difficult enough. As for taking a more active stance, that's quite beyond me. In any case, from a Buddhist point of view, to act is abnormal. "All actions are like a dream, a shadow, dew, or lightning." This makes it even more difficult to do anything positive.'

'Isn't that a quotation from the *Diamond Sutra*?'

'I'm impressed that you should have such an extensive knowledge of the scriptures. Where did you acquire such a wealth of knowledge? In Beijing, or in your hometown? Who was your teacher?'

'My teacher was the Gentleman of Jiujiang—Zhu Ciqi.'

'Ah, so you are a student of Mr Zhu's. He was a *jinshi* who wore only a plain cloth robe, was he not? I seem to remember that when he was serving as an official in Shanxi he insisted on walking everywhere, performing physical labour and eating only the simplest of meals.'

'That is correct.'

'Were you with Mr Zhu in Shanxi? Surely you are not old enough?'

'No, I hadn't even been born then. Mr Zhu was fifty-one years older than me; he was actually my late father's teacher, and a close friend of my grandfather's. I became his student when he was sixty-nine; I studied under him for six years until he died at the age of seventy-five. Before he died, he said that the books he had written would bring no benefit to China in the future; he burned them all. He was truly a great man.'

'What a waste.'

'I was twenty-four when he died. I already had a solid grounding in the Confucian classics, history, philosophy, and literature, and I had my feet set on the conventional path for a Chinese intellectual—reading old books, and preparing to take the imperial examinations for civil service. But Mr Zhu's actions had a profound effect on me, particularly when he burnt his own works one by one before his death. His *Record of the Dynasties*, his *Record of the Sayings and Deeds of Meritorious Ministers*, his *History of Mongolia*, his collected essays and poems . . . he burned them all; the floor was covered in ashes. I cried seeing him do it, I begged him to stop but he wouldn't listen. Mr Zhu was always a solemn man, when he burned his books he did it with the same calm detachment as always. Despite being so well read in the classics, and despite having secured the *jinshi* degree in the civil service examinations, before his death he demonstrated by his own actions that this was not the road that Chinese intellectuals needed to follow. He showed that we need to abandon the old paths of learning and take action to save the nation. It wasn't so much that he told us how we should act or what we should do; in fact, he said very little. All he did was demonstrate to us by example, in this way, before he died. When he passed away, it had been more than thirty years since he last served as an official. And yet, before he died he effectively disowned all that he had taught and all that he had written, on the grounds that it had no practical value. The burning of his books and his death came as a great shock to me. After his death, I came to Beijing to try to broaden my vision and to be able to think deeply about China's future. What had the most impact on me was walking through the *Kuozijian* Academy, or Directorate of Education. This is China's highest seat of learning for the cultivation of intellectuals. I walked through the door, walked into the *Liulifang,* or Lapis Hall, saw the Drum Tower and the Bell Tower; I saw the steles carved by Jiang Heng, and thought how he had spent twelve years carving those eight hundred thousand characters of The Thirteen Classics. The leading intellectual of his day spent all that time on it, and yet what use is it to China now? China needs to be saved, but The Thirteen Classics can't accomplish it! I bought a lot of books when I was passing through Shanghai. I purchased a large quantity of books on modern knowledge, published by the Jiangnan manufacturing office and by foreign missionaries. I shut myself away to study them for five years at our house at Xijiaoshan in Nanhai. I don't read any foreign languages, so I can only read works in translation, but what I've been able to learn from the translations is enough. What I learnt in those five years is that to save China we need to learn from the foreigners. We need to overhaul the legal system and undertake a comprehensive program of self-strengthening. That's why I have come to Beijing, to see whether there is any chance for me to put my ideas into practice. With it being New Year, I've taken the opportunity to indulge my interest in steles—that's why I came here today and had the good fortune to meet you. Although you've shared with me only a tiny fragment of your knowledge and wisdom, I'm already very impressed.'

'You are too kind. As a monk, I do not deserve such a compliment. You studied under Mr Zhu, and have steeped yourself in both Chinese and Western knowledge. We monks can only read a few books at best; there's no way we can stand comparison with true intellectuals such as yourself. What's more, you have set yourself the task of saving the nation and the people—this is not something that any monk could hope to do.

At that moment, they saw the young novice Pu Jing walking over towards them. The monk asked him, 'What is it, Pu Jing?'

'I finally got rid of that monk from Wanshou Temple.'

'Well done.'

Pu Jing was embarrassed, and laughed. He nodded to Kang Youwei, then turned to his master and said, 'It's almost lunch-time.'

'I know. Place a table in the small refectory; I am going to ask Mr Kang here to share our simple fare with us.'

Kang Youwei took a step forward and said 'Master, I don't want to put you to any trouble.'

'On the contrary, we would be honoured to have you eat with us. It's nearly lunchtime anyway, so why make a fuss about it? It's not as if we prepared anything specially for you, you will only be eating the same food that we eat.'

'In that case, I accept.'

'I'll go and get everything ready.' Pu Jing turned round and was about to leave; the monk called him back. 'Pu Jing, let me introduce you. This is Mr Kang, a scholar whom I admire very much, and who happens to be from my native area. Although Mr Kang is a real Cantonese, I can hardly compare with him.'

The novice joined his hands in greeting, and Kang Youwei did the same. Kang Youwei said, 'I seem to have been causing trouble for you ever since I arrived.'

'Not at all,' said the novice. 'If our master is so full of admiration for you, then we share that admiration. Our master would never invite anyone to eat with him unless he held great respect for that person.'

'All right, Pu Jing, you may go.' The monk smiled. 'You mustn't let your mouth run away with you. Go and get everything ready.'

'I'm going. You're in luck, Mr Kang; we're not eating steamed bread today.'

'Ha ha.' Kang Youwei laughed. 'This young novice of yours has quick reactions. He knows that Cantonese can't stand steamed bread.'

'And another thing, Pu Jing. Fry a couple of extra eggs, and come and eat with us.'

'Yes, Master.' The novice turned and walked off.

'He's quick-witted all right. Talking about steamed bread, that reminds me of another story about him. The first few days he was here, when he was given his piece of steamed bread for breakfast he would just eat half of it, and keep the other half. Sometimes when we had steamed bread for lunch too he would just eat one of the two he was given and keep the other one. Eventually, one of the monks who was sleeping in the same room with him told me that his bundle was getting bigger and bigger. I thought of an excuse to get him to open his bundle, and found that it was full of steamed bread. He had grown so used to adversity, and he was worried that his brother might be roaming around hungry, so he had only eaten half of his share of food. He opened his eyes wide, looked down at the steamed bread, looked up at us, looked down at the bread, looked up at us again, and asked haltingly if he could take the bread away when his brother came back for him. Listening to him, I couldn't help crying. When he and his brother had been fleeing the famine, they had eaten dead rats, tree bark, grass, maybe even human flesh. He remembered one time when his brother brought back a piece of meat that tasted funny. He asked his brother, "What kind of meat is this?" His brother frowned and said, "Don't worry about that, hurry up and eat. I'll eat what's left over."'

'That's what misgovernment does to the people.'

'But sometimes it's the result of natural disasters which you can't blame those in power for. From our point of view as monks, calamity is hard to avoid.'

'Master, you have a natural tendency to sympathize with others, so you are bound to forgive those in government for failing in what is actually their duty. While I was studying at Xijiaoshan, I read a lot about famine in Chinese history. When people refer to "natural and man-made disasters" as being one and the same, it's not without reason. Whenever a natural disaster occurs, we think of it as being a wholly natural event, but in fact there are human causes at work too. Take floods, for example. A flood happens because a river contains more water than it can disperse. But the reason why the river contains more water than it can disperse is because the irrigation and drainage canals are controlled by rich families who are in collusion with government officials. The land near these canals is fertile and easy to irrigate, so the rich and the officials collude with one another to stop up the canals. They not only refuse to open the canal gates, they actually increase the height of their own fields, so that the fields belonging to ordinary farmers become low-lying areas that are more liable to flood. This kind of flood is actually man-made, not natural in origin. It's unfair to put the blame on Heaven.'

'Fancy that. Well, I'm a city dweller; I don't know much about these things.'

'And am I not the same? If I hadn't had the urge to start studying works of practical value, and had read only the Four Books and Five Classics, then all I would know would be the reference in the *Book of History* to "flood waters rising so high that they engulfed Hsiang Ling", or the passage in *Mencius* about "floods devastating the land". I could only be helpless, blaming Heaven too, not man. But since I started to study works of practical use for government, I've gradually started to see the light. When I was reading the section of *A Comprehensive Report of Industries*, "Monetary System and Taxation System in the Song Dynasty", and I read references to "lakes being dyked off and turned into fields", describing how after the land immediately adjacent to the lakes had been converted into fields, "the inhabitants of two prefectures were affected either by drought or by floods every year", and how "the area of fields that were abandoned ran into the tens of thousands", I realized how drought and flood are actually the result of human action. And when I read Shao Bowen's *Record of Things Heard and Seen*, describing how when the Yin River and Luo River flooded, "the local inhabitants' houses were all destroyed; only to the east of the Yin River where the holes in the dykes were stuffed full of brushwood was the land belonging to the chief minister of state saved from flooding", I suddenly realized what was going on.'

'You are obviously skilled at making connections when you read. I am filled with admiration.'

'You are too kind. I was lucky to benefit from the example of Mr Zhu, to be able to shut myself away for five years, and to avoid the traditional methods of studying old books. That is the only reason why I was able to gain the insights I have.'

'What has brought you to Beijing this time?'

'I've been thinking it out over and over, and I've come to the conclusion that the only thing I can do is to submit a petition directly to the emperor. The only way the nation can be saved is if I can convince the emperor to undertake large-scale reforms; that would solve the problem at its root.'

'How many times in history has anyone ever been successful in bringing about reforms through a petition? The only example I can think of is Wang Anshi, a prime minister in the Song Dynasty, and even he failed in the end. The reactionary forces and the forces of self-interest have always been obstacles for reform; unless you can overcome these two obstacles, you can expect the end result to be tragic.'

'From my point of view, it's still too early to talk about a tragedy, because I still haven't been able to get my petition submitted. You know how it is, if there is no high official who is willing to present your letter on your behalf then the emperor won't see it, commoners are not permitted to submit communications directly to the emperor. If a commoner did try to submit one directly, they might end up being exiled to the frontiers to become a slave; there were cases in the Qianlong era when that happened.'

'So you haven't found a high official willing to deliver your letter for you?'

'I've asked many, and none of them has been willing to do it. None of them wants to burden themselves with any extra work. They are happy enough to hold official posts, but they don't want to do an official's work.'

'So that's why you have come to this old temple to look at steles on the second day of the Lunar New Year?'

'Talking about old steles, I must admit that's something I am really interested in. Since I've been in Beijing I've bought many books on stele rubbings, with the idea of teaching myself something completely useless to sharpen my mind. You never know when something that seems totally useless may come in handy. Take Wang Xizhi's Cao E stele, for example. Who would have thought that it would be seeing that inscription that would have led Xie Fangde to starve himself to death in this temple, so that he ended up dying a noble death?'

'As far as dying a noble death is concerned, Xie Fangde was already thinking about death; he already had his feet planted on that road. When he saw the Cao E Stele in this temple, that merely put the finishing touches to his plans to kill himself—the idea of doing so was already there. The same is true of you. You have already mapped out the path you wish to take, which is to save China, and spent many years preparing yourself. All that is left is the final touches. Get it right, and you will be like a dragon flying up into the heavens; get it wrong, and you will be like a dragon plunging into the sea. Either way, you will have achieved self-fulfilment.'

'And you?'

'I am a monk.'

'Surely that doesn't preclude you from taking an interest in China's future?'

'I am concerned about the nation's future.'

'Being concerned isn't the same as doing something about it.'

'It can be.'

'Didn't you just say that a good deed has to actually be performed, that it isn't enough just to have the intention to perform a good deed? Surely, judged by this standard, you are not doing enough.'

'I am only a monk. What do you expect me to do? I have very little power. The most I can do is to refrain from doing evil myself, to not allow myself to be stained by the general atmosphere of corruption, to not go to Wanshou Temple to fawn upon those in power, to keep my hands clean, like a, like a, like a what?'

'Like the lilacs in the temple here.' Kang Youwei pointed to an array of purple flowers.

'Alright, then. Like the lilacs in the temple.'

Source of Law Temple was famous in Beijing for its many lilacs. The first of them had been brought to Beijing from Guangdong several hundred years previously. In China, lilacs are used to produce medicine for treating stomach complaints, cholera, for removing abscesses, and curing bad breath.

'Lilacs are beautiful to look at, and they have a nice scent. But to turn them into medicine, you have to grind them up into powder or use them to make broth. If you don't crush them and grind them up, they are only good for looking at and smelling,' said Kang Youwei.

As he listened, the monk stared at Kang Youwei motionlessly. Finally, he nodded, turned round, and extended his right arm. 'Let's go and eat.'

CHAPTER THREE

Put Aside Your Fear of Death

The two men continue their conversation over a meagre vegetarian lunch. Pu Jing, the young novice, occasionally joins in. They discuss the fine distinctions between traitors and loyalists, with a historical revue of several figures who were wrongly labelled as one or the other. They discuss the nature of loyalty and the relationship of outstanding individuals to their peer group. Abbot She warns that the group will ultimately reject its outstanding individuals and even attack them. Finally, the meal finished, the three retire to the study, where a scroll hangs containing a poem which they read and discuss. Abbot She asks Kang Youwei to write some calligraphy to leave at the temple as a memento of his visit. Kang Youwei, an accomplished calligrapher, agrees. After he is finished they discuss the latent meaning of the poem, which was first written by the famous Chinese poet Du Fu. At last the men part company.

──◦◦◦◦◦──

When they entered the refectory, the meal had just been served. Instead of rice there was sorghum mixed with millet; ordinary people in Beijing rarely ate rice, because it was too expensive. There were only three plates of side dishes, two large and one small. There was one large plate of stewed cabbage and tofu, one large plate of fried eggs and one small plate of squash in soy sauce. The monk invited Kang Youwei to sit; the chairs were hard wooden ones which allowed only a rigidly erect posture. The food was placed on a rectangular table; it was an ordinary table, coated with red lacquer so that it would not be damaged if hot soup were spilled on it. A poem was hung up on the wall facing the table. It read:

> *Once there was a minister named Gong Shengzu in the West Han*
> *Dynasty, who could fast for fourteen days.*
> *Now I have been fasting for half a day, suffering from hunger and thirst;*

While I am hoping to fulfil my desire for death, I have yet found no way
    to accomplish it.
High is my spirit, as high as Heaven,
Food holds no interest for me.
It may be either that I have not accomplished my assigned task, or that I
    have not repaid to the world what I owe.

This was the poem which Xie Fangde wrote while fasting to death. To hang this poem by a martyr who starved himself to death in the temple refectory made for a highly meaningful contrast.

The monk waited until Kang Youwei had finished reading the poem hung on the wall, and then invited him to start eating.

'As I said just now, we haven't prepared anything special for you. You are eating the same food that we eat. Please go ahead. By conventional standards I should be ashamed to present you with these meagre dishes, but I am sure you will not object.'

'Not in the least.'

The three of them began to eat. Before the monk started to eat, he split his portion of egg into two halves, and said, 'You two can have the egg; I don't eat eggs. The poem which you read just now was copied out by a monk of this temple a little over a century ago. You are an expert, Mr Kang. What do you think of the calligraphy?'

Without needing to look back at the poem, Kang Youwei answered straight away, 'It's well written; a fine example of the Zhao style. Although, using the style of calligraphy developed by Zhao Mengfu to copy out Xie Fangde's final poem isn't really very appropriate.'

'Why is that? The reason escapes me.'

'They were contemporaries! Zhao Mengfu surrendered to the Yuan regime, while Xie Fangde refused to collaborate with the Yuan. If Xie Fangde knew that his final poem had been copied out using the Zhao style of calligraphy, he'd roll over in his grave!'

'Of course! You're right. We're all too ill-educated to have noticed. You are right, it's quite ridiculous.'

Kang Youwei smiled, with a slight air of self-satisfaction. The monk asked him:

'Why would the monk who wrote this over a century ago have used the Zhao style? What would be the reason?'

'There's a very good reason. One hundred years ago was the Qianlong era, and the Qianlong Emperor liked the Zhao style! So the Zhao style became very popular. Prior to that, Qianlong's father and grandfather, Kangxi and Yongzheng, were both fond of Dong Qichang, so Dong Qichang's style of calligraphy went through a period of popularity during their reigns. It all boils down to imitation of those in power; that's one of China's main characteristics. That's why if you want to get anything done in China, you have to do it from the top down.'

'The Qianlong Emperor's fondness for Zhao Mengfu's calligraphy can't have been as simple as all that, surely. There must have been some political motivation.'

'The political motive is fairly obvious. The Yuan Dynasty were Mongols: in Chinese eyes they were barbarians. Zhao Mengfu was not only a Chinese, he was a member of the Song imperial family. For the Yuan to have someone like this come over to their side was very useful for them in ruling China. The Qianlong Emperor was a Manchu; in Chinese eyes he also was a barbarian. So of course he would want to make use of Zhao Mengfu, all the more so since he really was fond of Zhao's style of calligraphy.'

'So Zhao Mengfu was a traitor to the Chinese race?'

'Deciding whether someone is a traitor depends on what standard you use to judge them by. If you take the view that Han Chinese, Manchus, Mongols, and Tibetans are all part of the Chinese people, then there can be no such thing as a traitor to the Chinese race. And of course questions of loyalty and treachery aren't that simple or clear-cut to begin with. The more history you read, the more you come to realize that the opposites we are used to thinking in terms of, like right and wrong and good and evil, are not as straightforward as they seem. Often, it isn't that clear who is on which side; both parties may have elements of both in them. Sometimes, you have the embarrassing situation of things being the exact opposite of what they seem. Starting from the *New History of the Tang Dynasty* compiled by literary giant Ouyang Xiu of the Song Dynasty, the dynastic histories have always contained "Biographies of Loyal and Disloyal Officials"; the *History of the Song, History of the Liao, History of the Yuan,* and *History of the Ming* all followed Ouyang Xiu's example, and, as a result, the division made between loyal and disloyal officials has come to be more and more pronounced. Besides the official dynastic histories, the judgements in popular novels and operas as to which officials were loyal and which were disloyal have also been very influential. In opera, in particular, in order to help the audience to tell at a glance which officials were loyal and which were disloyal, red and white face paint started to be used. Loyal officials like Guan Gong were given red faces; traitorous characters like Cao Cao were given white faces. This kind of distinction is very convenient for the audience; it helps them to know who to root for and who to hate. The problem arises when you get it wrong. If you look at the list of names included in the "Disloyal Officials" section of the *History of the Song,* many of them were not disloyal at all, people like Chao Si. And some people who should have been included as "disloyal officials", people like Shi Miyuan, got left out! So making a distinction between the loyal and the disloyal is not as simple as it seems in the histories and in popular legends. Take Cao Cao, for example. Not only was he not a treacherous official, he was actually a heroic figure. The judgement made on him is one of the easiest to be overturned. With others, like Feng Dao, the situation is more complex. In the chaotic era of the Five Dynasties, Feng Dao refused to conform to conventional definitions of loyalty and disloyalty. He was willing to serve any emperor, any dynasty, if it would enable him to achieve some benefit for the people. During the Song Dynasty, Tang Zhixiao, a fellow high-ranking official asked Wang Anshi whether Feng Dao could be considered a pure official when he had served four different dynasties and ten different rulers. Wang Anshi's reply was that Feng Dao was the epitome of a pure official. Wang Anshi took Yi Yin as an example. He said, "Yi Yin served King Tang five times, and he served King Jie five times. His motivation for doing so was to help the people." In shifting his allegiance back and forth between King Tang of the Shang Dynasty and King Jie of the Xia, Yi Yin was not concerned about being loyal to any given ruler; he was concerned only with looking after the interests of the common people. Wang Anshi felt that Feng Dao's willingness to humiliate himself was a sign of almost Buddha-like greatness. For example, when the Khitan invaded China, butchering the people and destroying cities, none of China's heroic generals was able to save the people. And yet Feng Dao was able to save the people of China by talking the Khitan emperor into sparing their lives. When Ouyang Xiu was writing the *New History of the Five Dynasties,* although he was generally critical of Feng Dao, he had to admit that it was thanks to Feng Dao that the Chinese people were spared genocide. Feng Dao saved the lives of millions of Chinese; that's far more than any other patriot has ever achieved. Is it really fair to call him a "traitor to the Chinese race" for collaborating with the barbarians in this way?'

'So judging by this standard, wasn't Xie Fangde's death a meaningless one?' asked the monk.

'The value of Xie Fangde's death lay in the fact that he died for something he believed in. As to whether his belief was a correct one, and as to whether his death was worthwhile, that is another matter. This kind of thing may come to seem unimportant or even wrong-headed with the passage of time. For example, Xie Fangde was loyal to the Song Dynasty, but how did the Song take power? They stole it from out of the hands of widows and orphans. Xie Fangde must have been aware of this. The founder of the Song Dynasty was a minister who betrayed the dynasty he served, the Later Zhou; you have to say that he was a "disloyal official". So the loyal official Xie Fangde died for a regime established by a disloyal official. If you go back far enough in this way, his death comes to seem totally meaningless, doesn't it?'

'Did Xie Fangde himself know this?'

'I think he must have, but he chose not to think about it too carefully.'

'Why?'

'Because by his time there had been eighteen Song emperors; three hundred and twenty years had elapsed. Xie Fangde died ten years after the Song fell; for him, an old debt dating back three hundred and thirty years had no meaning at all.'

'So it was not important.'

'You can't say that it was not important; it was just that he did not want to think about it that way.'

'Why?'

'Because loyalty had already become a habit to him. The Song Dynasty had been in power for three hundred and twenty years; three hundred and twenty years in which officials had been taught they had to be loyal to their ruler. Enough time had passed for everyone to come to see the Song regime as legitimate. The passage of time can make the unlawful seem lawful, "loyal officials" are created by time. If enough time hasn't elapsed, it won't work. In the Five Dynasties era which preceded the Song, in the space of fifty-three years there were five different dynasties, eight different ruling houses and thirteen different rulers. All this in the space of just fifty-three years. With one regime succeeding another at such a rate, how could you say who the empire really belonged to, and how could you distinguish between loyal and disloyal officials? In reality, there was no reason why you should have had to be loyal to the ruler. All of those dynasties were very short-lived; there wasn't enough time for anyone to become loyal to them. The Song Dynasty was different; the Song had been in existence long enough for loyalty to become a possibility.'

'You can shut a dog up in a cage, but if you want him to wag his tail when he sees you, only time will achieve that,' the young monk broke in suddenly. The older monk glared at the young monk, who lowered his head. But Kang Youwei said,

'Your analogy is a very apt one. Standards of behaviour among humans aren't really that high. In fact, what passes for loyalty among humans is often on the same level as the loyalty of dogs, or even lower.'

'Just now, you said that it takes time to create loyal officials. How long does it take?' asked the monk.

'There's no hard and fast rule as to how much time it takes. You can only tell that enough time has elapsed when everyone is loyal. The problem of loyalty and disloyalty is one that has plagued Chinese people for millennia. But if you study the classics closely, you will find that traditionally, the concept of "loyalty" has always had two sides to it. There is "relative loyalty" and "absolute loyalty". When Duke Zhuang of Qi was murdered, the great Yanzi refused to commit suicide to follow his lord in death. The reason he gave was an admirable one. He said, "If one's lord dies for the state, then you should die with him. If one's lord dies for personal reasons, then unless you have a deep personal attachment to him, there is no reason to die with him." Those with a "deep personal attachment" would be the ruler's personal retainers and lackeys. Actually, the origins of the word "loyalty" are quite interesting. In the earliest records, the word does not appear at all. It first makes its appearance in the Spring and Autumn Period, but at that time it referred to the "pheasant-like loyalty of a minister". For the ancients, the pheasant was a symbol of unsullied virtue, while the word "minister" originally meant a captive or a slave. "Pheasant-like loyalty of a minister" was thus the loyalty of a personal retainer to one's lord. This kind of loyalty was unconditional and absolute.

By contrast, the kind of loyalty that Yanzi was advocating was conditional. It had as its precondition the loyalty of the ruler towards his people, in return for which the minister owed loyalty to the ruler. This kind of loyalty was relative. Unfortunately, in traditional Chinese thought the concept of relative loyalty was not developed fully, while the concept of absolute loyalty became the mainstream. The role of "ruler" came to take on the aspect of a father, while the role of "minister" took on the aspect of a son. The absolute and unconditional loyalty of a personal retainer became the mainstream of the concept of loyalty in China, and the idea that one should die for one's lord became an important concept in traditional Chinese thought. But if you look into the reality of the situation, it doesn't stand up to scrutiny.

Let me take two examples from the transitional period between the Tang and Sui dynasties. Let's take Qu Tutong as the first example. Emperor Wen of the Sui Dynasty dispatched Qu Tutong to Gansu to inspect the state horse-breeding operations there. He discovered that twenty thousand horses had been appropriated by private individuals. When the Emperor heard of this, he at first planned to execute fifteen hundred of the government officials responsible for horse-breeding. Qu Tutong told him that it would be wrong to kill people for the sake of horses, and said that he was willing to offer his own life in the place of those of the fifteen hundred officials. Emperor Wen listened to him, decided not to kill the officials, and promoted him.

As an official, Qu Tutong enforced the law with great strictness; his brother Qu Tugai was the same. There was a popular saying at the time: "I would rather eat nothing but mugwort for three years than run into Qu Tugai; I would rather eat nothing but spring onions for three years rather than run into Qu Tutong." You can see from this the kind of fear they inspired. When Tang Gaozu first rebelled against the Sui, Qu Tutong was in charge of the garrison at Yongji in Shanxi. He led his army to relieve the Sui capital at Chang'an, but was trapped by Tang Gaozu's forces. The Tang army sent one of his servants to ask him to surrender; he refused, and killed the servant. They then sent his son to ask him to surrender. Again he refused, and he berated his son in front of the whole army: "Before, we were father and son; today, we are enemies!" He ordered his archers to shoot his son.

In the meantime, the capital had fallen to the Tang forces. Tang Gaozu sent agents to conduct psychological warfare in Qu Tutong's camp, and his troops mutinied. Qu Tutong dismounted from his horse and kowtowed three times facing south-east. Weeping, he cried out, "I have done my utmost, and I have still been defeated; I have not failed you, my lord." His mutinous subordinates sent him under guard to Tang Gaozu. Tang Gaozu urged him to come over to his side. Qu Tutong said, "I have not been able to die for my lord as I should; to have been taken prisoner by you like this is too shameful." Tang Gaozu said to him, "You are a loyal minister," and sent him to serve as the general chief of staff to Tang Taizong.

When the pacification of the empire had been completed, Tang Taizong had portraits of twenty-four meritorious officials painted on the walls of the Ling Yan Hall; Qu Tutong was one of them. Qu Tutong has been described as a loyal official of both the Sui Dynasty and the Tang Dynasty. The reason is that he displayed whole hearted devotion to both of the rulers he served. As a result, after his death Wei Zheng, a leading figure in the imperial court, described him as having been "a man of unblemished purity, loyal unto death". His loyalty and reliability were widely admired at the Tang court.

There is another example from the time of Qu Tutong, which is Yao Junsu. Yao Junsu had been one of Qu Tutong's subordinates. After Qu Tutong went over to the Tang, he came to see Shao Junsu to invite him to surrender. When they came face to face, both of them wept. Qu Tutong said, "My troops have been defeated, but the army I have surrendered to is fighting in a just cause. Everyone is going over to them. Given the way things are, why don't you surrender?" Yao Junsu replied, "You are a minister of state; how can you go over to the enemy? Look at the horse you are riding; this horse was given you by the Emperor. Don't you feel ashamed to be riding it?"

Qu Tutong tried to defend his actions, saying, "Junsu, I did all that I could!" Yao Junsu replied, "I still haven't done all that I can! I can still do more!" Yao Junsu refused to surrender. The Tang army that had surrounded the city he was defending sent his wife to beg him to surrender. His wife said, "The Sui Dynasty has fallen; it has already become clear who Heaven wishes to be emperor. Why make life difficult for yourself?" Yao Junsu replied, "What do women know about affairs of state?" and shot her with an arrow. These two men were contemporaries. Qu Tutong shot his own son, and Yao Junsu shot his own wife.

Here you have examples of two "loyal officials" who hadn't yet done their utmost to fulfil the demands of loyalty killing members of their family first as a blood sacrifice. Yao Junsu won himself a mention in the *History of the Sui*; Qu Tutong had his biography included in the *History of the Tang*. They were contemporaries, and yet their lives ended up being recorded in the histories of two different dynasties. Why? Because Yao Junsu died for the Sui Dynasty; he was their man. Qu Tutong did all he could to save the Sui, but did not die for them, so he was not their man. And yet the fact that Qu Tutong did his utmost to save the Sui did not prevent him from being honoured as a loyal official by the Tang. How can you explain this? The only reasonable explanation is that by the time Qu Tutong had done all that he could for the Sui, the object of his loyalty no longer existed. Furthermore, the new regime that was replacing them appeared to have the favour of both Heaven and the people. The regime to which he had been loyal could not match the new one in this respect. Even if he had continued to resist, there would have been no benefit to the state. So instead, he became the devoted servant of the new regime.'

'So how do you explain Xie Fangde?' asked the monk.

'As I just said, Xie Fangde died for something he believed in. The belief itself may come to seem trivial or even wrong-headed with the passage of time. For example, as Xie Fangde saw it at the time, the Mongols were not Chinese. His concept of the state was confused. He felt that China had been destroyed. In fact, what had been destroyed was the Zhao ruling house of the Song Dynasty—China itself was perfectly fine. Nevertheless, when you are evaluating a historical figure you have to put yourself in their shoes. From Xie Fangde's point of view at the time, his death was not meaningless. The reason why we respect him is because he died for his beliefs, not because of what those beliefs were. After five or six centuries, those beliefs no longer stand up. The Song Dynasty was a part of Chinese history, and so was the Yuan.'

'And what about the Ming and Qing dynasties?'

'The same. Take this queue on my head for example. When the Manchus invaded China over two hundred and forty years ago, they issued an order that all inhabitants of China must cut their hair. The order was to be implemented within ten days; anyone who hadn't changed their hairstyle by the end of that time was to be killed. All Chinese, except for you monks and women, had to adopt the Manchu hairstyle. At the time, some people refused to change, and were killed, but today, two hundred and forty years on, people have got used to it. Not only have they got used to it.' He paused, and cast a glance in the direction of the young novice; 'They wag their tails, too!'

The novice laughed, and then lowered his head. The monk laughed too. Kang Youwei went on:

'If you look at it from the point of view of Han Chinese two hundred and forty years ago, you can't say that they were wrong to oppose the Manchus. But today, two hundred and forty years on, the same reasoning no longer applies. Two hundred and forty years ago, foreigners weren't knocking on China's gates. The Han Chinese of that time had never seen real foreigners, so naturally they viewed the Manchus as being foreigners. Now we know who the real foreigners are; the Manchus are actually Chinese like us.'

'The Manchus are the rulers; surely there is inequality between them and the Chinese. And surely the Manchu regime is corrupt?' asked the monk.

'It's true that there is inequality and corruption, but that is an internal contradiction within China. Internal contradictions have to be solved internally. Whichever way you look at it, I can't see any reason for setting up a racial divide between Manchus and Han Chinese. As I see it, the Manchus are Chinese too; the Manchu emperor is a Chinese emperor. Just as in Feng Dao's eyes, the Khitan were Chinese, and the Khitan emperor was a Chinese emperor. As long as the common people benefit, who cares whether the emperor is Han Chinese or a barbarian?'

'So that's why you are going to submit a petition to the barbarian Manchu Emperor?'

'Yes. The fact that I am submitting a petition shows that I am unhappy with the actions of this regime, but that I am not attacking them on racial grounds. After two hundred and forty years, I don't believe that that historical problem still exists.'

'Has it occurred to you that the Manchus themselves may not think in those terms?' the monk retorted.

'Uh, that's possible, I must admit. But in terms of external appearances, at least, as soon as the Manchus entered China they announced that intermarriage would be permitted between Manchus and Chinese, and opportunities to obtain official posts and administrative power would be shared between Manchus and Chinese. Of course, there is bound to have been some discrimination, and they are bound to have tried to maintain certain special privileges for themselves. But I am sure that a cultured Manchu like the Emperor would see no reason to make any distinction between Manchu and Chinese. The time for that is long past. It's been more than two hundred and forty years; it makes no sense for either Manchus or Chinese to harp on about it now.'

'So basically you support the Manchu government?'

'I support anyone who is of benefit to China. If the Manchu government rules China well, why should I not support them? This regime has been in power for more than two hundred and forty years now; that's a very solid foundation. It's no easy task to build up a solid foundation like this, and having a foundation like this to work on should make saving China a much easier task. I just wish I could inform the emperor of my plan to save the nation. Unfortunately, there is no one willing to submit it on my behalf.'

'As to whether there is someone who could do this for you in Buddhist terms—that is a matter of fate. The cause starts from nowhere, and one's destiny is to go where fate leads. As long as the conditions exist for it, I think it is not only possible that you might find someone to submit your petition for you, you may well find that the emperor is susceptible to your ideas, so that you are able to put your plan into practice in the same way that Wang Anshi was able to do.'

'It's hard to guess what the future will be, but listening to you has made me more hopeful. At any rate, I have been extremely fortunate to have the chance to meet you, both you and the young master here.'

As Kang Youwei spoke, he glanced at the young novice, who smiled. The monk also looked at the novice and smiled. He then pointed at the fried egg; the novice nodded and began to eat his portion. The monk also suggested that Kang Youwei should eat up his egg. Kang Youwei seemed slightly surprised.

'Thank you. But aren't you having any?'

'You know that we monks are vegetarians. Strictly speaking, we are not supposed to eat eggs either. I abide by this prescription, but I am in favour of allowing other monks to eat them, so I allow Pu Jing and the others here to eat eggs.'

'Isn't that in violation of the principles of vegetarianism?'

'Being a vegetarian is a spiritual thing; one's spirit affects one's actions. Most people don't understand this, they have completely the wrong idea. Meat and fish are called *xing*; pungent vegetables like green onions, garlic and celery are called *hun*. Everyone thinks that *hun* is meat and fish, so that being a vegetarian is just a matter of not eating fish and meat, and that you can eat as many pungent vegetables as you like. This is due to a failure to understand the spiritual significance of vegetarianism. As for those temples which cook "vegetarian chicken" and "vegetarian duck", in spiritual terms they are eating *hun*; that is not true vegetarianism.'

'According to what you just said, Master, I shouldn't eat egg either,' said Pu Jing.

'You should eat it. You're young, and you need the nutrients.'

'But I am a monk, the same as you.'

'Not yet. Monks aged between fourteen and nineteen are only novices; you aren't a real monk yet,' said the monk, laughingly.

'So when will I be a real monk?'

'You don't necessarily have to ever become one.'

'Why?'

'Because you don't have to stay in this temple forever.'

Pu Jing became nervous, and started to bite his lower lip. He grasped his left hand, and placed his thumb under his index finger. That was a habit of his; he did this whenever he became nervous. He stared at the monk, and asked:

'Do you mean that there may come a day when you will ask me to leave?'

'Not at all. Of course not,' said the monk, gently. He put down his chopsticks and placed his hand on Pu Jing's left hand. 'What I meant was, a monk's purpose is to do good in this world, and there are many ways of doing good. Living inside a temple is not necessarily a good method, or at least, it is not the only one.'

'What about yourself, Master?'

'My situation is slightly different.'

'In what way?'

'One day you will understand. All I can say is that I did not become a monk until I was thirty. Before the age of thirty, although I had studied Buddhism, I was not a monk. You don't know anything about my life before the age of thirty; one day you will find out about it.' Having said this much, the monk was somewhat gloomy, and seemed unwilling to say more.

At this point, Kang Youwei broke in:

'I thought you must have become a monk as a boy. To judge from your age, you can only have taken holy orders a few years ago.'

'More than just a few years. How old would you say I am? I'm forty-one; I have been a monk for eleven years now.'

'Eleven years? I had no idea you had only been a monk for eleven years, master,' said Pu Jing.

'Only eleven years,' said the monk simply.

'Have you been here at this temple all that time?' asked Kang Youwei.

'Always. There is a close relationship between this temple and my ancestors. When my ancestor stole the body of Governor General Yuan in the middle of the night and carried it away from the execution grounds, it was brought to this temple first. The funerary rites were performed here for Governor General Yuan in secret before his body was carried to the Guangdong cemetery to be buried. My ancestor was a friend of the abbot, and the abbot had a great respect for Governor General Yuan, so he was happy to perform the funerary rites for him. Since then, whenever anyone in my family has needed to have Buddhist services performed, they have come to this temple. So naturally when I decided to become a monk eleven years ago I came to this temple. Because this is a poor temple as Beijing temples go, with a high rate of turnover among the monks, I was able to rise to the position of abbot in only eleven years.'

'The reason for building this temple was to commemorate the Chinese soldiers who died in the north-east. Governor General Yuan also died trying to help the garrisons in the north-east. It seems only right and proper that the funerary services for the Governor General should have been performed here.'

'That had never occurred to me. Perhaps that was another reason why the abbot was willing to perform the funerary services for the Governor General.'

'Did anyone erect a memorial stele to the Governor General in the temple?'

'At the time, no one dared. The Governor General was accused of conspiring with the Manchus; he was executed for treason. No one would have dared admit they sympathized with him.'

'Governor General Yuan died in the third year of the Chongzhen era; the Ming Dynasty fell fourteen years later. When the Manchus conquered China, what attitude did they take towards this man who was supposed to have been in collusion with them?'

'The Qing government knew full well that Governor General Yuan had been falsely accused, because they were the ones who framed him. But they kept quiet about it. On the one hand, it was a low trick to have used. On the other hand, if they had rehabilitated him, that would have amounted to honouring him as a hero who had fought to protect China from the Manchus, so from the Manchus' point of view that wouldn't do either. As a result, the fact of Governor General Yuan's martyrdom has never been made public. Before he died, Governor General Yuan wrote a poem: 'My achievements are known to the emperor; my sufferings will be known to later generations'. His achievements were significant all right, but the Emperor wasn't aware of them. In fact, he had him executed as a traitor. His sufferings were real enough, too, but how much have later generations known about them? Two hundred and fifty years later, a hero who was wrongfully executed still hasn't been rehabilitated—there is no justice in it.

Governor General Yuan was unfortunate in living around the time of the Ming–Qing transition. The Ming said that he was a servant of the Qing; the Qing said he was a servant of the Ming. After the Ming fell, he still didn't have his name cleared. More than two centuries of Qing rule have elapsed since then, and his name still hasn't been cleared. It really is difficult to predict how your life will turn out. When an individual finds himself caught up in a struggle between two groups, it's bad enough having to sacrifice oneself for the group. It's even worse when one's sacrifice isn't known even after one's death. Why do groups always treat individuals so brutally?

Individuals can survive only if they align themselves with the majority within the group; that's the only way to avoid a tragic end. If an individual is too upright, too independent, then they are likely to find themselves being attacked by the group. Groups are brutal; individuals are better than groups. Groups run to extremes; they are either much better than the individual or much worse. So if an upright individual is too upright, he can expect to be made to pay a heavy price for it by the group. When an upright individual works in the service of the group, they have to mentally steel themselves for the possibility of being sold out by the group. I think Governor General Yuan must have known this. His predecessor, Xiong Tingbi, was also wrongfully accused and executed; he must have been aware of the possibility that he would meet the same fate. The fact that knowing what might happen to him, he didn't flee from his responsibilities, shows that he was mentally prepared to sacrifice himself for the group.

As to you, Mr Kang, do you wish to save China? If you plan to go down that road, you have to prepare yourself; you have to keep in mind that the group is changeable, ungrateful, and cruel. The greater the people, the more true this is. If you do end up meeting this kind of fate, you may find that you love China, but hate the Chinese. When that happens, please remember this: that is the way groups are, you mustn't expect too much from them. If you seek to be a righteous man, then righteousness must suffice for you, and you must be ready to face death lightly. If the group comes to eulogize you, that won't be for another two hundred and fifty years. Just as we commemorate Governor General Yuan, think about him, pay tribute to him and visit his tomb. This shows that there is justice in the human heart.'

When the abbot finished speaking, Kang Youwei nodded. His expression seemed slightly morose, and he did not speak. At this point, the novice spoke up:

'Master, you just said that you've only been a monk for eleven years. You're forty-one now, so eleven years ago you must have been thirty. What did you do before the age of thirty?'

When the abbot heard this, his face lost its serenity; he knit his eyebrows, and his piercing gaze moved from the novice's face to the window and then up into the sky. The whole room suddenly seemed to take on an atmosphere of deathly stillness; no sound could be heard. Kang Youwei sat quietly without moving. He noticed a faint odour of lilac; as he breathed it in, he felt that there was a kind of vitality within the stillness. Only his eyes moved. He glanced over at the novice, who had lowered his head and was staring at his empty rice bowl. The novice was feeling the edge of the bowl with the thumb and index finger of his right hand. Other than that, he also was motionless.

A long time passed. Finally, Kang Youwei pushed his chair back with both hands, and stood up. 'I've taken up too much of your time, master.' The abbot awoke from his reverie, and looked at him. Kang Youwei added, 'I'd better be on my way.'

'But it's still early, Mr Kang,' the abbot said, hurriedly. 'Have some tea before you go. Let's go to the guest room and have some tea. Pu Jing, you come too, you can clean up the dishes later.'

<hr>

The guest room was very small and simply furnished. On the south side was a window, under which was placed a wooden armchair. There were low tables on both sides of the chair, and more chairs placed at right angles to the tables facing east and west. On the north side a bookcase was placed against the wall, filled with sutras. In the middle of the room there was a long table on which were placed writing brushes and other writing instruments. There were chairs on both sides of the table. The room appeared to function both as a guest room and study. The most striking thing about the room was the scroll hanging on the wall at the back, which bore the poem Wei Zhixiu wrote after visiting Minzhong Temple:

> *In the depths of the huge temple where pine trees line up in long black rows;*
> *Sorrows and miseries have gone through the Repentance Terrace of Buddhism.*

Where Monk Miaofa was fortunate enough to have been witness to a
    prosperous age, the lonely loyalist general could hardly expect any
    mercy from the Tang Emperor.
While the abbot enforces the house rules both mild and strict,
Visitors to the temple are in high spirits.
One should not talk about the An-Shi rebellion, referred to on the remnant
    of the stone tablet, because the story of the emperor hanging himself
    on Coal Hill was even more miserable.

Standing in front of the scroll, Kang Youwei found himself
deeply moved by the poem. One hundred years after the building of
Minzhong Temple, the generals An Lushan and Shi Siming were
stationed in Beijing; they had two pagodas built at Minzhong Temple.
Later on, An Lushan and Shi Siming launched a rebellion, and nearly
brought down the Tang Dynasty. The Tang court imported foreign
mercenaries to put down the rebellion, and An Lushan and Shi Siming
fell out among themselves. As a result, the dynasty was saved. When
the dynasty did eventually fall a century later, An Lushan and Shi
Siming were long since dead. All that remained were the pagodas
they had built, standing stark and forlorn. Another century elapsed,
and another, and another. The pagodas finally fell, no one knows
exactly when, and all that remained were ruins. A poet came to the
temple, viewed the ruins, and thought about how all the emperors
and princes and heroes of the Tang era had disappeared like smoke.
Neither An Lushan nor Shi Siming received a proper burial, and even
the tomb of Tang Taizong—who built Minzhong Temple—had been
robbed and destroyed. The glory of the great Tang Dynasty had
disappeared from China, and yet in this small temple a trace of it still
remained. Minzhong Temple was too small for most people to notice,
but for those astute enough, or for a poet, it held a great and sombre
symbolism. A poet can see the world in a grain of dust, or see heaven
in a flower, and Minzhong Temple had no shortage of either dust or
flowers. At Minzhong Temple, a poet could visualize the glory and
fall of past dynasties, the laughter and the tears, the life and death,
the steles erected in commemoration of the dead, and even the
eventual disintegration of those steles into dust and fragments.

The Tang Dynasty was followed by the Five Dynasties; the
Five Dynasties were followed by the Song; the Song was followed
by the Yuan; the Yuan was followed by the Ming. Eventually the
Ming too grew old and its glory became tarnished. Just as the dynasty
itself entered the dark of night, one night the gates of Minzhong

Temple were opened to receive the coffin of Yuan Chonghuan. Fourteen years after Yuan Chonghuan's body was placed in its coffin, the Ming Emperor, who had had him executed, climbed forlornly up Coal Hill behind the palace to the sound of drums and hung himself from a tree. Thus, the story of the Emperor hanging himself on Coal Hill was even more miserable. From the poem that was written to commemorate this event, one could see that to the poet it was as though all of this was past, and yet not gone.

Past, and yet not gone. It all seemed to be gone, and yet it was not, it was all still there. Chinese philosophers had long since developed the concept that the essence of a thing survives after the physical form has disappeared. In any given physical space, the 'shadows' of people and actions are constantly being produced. These shadows are changing all the time; the shadows that exist now are not the same as those that were there before, but the old shadows still remain in the same place, even though you can't see them. In any space, in any ancient monument, even if only ruins remain, the more historic the remains the more layers of these shadows there are. Only spaces, ancient monuments, and ruins constantly face the passing of the generations. Time passes in front of them in a long line; they are the examiners of time, the witnesses of history. The poet felt this truth very strongly. He put his impressions down on paper, and hung the paper on the wall, creating a new shadow. The poet projected his shadow onto the paper, and the paper projected its shadow onto later generations, creating a complete cycle.

'This seven-character eight-line poem is very well written.' Kang Youwei seemed to have come out of a dream. 'Everything that I would have wanted to say, he has said.' He turned round and saw that the abbot was watching him silently, as though he had had that same impression. Finally, the abbot pointed to the table on the north side of the room:

'We have paper and writing brushes here; we would like to ask you to write a poem as a memento of your visit here.'

'It is very kind of you to ask me, but it would be too presumptuous of me to accept,' said Kang Youwei, smiling.

'Not at all. Someone whose knowledge of the past is as deep as yours is bound to be a first-rate calligrapher. If you could leave us a poem to commemorate your visit, in another hundred years or so it will have become one of the temple's treasures.'

'I doubt that very much. I am honoured that you should think
so highly of me. Calligraphy is a trifling accomplishment which
Chinese people waste too much time on. Nevertheless, for cultivating
one's character and as a social activity, there is something to be said
for it. Since you've asked me to write a poem I had better do as I am
bid.' Kang Youwei walked over to the side of the table, sat down,
and began to write slowly on a sheet of fine, white, thin paper called
xuanzhi:

> *Soft and fragile is the lilac,*
> *with seeds all over its stem;*
> *Pretty are its leaves and flowers,*
> *though the beauty is restrained rather than gaudy.*
> *Deeply planted behind the house,*
> *it is meant for thinking people to enjoy.*
> *Emitting a strong scent morning and evening,*
> *Even the prospect of ending up ground into powder instils no fear in it at all.*

He finally added in small letters, 'The Lilac Poem of Du Fu
written by Kang Youwei, in the first month of 1878.' When Kang
Youwei wrote out the first line of the poem, a touch of surprise
showed on the abbot's face. When the poem was finished, the monk
read it over and over again, clearly highly appreciative. Kang Youwei's
calligraphy was superb; he had a strong, powerful style which was
at the same time uniquely his own. The abbot said:
'As soon as you started to write, I could tell you were an expert
calligrapher. You could achieve fame through your calligraphy alone;
why bother with politics? Ha ha ha.'
'The ancients said that the three things one could obtain
immortal fame for were moral rectitude, meritorious deeds, and wise
words. Calligraphy wasn't one of them! Even if one could win fame
through one's calligraphy, what kind of fame would that be? What
benefits can calligraphy bring to the state or to the people?'
The abbot nodded. 'Your aim is to help mankind; that is a very
virtuous purpose. Nevertheless, this poem is very well written. You
are obviously a man of wide learning with a powerful memory, to
think of matching Du Fu's poem about lilacs with our Minzhong
Temple, which is famed for its lilacs. It really is a very fine piece of
work. Look, Pu Jing, see what a fine calligrapher Mr Kang is!'
The novice had been standing behind them, watching with great
curiosity. Having been addressed by the abbot, he joined in the
conversation:

'Master, what does the poem mean?'

'Poems are like Buddhism; there is much that can only be felt, and cannot be put into words. There is a saying that no exact interpretation can ever be given of a poem. One person may interpret it in one way, another person will interpret it in another. Isn't that true, Mr Kang?'

'Very true.' Kang Youwei nodded.

'But with this poem by Du Fu, it is possible to sense roughly what the poem was intended to mean. As I see it, the meaning of the poem as a whole is this: The lilac is soft and fragile. It has many seeds, and its leaves and flowers are pretty, but with a restrained rather than gaudy beauty. The lilac is planted behind the house to be enjoyed by thinking people. And the lilac itself? It produces its strong scent both in the morning and in the evening, without thinking about the fact that it will eventually be ground up into powder. What the poem really means is this: a soft, weak, beautiful living thing should be aware of its own characteristics and fulfil its destiny, even if its destiny is to be ground up into powder. What do you think, Mr Kang? Am I too far off the mark?'

'You have explained it very well, very well indeed. That's how I would have explained it, too. Du Fu wrote this poem to have an active meaning, to show that even a soft, weak creature can be strong. People use the lofty pine and cypress as symbols of resilience and tenacity, without noticing that the soft, weak lilac also has a tough side to it. The lilac emits its scent throughout its life and also after its death, although it is not at all hardy to look at. In other words, it isn't always the strong who perform great deeds; there is much that the weak can accomplish, too. Knowing that they are likely to end up being ground up into powder, the weak might be put off from acting. But if they cease worrying about their fate, they may yet end up achieving something of importance.'

'You've explained it even better,' said the abbot. 'Du Fu would have been amazed to learn that you have extracted this message from his poem so many hundreds of years later.'

'And you too,' added Kang Youwei.

'Both of us,' they added together.

Everyone laughed. Looking at the poem, the novice nodded in understanding.

After they had finished drinking their tea, Kang Youwei stood up to say goodbye. 'When I go back home to Guangdong, is there anything I can do for you while I am there?'

'No, nothing. My native place is very distant from me, in spatial and temporal terms. That's the thing about Beijing, it makes you feel as though it is your home.'

At this point, a monk came in and said to the abbot, 'A monk from Yongqing Temple is here. He says he wants to go with us to Wanshou Temple to attend the funerary services for Chamberlain Li's mother. What shall I tell him?'

The abbot smiled ruefully, and shook his head. 'Ask him to wait for a minute. I will go and talk to him myself.'

The abbot and the novice walked with Kang Youwei to the temple gate, where they said goodbye. As Kang Youwei started to walk off, the abbot suddenly called out to him: 'Have you visited the Xie Wenjie Shrine down that road?' Kang Youwei said he hadn't. The monk said, 'It's worth a visit. If you want to gain a better understanding of Xie Fangde's martyrdom, you should go there.'

CHAPTER FOUR

Empress Dowager Cixi

*Returning to historical background, the Empress Dowager rises to power.
Beginning with the history of the Qing Dynasty, we follow the waxing
and waning of its power. At its height, the Qing Dynasty boasted the
largest royal garden in the world, the Yuanmingyuan (Garden of
Perfection and Brightness). In 1900, this opulent garden was sacked,
looted, and burned by Franco-British forces in revenge for a diplomatic
incident. The Empress Dowager's rise to power parallels China's decline
and fall into the era of domination by various Western powers, and
eventually Japan. The Empress Dowager's unbelievable acts of treachery
and political intrigue, motivated solely by her thirst for power, make for
harrowing reading. She utilized eunuchs to exercise her power, and
there is a brief account of the historical status of eunuchs and efforts to
prevent their amassing power.*

Beijing's north-west gate was known as Xizhi Gate. After you pass
through the gate, you can see a river running west to east. If you
follow the river upstream for seven kilometres, on the right bank
you will see the famous Wanshou Temple.

Wanshou Temple was built in the sixteenth century, in 1577
(the fifth year of the reign of the thirteenth Ming emperor, the Wanli
Emperor). The temple was built by the eunuch official Feng Bao. At
the time of its construction the imperial treasury was full, so there
were plenty of funds available, and the temple was built on an
impressive scale. The Dayanshou Hall in the centre of the temple
had five main columns, while the two Arhat Halls on either side had
nine columns each. The sutra repository at the rear of the temple
was a very tall building; the Vitasoka Dama Halls that flanked it had
three central columns each. One hundred and seventy years before

this large temple was built, the third Ming emperor, Chengzu, had been helped by the monk Yao Guangxiao in his seizure of the throne from his nephew. To show his gratitude to Yao, Chengzu invited him to supervise the casting of a great bronze bell twelve feet in diameter and weighing 87,000 catties (one catty is the equivalent of 0.6 kilogram). This bell was called the Huayan Bell, because Shen Du carved the full text of the eighty-one chapters of the Huayan Sutra on its sides, along with a condensation of the Prajnaparamita carved in characters the size equivalent of thirty-two font. Chengzu ordered that six monks should strike the bell one character at a time every day. In this way, once every character had been struck, one cycle of the prajna or highest wisdom was completed. When the Wanli Emperor ordered the building of Wanshou Temple, he had this great bell installed in it, and the bell was struck consistently from then until the reign of his grandson Xizong. When the bell ceased to be struck, the Ming Dynasty fell.

One hundred years after the founding of the Qing Dynasty, in 1751 the fourth Qing emperor, Qianlong, ordered that the bell be moved to Juesheng Temple outside Xizhi Gate, where a bell tower was specially constructed for it. Once the bell was installed, people in Beijing stopped using the name Juesheng Temple and started to refer to it as Big Bell Temple.

With the bell removed, Wanshou Temple was able to breathe a sigh of relief. The temple was in a position to better ingratiate itself to the current regime. During the Ming Dynasty, the rulers had often visited the temple, stopping to rest there on their journeys, a fact of which the temple had been very proud. The temple had been built at the behest of a Ming ruler and his eunuch official, so right from the start the history of Wanshou Temple had been intertwined with the rulers and their eunuchs. Now, on its three hundredth birthday, the temple was continuing to link itself with the current ruler and their eunuchs; that is, with the Empress Dowager and Chamberlain Li Lianying.

If one headed upriver from Wanshou Temple towards the north-west, at a point twenty kilometres from Xizhi Gate one would come to Wanshou Hill. Wanshou Hill was originally known as Weng Hill; in the same year in which the Qianlong Emperor ordered the removal of the great bell to Juesheng Temple, he also had Weng Hill renamed Wanshou (Longevity) Hill in honour of his mother's sixtieth birthday. There was a lake in front of the hill, known as West Lake. The Qianlong Emperor had the lake widened and deepened (to twice its original depth), and changed its name to Kunming Lake. This lake now functioned as a reservoir, providing part of the water supply for the city of Beijing. The Qing regime not only turned it into a reservoir, they also used it as a training ground for the navy. A large number of sailors from Fujian were stationed there, and the lake's name changed to Kunming Lake in memory of Emperor Han Wudi's campaign against the state of Kunming in south-west China. When Han Wudi was preparing for this campaign, he realized that he would need to be able to fight on water, as the territory of Kunming encompassed the huge Lake Dian. In order to make his preparations as realistic as possible, Han Wudi ordered the construction of a replica of Lake Dian to the south-west of his capital, Chang'an, and conducted military exercises there. It can thus be seen why, in the Qing Dynasty, the Qianlong Emperor chose to rename West Lake as Kunming Lake.

Wanshou Hill and Kunming Lake were more than just a reservoir for Beijing and a naval training ground; they also constituted a suburban park for the Qing royal family. The mountain and lake scenery here were collectively known as the Haoshan Park; Qianlong renamed it the Qingyiyuan Park. Although the park had a circumference of 16.4 *li* (1 *li* = 0.6 kilometre), it was not the largest imperial park. The largest was the Yuanmingyuan to the north-east, which had a circumference of over 20 *li*. The Yuanmingyuan was the largest royal park in the entire world. Its construction began almost as soon as the Qing Dynasty had been established. During the reign of the Qianlong Emperor it was kept in superb condition continuously for sixty years. It was not a purely Chinese construction; some of the buildings were the product of several decades' sweat and toil by Western missionaries. One missionary who had seen the palaces of Europe and was in a position to make comparisons called it the 'garden of gardens'. The Yuanmingyuan contained over one hundred scenic spots, both eastern and western, including representations of Taoist immortals' grottoes and scenes from Buddhist sutras. It was not just one palace, but rather a series of over one hundred palaces linked together by a long corridor. It was estimated that each palace cost the equivalent of four million francs to construct, not including the interior decoration. The gardens of Versailles, only half a kilometre in length, were diminutive by comparison.

The Qing emperors were much fonder of the Yuanmingyuan than they were of the imperial palace in Beijing itself; on average, they stayed here for around two-thirds of the year. As a result, the

Yuanmingyuan became a glittering royal city. It was guarded by more than five thousand troops; there were no commoners inside, only people play-acting at being commoners. At the emperor's whim, the palace women and eunuchs would dress up as judges, merchants, artisans, entertainers, storytellers, and thieves; there were magistrates' offices, shops, markets, wharves, inns, and prisons, all of them filled with people bustling about. It was a Chinese-style masquerade party. Entertainment of this kind had been held in imperial palaces at least since the second century BC. Sometimes the emperor himself would participate, dressing up as a merchant, for example, enjoying himself as he pretended to be an ordinary citizen. They were a class apart, shutting the commoners outside the walls of their gilded palaces, while they played at being commoners inside.

After the Qianlong Emperor, the Qing Dynasty started to weaken. The impoverished masses were already showing signs of revolt. The fifth Qing emperor, Qianlong's son the Jiaqing Emperor, began an investigation into corruption among his father's officials in the fourth year of his reign. One of these officials was named He Shen; after his property had been confiscated, it was discovered that his wealth was equal to ten times the total government revenue for the whole of China! The Jiaqing Emperor was actually relatively lucky; he only had to deal with internal troubles. His son, the Daoguang Emperor, found himself having to deal not only with increasing internal difficulties, but also with attack by the white man—it was in his reign that China was defeated by Britain in the Opium War. The Treaty of Nanking, signed in 1842, gave the 'foreign devils' the privilege of extraterritoriality, internal navigation rights along China's rivers, most favoured nation status, control over customs duties, control over their settlements in several port cities, the opening up to trade of ports that had previously been closed to them, a large indemnity, and the ownership of Hong Kong island. Never in three thousand years of history had China suffered a humiliation of this sort. The Chinese simply could not accept the new situation. Fifteen years later, in 1857, the seventh year of the reign of the Xianfeng Emperor (the Daoguang Emperor's son), a major conflict erupted. A combined French and British force stormed and took the city of Canton (Guangzhou), taking prisoner the Governor General Yeh Mingchen, who was derided for 'refusing to fight but refusing to make peace; refusing to defend the city and refusing to commit suicide; refusing to surrender but refusing to leave'. They then linked up with the Americans and Russians and moved north. The Qing government was too weak to resist, they signed another unfair treaty, the Treaty of Tianjin, which meant increased indemnity payments and a further loss of sovereignty.

The year after the signing of the Treaty of Tianjin, the British and French governments sent representatives to Beijing to exchange ratification of the treaty. Conflict arose because the location at which the ambassadors landed and the number of persons in the delegation was not in accordance with Chinese protocol and international law. The British launched a sudden attack on the Dagu Forts; the garrison returned fire, and succeeded in sinking four British vessels, killing eighty-nine Britons. This sparked off another war. In 1860, a Franco-British army landed in China and marched on Beijing. The Chinese were unable to resist their advance; the thirty-year-old Xianfeng Emperor fled from the Yuanmingyuan to take refuge in Jehol. British and French troops occupied the Yuanmingyuan and began to pillage it. One British officer recorded his memories of the event. He wrote that everyone seemed to have gone mad. French troops went so far as to steal the loot that had been set aside to be presented to Queen Victoria. Another British officer recalled that everyone was in a supremely good mood. Soldiers kicked down doors rather than be bothered to open them; rare books had their pages torn out to make tapers for lighting pipes; all the mirrors in the palaces were stolen; the statue of Venus had a moustache added to it and was used as a puppet. . . . These 'civilized' people destroyed everything of China that could not be carried away.

Looting was not enough for them; they had to destroy as well. In the end, merely damaging the palaces was not enough for the British; they wanted to burn the whole place down as punishment for China's uncivilized behaviour. The French took the view that burning the palaces would alienate those members of the Chinese government who were in favour of ratifying the treaty, and refused to go along with this, but the British insisted on going ahead anyway, using this uncivilized action to display their piratical civilization. The British assigned troops to set fire to the Yuanmingyuan palaces. As one of the British remembered it, they set fire to the Yuanmingyuan and all the neighbouring palaces on 18 October. The palaces burned for two days and two nights, and a dense carpet of black smoke spread over the sky. Black clouds hovered over the city of Beijing, blotting out the sunlight; it seemed like a long, drawn-out eclipse.

The leading Chinese peace negotiator, the Emperor's brother Prince Gong, asked the British and French why, as representatives of civilized nations, they had done such a thing. What do our three countries have to contend over?

Who could answer a question like this?

A long, drawn-out eclipse.

Burning the Yuanmingyuan whetted the appetite of these 'civilized' armies. While they were at it, they set fire to the Jingmingyuan at nearby Yuquanshan, and to the Jingyiyuan at Xiangshan. Forty-four scenic spots and eighty-one gilded bronze halls were burnt to the ground. At the same time, the Qingyiyuan at Kunming Lake, Wanshou Hill was also burnt down. In the advance on Beijing, the British had lost thirteen men and thirteen were injured; the French had seven dead and six injured. China agreed to pay an indemnity of 500,000 *liang* of silver. The French were willing to accept this, but the British refused, and set fire to the Yuanmingyuan. Over three hundred Chinese perished in the fire. In exchange for twenty European lives, the number of Chinese who were killed in battle, burned to death or committed suicide must have been several hundred times greater.

When the terrible news reached Jehol, the Xianfeng Emperor became apoplectic and spat blood.

When the Xianfeng Emperor was resident at the Yuanmingyuan, four Han Chinese women were assigned to four palaces within the gardens—the Mudan Chun, Haidai Chun, Wuling Chun, and Xinghua Chun palaces. In addition, a Manchu woman was assigned to the Tiandi Yijia Chun palace. These five palaces together were known as the Wu Chun (Five Springs). The Manchu woman, surnamed Yehonala and named Lan-er, bore the Emperor a son. At the time of the Xianfeng Emperor's death, the boy was only six years old; he succeeded his father as the Tongzhi Emperor, the eighth Qing emperor.

When the Manchu woman first entered the palace, her status was very low. There has been considerable controversy regarding her birth. According to the official records she was a Manchu; her father, grandfather, and great grandfather had all served as middle-ranking officials; none of them had risen very high. When she was three, her father died in Anhui. Up to the age of sixteen, she had always lived in the south; legend has it that she was actually a Han Chinese, from Guangdong. Her father was supposed to have been a minor official surnamed Zhou, who was executed for some offence; she was sold into a Manchu family as a servant, and was later able to exploit this fact to claim Manchu ancestry. When she was sixteen, she and her younger sister came north and were selected for palace service; they were assigned to the Yuanmingyuan. As she had lived in southern China for a long time, she was able to sing the popular songs of the south. This caught the attention of the emperor, and she began to be promoted in rank.

The classification of palace women at that time was as follows: The most senior woman in the palace was the emperor's grandmother, who was given the title Taihuang Taihou. Next came the emperor's mother, the Huang Taihou. Then came the emperor's principal wife, the Huang Hou or empress. In the fourth rank came the principal concubine, followed by two secondary concubines, four tertiary concubines, and six minor concubines; these in turn were followed by an indeterminate number of concubines, subordinate concubines, and ordinary concubines, followed by an indeterminate number of palace women. Palace women had the status of servants rather than concubines; they could not rise to the status of concubine until the emperor had had sexual relations with them. The total number of concubines and palace women at the Qing court was under two thousand. By comparison with other Chinese dynasties, this was a relatively low figure; at one point in the Tang Dynasty there were over forty thousand. This gives some idea of the level of dissipation of the emperors under an autocratic regime.

This Manchu woman who could sing southern Chinese popular songs steadily climbed higher and higher within the Yuanmingyuan. Having borne the emperor a son automatically increased her status to an immeasurable extent. In addition, the emperor's mother enjoyed her company. As a result, she soon rose to the status of *guifei*, or primary concubine. She was generally known as Yi Guifei.

Prior to Wenzong's death, power had actually rested in the hands of three Manchus: Zai Yuan (Prince Yi), Rui Hua (Prince Zheng), and Rui Hua's younger brother, Xiao Shun. Xiao Shun was the most far-sighted and able of the three. Of all the Manchu nobility, Xiao Shun was the most aware of the need to collaborate with the Han Chinese; he knew that there were many men of talent among the Han, and that only with their help could China be ruled effectively. He made a deliberate effort to change the Manchu practice of keeping the Chinese down, and associated with a number of leading Chinese officials. Zeng Guofan would not have been able to achieve all he did without Xiao Shun; without Xiao Shun, Zuo Zongtang would have been stabbed in the back much sooner. Many other leading Han Chinese officials, including Guo Songdao and Wang Kaiyun, also benefited from Xiao Shun's sponsorship. He was an affable man, who often invited eminent Chinese to his house to drink with him. In comparing Manchu and Chinese, he once said: 'There are many rogues among the Manchus, and most of us are woefully ignorant. Never make an enemy of a Chinese; they can destroy you using only their pen!'

In his attempts to reform the government, Xiao Shun made many enemies. For example, he felt that the Manchu troops—the 'Eight Banners'—were militarily useless, and tried to reduce their stipends; this made him a lot of enemies. He made many more by coming down hard on cheating in the civil service examinations and on official corruption. The fact that he was young, energetic, and outspoken made him even more unpopular; it was these characteristics that caused him to make an enemy of a woman—that Manchu woman.

When the Franco-British army was approaching Beijing, the Xianfeng Emperor's flight from the Yuanmingyuan was so hurried that he was not able to take all of his concubines with him. When the British and French troops entered the Yuanmingyuan, those left behind committed suicide by drowning. On the first day of his flight to Jehol, all the Emperor had to eat for dinner was pancakes, millet cakes, and gruel; it was not until the second day that his entourage were able to get hold of some pork for him. If even the Emperor, who was accustomed to dining on exquisite delicacies every day, was reduced to eating food as simple as this, it is no surprise that those accompanying him had to make do with soya bean milk.

Some of the concubines, who were used to lives of comfort, were unhappy with this treatment, and vented their anger on the person directly responsible for the supply of food—Xiao Shun. On the road, that Manchu woman complained that the carriage she was riding in was too uncomfortable, and asked Xiao Shun to find her another one. Xiao Shun, who was on horseback, replied impatiently, 'We're in the middle of a war; you should be thankful you've got this carriage.' When they arrived at Jehol, food was still in short supply, and the concubines were unable to live in the style to which they were accustomed in Beijing; this made Xiao Shun even more unpopular.

When the Emperor arrived at Jehol, he was in a foul mood. He sent for a troupe of actors from Beijing to perform operas for him. Apart from the play of 'The Peaceful World', he displayed far more interest in the opera than he did in affairs of state. He listened very carefully to the performances; if as much as a single note was sung out of tune he would insist on correcting it. On one occasion, he told one of the actors that he had sung the wrong note; when the actor replied that that was how it was supposed to be sung according to the score, the Emperor replied, 'The score is wrong!'

The Emperor's health was failing him, although he was still alert enough to be able to correct a wrong note in an opera. Nevertheless, he had to start thinking about the succession.

According to the Qing Dynasty's family tradition, the succession had to go from father to son, but not necessarily to the eldest son. Prior to the Xianfeng Emperor's own accession to the throne, the other candidates to succeed his father had included his younger brother Yi Xin, who was more able than he. Their father, the Daoguang Emperor, had found it very difficult to decide who he should make his heir. On one occasion when they were out hunting, his younger brother returned with a bag full of game, but Wenzong was empty-handed. His hunting instructor told him that if the Emperor asked why he was such a useless huntsman, he should answer, 'Spring is a time of growth. Killing animals at this time is harmful to both heaven and earth; I would rather return empty-handed.' This explanation led the Emperor to feel that Wenzong would make a more stable ruler than his younger brother, and so he chose him to be his heir, while his younger brother was given the title Prince Gong.

Now that he was about to die, with his son being only six years old, he was concerned that Prince Gong might try to seize the throne. On the day before his death, therefore, while announcing that his son was to succeed him as emperor, he also announced the names of eight men, including Prince Yi, Prince Zheng, and Xiao Shun, who were to serve as regents: Prince Gong was not on the list.

The emperor's wife also had no role to play. The emperor's mother could not interfere in government; this was not only a tradition of the Qing Dynasty, it was a long-standing practice at Chinese courts. Traditionally, rule by a woman was thought to lead to calamity. The earliest women to achieve fame in China such as Mei Xi during the Xia Dynasty, Da Ji during the Shang Dynasty, Bao Si during the Zhou, and Xi Shi during the Spring and Autumn Period, were all famous for having caused the downfall of a state. In the early years of the Han Dynasty, Empress Lu, the wife of the first Han emperor, Liu Bang, seized power after her husband's death, further damaging the reputation of women as rulers. This was why, when the fifth Han emperor, Han Wudi, appointed his young son to succeed him as emperor, he had the boy's mother killed. His reasoning was that as the boy was so young, his mother was bound to seize power, which would lead to the downfall of the state. The Xianfeng Emperor was aware of cases like these, and he felt that his son's mother, Yi Guifei, was a strong, ambitious woman, so he arranged for a group of regents to assist his son; women could not be appointed regents.

When the emperor died, his six-year-old son succeeded him. In order to demonstrate respect for the emperor, it was inappropriate that his mother continue to hold the position of concubine, so she started to rise in rank, getting ever closer in status to Empress Dowager, who had had no sons of her own. As a result, there were now two empress dowagers; the original Empress Dowager was given the title of Ci'an Taihou, while Yi Gui Fei was given the title of Cixi Taihou. As the latter resided in the Xi Gong, or Western Palace, she was generally known as Xi Taihou (Western Empress Dowager).

Xi Taihou was a highly ambitious woman; she saw an opportunity. She said to the Ci'an Empress Dowager, 'Now that our husband is dead and Xiao Shun and these others have taken power, you and I have no future. Let's get in touch with Prince Gong, and organize a coup.' She managed to convince the Ci'an Empress Dowager; in secret, they contacted Prince Gong, who was in Beijing sorting out the mess left by the Anglo-French occupation of the capital, and they planned their coup.

The coup began when the Xianfeng Emperor's coffin was being transported to Beijing for burial. Zai Yuan and Rui Hua were given satin ropes and forced to hang themselves. At that time, being allowed to commit suicide rather than being executed was considered a mercy. Chinese traditionally prefer the body to remain whole after death, so allowing someone to kill themselves rather then chopping off their head was a kindness, although having one's head cut off is a quicker death than hanging.

Xiao Shun, whom Xi Taihou hated, was ordered to be executed in the public execution ground at Caishikou in Beijing. On the day of the execution, Xiao Shun was brought to the execution ground, trussed up on an ox-cart. As everyone was in mourning for the Xianfeng Emperor, Xiao Shun also wore white garments, with cloth shoes. The atmosphere was sombre; nevertheless, Xiao Shun remained defiant right to the very end, cursing Xi Taihou for her scheming. He refused to kneel down, and the executioners had to break his legs with iron bars before they were able to force him down and cut off his head. After his death, his property was confiscated, and ended up in Xi Taihou's private treasury. One of the crimes for which he was sentenced to death was failing to provide the Empress Dowager with appropriate supplies; this kind of ridiculous charge shows that Xi Taihou was taking revenge for the incident on the road to Jehol. In this way, because of one woman's hunger for power and her personal animosities, the Qing Dynasty's traditional practice was overthrown, the Emperor's dying instructions were disregarded, and the forces of reform were destroyed.

China was going downhill.

At the same time, however, the Manchu woman was becoming increasingly powerful. Xi Taihou and Ci'an Taihou began to 'order state affairs from behind the curtain' as the true power behind the throne. They would both sit behind the curtain, while the Emperor sat in front. The curtain was a yellow curtain, usually hung in the Mental Cultivation Hall. On entering the hall, an official would take three steps and then kneel down and announce, 'Your slave so-and-so requests audience with the emperor.' They would then take off their hat and kowtow, saying 'Your slave kowtows in appreciation of the imperial favour.' They would then replace their hat and walk forward to kneel on a cushion placed before the emperor.

According to regulations, ministers could not look the emperor in the eye; they had to keep their eyes down while entering the hall, during the audience, and while leaving. The hall was very large, and lit only by candles. On entering the hall, it would be some while before you were able to see clearly. The usual practice was to look at a point just below the emperor's chin; in this way, you could avoid showing disrespect by looking directly at the emperor, while also getting some idea of the expression on his face. Strictly speaking, therefore, unless you were skilled enough to take a quick peek without being noticed, a person having an audience with the emperor would never actually see the emperor's face.

When Xi Taihou began to 'order state affairs from behind the curtain', she was only twenty-seven years old; she had plenty of time ahead of her to seize power and spend money. She had received no education, she relied solely on her unschooled intelligence and spite to help her take control of government. The Emperor was her son, and was only six years old; he was therefore no obstacle to her. There were only two people who could stand in her way; one was Ci'an Taihou, the other was Prince Gong. Back when Xi Taihou still held the title of Yi Guifei, Ci'an Taihou was already empress. Although Xi Taihou had been promoted to the rank of Empress Dowager at Emperor Xianfeng's death, this did not alter the fact that she had never been empress. As a result, she was always ill at ease when in the presence of Ci'an Taihou. Before the Xianfeng Emperor's death, he had given Ci'an Taihou a secret edict which stated that if Yi Guifei caused trouble the empress could convene a meeting of the leading ministers of state, make public the secret edict, and have Yi Guifei put to death. After the Xianfeng Emperor's death, Xi Taihou behaved very respectfully towards Ci'an Taihou, sufficiently so to make the latter completely satisfied with her attitude. On one occasion when Ci'an Taihou had been seriously ill, she noticed after her recovery that Xi Taihou was wearing a bandage on her arm. When she asked why, Xi Taihou replied: 'While you were sick I prayed for your health; I cut a piece of flesh from my arm and mixed it in with your medicine to cure your illness.'

This practice of cutting off one's flesh and mixing it in with medicine was based on a long-standing Chinese superstition that if children performed this act when one of their parents was ill, Heaven would be moved by their action and the patient would recover. After listening to Xi Taihou's explanation, Ci'an Taihou was deeply moved. She said to her: 'Who would have thought you would do something like this for me? You are just like a sister to me; the Emperor was wrong about you!'

She then told Xi Taihou about the secret edict which the Xianfeng Emperor had given her. She took out the edict and burned it in front of Xi Taihou.

From then on, their relationship changed dramatically; all of Xi Taihou's politeness towards her vanished.

The situation whereby the two Empress Dowagers had ruled together gradually changed; Xi Taihou increasingly became the dominant partner. Her method of ruling was to make extensive use of the eunuchs. These were men whose reproductive organs had been cut off, and who were used to perform menial tasks in the imperial palace. There were a great many tasks to be performed in the palace, but at the same time the emperor had a large army of wives and concubines; it would not do to have men working there, but men were more effective workers than women. This was why the emperors needed eunuchs. The imperial palaces of the past were truly a monstrous entity. They housed thousands or even tens of thousands of women capable of reproducing, hundreds or even thousands of men incapable of reproducing, and only one man, the emperor, whose reproductive organs were intact.

The eunuchs spent their whole lives in the centre of power attending to the Emperor's needs. They had to watch the Emperor's moods, and relay orders for him. Naturally, there was a tendency for them to win the Emperor's trust. They were in a position to exercise power, and this, coupled with their warped psychology, was one more cause of trouble in times of chaos.

As a rule, the eunuchs were ignorant, self-interested people who abused their power. The first famous eunuch in Chinese history, Zhao Gao, caused the downfall of the Qin Dynasty through his interference in government affairs. One time, he pointed at deer and declared them to be horses while at court and nobody dared challenge him. In the Han Dynasty, eunuchs caused even more trouble. One eunuch was reported to have confiscated three hundred and eighty-one houses belonging to ordinary citizens. Towards the end of the dynasty, soldiers broke into the palace and killed over two thousand eunuchs. But it was no use.

In the Tang Dynasty, the eunuchs' power increased still further; they bullied not only government officials and commoners, but even the Emperor himself. One-third of all the Tang emperors were raised to power by the eunuchs, and once again it was eunuchs who finally brought down the dynasty. Once again, soldiers broke into the palace to kill the eunuchs; any man without a beard was liable to be killed on suspicion of being a eunuch.

In the Ming Dynasty, the eunuchs staged a comeback. The first Ming emperor was afraid that the eunuchs would seize power, and gave orders that eunuchs be prohibited from learning to read or write. This only served to make their abuse of power even greater. One Ming eunuch, Wang Zhen, collected a private hoard of gold and silver that filled sixty storerooms; another, Wei Zhongxian, came to exercise control over the cabinet and the six ministries and over the appointment of provincial governors. It reached the stage where everyone in the country was grovelling before him. The particular form this took was in the construction of shrines.

A shrine was normally only built to honour someone after their death, but someone had the idea that Wei Zhongxian might enjoy this honour while he was still alive. As a result, officials of all ranks throughout the country started building shrines in his honour. They were extremely expensive to build, and required the felling of large numbers of trees, but no one dared not build one. In the city of

Kaifeng alone, two thousand commoners' houses were levelled in order to construct a shrine to Wei Zhongxian. The emperor was referred to by the title of 'Ten Thousand Years'; Wei Zhongxian was referred to as 'Nine Thousand Years', only one thousand short of the emperor. In the end, the last Ming emperor had Wei Zhongxian executed, but this could not stave off the fall of the dynasty.

In the early years of the Ming Dynasty, in order to prevent the eunuchs from seizing power, an iron plaque had been hung outside the palace gates. It said that eunuchs were forbidden to interfere in government affairs, and that anybody who did so would be executed. Nevertheless, eunuchs still managed to bring about the fall of the dynasty.

A similar iron plaque was produced in the early years of the Qing Dynasty, proclaiming even fiercer punishments; eunuchs who interfered in government affairs were to be not merely executed, but sliced to death, cut by cut. Despite this, eunuch power continued to increase. During the Qing Dynasty, eunuchs were forbidden to leave the palace without permission, to interfere in matters not relating to the palace, to meet with government officials and to own property under an assumed name. The punishment for all of these offences was death, but the eunuchs, secure in the emperor's favour, ignored this.

In order to secure her hold on power, Xi Taihou used eunuchs as her agents. Initially, the eunuch she relied on most heavily was named An Dehai. Having already caused great disruption within the palace, he proceeded to carry on his activities outside it. In the ninth year after Xi Taihou started to participate in government (1869), An Dehai set off on a trip to Shandong. His squadron of boats sailed under a large dragon banner, which bore the title 'Imperial Servant Undertaking Purchasing'. On the boat with him were his nineteen-year-old adopted daughter, his uncle, younger sister and niece, footmen, bodyguards, cooks, barber, chiropodist, and storytellers, along with a monk and the monk's cook. They spent their time on the boat singing and partying; singing girls were hired to entertain them, and the monk joined in the fun along with the rest of them. When they reached Shandong they switched to carriages and sedan chairs, commandeering twenty-two mules, seventeen horses, and a donkey, and set off again in grand style. Angered by their activities, the Governor of Shandong Province, Ting Baozhen, sent a secret communiqué to Prince Gong informing him of the goings on. Prince Gong decided to teach Xi Taihou a lesson, and ordered Ding Baozhen to have An Dehai executed. When the news reached the ears of Xi Taihou, who was listening to an opera at the time, she fell into a rage. Convinced that Prince Gong and Ci'an Taihou were plotting against her, she was determined to have her revenge on them. At the same time, she continued to cultivate her control over the eunuchs.

Eleven years passed. By 1880, Xi Taihou had solidified her power still further. In the eighth month of 1880, she ordered the eunuch Li Sanshun to go outside the palace to deliver a gift to her sister. According to palace custom, eunuchs could not go in or out through the main entrance, they were only permitted to use the side entrance. Li Sanshun insisted on going out through the main entrance, and refused to submit to inspection. As a result, he and the gate guards became involved in a fight. The eunuch ran back into the palace and reported the incident to Xi Taihou, embroidering it extensively. She called for Ci'an Taihou, and said to her, 'I'm not even dead yet, and already they are treating me as though I did not exist. Either the guards pay for this with their lives, or I don't want to go on living.'

Ci'an Taihou was afraid, and issued orders to have the guards killed. The palace official in charge of justice said that this would not do. He said that the guards had not committed any offence, and that in any case according to the ancestral regulations they were required to refuse passage to Li Sanshun as they did. Ci'an Taihou said, 'What ancestral regulations? When I'm dead, won't I be one of the ancestors myself?' She insisted that the guards be killed. The Minister of the Board of Punishments, Pan Zuyin, said that since the guards had been delivered to the Board of Punishments the case would have to be dealt with according to law, which meant that the guards were declared not guilty. He said that if the Empress Dowager was determined to kill them she should find some other way to do it; she could not order officials responsible for upholding justice to kill people in violation of the law. Ci'an Taihou reported this to Xi Taihou, who called for Pan Zuyin. When he arrived, she wept, yelled, and cursed him.

Eventually, they agreed to a compromise. The guards would not be executed, but they would be publicly flogged on the buttocks. Prince Gong pointed out that this was a cruel punishment that the Ming rulers had used, and that the Qing should not copy them. Xi Taihou said, 'Why do you have to oppose me in everything? Just who do you think you are?' Prince Gong said, 'I am the sixth son of the late emperor.' Xi Taihou said, 'I strip you of your rank.' Prince

Gong said, 'You can strip me of my rank, but you can't take away the fact that I am an emperor's son!'

Xi Taihou was furious. In the end they got her to agree to a further compromise, and the matter was settled with the punishment of men who should not have been punished.

This kind of thing went on unchecked until the Tongzhi Emperor's eighteenth birthday, when things started to change. When he reached the age of eighteen the emperor had to marry, and once he was married he was considered to be an adult—Xi Taihou's involvement in government affairs would have to cease. The formal transfer of power from her to her son was thus drawing near.

The two Empresses each had a different candidate to be the Emperor's wife. In the end, the Tongzhi Emperor appointed the woman recommended by Ci'an Taihou to be empress, while the candidate put forward by Xi Taihou was given the title Hui Fei. Xi Taihou was very unhappy about this. After the wedding, she took every opportunity to encourage the Emperor to spend time with Hui Fei rather than with his Empress. Tired of being bossed around by his mother, the emperor started going out into the city in disguise, and eventually got sick as a result. The Empress rushed over to look after him; they had no idea that Xi Taihou was hidden behind a curtain listening to them. Xi Taihou heard the Emperor say, 'You'll just have to put up with it for now; one day we'll be able to take control from her.'

On hearing this, Xi Taihou leaped out, grabbed the empress by the hair and starting hitting her, while calling out for someone to bring her a stick. The Emperor died of fright; two months later, the eighteen-year-old empress committed suicide by swallowing gold. Once again Xi Taihou was able to rule again from behind the curtain; two years after having formally lost her power, she regained it by driving her son to his death.

Following the death of the Tongzhi Emperor, according to custom he should have been succeeded by someone from the next generation. However, having someone from the next generation take power would have meant that Xi Taihou would be that much further removed from power. Unable to bear this, she had her younger sister's son, her nephew, installed as the ninth Qing emperor—the Guangxu Emperor. When the boy became emperor he was only four years old, even younger than his predecessor, who had been six when he assumed the throne. This meant that Xi Taihou would have even more time in which to exercise power.

In the seventh year after the enthronement of the Guangxu Emperor, Xi Taihou had Ci'an Taihou poisoned, and in the eleventh year she divested Prince Gong of his rank. She now held absolute power, which she wielded blindly and selfishly. The government began to rot, and China went further and further downhill.

In the year in which Xi Taihou convinced Ci'an Taihou and Prince Gong to join her in a coup, she was twenty-seven, Ci'an Taihou was twenty-five, and Prince Gong was thirty. These three young people had to deal not only with foreign aggression but also with internal disturbances. Of these, the most serious were the rebellions that were taking place throughout China. When the coup took place, rebellions had already been underway for eleven years; they subsequently continued for another seventeen years after the coup. During the course of these rebellions, the population of Zhejiang Province fell from thirty million to ten million; within Zhejiang, the population of the city of Hangzhou, which had had the reputation of being a paradise on earth, fell from 800,000 to under 100,000; and the population of Jiangsu Province fell from forty-five million to twenty million. The troubles were not limited to Zhejiang and Jiangsu; every other province was littered with deserted villages, starving people and whitened bones, and cannibalism was common.

Nevertheless, despite the fact that both the internal and external threats to the regime were becoming increasingly serious, the Manchu woman continued to live a life of luxury in Beijing. In the thirty years after she took power at the age of twenty-seven, she remodelled the Qingyiyuan Gardens in the suburbs of Beijing to create the magnificent Yiheyuan park, or the Summer Palace.

The Summer Palace was the greatest garden park ever constructed in China. It contained over one hundred buildings in classical style, including palace halls, towers, pavilions, theatres, temples, pagodas, waterside pavilions, long corridors, piers, arched bridges, and a marble boat. This site had been a summer palace on and off for eight hundred years. When Xi Taihou took charge of it, she completely remodelled and expanded it, turning it into a park for her own private use. In the early years of her rule she moved to the Summer Palace on the first day of the fourth lunar month every year, and then moved back to the imperial palace in Beijing on the tenth day of the tenth month. Later, she spent the greater part of the year at the Summer Palace.

The extravagant life the Manchu woman led at the Summer Palace was staggering. She would insist on having one hundred and eighty-two dishes for one meal, costing a total of one hundred *taels* of silver; this amount of money could have bought enough millet to feed fifteen thousand Chinese peasants. In other words, the money she spent on food in one day would have been enough to feed forty-five thousand peasants. Although by this stage ordinary people in China were lucky to get even millet. They were reduced to eating bran and even tree bark; millet had become a luxury!

On her way from the imperial palace in Beijing to the Summer Palace, Xi Taihou would always stop and rest for a while; the place she chose to stop at was Wanshou Temple. In this way, Wanshou Temple became a very 'hot' temple, and it was no surprise that her trusted subordinate Li Lianying should choose to have the funerary rights for his mother performed there.

CHAPTER FIVE

Kang Youwei, the Presented Scholar

Kang Youwei passes his jinshi exam, while also progressing towards his goal of pushing political reform in China. This progress comes in the form of gaining entree to a high official, Weng Tonghe (former tutor of the emperor), and the Emperor. Concurrently, in light of the various unfair and humiliating treaties that have been forced upon China, the Japanese take the opportunity to declare war on and defeat China. This causes China great humiliation. China had always dominated Asia, and Japan now reverses China's dominant position seemingly overnight. Kang Youwei eloquently makes his case for reform, seeking Weng Tonghe's support in submitting his petition for political reform to the Emperor. He expresses what Weng Tonghe knew in his heart, but had refused to face politically—China's severe state of backwardness and even decline under the current leadership. The climax comes with the humiliating defeat at the hands of the Japanese. Weng Tonghe had been an important official in the government over the past decades, and feels responsible for his own inaction when it comes to reversing the country's decline, for continually supporting the personal agenda of the Empress Dowager over the welfare of the country as a whole. Consequently, he agrees to support Kang Youwei's petition, even at the possible expense of his own career. Thus, despite various other setbacks, Kang Youwei has renewed hope of succeeding in gaining an audience for his ideas in the Emperor.

◇◈◇

Just as the Empress Dowager resumed her excursion from Temple of Longevity on to the Summer Palace, Kang Youwei walked out of Fayuan Temple alone and headed back south to Guangdong.

His Beijing trip had been a failure. He had come to the capital for the purpose of submitting a petition to the emperor, asking for political reform. Before that, he had spent five years at Shiqiaoshan, Guangdong, preparing for this trip. At Shiqiaoshan, he delved into ancient books and studied the translations of new publications from the West. He did not know any foreign languages, but he had collected foreign books in Chinese translation in order to learn about other countries. The conclusion he drew from his studies was that China must be modernized in order to be saved. To take on the path of modernization, one person, the Emperor, had to be won over. It was practically hopeless to persuade that stodgy old conservative, the Empress Dowager. Things would move along if the Emperor gave the go-ahead.

Thus he decided to make an appeal to the Emperor. This Beijing trip had been an experiment, but a failed one. Despite the brilliant ideas presented in the petition, he could not find a way to get it delivered to the Emperor. In the imperial politics of China, the petitions of commoners almost never reached the emperor directly. If you wanted to submit a petition, you had to be connected with some powerful official who would make the delivery for you and be essentially responsible for its contents. But who would want to risk this kind of trouble? Besides, it was not that easy to establish contact with someone that well connected.

Disheartened, Kang Youwei decided to go back south. He planned to renew his efforts after building up his social status in order to be taken more seriously. The starting point was to pass the imperial civil service examination at the county level (a *xiucai* or Cultivated Talent), then at the provincial level (a *juren* or Recommendee), and finally at the national level (a *jinshi* or Presented Scholar). Kang was already a *juren* at that time. So he decided to take the exam for *jinshi* and start running classes to cultivate his own cadre of aspirants.

Although the Beijing trip had floundered, there was one thought that comforted to Kang Youwei. He had established a contact, however tenuous, with an influential official, the Emperor's tutor, Weng Tonghe. When he had first written to Weng, Weng refused to meet with him. He then asked Sheng Yu, the Chancellor of the Directorate of Education, to introduce him to Weng. Still Weng refused to deliver his petition on the grounds that the tone of the petition was too straightforward and the views expressed had little value.

Nevertheless, Kang had left a strong impression on this old scholar. It so happened that Weng was a calligrapher who had spent considerable time and effort in studying the inscriptions on old tablets. Kang himself was also an accomplished calligrapher and a scholar of old tablets. After returning south, Kang spent seventeen days writing *A Diversified Artistic Boat with Two Paddles*, which described what he had learned by studying the calligraphy and old tablets during his stay in Beijing, and sent it to Weng. Weng was astonished by the capacity of this young man and from then on considered him to rank as a person of comparable taste.

Naturally something in the nature of *A Diversified Artistic Boat with Two Paddles* was not the usual theme of Kang's writings. His writings generally advocated a government administration that would benefit the people, or provide guidance for China, or provide a direction for the intellectuals. His master work came in three parts: Part One was the *New Doctrines Against the Old Classics*, meant to break the hold of traditional doctrines and advise intellectuals to have the courage to break away from the bondage of tradition; Part Two was *Confucius as a Reformer*, which pointed out the true nature of Confucius and urged intellectuals not to fear changing the status quo; Part Three was *An Advocacy on the Utopian World*, a vision for the future, telling intellectuals that the prerequisite for creating a utopia was to first build a state of modest prosperity.

Aside from writing books and propounding his own set of theories, Kang opened a private school and recruited a dozen students. One of them was Liang Qichao, a child prodigy who had passed the exam for *juren* at the age of seventeen. Liang was eighteen years old when he came under Kang's tutelage. It might have seemed strange since both of them were *juren*. But this eighteen-year-old *juren* truly admired the thirty-three-year-old Kang *juren*. Liang was well versed in ancient literature. But one day he and a friend chanced upon Kang and discovered that Kang's scholarship was as loud as the tidal wail and the lion's roar. He and his friend were amazed and glad, yet bitter and sad. They were glad to learn that the world of knowledge was so immense, and felt fortunate to have encountered an intelligent person like Kang. They were also bitter to learn that the knowledge they had attained led to a dead end. They had toiled in the wrong direction, although it was the same path the majority of Chinese intellectuals had taken. After listening to Kang's eloquent discourse, they decided to follow him.

The second year after his return from Beijing, Kang opened his private school, named Wan Mu Cao Tang, or Ten Thousand Woods and Grasses School, in Guangzhou. The courses taught at the school ranged from the classics to modern subjects, from religion to rhetoric, from mathematics to physical education. The teachers and the students totalled a dozen people. But everyone got an assignment, be it assisting in teaching, monitoring student conduct, leading exercise sessions, or safekeeping books and instruments. Teachers and students lived and learned together with a new conviction, longing for that great, though unattainable, future.

Three years passed. What transpired in those three years was quite different from the first five years Kang had spent in preparation; Kang had struggled alone for those five years. During the past three years, Kang had enriched his mind and published *New Doctrines Against the Old Classics* and *Confucius as a Reformer*. He had also gained more fame. With Liang Qichao as his student and assistant, he was no longer alone.

The year 1894 was a troubling one for the imperial court insofar as foreign encroachment was concerned. The foreign barbarians that had tried to bully China in the past had blond hair and blue eyes, mainly the British and the French. In ancient times when China was strong, there were no encounters with these foreign devils. The predominance of the Chinese Empire was extended primarily to the yellow race, including Japan and Vietnam. The title of 'Kingdom of Dwarfs' was conferred on Japan during the Han Dynasty and China once invaded Japan during the Yuan Dynasty. That country was never a threat to or taken seriously by the Chinese.

But by the end of the nineteenth century, Japan had grown so strong as a result of reform that she now eyed China as potential prey. The Japanese had witnessed China's decline: the country was forced to sign the Treaty of Nanking with England in 1842; the Treaty of Tientsin with England and France in 1858; and the Treaty of Peking (now Beijing) again with Great Britain and France in 1860. The signing of a series of humiliating treaties had taken place. Japan decided that she wanted a piece of the pie. Thus in 1894 the Sino-Japanese War was launched over the issue of Korea.

The Sino-Japanese War was formally declared on 1 July 1894, and China was defeated. After the defeat, everybody blamed Li Hongzhang, the administrator responsible. But Li countered: 'I am not to be blamed for this disgrace.' He said he had been through much adversity and knew about the world and affairs of state. He had warned against the war. But everybody was so gung-ho about fighting the war that any dissenter was branded a traitor. Now China had lost the war and he was still called a traitor for losing the war. He did not think he should be held responsible under these circumstances.

In this ill-fated war, China dispatched fifteen thousand soldiers to Korea to put up a land defence, while Japan sent in a force of forty thousand soldiers. At sea, China's Yellow Sea Fleet had not acquired a new ship for six years. The British had recommended the purchase of two cruisers some time previously. But the Empress Dowager diverted the funds earmarked for the navy, using them instead to fix up her Summer Palace. The cruisers were eventually bought by the Japanese; one of them, the battleship Yoshino, proceeded to defeat the main naval force of imperial China.

The national sentiment regarding the war was most peculiar. At the start of the war, everybody in Japan from the emperor down was concerned about the war situation. But in China, everybody from the Empress Dowager down was busy watching Chinese opera as if some other country were fighting the war. With such a mentality, absurdity abounded. The imperial navy had different divisions—Beiyang (northern sea), Nanyang (southern sea), Mingnan (Fujian), and Yueyang (Guangdong)—each going their own way. In the grand inspection prior to the Sino-Japanese War, the Yueyang division dispatched three ships, the 'Guangjia', 'Guangyi', and 'Guangbing'. The war broke out before the inspection was over, and those three ships stayed on to make a show of force. During the war, the 'Guangjia' was stranded, the 'Guangyi' was sunk, and the 'Guangbing' surrendered. After the war, the head of the Yueyang division wrote to the Japanese general who had accepted the surrender, asking for the return of these three ships. He claimed that these three ships, each with a prefix of 'Guang', belonged to Guangdong, which had nothing to do with the war.

Some foreigners commented on the Sino-Japanese War saying that in same respects, it was not a war between China and Japan, but a war between Li Hongzhang and Japan. With Li fighting alone against thirty million Japanese, the outcome of the war was predetermined.

During the past two thousand years, Japan had been a tiny state, an insignificant neighbour, and a small protectorate in the eyes of the Chinese. Now, powerful China had been defeated by the Japanese devils. The experience was more humiliating than the defeat at the hands of the British. This defeat prompted the intellectuals to take drastic actions, of which the act of petitioning the emperor by *juren*, or recommendees, was the most unusual.

According to tradition, after a *xiucai* or cultivated talent passed the exam for *juren*, the *juren* could take the exam for *jinshi*, or presented scholar, in the capital city. With *juren* submitting a petition to the emperor, it amounted to the exam candidates submitting a petition to the ruler. This kind of skip-order petition, although rare, was not unprecedented. In the second year after the end of the Sino-Japanese War, *juren* from all provinces arrived in Beijing to take the exam for *jinshi*, as did Kang Youwei and Liang Qichao. In fact, soon after the news of the signing of the Treaty of Shimonoseki was heard, Liang gathered the signatures of one hundred and ninety *juren* in Guangdong in a petition that discussed the current political situation. Two days later, Kang held a meeting at the Songyun Buddhist Convent attended by twelve hundred *juren* from all over the country, and prepared a petition for political reform. In the course of this action, the *juren* from Taiwan were the most bitter, because Taiwan had been ceded to Japan as a result of the treaty. Kang spent one day and two nights drafting this petition of over ten thousand words.

But petitions to a regime in decline were ineffectual. The Court of Censors refused to forward the petition on the grounds that the Qing government had already approved the treaty and the issue was closed.

The issue might have been closed on the surface, but the Qing government could not entirely ignore the views of over one thousand people, particularly when these people were *juren*. The most prominent of these *juren* was Kang Youwei, who became Kang *jinshi* the day after the petition was submitted.

Kang Youwei had been well known among high-ranking officials prior to becoming a *jinshi*. He had earned a reputation for submitting his petition six years earlier, and had gathered more fame since, partly owing to the fact that his work, *New Doctrines Against the Old Classics,* had been banned in its first year of publication. The conservatives in the Qing court viewed him as a potential troublemaker. After passing the exam for *jinshi*, Kang attained a new level of pre-eminence, and his third petition was finally brought to the attention of the Emperor. Nevertheless, there was a long way to go before his words could produce any effect.

After Kang became a *jinshi*, he founded a newspaper called the *Chinese and Foreign Gazette*, to advocate reform. At that time, there was no such thing as a newspaper subscription. If it was to be read, a newspaper had to be provided free. Thus Kang and his colleagues printed three thousand copies each day and hired young boys to make daily door-to-door deliveries. But not knowing what the newspaper was about, most families turned it down. Before long, even the delivery boys became suspicious and refused to continue the job for fear of being implicated in some scandal.

Soon after his newspaper publishing business began, Kang founded an organization called the Qiangxuehui, or Learning Strength Society, which published books and periodicals and advocated new thoughts. The Society was well received among more open-minded people. Even the British and American envoys donated books and printing presses. But the shadow of intransigence soon loomed, and Kang felt that his days in Beijing were numbered. He decided to go south and develop something there. Thus on the evening before the Qiangxuehui was banned, he left Beijing.

Despite the fact that all his activities in Beijing in the past year had fallen short of success, Kang did make some progress on his long journey towards winning over the Emperor. The most significant gain was that Weng Tonghe, the Emperor's tutor who had refused to see him six years earlier, now agreed to meet with him. Weng recalled that Kang had predicted the defeat of China at the hands of the Japanese six years earlier. He also felt that he had slighted this calligrapher called Kang Youwei who was now a fellow *jinshi*. In his meeting with Weng Tonghe, who had the honest, sincere look of an old farmer, Kang made the following remark that left an indelible impression on this high-ranking official:

'Grand Secretary, you are certainly familiar with the Opium War of fifty-five years ago. It was caused by foreigners shipping to China the opium they didn't smoke themselves. But the real reason for China's defeat in that confrontation was her backwardness. The Chinese government, officials, intelligentsia, army, weaponry, and people were all backward. But their backwardness was understandable, because China didn't have much contact with the outside world at that time. But it was inexcusable that the country slept for another twenty years of inaction and ended up with the Anglo-French force setting fire to the Garden of Perfection and Brightness. After that, some people began to wake up. For example, Prince Gong launched the self-strengthening movement. But the conservative attitude prevalent throughout the Qing court from the Empress Dowager down and Prince Gong's half measures had precluded any real progress over those thirty-five years.

The truth about the state of our country was revealed in our war with Japan. We have failed to recognize our situation for the past fifty-five years since the Opium War, while the Japanese were moving forward, leaving us way behind. Let's look back. If we had learned our lesson in the Opium War and moved in another direction in the ensuing fifty-five years, we would not be in the predicament we find ourselves in today.'

'In your view, why didn't we have some kind of realization after the Opium War?' asked Weng.

'The main reason was that the majority of people, from the top down, were opposed to change and unaware of China's real position in the world. But those scholars who did know, chose not to get involved and kept their mouths shut. This was the more important reason. Take the example of Lin Zexu, a most esteemed and illustrious official fifty-five years ago, a man of integrity. He was sent to Guangdong to ban the opium trade under the commission of Emperor Daoguang. He had the total trust of the Emperor and full confidence in himself. He was convinced that he could crush the Westerners. But Lin was no ordinary person. Once he had arrived in Guangdong and had a look at the actual situation, he knew that Chinese weaponry was inferior and confidence alone could not defeat the enemy. The guns and cannon used by the imperial army were relics from the seventeenth century and no match for Western weaponry. Therefore he recommended buying foreign cannon and ships, and had foreign publications translated. Later he turned over the materials to Wei Yuan, who compiled the *Map Journal of Sea Power,* which advocated fighting Westerners with Western weaponry. The Japanese translated this book into their own language, which greatly helped their efforts at reform.

Given Lin's status and his understanding of China's situation in the world, he had hardly done enough. Why? Because he made the same mistake as the great majority of Chinese intelligentsia— minding their own business, fearing peer criticism, and staying out of trouble. In his letter to a friend two years after the Opium War, Lin wrote: "The cannon of the Westerners can shoot much farther and faster. Despite the combat experience of our army, the cannon fired from a long distance can destroy them before there is any face-to-face encounter. If we don't deal with this problem, an army of one million soldiers is only good for one big offensive. Without cannon, even the famous generals Yue Fei or Han Shizong would have been at a loss." Lin asked his friend to keep this letter confidential. This behaviour spoke volumes. Lin himself knew very well the problems of China. But he refused to voice his opinions despite his position. It was not that he was losing favour with the court when he wrote that letter—he was subsequently appointed governor-general of Shanxi and Gansu, and later Yunnan and Guizhou. If even prominent and competent officials like Lin chose to stay passive about the affairs of the country, how could there be any hope?'

Weng Tonghe listened attentively and in silence to Kang's remarks. He was apparently touched by the example of Lin Zexu. When Lin died in 1850, Weng was only an unknown young man of twenty. Now he was sixty-five, and feeling the time slipping away. He was uncertain whether or not he had achieved anything in his service to his country in the past few decades, and he had only a few more years left. The country, he felt, needed a new generation to save it. It would be good if he could make use of his vision and influence to recommend to the court some good people before his retirement, and Kang was a good prospect.

After thinking for a while, Weng replied in a kindly tone, 'I can see that you are a competent, outstanding young man. You probably know what I think of you. Otherwise you wouldn't have tried again and again to see me. It's my responsibility to recommend competent people to the court. It is actually wrong to hold back such knowledge.

'But you are aware of how complicated the political situation is in China. Even with my position, I have to do things by a circuitous route. However I will try to figure out a way as soon as I can to recommend your ideas to the Emperor. I am not sure if it can be done. But I can assure you of one thing, and that is that I will no longer just mind my own business. You know I tutored the last and the present emperors when they were young, and I am doing modestly well at court. I won't hold back this time. I'll find the opportunity to recommend you to the Emperor. It doesn't matter what consequences I must face.'

Weng Tonghe was from Changshu, in Jiangsu. He was the number one scholar when he passed the imperial exam for *jinshi* nearly forty years previously, before Kang was born. In the past forty years, his star had been on the rise, but that of China was in decline. His sense of guilt and self-blame deepened with advancing age. On his sixtieth birthday five years previously, the Empress Dowager had bestowed upon him a myriad of gifts and received him the next day, praising his loyalty. These special honours had made him feel all the more remorseful, because his loyalty was of questionable value.

For many years, he had been loyal to the private affairs of the Empress Dowager, not to the welfare of the entire country. The matter of the naval budget being diverted to fix up the Summer Palace caused him the most guilt, for he was in charge of government finance at that time. Was he not the one who failed to put up a good fight against it? Was he the one who failed to risk his job to fight the decision to build the palace? Was he not the one who finalized the government policy of no additions to naval artillery for fifteen years? The war was lost and he was partly to blame. Now he was old. He felt he must do something to redeem himself, even if he risked offending the Empress Dowager.

CHAPTER SIX
The Emperor

The Emperor is under the thumb of the Empress Dowager from the time he comes to the throne at four years of age. Things do not change, even though she nominally hands power over to him when he reaches the age of nineteen. The Empress Dowager skilfully manipulates the Emperor's environment to ensure that he has no support from anyone besides her. One exception is his tutor Weng Tonghe. He tutored the Emperor for twenty-four years when he came to recommend Kang Youwei to the Emperor. In the interest of saving his country, this high-ranking official thereby brings ruin upon himself.

On the same day that the Emperor summons Kang Youwei to an audience, Weng Tonghe is stripped of his rank and all privileges under pressure from the Empress Dowager. Kang Youwei persuades the Emperor to take up reform, beginning with the abolition of the eight-part essay examination system for the civil service system. Along with the abolition of the outdated examination system, the Emperor appoints several junior officials, including Kang Youwei, to assist in effecting reforms as a means of circumventing the Empress Dowager's firm control over high-ranking officials. Thus the reform movement begins to be realized, as the plot thickens.

———◇◆◇———

Weng Tonghe went to court and secretly related the ideas of Kang Youwei to the Emperor. He asked the Emperor to heed the words of this thirty-eight-year-old reformer. This was the second year after the Sino-Japanese War which China lost, and as a result of which China ceded Taiwan to Japan and paid an indemnity of two hundred million *taels*. The Emperor was in a dejected mood.

Ever since he was enthroned at the age of four, the Emperor had been growing up under the stern gaze of the Empress Dowager. Not one day went by without him feeling that dreadful gaze behind his back. When he was little, he sat on the emperor's throne with a screen behind him. The Empress Dowager sat behind the screen to attend to the affairs of state. Her silhouette was indistinct, but her words, not his, were the commands to the courtiers and officials. He was too young to govern the country, so his eldest aunt, the Empress Dowager, who was thirty six years his senior took charge.

Each time he was put on the throne, the back of his boots pointed squarely at the faces of the officials. He didn't understand a word they said. In sheer boredom, he entertained himself by aiming his shoes, with tips propped against each other, at whichever official was doing the talking. That tended to block the face of the speaker. Then he would part the heels and squint at that talking mouth from the triangular gap created. Each mouth looked different, but they all had rotten teeth. He compared the mouth and teeth of each official and found it quite funny. But he dared not laugh out loud. The Empress Dowager was sitting behind him.

When he was small, he often heard the word '*yi zhi*' and learned later that it meant the Empress's decree. He also heard the word '*yu zhi*' and found out later that it meant the imperial or his own decree. Gradually he realized that '*yi zhi*' was real, while '*yu zhi*' was a sham. His tutor, Master Weng, taught him about these '*zhi*'. He remembered his first lesson with Master Weng when he was only four years old was to learn to write the Chinese characters for the name of his teacher—Grand Secretariat Scholar Weng Tonghe. That was really difficult. Whenever he cracked up thinking about those talking mouths framed in the triangular gap of his boots, Master Weng admonished him that an emperor must appear dignified; no smiling or laughing.

So he grew up in the court without smiles. People kowtowed to him all day, and he kowtowed to the Empress Dowager. He was sandwiched between two poles, where he stood all alone. He was faced with walls of people and palaces all day. The walls of people were always on their knees, appearing so low; the walls of palaces were always standing, looking so lofty. He had no playmates; he had to play by himself. But there were always people nearby looking after him, peeking, as if he were acting on stage. He accompanied the Empress Dowager when she watched plays on the court stage. Now he was watched playing by himself. The difference was he had a smaller audience than Liu Gansan, the court performer.

He really enjoyed the plays of Liu Gansan. He remembered how when he got married at the age of nineteen, the Empress Dowager returned power to him and removed the screen behind his throne, making him look like a real emperor. But when he watched plays with the Empress Dowager, he still had to stand respectfully at her side. One day, Liu Gansan was playing the emperor on stage. The other actors ridiculed him, saying that he was a fake emperor. He suddenly blurted out: 'Don't make light of this fake emperor. At least I have a chair to sit on!' In the height of the moment when everybody was enjoying the play, Liu's words surprisingly amused the Empress Dowager. She nodded with a smile and slowly lifted her index finger, saying: 'Then let's give our real emperor a chair.' From then on, he was able to watch the plays sitting down.

The Empress Dowager was his mother's elder sister. She had practically tortured her own child Emperor Tongzhi, to death, so she put her nephew on the throne. Not long after he was born, the Empress Dowager asked his mother: 'Have you prepared the lock?' His mother replied: 'No, we are waiting for the Empress Dowager's grace.' The so-called lock was a plate that hung on the neck of a newborn. The Chinese believed that to have a child grow up safe and sound, securing him with a symbolic locking plate would prevent him from walking back to where he came from. Following tradition, the Empress Dowager gave him a gold locking plate. It turned out that this eldest aunt, who gave him the plate, was actually the person who was to have him completely shackled.

According to the system adopted by the imperial forefathers, the Empress Dowager should have chosen a crown prince from among the nephews of Emperor Tongzhi after he passed away without an heir. But she did not, for this would have made her a 'Great' Empress Dowager, in which case it would have been highly inappropriate for her to sit behind the screen to attend to affairs of state. So she chose her own nephew as the new emperor. Censor Wu Kedu openly remonstrated against this choice at the time. He presented a petition and then committed suicide, but to no avail. When her brother-in-law Prince Chun learned that his own son was to become the emperor, he knelt before her and tearfully pleaded against it, but couldn't reverse her decision. It was an extraordinary honour for his son to be emperor. But it also meant that they would be separated for good, and their father–son relationship would turn into that of sovereign–minister.

One evening the four-year-old boy was awakened and carried into an imperial palanquin. The only face familiar to him was his wet nurse who was permitted to come along under a special edict from the Empress Dowager.

The wet nurse was a familiar feature in families of wealth and rank. By Chinese custom, nursing a baby boy required the work of a specialist since the biological mother was physically weak after ten months of gestation. The so-called specialist usually came from a peasant family. Peasant women lived close to nature and tended to be healthy and simple. The best wet nurse was a woman who had given birth less than two months earlier, looked upright, and produced dense breast milk. After the wet nurse was chosen, the parties entered an agreement that usually prohibited her going home or visiting her own child, and required that she eat a bowl of unsalted pork each day to facilitate milk production. Soon she became no longer a woman, but a milk cow. Many peasant women were willing to become a wet nurse to save their families from starvation. But it was a common scene for a wet nurse to go home to visit her family after the child she had nursed grew up, and find that her own child had died of hunger many years earlier.

After the wet nurse carried the four-year-old boy into the imperial palanquin, she herself got into a sedan chair of shoulder height, and entered the palace at the end of the procession. She and the little Emperor depended on each other in the unfamiliar environment. Still, the little Emperor was a tad better off; he could still sneak a glimpse of his family among the throng of officials. She could only see her own family in her dreams.

The imperial palace was called the 'Forbidden City'. In Chinese legend, the heavenly palace where the supreme deity resided was dubbed Zi Palace, or 'Purple Palace'. Zi meant *ziwei*, the 'Northern Star', which was situated at the centre of the sky with clusters of stars surrounding it, signifying the sovereign descent of an emperor. The layout of the Forbidden City was created accordingly. The Taihedian, or 'Hall of Supreme Harmony', stood magnificently in the centre, overlooking the other structures. The emperor's sleeping quarters, called Qianqinggong or the 'Palace of Heavenly Purity', and the empress's sleeping quarters, called Kuninggong or the 'Palace of Earthly Peace', were positioned as heaven to earth. Rijin Gate or 'Sun Essence' Gate in the east, and Yuehua Gate or 'Moon Splendour' Gate in the west, were arranged on either side to represent the sun and the moon. The twelve palaces represented the twelve time periods of the day. The rows of garden houses behind the palaces on the east and west symbolized the galaxy of stars. The true son of heaven stood out in the palaces of heaven, earth, sun, moon, and stars.

The Forbidden City was all splendour and radiance during the day. But when night fell, a ghastly aura pervaded there. There was only the shrilling sing-song of the eunuchs emanating from the silent

Palace of Heavenly Purity, yelling: 'Lock the doors, take care of your valuables, be careful with the lights . . .' The lingering voice of one eunuch was echoed by other eunuchs on duty. The waves of sound that permeated every corner of the Forbidden City emitted ghostly ripples that sent chills down the spine.

For the little Emperor who was only four years old, a sense of terror was with him night and day. The sight of his awe-inspiring aunt during the day, no, the 'dear papa' as she preferred to be called, always petrified him. The shadows of the grand palaces and the look of those asexual eunuchs at night also scared him. The only comforting sight in all his fears was his wet nurse. But she was not with him all the time. He was mostly alone, with no one to depend on. His knowledge of the world did not develop until his tutor Weng Tonghe started giving him lessons at the age of six. Since then they forged a strong bond as teacher and student. Under Weng's tutelage, he learned about himself, China, and the world beyond. There was much more to life than the array of palaces; outside the palace, there was the great land of China, and the universe.

The Empress Dowager returned power to him when he was nineteen, but he remained only a figurehead. The Empress Dowager possessed the real power. Although she no longer sat behind the screen, she set up an invisible net of influence from the Summer Palace that covered the entire city of Beijing.

The affairs of the state were in a shambles when he was given back his power. The Empress Dowager was fifty-five years old and had been ruling China for thirty years. The encroachment of the Anglo-French forces had first put her in power three decades back. But owing to her selfishness and ignorance, the country was now further debilitated and faced with a new threat of foreign aggression posed by the Japanese. As the state situation worsened and as he grew older, he decided to climb over the walls of the palaces and become a competent ruler. He knew that the land outside the palaces was his land, waiting to be ruled by him. But the palace walls that were still in his way, not only physically but also invisibly, extended to the Summer Palace. He had to go there five or six times a month to pay his respects to and seek instructions from the Empress Dowager. Even with the prestige of an emperor, he was not allowed to go into the Empress Dowager's palace directly. He had to kneel outside and wait to be summoned. Like other senior-ranking officials, he had to give head eunuch Li Lianying packets of money so he could be seen sooner. What kind of emperor *was* he?

There was practically no man in the enormous court with whom
he could have heart-to-heart talks. After he was given back his power,
there were rumours of 'the Empress Dowager's faction' and 'the
Emperor's faction'. The former was facetiously dubbed the 'mother's
gang', and the latter the 'kid's gang'. But the leader of either the
'Emperor's faction' or 'kid's gang' was a loner. He had no real
supporters or followers. Everybody had become the eyes and ears of
the Empress Dowager. His Empress Long Yu, a niece of the Empress
Dowager, was no exception. He had no women other than his
beloved Zhenfei, the 'Pearl Concubine', with whom he could
exchange intimate words. But his love for her brought her disaster.
To remind the Emperor of her authority over him, the Empress
Dowager often punished Zhenfei by having her kneel down for a
long time or ordering head eunuch Li Lianying to slap her. Many
times when he visited Zhenfei, he found her sobbing in her room.
Then he knew that it had happened again. But all he could do was
pat her back, his feelings a mixture of hurt, rage, guilt, and futility.

<hr />

Many a time he left Zhenfei with both a sense of comfort and a
nightmare. The nightmare was a frequently recurring one. It always
began with his eldest aunt, the Empress Dowager. Her long, cold,
and stern face pressed upon him in total silence. He dared not cry;
he only stretched out his arms wishing to grab something that could
bring help and warmth. He seemed to have grabbed a soft hand, the
hand of his wet nurse. But soon the hand was slipping away, until
he could no longer hang on to it. In a stupor, he felt another softer
hand grab him, the hand of Zhenfei. But his own hand was so weak,
so powerless. Finally, Zhenfei's hand was slipping. Suddenly, the
Empress Dowager started to back away. But there was a noise coming
from a distance. He went over to have a look and saw that horrible
scene: the Empress Dowager sitting high and mighty in the big
palanquin with people crowded around her, while his beloved
Zhenfei was on her knees with torn clothes, and Li Lianying grabbing
hold of her hair. Lee was slapping her while he counted: 'One, two,
three, four . . .'
    He dashed forward and yelled: 'Stop! Stop!' He seized Li's
shoulder and smacked him. Li broke loose and threw himself before
the Empress Dowager, crying out: 'I did this for the Venerable Buddha!
I did this for the Venerable Buddha! How could the Emperor do this

to me! I won't do this job anymore! No more!' He then did five
kowtows, pleading: 'I ask for the grace of the Venerable Buddha! Let
me go home!'

Suddenly the Empress Dowager flew into a rage.

'What audacity the Emperor has! How dare you slap my people!
You have to make sure who the master is before you kick the dog. If
you have no Li Lianying in your vision, how can you see me?'

'Dear Papa! Dear Papa! I'm sorry.' The Emperor knelt down
immediately.

'Alright,' said the Empress Dowager in a chilling tone. 'Since
we can't afford to offend you, we might as well hide in the Summer
Palace. But I can tell you, we'll just wait and see. Don't think that
now you are the emperor, you can have more concubines and forget
all about your mother. I can make you an emperor and I can drag
you down. You can figure out yourself what kind of emperor you
want to be.'

The voice of the Empress Dowager lingered and her cold, stern
face began to press upon him again. He had no one to hold on to.
His wet nurse disappeared and Zhenfei fell down. He awoke abruptly,
covered in sweat. Only one candle flickered in the darkness, bringing
his life pitifully little brightness.

⸺◦◦◦⸺

The Emperor couldn't go back to sleep. It was two o'clock in the
morning. 'I should get up,' he mumbled. 'Many officials are on their
way to the court.'

The teachings of the forefathers were that 'the best time of the
year is spring' and 'the best time of the day is *yinshi*', that is, from
three to five o'clock in the morning. These hours were the time for
working, not for getting ready for work. Officials who lived far from
the palace usually left home at one o'clock in the morning. Officials
of varying levels passed through one of the three gates before entering
the imperial palace. There used to be a rule that required a body
search at the gate. But with too many officials passing through each
day, the rule was formally waived. But another custom was still in
practice: when an official entered the Forbidden City, the guard had
to yell out 'Oh!', meaning, 'I know you are here.' For senior officials,
the 'Oh!' lasted longer; for petty officials, the 'Oh!' was brief.
Sometimes the sleepy guard could get away with yelling 'Oh!' while
still inside his matted sleeping bag in the gateway. So every morning

the officials, each with a small lantern in their hand, paraded into the palace from the three gates to the accompaniment of 'Oh!' Naturally elderly, venerable officials might receive preferential treatment. At times the emperor allowed them to ride in a two-man palanquin or ride a horse into the Forbidden City. But such preferential treatment stopped at Longzong Gate, the same being true for the Emperor's tutor, Weng Tonghe. Today, he stepped out of the palanquin and walked into the Yangxin Hall or Mental Cultivation Hall with a heavy load on his mind.

———<><>——

Beijing had three main city gates. Zhengyang Gate was in the middle, Xuanwu Gate on the left, and Chongwen Gate on the right. If one entered the city through Zhengyang Gate, one came next to Tiananmen or 'Gate of Heavenly Peace', and farther in, Wumen or 'Meridian Gate', a massive structure with three sides that featured a big tower at the front and four corner towers on the two sides. The courtyard in front of Wumen could hold an audience of twenty thousand, and many national ceremonies of the Ming and Qing dynasties had taken place there. Naturally, the courtyard was also used on other occasions. For example, in the Ming Dynasty, when an irate emperor wanted to assert his authority, he would flog a minister there; in the Qing Dynasty, when an emperor wanted to reprimand an official, a eunuch would carry out the job for him there. Also, when groups of senior officials thanked the emperor for his grace, they knelt in front of Wumen to show their appreciation.

After Wumen, there was the Jinshuiqiao, the 'Golden Stream Bridge', and then further down into the heart of the Forbidden City, Taihemen or 'Supreme Harmony Gate'. After Taihemen, the greatest and grandest structure in the imperial city, the Taihedian or 'Hall of Supreme Harmony' was situated. Three terraces of dragon-ornamented steps flanked the frontage of the palace; the first terrace had twenty-one steps and the second and the third nine steps each. Each terrace was bound by dragon-shaped marble balustrades winding up the steps. Overlooking the top was the largest and most splendid wood-framed structure in China. Supported by eighty-four *nanmu* pillars, the building was thirty-three metres tall with a six-metre long foundation.

Taihedian was the main hall of the outer court where major ceremonies were held. Behind it were two smaller halls, Zhonghedian, the 'Hall of Middle Harmony,' and Baohedian, the 'Hall of Preserving Harmony,' that together constituted the three great halls, the political centre of the outer court.

Beyond the three great halls were Heavenly Purity Gate, where the inner court began, and then the Palace of Heavenly Peace, where the emperor resided. The emperor carried on his daily activities, such as receiving officials or holding banquets at the Mental Cultivation Hall, situated on the right flank of the Palace of Heavenly Peace. The emperor had a small suite in this hall that enjoyed a relative degree of warmth in the immense and depressing Forbidden City. The name 'Mental Cultivation Hall' came from a quotation from the *Book of Mencius*: 'To cultivate one's mind begins with fewer desires.' Actually, to have few desires or to cultivate one's mind were both difficult in this nerve centre where so many troubling issues were handled.

This day, the Emperor received Weng Tonghe alone in the Mental Cultivation Hall.

Weng gave the Emperor a summary report of the current situation facing China, unprecedented in her three thousand years of history, and asked him to consider fundamental changes.

'Our country has been evolving. We started making changes over thirty years ago,' the Emperor replied. 'In the first year of Tongzhi, Zeng Guofan set up the Ammunition Depot in Anqing and Li Hongzhang established the Artillery Manufacturing Bureau in Shanghai. Then there were the Shanghai School for Foreign Languages, the Nanking Arsenal, the Jiangnan Machinery Bureau in Shanghai, the Maritime Administration Bureau in Fuzhou, the Machinery Bureau in Tianjin, the Dagu Forts, and China Merchants Steamship Company. These were changes made in previous reigns. In the present reign, we established the Armoured Ship Factory and Bureau of Western Knowledge in various provinces in the first year. Later on, there was the Telegraph Bureau, Railway Bureau, Mining Bureau, Military Academy, Navy of the Northern Ports, and Hanyang Arsenal. Even today . . .'

'Your Majesty is right,' answered Weng Tonghe. 'Our country has indeed been making changes over the past thirty years. But our changes have concentrated on imitating the apparent strengths of the foreigners, that is, their naval power and artillery. But these things are not why they've become strong. The root of their strength lies in political progress brought about by reform. That is their true strength. But we missed it. The result is that we were defeated not only by the Westerners, but also by the Japanese, who implemented reform modelled after the real strengths of the Westerners. This lesson tells us that only political reform can save China. I ask Your Majesty to think about it.'

Sitting on his throne rubbing his face, the Emperor contemplated Weng's words. He was twenty-five years old. Although he was not particularly well built, he had youth and vigour. He had developed some concrete ideas about reform thanks to Weng. But to undertake a reform movement, he needed new assistants. Who would be his aides? Master Weng?

'I am too old. Not only am I sixty-four years old, my thinking lags behind the times as well,' answered Weng wearily. 'But the young man Kang Youwei whom I mentioned to Your Majesty earlier will be a good assistant. I recommend him strongly. Kang was ranked number five in the imperial exam for *jinshi* this year. On the surface, it might look like he is just another good scholar. But he's much more than that. He is extremely knowledgeable, passionate, and competent. When he was a *juren*, he wrote *New Doctrines Against the Old Classics,* which was banned by the local officials under the command of the then Governor-General of Guangdong and Guangxi. This shows that he is no ordinary person. When he heard the news of Taiwan being ceded to Japan, he drafted a petition signed by twelve hundred *juren* scholars asking for reform. Now he has founded the Qiangxuehui in Beijing, advocating new ideas. Yuan Shikai is a member and Zhang Zhidong donated money to the organization.

According to Kang, you can't even find a world map in the whole city of Beijing. That tells how ill-informed the Chinese are about the world. If this is the case in the capital city, it's certainly worse in other places. A country with ignorant people won't have a place in the world. It's not entirely true to say that foreigners are not willing to see China strengthen itself. Some Britons have participated in the meetings of Qiangxuehui. The British and American envoys also donated books. Anyway, a progressive China is welcomed by most countries. I beseech Your Majesty's consideration of the situation.'

The Emperor nodded without uttering a word and gazed into the distance. The Mental Cultivation Hall didn't provide a good field of vision, which depended on the imagination of the ruler. A pair of scrolls hanging in the Western Warmth Pavilion in the hall emerged in his mind's eye that read:

> *The world may be dependent on one,*
> *But it is not the case that everyone in the world is supposed to support one*
> *person.*

As an emperor, the whole country of China served him alone. But now China was crumbling. How could he save China? He felt the burden on his shoulders growing heavier.

⊸◈⊶

Two years went by. Emperor Guangxu was twenty-eight years old. He had been on the throne for twenty-four years and didn't want to wait any longer. He had read the writings of Kang Youwei on *The Reform of Japan* and *The Reform of Peter the Great*, which bolstered his desire to follow their examples. He was resolved not to see the ruin of the Qing Empire under his hands.

On the eve of the Emperor's speeding up of reform efforts, Weng was dismissed from office. This seasoned government official of forty years was barred from entering the palace under a callous imperial decree, obviously issued under pressure from the Empress Dowager. Weng went to the court the next day to finish up the formalities of leaving office, and saw the Emperor come out of the palace. Weng knelt on the road to see him leave, and the Emperor turned his head to take a look at him without saying a word. Was this separation temporary or permanent? Both the teacher and the student were flooded with unspeakable feelings. Their twenty-four years of companionship and teacher–student relationship came to an abrupt end.

Six years later, the seventy-five-year-old Weng Tonghe died under house arrest in his home town. He had paved the way for reform. He had become a stepping stone for other people to advance. His distinguished career as a teacher of two emperors and a senior statesman serving four regimes was but a preparation for others to move forward. He was old and left with little energy to carry out reform. In fact, the reformists of yesterday often became conservatives in the eyes of the new generation of activists. A living example was the younger brother of Emperor Xianfeng, Prince Gong, who in his prime had been a gallant, imposing reformist. But he became a stumbling block as he aged. He had been strongly opposed to the Emperor seeing Kang Youwei, as recommended by Weng Tonghe. Four months later, the Prince passed away at the age of sixty-seven, and the Emperor received Kang eighteen days later.

———⟶∘✦∘⟵———

The day the Emperor summoned Kang was the day he and his teacher Weng Tonghe parted. Weng's recommendation of Kang drew the wrath of the Empress Dowager upon himself. He shouldered all her resentment silently. The Emperor was to see Kang Youwei in the Renshou Hall of the Summer Palace, where he often held court during the spring and summer. To be summoned by the Emperor was a major event. The official had to learn something about court protocol and customs in advance. Just as Kang was going to seek advice from some experienced officials, an invitation from that big-headed fatso Yuan Shikai (then a judicial commissioner), arrived. So Kang got into the carriage dispatched for him and headed for Yuan's Haiding Villa.

'Haven't seen you for a long time,' Yuan welcomed him at the door. After the greeting, Yuan indicated the purpose of his invitation. 'I hear the Emperor is going to see you tomorrow morning. Since this is your first time, you should get acquainted with some etiquette.

First of all, you should arrive at the reception chamber outside the Summer Palace before dawn. A eunuch will take you through the palace gate to Renshou Hall and then retire. Make sure you watch the threshold at the entrance of the hall. It's about two-thirds of a metre high hung with a thick, wide cotton curtain. The eunuch inside will lift the curtain to let you in. But you have to hurry. Otherwise when the curtain drops, you might have one foot in and one foot out of the threshold. The falling curtain might hit your headpiece and it's considered a breach of etiquette. But I've taken care of this for you. . . . Also,' Yuan stood up and picked up a package from the table, 'here is a pair of knee guards. Tie them over your knees. You have to kneel down when you see the Emperor. If you can't stand up properly afterwards, it's also considered a breach of etiquette. These are my first-hand experiences for you. I have to rush back to Beijing. But I've given instructions to my head butler to provide you with everything you need. He'll take you to the Summer Palace today and wait for you at the gate tomorrow morning to take you back to Beijing after you see the Emperor.'

Kang thanked Yuan Shikai profusely for his help. In his view, Yuan was attentive, smooth, and experienced. He had even donated money to the Qiangxuehui three years ago. Although they didn't really know each other well, he was providing needed assistance at a critical moment.

————◦◦◦◦————

The Summer Palace always seemed chillier than Beijing in the wee hours of the morning, maybe because of the myriad of hills and lakes, and the omnipresence of the Empress Dowager. Kang was the third in line to be seen by the Emperor that day. It was close to daybreak when he was summoned. He walked into the dark hall lit only by two candles on the table in front of the emperor's seat, and knelt down on the pad in front of the table, waiting to be questioned.

When the Emperor summoned an official, a eunuch usually handed over a green-tipped stick stating the age, birthplace, brief family background, and current title of the summonee. But the Emperor did not bother to check the stick this time, indicating that he was sufficiently familiar with Kang Youwei, even though it was their first meeting.

'I know you quite well,' said the Emperor quietly. 'Weng Tonghe recommended you many times. I asked Weng Tonghe, Li Hongzhang, Rong Lu, and Zhang Yinhuan to talk to you at the ministry in January this year, and they related to me what you said. On that day, Rong Lu said the rules of the ancestors shouldn't be changed. You answered: "The rules of the ancestors are used to govern the land of the ancestors. But if we can't keep the land, what are those rules for? Or we could take this Ministry of Foreign Affairs for example. The rules of our ancestors never mention it." I was impressed by your arguments, and so were other senior officials. Later on I read your petitions and was convinced that I'll be an emperor without a country if we don't undertake reform. I've carefully studied *The Reform of Japan* and *The Reform of Peter the Great* you submitted. How long do you think it will take for things to start to take shape if China takes on reform?'

'Your Majesty's comments are greatly appreciated. According to my view, the West took three hundred years to establish a workable political system. Japan became strong after thirty years of reform. Given China's vast land and population, we should be able to see some results of reform in three years,' replied Kang with composure.

'Three years,' the Emperor pondered. 'If the entire country devotes its efforts to reform for three years, I believe we can achieve something. Why don't you elaborate?'

'Your Majesty has the vision. But in fact, if Your Majesty had opted for reform three years ago, the situation in China would be different today.'

'I realize that,' said the Emperor, his eyes lingering outside the curtain with a sad expression. 'But there were too many forces of resistance. What do you think should be done under the circumstances?'

'According to my view, the real problem lies with those diehard high-ranking officials. Why are they so conservative? The system is to blame. China recruits talent through the imperial civil service exam featuring an eight-part essay that is rigid in form and weak in ideas. Candidates who learn to write such an essay do not read books dating after the Qin and Han dynasties and do not learn about the world situation. They know that passing the exam is the only route to officialdom. These people are scholars, but they don't know the hows and whys. They are behind the times, without realizing it. Consequently, they spoil the country instead of saving it.

Fundamentally, the way to begin reform is by abolishing erroneous systems such as recruiting officials through the eight-part essay. But to expedite the process, Your Majesty should issue an edict directly, instead of turning the matter over to the ministries. Any good plan or idea is ruined once it is turned over to the officials for discussion. Who can carry out the reforms if most of the high-ranking officials are opposed to change? Your Majesty can make exceptions in promoting junior officials. Replacing senior officials with low-ranking ones will bring fresh vigour to the country, and things will take on a new perspective soon. Your Majesty can give assignments and authority to junior officials who are willing to serve the country without promoting them or dismissing high-ranking officials. To proceed with reform in this fashion can minimize resistance to reform.'

The Emperor talked to Kang for a long time, probably knowing that such an occasion would be rare. After Kang was dismissed, the Emperor issued his new appointment as secretary of the government office in charge of foreign affairs, comparable to a mid-level official in the ministry of foreign affairs. Given that the appointment and dismissal of a high-ranking official required the approval of the Empress Dowager, giving Kang Youwei the title of a junior official was designed not to draw attention. But five days later, the Emperor gave him a special privilege that permitted him to report to the Emperor directly without going through other officials.

Since his first attempt to submit a petition to the Emperor ten years back, Kang had exhausted all means of finding a way to the ruler. After a decade of unceasing efforts, he had finally established a direct channel. His ideas and opinions could reach the ears of the Emperor without going through another person or being intercepted. The feeling of having the support of his Emperor gave him hope. He was forty-one years old now, and willing to be a junior official at the side of the Emperor, offering his ideas about the country.

Subsequent to the summons, he submitted more of his writings, *An Examination of the Reform of Japan*, *The Disintegration of Poland*, and *An Examination of the Reform of France*, to encourage the Emperor to look at China from the perspective of the world. This constituted a horizontal endeavour. His writings *New Doctrines Against the Old Classics* and *Confucius as a Reformer* constituted a vertical endeavour. He argued with massive evidence and solid scholarship that the much-worshipped Confucius was a champion of reform. With Confucius as his shield, the diehards would have a difficult time rebuking his ideas. Now his efforts in both directions arrived at the juncture of a final trial. He felt immensely gratified, excited, and confident.

Seven days after his meeting with Kang Youwei the Emperor issued an imperial edict abolishing the eight-part essay system. Subsequently, under Kang's planning, many junior officials were placed in important positions. Three months later, the Emperor issued another edict, conferring grade-four ranking on four junior officials and assigning them as secretaries attached to the Grand Council of State to participate in matters concerning the new policies. The secretary to the Grand Council of State was an official of grade four or under, comparable to the confidential secretary to the Emperor. The head of the Grand Council of State was a high-ranking official of grade three or higher, whose assignments were under the firm control of the Empress Dowager. So the Emperor could only circumvent the situation by appointing four secretaries to share the power of the high-ranking officials in the Grand Council. It took great effort to arrive at such an arrangement.

Among these four secretaries, Yang Rui and Liu Guangdi were students of Zhang Zhidong; Lin Xu was a student of Kang Youwei. All three of them had attended the meetings held by Kang and had known him for some time. The last one had never been associated with Kang before. He was a new arrival, originally from Liuyang, Hunan, but born in Beijing, aged thirty-three. His current status was the expectant appointee for Prefect of Jiangsu Prefecture. His father was the governor of Hubei, a friend of Weng Tonghe. Weng once met this son of his old friend and entered in his journal: 'has a good command of foreign affairs, arrogant, carrying the air of a person with an illustrious pedigree'. The secretaries to the Grand Council of State were divided into two groups. This person was assigned with Liu Guangdi. On his first day in office, he strutted into the court. When asked by the censor and eunuch for his name, he picked up the writing brush without a word and jotted down three large characters on the paper—Tan Sitong.

CHAPTER SEVEN

The Turn from Theory to Practice

Liang Qichao visits Fayuan Temple, after having been ousted from the premises of the Qiangxuehui, as it was closed down by government troops. While in the Temple, he happens upon another visitor, a stranger to him, who later turns out to be Tan Sitong. The two discuss Buddhism and they discover that their views are very similar. Notably, they observe that most Buddhist followers are focused on attaining buddhahood through accumulating merit, worshipping, and meditating. However, most followers do not focus on the goal following the attainment of buddhahood, which is to return to the world and save the multitudes. These two men are very conscious of their own goals—to save the multitudes by bringing political changes to China and thereby relieving the suffering of the Chinese masses. They believe that Buddhism has been misunderstood since its importation into China as a 'passive' religion, whereas these two see it as a call to action to save their fellow man.

They further discuss their own backgrounds and punctuate their discussion with examples from Chinese history. Finally, after the two part ways, Liang Qichao contemplates some poems written by Tan Sitong, which he had given to Liang Qichao. The poems are filled with allusions and references to historical figures and Buddhist concepts, which Liang Qichao elaborates on. This chance meeting of two intellectuals, both having the goal of political reform, is just the beginning of their camaraderie as they work toward this common goal.

———◦◦✦◦◦———

Beijing had turned cold in October. But there was a jet stream of warm air, dubbed 'warm snow', meaning snow was about to fall.

Tossing and turning in bed in the middle of the night, unable to sleep, Liang Qichao lit a candle and started to read a book with a blanket wrapped around him. It was a book about the historical sites of Beijing, written under the patronage of Emperor Qianlong. The book said Beijing used to have eleven gates, which were later reduced to nine gates. The 'Nine-gate Commander-in-Chief' was the general in charge of security inside Beijing. If the city hadn't shrunk in size, the general would have been called 'Eleven-gate Commander-in-Chief', figured Liang Qichao. He then counted while trying to memorize the names of those gates. A doggerel verse about the gates of Beijing went: 'Nine inside, seven outside and four in the imperial city'.

Different gates saw the passage of different carriages. Zhengyang Gate in the middle of the city walls on the south was for imperial carriages; Chongwen Gate, east of Zhengyang Gate, was for wine carts; Chaoyang Gate, in the middle of the city wall on the east, was for grain carts from the South. That was why there were so many grain warehouses in the vicinity of Chaoyang Gate. Dongzhi Gate, east of Chaoyang Gate, was for timber wagons, with many timber factories in the vicinity.

Through Anding Gate on the north side travelled dung carts. Through Desheng Gate, west of Anding Gate, passed army wagons. The gate was named Desheng, meaning 'victory', for the sake of good auspices, although the army often lost the battles it fought. Through Xizhi Gate on the west travelled the water carts, and water from Yuquan Mountain was loaded onto mule carts here and shipped to the imperial palace. Through Fucheng Gate west of Xizhi Gate in the middle of the city wall on the west travelled the coal carts; there were several coal shops in its vicinity.

Xuanwu Gate on the south saw the passage of the prisoners' vans. The famous execution ground, Caishikou, was outside Xuanwu Gate. Inmates on death row were paraded from inside the city through Xuanwu Gate for their execution. To Liang Qichao, a Cantonese, the south-western district outside Xuanwu Gate was most familiar to him. The Cantonese Association was on Nanheng Street, and the Nanhai Association he frequented was in Mishi Hutong, where his teacher Kang Youwei resided. He himself had lived there for a while until the establishment of the Qiangxuehui. After that, he moved to Housun Park so he could see to the business of the organization.

It was 1895. Kang Youwei went back south after an unsuccessful year in Beijing. His petition to the Emperor never bore fruit; his newspaper folded, and the save-the-country society that he organized, the Qiangxuehui, was on the brink of collapse. On the evening Kang left Beijing, the word spread that Qiangxuehui was about to be banned. This organization had the incipient form of a political party and was meant to be a transitional body under the prevailing conservative atmosphere. Nevertheless, it did not evade the attention of the conservative forces. After Kang headed south, the infantry commander of Beijing forced entry into the place and seized all books and equipment, and even some personal belongings of Liang Qichao. Liang himself was evicted from the premises.

Liang was only twenty-three years old. One morning, he strolled into the Xizhuan Hutong and stepped into Fayuan Temple. The winter sky of the northern country was clear and desolate. The Hall of Maharaja-devas in Fayuan Temple was covered with snow from the eaves down to the front court. The glistening white snow gave an aura of freshness. Liang had long heard of Fayuan Temple from his mentor, but his busy schedule in Beijing over the past year had kept him from paying a visit. With the closure of the Qiangxuehui two days before, he had lots of free time, and Fayuan Temple was the first place he thought of visiting.

Liang stood in front of the first old stone tablet near the steps of the Great Hero Treasure Hall. His proficiency in calligraphy couldn't keep pace with that of his mentor, but his comprehension of the Buddhist doctrines was gaining ground. So he looked at the inscriptions on the tablet from the viewpoint of Buddhist teachings, instead of calligraphy.

Liang was a child prodigy. He had started reading the Four Books at the age of four, finished the Five Classics at six, learned composition at eight, wrote articles of more than one thousand words at nine, passed the county civil exam for *xiucai* at twelve, and the provincial civil exam for *juren* at seventeen. His mentor Kang Youwei didn't become a *juren* until four years afterwards, at the age of thirty-six. In the year of the Sino-Japanese War, he and Kang came to Beijing together to take the imperial exam for *jinshi*. At that time, Kang was already a well-known figure. Fearing that passing the exam would add to Kang's fame, the chief examiner decided to block his passing. In the process of grading, the examiners came across an outstanding essay, thought it was written by Kang, and failed it deliberately. On the day the list of successful candidates was posted, Kang's name was on it, but Liang Qichao didn't pass. In fact, that essay was written by Liang. Those diehards had got it all wrong.

Despite his unsuccessful bid for *jinshi*, Liang had received a lot of attention and praise while accompanying his mentor in his travels about the country. Although he had gained considerable fame at the young age of twenty-three, he maintained his modesty. His aspiration was to save the country. He immersed himself in Confucianism, Mohism, then Buddhism, in an attempt to build a consistent belief. Belief in Buddhism pertained to idealist and abstract conceptions, while the temples represented the materialistic. Was the presence of a temple necessary for belief? Pondering these questions of mind and matter, Liang walked up into the hall and examined a wooden board with the inscription 'Fahaizhenyuan', or 'the true source of law', written by Emperor Qianlong. His doubt deepened. The true source of law resided in the invisible self, not in this temple of wood and mortar. He shook his larger-than-average head and mumbled to himself.

Another young man in the hall noticed his presence and approached. The man looked thirtyish, with a demeanour of fortitude and a pair of bright piercing eyes.

'From your looks, you must be a southerner,' said the young man.

Liang turned around and nodded his head. 'You are right. I am from Guangdong. You seem to come from the south as well, judging from your Hunanese accent.'

'Yes, I am from Liuyang, Hunan, and you?'

'Xinhui, Guangdong,' said Liang. 'Oh! The Liuyang Association is just nearby.'

'Yes, it is. I just came from Shanghai yesterday. I am not familiar with Beijing, so I am staying at the Liuyang Association.'

'Since you came straight to a temple, you must be a Buddhist.'

'Yes and no. I am interested in Buddhism, but I'm not a worshipper.'

'Neither am I. We share the same values in this regard. I like to study Buddhism and enjoy visiting temples. But I always think that the presence of a temple is in conflict with the essence of Buddhist doctrine. When Emperor Ming of the Song Dynasty built the Xiangong Temple, he said, 'I have earned great merit by building this temple.' But Yu Yuan told him the truth: 'Your majesty used the hard-earned money of the people to build this temple. If the Buddha knew, he would weep with grief. So where is the merit?' There have been so many temples like Xiangong through the ages and they are getting bigger. But they seem to depart ever further from the true ideals of Buddhism. Of course, this Fayuan Temple might be an exception. It was built as a martyrs' shrine in the Tang Dynasty and was devoid of the Buddhist atmosphere it has today.'

Liang's Cantonese-accented Mandarin sounded strange, but his views were even more unorthodox. In a place where people worshipped Buddha, he didn't deny Buddha, he simply denied the meaning of such a place. His words intrigued the Hunanese in front of him.

'I think your views are brilliant. Here we share the same ideas again. Strictly speaking, material manifestations such as temples might have some artistic, architectural, and a little bit of cultivation value. But as you say, they are far from the true spirit of Buddhism. Ever since Buddhism was brought into China, its evolution has deviated from the true path. It seems the majority of people fail to grasp its substance, but instead spend a lot of energy and effort on form.

The path to Buddhism is intangible, but those who call themselves Buddhists make it all the more tangible. They build temples, chant scriptures, meditate, perform rituals, and such. These practices are far from the heart of the Buddha. The Avatamsaka Sutra has a chapter on "returning", which maintains that people who have attained Buddhahood should return to the world to give their lives to the multitudes. Such sacrifice, returning from beyond the world back to this world, illustrates true Buddhism. But after Buddhism came to China, the Chinese got it only half right. We only know about attaining the realm beyond this world. People set their life's goal on attaining nirvana, thinking passivity, nihilism, and extinguishing the will, as the paths leading to their goal. They are all wrong. They don't realize that they have only grasped half of the quintessence of Buddhism. To complete the other half of the journey, they must return.

Speaking of the sacrifice of returning to the world, some Buddhist adherents have done it, but in an aberrant way. Emperor Shizong of the Later Zhou in the Five Dynasties pointed out, "Monks, nuns, and laymen claim to be making a sacrifice by burning their arms, piercing their fingers, amputating their arms and legs, or they carry bells, use props, and then rave they can transform the body, call the spirit, and dispense holy water and lamps. All these practices are fallacies and deceptions and will be banned from now on." These so-called sacrifices were actually tricks.

In the later period of the Five Dynasties, the whole country was financially strapped. So Emperor Shizong ordered the melting of all bronze statues of Buddhist deities for the casting of coins. His reasoning was that the Buddhist doctrines teach that body and life

are unreal, and doing whatever benefits others is the first priority. If
the Buddha himself were here today, he would give his life to save
sentient beings, not these fake bodies made of bronze. Such theory
embodies the true understanding of Buddhist doctrines.

In the late Ming Dynasty, rebel Zhang Xianzhong slaughtered
civilians wherever his troops had passed. One day, his subordinate
Li Dingguo met Monk Poshan, who pleaded with Li to stop the
slaughtering. Li ordered his soldiers to bring forth mutton, pork, and
dog meat and told Poshan, "If you eat this meat, I'll stop!" Poshan
answered, "What does it matter if I break a commandment of Buddha
if I can save millions of lives?" He then finished the meat, and Li kept
his promise.

Both Emperor Shizong and Monk Poshan were first-rate masters
of Buddhism, because they could break a "holding" or "tenet". There
are two kinds of holdings in Buddhism. One is holding onto the
concept of ego, which has to do with the subjective self; the other is
holding onto things as reality, which has to do with the objective
universe and is actually a false tenet. Regular Buddhist adherents
talk about the law of this world and the law beyond this world all
day without truly understanding or practising these laws. If
Sakyamuni had known such people were to be his followers, he
would probably have died of grief.' The Hunanese became more
irritable as he talked.

'Your views on Buddhism are outstanding. You referred to the
Avatamsaka Sutra earlier. It seems you prefer the Huayan sect?'

'Actually all the sects are messed up, including Huayan. Only
Huayan was discriminated against at the very beginning. The
translator of the Avatamsaka Sutra, Buddhabhadra, came to Chang'an
around the year AD 408, but was forced out by the hostility of three
thousand monks. After a dozen years, he finished the translation of
the Avatamsaka Sutra. The birth of this book came out of hardship.
I am particularly fond of it. Its propagation was also a legend. After
Buddhabhadra was killed, his friend Nagarjuna lived to disseminate
his thoughts.'

The Avatamsaka Sutra is said to have been collated by Manjusri,
the bodhisattva of wisdom, and Ananda, and collected by the dragon-
god in his palace. Nagarjuna attained enlightenment after reading it,
and passed it on to the world. This sutra has three volumes. The one
that came into China was the abridged version of the third volume.

Nagarjuna was an apostle of Sakyamuni seven hundred years
after his death, and the disciple of Bodhisattva Asvaghose. The story

goes that he learned the practice of invisibility with two other friends and sneaked into the imperial palace. The Emperor ordered his guards to wield their swords all around to hack these invisible intruders. In the end the two friends were killed. But Nagarjuna got away, for he hid near the Emperor, whom the soldiers were afraid to hurt accidentally. Recalling these stories, Liang Qichao became all the more curious about this Hunanese, thinking to himself, 'He likes Nagarjuna. That means he must be a chivalrous person himself.'

Then Liang said, 'You talk about the conduct of Emperor Shizong and Monk Poshan. It shows that you approach Buddhist doctrine from its greater meaning. A person must have extraordinary vision and valour to offer himself to this world with an otherworldly spirit. Buddhism talked about transformation from the worldly to the otherworldly. But the problem is that if Buddhist believers only know about the common principles, not the truth or reality, then where do they start the transformation from, and where does it lead to? Your comments about them not truly understanding or practising the laws are spot on.'

'I appreciate your compliment. But in my view, being right is just talk—hitting the target with one stroke requires action. People with ideals and integrity have also lived in this squalid and treacherous world through the ages. This is what the Buddha called adhering to their original vows, or what Confucius called seeking virtue and acquiring it. In the end, they all vow to shed blood for the multitudes, even if it means losing their lives and their families. This is true sacrifice.'

The Hunanese then pointed to the Buddhist statutes in the hall: 'Here we have Vairocana, Manjusri, and Samantabhadra, commonly referred to as the three holy deities of Huayan. The Buddha has Tridaya or three embodiments: Dharmakaya or the true body of the Buddha, Sambhoga-gaya or the reward body, and Nirmanakaya, or any incarnation of Buddha. The true body of Buddha is Vairocana. But according to *On Buddha Stages*, there are three incarnations; the incarnation of self, the incarnation of others, and the incarnation of non-physical form. In the incarnation of others, the King of Maras was transformed into the Buddha, and Sariputra was transformed into Devakanya, the goddess. To me, these incarnations comprise the true body of the Buddha. Vairocana sitting in the middle and Manjusri and Samantabhadra on his sides are false bodies. These statues of them only demonstrate the unreality of these forms. You would think the real Buddha and bodhisattvas just want to be worshipped here. Instead of attaching their spirit to these wooden statues, they would probably rather live as idealists and patriots of integrity who sacrifice their lives in the practice of Buddhist doctrines. What do you think?'

Nodding his head, Liang smiled and said,

'Since the King of Maras can be transformed into the Buddha, naturally the Buddha can be transformed into idealists and patriots. I think such a deduction is acceptable. So, let's say the martyrdom of idealists and patriots embodies both their sacrifice and the death of the Buddha and bodhisattvas. Don't you agree?'

'You may say so,' the Hunanese grinned. 'However, the Buddha and bodhisattvas can have tens of thousands of incarnations to live as idealists and patriots. So when these people die, only one ten-thousandth of the Buddha and the bodhisattvas dies. But for idealists and patriots, they give it all when they die. It's not quite fair, is it?' The smile of the Hunanese was gone.

'Your argument is unique. But your readings of the Avatamsaka Sutra might contain too much of your own interpretation.' Liang paused a while. 'There is the so-called "Realm of One Reality" in the world of Huayan, where reality and unreality, sentient beings, and the Buddha become indistinguishable. It supersedes all approaches. The original body is a phenomenon and vice versa. Everything is absolutely equal. In the realm of one reality, all laws and truths converge into one. In terms of quantity, one is not few, and tens of billions are not many. The infinite world can be discerned through a grain of sand. In terms of volume, dust is not a small amount and boundless space is not a large amount. The Sumeru can accommodate a mustard seed and vice versa. In terms of time, an instant is not short, a kalpa, (the period of time between creation and recreation), is not long. For creatures that die immediately after they are born, or live as long as pine trees and cranes, it's all just one life. In the realm of one reality, quantity and size are unreal. It supersedes existence, non-existence, time, and space. One thought might lead to or avert numerous disasters. Oneness is everything and vice versa.

So idealists and patriots who die for a cause are no different from tens and thousands of Buddhas and bodhisattvas who sacrifice themselves. To be more precise, Buddhas and bodhisattvas may incarnate in thousands of bodies. But if one of these bodies dies for a cause, it is the martyrdom of the whole. From the perspective of oneness, tens of thousands are one. But I think we are stretching it a little bit too far here. If the Buddha knew it, he might ridicule us as culprits misinterpreting the Avatamsaka Sutra.'

'No, I don't think so,' insisted the Hunanese. 'Avatamsaka Sutra is the king of all sutras. Think about it. The Buddha finished the teaching of Avatamsaka Sutra on nine different occasions. At that time, he said nobody understood its profound meaning, except for the great bodhisattva of intelligence. That's why this sutra was hidden in the palace of the dragon-god, until Nagarjuna recited it and passed it out. Although Nagarjuna memorized only one third of it, people are still having a hard time grasping its essence. The chapter on "returning" is the greatest. Simply unparalleled. Once you get a handle on the meaning of "returning", you find that the Buddhist doctrines are definitely not passive. Do you remember the poem of Wang Anshi on dreams?

> *Knowing that life is like a dream, that we shouldn't ask for anything,*
> *My mind is at ease all the time.*
> *Being with the dream wherever it goes,*
> *Any tiny accomplishment should be attributable to the dream.*

What a lofty state he describes! It parallels the realm of "returning" in Avatamsaka Sutra. Wang Anshi reckoned that life was but a dream. His heart was like still water and he had no desire to pursue anything. But from one dream to another, he left so many merits in this world. This realm embodies the true understanding of Buddhist teachings. These wise, virtuous, and courageous people who go beyond this world and then return are people who die first and then come to life. When they attain this stage, they are the Buddha and bodhisattvas. Their final act in this world is to die for a just cause. That means their dreams come true and their bodies are real.

But ordinary Buddhists have it all wrong. If you can see through the vanity of this world and come back to it, you achieve the state of visible form, but formlessness of the mind. Wang Anshi made great efforts to save the world, but he didn't mind his own gains or losses. Such is the real Buddha and bodhisattva. I believe you share this view?'

'Yes, I do,' replied Liang Qichao excitedly. 'Our chance encounter here is witnessed by the Buddha, the bodhisattvas, and the lohans. We only touch briefly on the realm of one reality, but our views are quite compatible. What a great pleasure!'

Liang bowed to the Hunanese and he returned the courtesy.

'Oh yes!' added Liang. 'I haven't asked your name yet.'

'Sorry! My last name is Tan and my first name is Sitong.'

Liang's eyes lit up and he grabbed the other's hands, smiling broadly. 'Aren't you the son of the Governor of Hubei?'

'How extraordinary!' Tan's eyes glistened as well. 'How do you know my name? Who are you?'

'I am a student of Mr Kang Youwei. My name is Liang Qichao.'

'My! You are Liang Qichao. What a pleasure to meet you!' Tan shook Liang's hands forcefully. 'I came to Beijing from Shanghai just to see you and your teacher. I heard in the south that you have something dynamic going on here, so I rushed here to join your Qiangxuehui. How about it? Will you take me to Mr Kang and let me become a member?' Tan entreated.

Liang forced a smile. 'It so happens that Mr Kang went back south the end of August, and you are too late for the Qiangxuehui as well. It was closed down three days ago and I was evicted.'

'That's really too bad. What's your plan? Do you have a place to stay? You can live with me at the Liuyang Association. My father donated the building twenty-two years ago. You'll feel very much at home there. How about it?'

'No thanks,' replied Liang. 'I am staying at the Nanhai Association and watching the residence of Mr Kang for him. But we can meet anytime since the two places are nearby. You said you came here to look for Mr Kang and me. Actually we are waiting for the arrival of more comrades to join us here. The Qiangxuehui had only two dozen members, and we really need more people sharing the same ideals and goals. We've long heard of your many talents. I am thrilled that we met here today. It's just too bad that I can't show you our organization.'

'You must have lost a great deal in the seizure?' asked Tan with concern.

'Yes, indeed. But the greatest shame in the whole embroilment is the loss of a world map. We spent almost two months in Beijing looking for a world map, but to no avail. Finally somebody in Shanghai found one. I remember when the map got here, everybody treated it like a treasure. In order to expand the vision of our fellow citizens, we publicized the map every day, hoping people would come to see it. Now this map has been seized as well,' lamented Liang. 'Although Beijing is the capital city, people here are very ill-informed, and that was what the Qiangxuehui wanted to exert its efforts on. But the organization was banned after merely three months. Still we have no regrets. The great poet Tao Yuanming of the Jin Dynasty expressed the same sentiment in his poem. He grew mulberry trees along the bank of the Yangtse River for three years. When he was about to harvest them, the flood washed everything away. He had no regrets, for "the trees weren't grown in the highlands. What is there to regret?"

We'll continue to grow mulberry trees, then raise our own silkworms that will produce silk. Only we have to consider a location other than Beijing. Mr Kang is in the south now. He has a whole set of plans. I am convinced we can take root in the south and gradually move up north. Saving the country is not a short-term undertaking. Maybe we won't see the day in our generation. But we won't give up any opportunity that could lead to some results. From the long-term point of view, running schools and newspapers to educate the public is the fundamental approach. So one of Mr Kang's endeavours is to nurture students, inspire them, and turn them into comrades in the great undertaking of saving the country. Although you are not a student of Mr Kang, we welcome your presence and cooperation. You also style yourself as?'

'Fusheng.'

'Alright, I'll call you Fusheng. And I also go by the name of Zhuoru. We are not fellow students, but we are comrades now.'

'Actually, we are fellow students in spirit. I admire Mr Kang tremendously, and revere him as my teacher. I read his *New Doctrines Against the Old Classics* four years ago when it was first published. The book was banned, but the thoughts of Mr Kang have spread. It's great scholarship and an immense achievement to write a book that repudiates the established beliefs of the past two thousand years. I am more than willing to become the student of such a great intellectual. Would you please pass on my intention?' said Tan Sitong earnestly.

'I surely will. I think Mr Kang will be thrilled to have a student of such uncommon valour, and as multi-talented and well travelled as you are.'

'It seems you know a lot about my background,' Tan cast a glance at Liang.

Liang grinned. 'I am seven years younger than you. I was born in a poor fishing village in Xinhui, Guangdong. Both my grandfather and father were *xiucai*. But we had to grow crops to feed ourselves. After I passed the exam for *xiucai* at the age of twelve, I still had to help the family in the fields. I didn't have the chance to travel and I am not an adventurous person, so I really envy the fact that you have been able to travel to every corner of the land and get to know so many outstanding people of different backgrounds and characters. I heard you've been to Gansu, Shaanxi, Henan, Hunan, Hubei, Jiangsu, Zhejiang, and Taiwan since the age of twelve, and are knowledgeable about the various local conditions and customs.'

'I haven't been to Taiwan. It was my second older brother, Tan Sixiang. He was asked by the Governor of Taiwan, Liu Mingchuan, to work in Tainan. But he died six years ago at the age of thirty-three. I was going to Taiwan to bring his coffin back. But Tang Jingsong sent me a telegram while I was in Shanghai and told me to wait there.'

'Maybe it was for the better,' said Liang. 'Taiwan was turned over to Japan this year. It's a place of painful memories.'

'Yes! China had spent so much effort and so many lives building Taiwan; my second older brother was one of them. Now it's been ceded to Japan. We have to recover it. As you said, I've travelled far. I am not as well versed as you in books, but I have more first-hand experience. You know, although I am from a well-off family, I am definitely not a pampered and ignorant person who can't even tell the difference between the different grains. On the contrary, I've been through some hardship in my life. I was infected in the plague of Beijing when I was twelve and stayed in a coma for three whole days. That's why I was also called Fusheng, meaning "born again". In five days, I lost my mother, eldest brother, and second older sister. I went back to my home town in Hunan at thirteen when my father took office in Gansu. On my way to Gansu the next year, we ran into a year of severe crop failure and famine in Henan and Shaanxi, and a dozen people in my entourage died on the way.

My favourite activity in Gansu was to explore the fields outside the Great Wall and to go hunting. But if you happened to run into the north-western wind, the flying sand and stones hit you like whips and arrows. The snow in the wintertime was a little bit better.

But snow can be disastrous as well. There was one time I got lost with a cavalryman in Hexi. We walked seven days in the snow for a distance of sixteen hundred kilometres without seeing anybody. When we finally came out safe, the flesh on our buttocks was cracked and bleeding, with blood all over our pants. Of course, life in the north-west has its unique side. You put up a tent on the sand at night, drink the blood of goats with snow, or gamble, perform a sword dance, engage in fencing, play the *pipa*, or listen to the sound of the bugle. That sense of gallantry and desolation in confluence is something you can't experience in books. Especially when you are in the midst of an ancient battleground, conjuring up the images of the non-Han people breeding horses, the Han generals on their mission of expanding the frontier, troops totally demolished, and the battle drums thundering from all around, there grows a sense of vastness and solitude. Your mind becomes crystal clear, but your heart is sorrowful and destitute. You feel the hordes of troops and soldiers charging past you, the roar of battle echoing to the sky and blood flowing like streams. Then suddenly, everything stops and all becomes still. The thousands of horses and soldiers are turned into dust and corpses. At that time, you seem to be the only man alive passing through a field of apparitions. It's not you mourning the ancient battleground, it's the battleground devouring you alive.

After that kind of experience, the rest of my life doesn't seem to matter. I was only eighteen. But my heart was as quiescent as that of an eighty-year-old man. I've immersed myself in books over the past thirteen years, particularly the study of Western natural and social sciences and Buddhism. I think my views toward life are maturing. Now I am thirty-one and feel that it's time to devote myself to the country. That's why I rushed here from Shanghai to follow Mr Kang, hoping I could do something with you all together. On my way here, I wrote *Four Poems of Reflection*. My life's sentiments are in these poems. I happen to have the manuscript with me and I would like your comments.'

Liang took the manuscript and the two of them walked out of the Great Hero Treasure Hall. It was almost noon. Liang said:

'There is a decent restaurant near the Liuyang Association where a lot of intellectuals meet. It's a good place for conversation. Since you just arrived in Beijing, why don't I buy you lunch there?'

Tan Sitong accepted the invitation and they left Fayuan Temple.

⎯⎯◦✦◦⎯⎯

Liang Qichao took care of a number of business matters after lunch. When he returned to the Nanhai Association, it was already ten o'clock at night. He couldn't sleep and decided to find something to read. He suddenly remembered the four poems Tan Sitong had given him that morning. Why not take a look at them now? He lit a candle and started reading:

The First Poem

Practising Zen meditation in the Paradise of Buddhists, life has been full of happiness;

Nonetheless, happy days do not last forever, for transmigration must continue.

The colours of the rainbow brighten the sky after the rain of Buddha's laws, but a black wind blows them from the sky.

Knowing that ill fortune is bound to fall upon me and that I cannot escape, I seek refuge temporarily in trivial sayings, if not nonsense, to get by.

For years I have been indulging in the study of Buddhism; the reading of sutras has become totally tasteless;

In a way, it also demonstrates why I haven't been able to become any of the ten categories of immortal.

The Second Poem

In a muddled state of mind, half asleep and half awake, incidents of the past appear suddenly.

I see a skeleton under the dim light;

Before my wine glass, there are dead bodies, sitting and lying down, while I dream of the good old days!

On a fine beautiful day when the sky is blue and high, the golden tiger is fighting the Almighty with vigour, bleeding from the mouth;

Elsewhere the sound of sorrow and grief echoes.

When Xu Jia repents after having witnessed what a man looks like after death,

Indeed there is nothing in life that matters at all!

The Third Poem

Transmigration of life and death never meets; however, the chance of a rendezvous does occur after the turnaround.

Glad I am that I have been relieved from the predestined connection;

Nothing remains crystal clear even when I try to trace what happened.

Gone are the days now that my hair has turned grey,

Even the pelican sheds tears in sorrow for me.

Just a snap of a finger, and a new baby is born again, holding in its mouth the golden ring from the last life;

Too soon, too real, everything becomes void.

The Fourth Poem

What's wrong with the fluttering willow leaves?

Drifting hither and thither without a fixed abode.

Separate today after having dropped into the water;

They may only meet again someday when the leaves become ashes.

How can I bear to see the way life has been treating me, and die the way
*   the willow leaves do?*
Even the Eternal Buddha encountered obstacles put up by Maras and
*   his relatives;*
That's only part of what one must encounter in the course of one's life,
*   and eventually death.*

As he read, Liang grew dumbfounded. These poems were masterpieces, melancholic, sad, and yet gorgeous. Every word was the outcome of learning. Usually poems couldn't be clearly defined. But reading these poems immediately gave a sense of expansiveness that begged for further interpretation between the lines. So Liang Qichao got up and started to deliberate on these poems.

'It's apparent in these poems that Tan is deeply influenced by Buddhism,' Liang said to himself. 'Buddhism views the lotus as the purest flower. The adherents of the Pure Land Sect even attach great significance to being reincarnated as a lotus, which, when in blossom, enabled them to see the Buddha. There is also the Pure Land in Buddhism, the Western paradise. In this state, disciples meditate to attain four dhyana heavens, starting from the first region, where the inhabitants possess only four of the six organs, and finally to the forth region, where only consciousness is left. At that time, the disciple has achieved such a high state that one laugh in the sky can spread far and wide. But just as disciples think about propagating Buddhist teachings and colours of the rainbow arch across the sky, a gust of dark wind brings clouds.

Lao Zi says, "All my obstacles and difficulties come from the existence of my body. I'll be free of them if I don't have this body." So long as I'm not concerned with my own life, I can become detached. This is the Buddhist teaching that a body has no fixed form. Without a fixed form, trivial talk, as mentioned in the book of Zhuang Zi, the famous Taoist philosopher, suffices to relieve a person from sadness and evil. But if a person looks back at a life with no desires, that life might become tasteless, as suggested in the Surangama Sutra. It may not be so, since you can travel with the ten immortals described in the Sutra.'

Liang couldn't remember exactly who these ten immortals were. He looked them up in the Surangama Sutra and found that they were the immortals of land, flying, travelling, air, heaven, path, Taoism, sunshine, essence, and uniqueness.

'Alright, I will continue on with the second poem,' Liang mumbled again. 'Buddhism says there are three births of incarnation, the so-called three lives. In *The Collection of Schools of Thought*, it talks about three periods—past, present, and future. In that poem by Bai Juyi, the great poet of the Tang Dynasty, it says, "If the talk of three lives is not heresy, then all of us were probably Chaoxu in our previous life."

Tan wrote: "In a muddled state of mind, half asleep and half awake, incidents of the past suddenly appear." He must be referring to the unconnected incidents from past lives suddenly appearing in this life. Buddhism says that reincarnation is determined by karma, which includes the karma in deeds, words, and thoughts. Karma bears the power of karma to produce good or evil fruit, that is, retribution for good and evil is an irresistible force. The force comes from the cause in a previous life and produces fruit and retribution in this life. For example, the Empress Dowager and her cronies act against the will of heaven. They bathe in a false sense of peace and prosperity, caring only about their high position, while living like walking corpses. They resemble the "skeleton" referred to by Zhuang Zi, and the "sitting like a grave and lying down like a corpse" which should be wiped out, that Mi Heng talked about.

One of Jia Dao's poems says: "Striking a bell and drinking wine that shoots up in the sky, the golden tiger is fighting the Almighty with vigour, bleeding from the mouth." When villains are in high places against the will of heaven, we should wage a bitter struggle against them. Born into a wealthy family, everything I have comes from the people and the land. I am but a skeleton. But while I am still all flesh and blood, I want to repent, I vow to sacrifice myself. I devote my body to my land and my people; I willingly let my body turn into a skeleton and the skeleton into dust.'

Liang continued to himself, 'The whole meaning of the poem turns on the last two lines: "When Xu Jia repents after having witnessed what a man looks like after death, he understands that indeed there is nothing in life that matters at all!" Legend has it that Xu Jia was once a servant of Lao Zi, the Chinese philosopher. In the many years he worked for Lao Zi, he was never paid. One day, he got mad and stood before Lao Zi, demanding that he be paid. Without replying, Lao Zi lifted his finger to turn Xu Jia into a skeleton. All of a sudden Xu Jia became enlightened and realized that there was really nothing to argue about, since we all die eventually. So he regretted what he had said to Lao Zi. In quoting the story of Xu Jia, Tan seems to suggest that we should die for a great cause that gives life meaning, and that other trivial things in life are insignificant.'

Liang Qichao continued his musing. 'As for the third poem, it's even more melancholy and disheartened. Buddhism talks about the transmigration of life and death. After an infinite number of reincarnations, I'll never have the chance to meet the person I miss. However, in times of turbulence, my beloved and we may come across one another once again. But our predestined connection from a past life seems lost. I am actually glad that I have been relieved of it. There have been so many sorrowful partings in life since the ancient times. Even though there are predestined connections in life, like Yangshuzi, who was the reincarnation of a seven-year-old boy from the Li family who died falling into a well. His reincarnation was proved by the presence of a gold ring, but so what? When we meet again in the transmigration of life and death, everything becomes void in the end, like in a dream.'

'The last poem also has elements of a love poem,' thought Liang. 'But it incorporates the essentials of the first three poems and intermingles sentiments towards one's life, country, and relationships. It talks about the fluttering willow leaves drifting apart and meeting again when they become ashes. The separation today carries the pain depicted in Lisao by Qu Yuan, the poet–politician of ancient China, but it also illustrates the boundless destiny from the philosophy of Zhuang Zi.

Buddhism relates that Mara-papiyan, leading an army of relatives, frequently puts up obstacles on the path to immortality. They have their own teachings that rival those of the Buddha. But these obstacles are transitory. In the *Record of the Buddhist Country*, it says, "The bodhisattva undergoes infinite sufferings and hardship, not caring about his life." Even the Eternal Buddha encountered obstacles on the path to immortality. But that's only part of the infinity one must pass in the course of life, and eventually death. The vicissitudes of life are but a process.'

Liang Qichao made a strenuous effort to interpret these four poems under the flickering candlelight. 'Tan Fusheng is truly an extraordinary man,' muttered Liang. 'His poems reveal the depth of his learning and the fact that he has found his way. His spirit is positive and invigorating. The true essence of Buddhism teaches that external appearances are insignificant. We are present in this world as one body with the multitudes and dispense benevolence. We don't touch anything, nor do we forsake anything. Since the power of a vow has no end, we might as well give in the present, instead of in the future. The Avatamsaka Sutra relates to "returning"—returning from the truth to the ordinary, from wisdom to pity—so the truth and the ordinary exist in harmony, and wisdom and pity merge into one. Such is the practice of Buddhism. Other practices of worship such as abstaining from meat, copying the Mahakaruna, or counting beads are all false.'

Feeling that they couldn't envision any concrete development in Beijing, Liang Qichao and Tan Sitong headed south separately four months after they first met. Liang launched the publication, *News of Current Events*, opened the Datong Rendition House, founded the Association for the Abolition of Foot-binding, and established a school for girls in Shanghai.

After learning that the governor of Hunan, Chen Baozhen, was an open-minded person, and that his son and a few subordinates were actually assisting in the promotion of the new policies, he went to Hunan to take up the post of headmaster at the School of Current Events. Tan Sitong also joined him there as a teacher. Liang Qichao had forty students at the school. He made use of his experience with Kang Youwei at Wan Mu Cao Tang School, where teachers and students intermingled with each other. He imbued his students with new ideas, the ideologies of reform, and democracy. He spent four hours in the classroom each day, and the rest of the time on school administration and commenting on the compositions and notes of the students. Some of his comments were over a thousand words long, and he often worked long into the night. His exhausting schedule finally took a toll on his health.

At the same juncture, the conservative forces in Hunan filed complaints against them, citing that they were spreading fallacies. Finally, the Governor of Hunan had no choice but to dismiss them, and Liang Qichao, supported by his students, boarded a ship heading east to Shanghai. The youngest of his students, only sixteen, was a thin-looking youngster with a keen intelligence. He had been with Liang for only a few months, but Liang's words and example had influenced him greatly. Liang expanded his students' horizons with the ten rules of learning, admonishing the students that to learn about one country, one had to read books from other countries. He imparted the idea that there was a world beyond China, and that you could appreciate the position of China only by gaining a comprehension of the whole world. 'The teachings of Confucius are not for the government of one country, but for all the land under heaven.'

Thus the purpose of learning was to acquire a means of governing the world. China's educational system at that time taught people to use studying as a means to achieve official rank, attain wealth, and bring honour to the family. But Liang discarded all these clichés. He urged the students to approach knowledge with a higher goal, so they had a new state of mind at the very start of their education. This sixteen-year-old boy, named Cai Genyin, was the smartest of all forty students and the one most engrossed in this new realm. He discussed at length the mission of the intellectuals and the future of China in his compositions and notebooks. Besides giving his own comments, Liang also held class discussions on the compositions of each student. Cai Genyin spoke little during the discussion sessions. But each time he talked, he gave focused and novel points of view. Both the teachers and his fellow students were particularly fond of him.

Cai Genyin was born in a farmhouse in Baoqing, Hunan. He began school at the age of seven, while at the same time working in the fields. In order to save on lamp oil, he often studied by moonlight. He had read all the books available to him by the age of ten, and started to look everywhere for places where books were open to outsiders. He often walked ten or even twenty kilometres to a place that allowed him to read and make notes. At the age of thirteen, he came under the tutelage of Fan Zhui, a personage of lofty thinking and vision from the same county. His articles 'Openness' and 'New Ideas' in *Xi'an News* moved Cai Genyin, but enraged the local conservatives. Finally, Fan Zhui was driven out of the county. It was a cloudy morning when Cai Genyin saw his teacher Fan Zhui off. In the midst of the hostile clamour, the teacher and his student walked silently toward the horse carriage.

As the carriage drove off, Fan Zhui waved goodbye to his young student who tearfully waved back until the carriage became a dot in the distance. He resolved at that moment to leave this place of imprisonment. Three years later, he went alone to Changsha and was admitted into the School of Current Events. He was fortunate to have run into Master Liang, a character even more brilliant than Master Fan. Fan taught him about China, but Liang introduced the world to him; from Fan, he learned that there was a world beyond his home village; from Liang, he learned there was a world beyond China. But their predestined connection was so fragile. Master Liang was dealt the same fate—being driven out. Now he was carrying Master Liang's sack as he went to see him off.

Supported by his students, Liang lay down on the sleeping berth and coughed strenuously. Cai Genyin rushed out to get a cup of water, and bumped into someone as he stepped out. It was Tan Sitong. Tan stopped him from falling, gave him a pat, then went into the cabin.

When Cai Genyin returned with the water, he heard Liang's words to the other students:

'The reason why we can't sacrifice ourselves to save the country is either because of our family or our body. Let's all agree on one thing—we can't save the country unless we shed the bondage of family ties. We can't attain virtue unless we sacrifice our life. Whoever agrees to this will be a comrade of ours.'

Everybody there nodded, and Tan Sitong added:

'Our chance encounter at the School of Current Events has probably come to an end. But our relationship as teacher and student, as friends of mutual understanding, as comrades in saving the country, has just begun. We all have great aspirations. From now on, we'll endeavour to save our country using different directions and different approaches. We cannot predict the success or failure of our efforts. But even if we fail, we will still adhere to our convictions. We might lose our family and our life at an unforeseen time and place as the evidence of our commitment made here today. But always remember that our spirits are together and remember the friendship we forged during the time we spent together at school.'

Tan Sitong got up, gestured goodbye to Liang Qichao and then walked out. Other people followed, with Cai Genren at the end of the file. With tears in his eyes he turned around to wave to his teacher. Liang smiled and beckoned him to approach:

'Genyin, I have no gift for you as we depart. I'll just give you a name, Cai E. "E" is the edge of the sword, tall and sharp, which describes exactly what your future is going to be. I'll also call you "Songpo", signifying the integrity of the pine tree and the free spirit of Su Dongpo, the famous Song Dynasty poet and painter, which is another aspect of your character.'

CHAPTER EIGHT

Big Sword Wang Wu

Unlike ordinary intellectuals of his time, Tan Sitong associates with people from all walks of life. One such associate is Big Sword Wang Wu, with whom he studied Chinese martial arts. These two maintain a close friendship. Big Sword Wang Wu is famous around Beijing for his chivalry, his loyalty to his friends, and for his martial arts expertise. He is the owner of an armed escort service and a member of a secret society that advocates opposing the Manchu-ruled Qing Dynasty and restoring the Han Chinese Ming Dynasty. They oppose the Manchus as foreign occupiers. As such, Big Sword Wang Wu and his gang are flabbergasted when their close and respected friend, Tan Sitong, goes to see the Emperor and agrees to serve as an official in the Qing government. After a brief bout of fisticuffs, Tan Sitong explains his goal of cooperating with the Emperor. He bolsters his argument with a historical review of the definition of 'foreigner' in China and how it changes again and again as enemies from the north were assimilated into mainstream China. He notes that the Manchus are of the Mongolian race, as are the Han Chinese. This confuses all of the gang members, who are now being told that their long-held goals (which the society held for about two hundred and fifty years) are apparently based on a false pretext. Tan Sitong acknowledges that his chances of succeeding in political reform are slim, but he vows to follow Kang Youwei and seek a bloodless road to political change. He tells the gang he will not blame them if they don't agree, that he plans to take the blame and sacrifice himself if things fail to work out. Then Tan Sitong departs.

It was the spring of 1898 when Liang Qichao returned to Shanghai, the twenty-fourth year of the reign of Emperor Guangxu. The efforts of the past years had finally borne fruit this year. First, on 28 April, the Emperor summoned Kang Youwei; seventeen days later, on

15 May, the Emperor received Liang Qichao and appointed him a grade-six official, responsible for handling the affairs of the Bureau of Publications. This was an unusual summons, for according to court custom, only officials above grade four were qualified to see the Emperor. At that time, Liang was only twenty-six, and did not hold official rank.

Even more unusual, after Tan Sitong was summoned in July the Emperor issued the appointments of four secretaries attached to the Grand Council of State on 20 July. These were low-ranking positions. But with their access to the Emperor, the secretaries held actual power akin to that of a prime minister. Fearing that Kang Youwei's reputation might incite the Empress Dowager, the Emperor arranged a position outside the court for Kang and maintained contact with him through these four secretaries. Thus the Nanhai Association and the Liuyang Association became their after-hours rendezvous points.

Meetings with Tan Sitong were not as simple. Kang Youwei, Liang Qichao and the other three secretaries—Yang Rui, Liu Guangdi, and Lin Xu—were conventional intellectuals with a limited circle of friends. But Tan Sitong was different. His associations were with intellectuals like himself, as well as people from all walks of life, including the so-called lower classes. Tan savoured a poem of Zuo Taichong that he remembered from his youth: 'There are exceptional talents to be found everywhere, but those living in swamps are most often missed.' And he believed it was the case, just as Confucius believed, that you could find the faithful within any ten houses.

In fact, extraordinary people were hard to find among scholars, as echoed in one of Huang Zongze's poems, which said: 'People who speak out with a sense of justice are often the butchers and the less well-educated'.

Tan Sitong desired to make friends with people from all circles of life, because he believed saving China took more than the words of intellectuals. They had to be accompanied by actions. People willing to act were mostly lower class characters, particularly those in the secret societies. The first example that came to mind was the Hongmen, also known as Sanhehui, or the Triad Society. The Hongmen was a secret society composed of the adherents to the restoration of the Ming Dynasty.

The origins of the organization could be traced back to Taiwan. After the Ming Dynasty was toppled, Zheng Chenggong, the leader of an anti-Manchu resistance army, retreated to Taiwan, and his subordinates entered a blood vow, pledging brotherhood and loyalty to the movement to restore the Ming Dynasty. Zheng Chenggong founded 'Han Liu' and dispatched five of his generals to sneak back to the Mainland. They later became the first five founders of Hongmen, headquartered at Shaolin Temple on Mount Jiulian in Fujian.

In order to trace the origins of Hongmen, Tan Sitong persuaded his second eldest brother, Tan Sixiang, to go to Taiwan and trace the footsteps of 'Han Liu'. But his brother wrote and told him the discouraging news that Taiwan was no longer the same as in the time of Zheng Chenggong. He saw only hoodlums there, no gallant men. So Tan Sitong decided to find his comrades among the lower classes in the Mainland. That was how he got to know Wang Wu.

Wang Wu was born in Beijing. His father's last name was Bai. Orphaned at the age of eight, he and his younger brother begged on the streets to survive. One day they begged at the door of Shunxing Armed Escort Service. The owner liked his uncommon looks, adopted him, and changed his last name to Wang. Eleven years later, when the owner passed away, Wang Wu took over the business. Owing to his chivalrous conduct, forthright character and good martial arts skills (Chinese kungfu), he was dubbed 'Big Sword Wang Wu'.

The armed escort service was a strange line of business. High-ranking officials and wealthy people hired these guards to escort people or goods on the road until they reached their destination. There were considerable risks involved, whether they travelled by land or by water. The risks were posed by bandits or pirates along the way.

Armed escorts could not possibly fight all the bandits they ran into, for the price in blood would be too high. So instead, they engaged in peaceful negotiations. When they ran into bandits blocking their way, the head guard usually approached them with a broad grin, bowed, and greeted them, saying, 'You must be working hard!'

The bandit leader, if tactful, would reply in the same manner. Then the bandit would ask for the name of the business. After the escort gave their name, the parties would talk in code.

The code words covered the lineage of the owners and their association with secret societies. If the parties were even remotely related, things became much easier. The bodyguard only needed to acknowledge the help and convenience given to them by the bandits through the following dialogue:

Bandits: 'Whose clothes are you wearing?'

Guards: 'A friend's clothes.'

Bandits: 'Whose meal are you eating?'

Guards: 'A meal provided by a friend.'

The exchange was basically true, because the bodyguards lived off the bandits. If there were no bandits, the business of the armed escort service would have no reason to exist.

After this dialogue in code, the bandits would let them pass. Prior to departing, the bodyguards had to show their appreciation by saying:

'Thank you for your road. If you need anything, I'll bring it back in a few days.'

'I can't think of anything.' The bandit repaid the courtesy. 'Don't work too hard.'

The bandits wouldn't ask the bodyguards to bring anything back. But sometimes they would go into town and the armed escort service would be obliged to protect them from government troops. If the bandits were caught, the bodyguards would have a difficult time on the road from then on.

The armed escort service owned by Wang Wu was only one of the eight establishments of its kind in Beijing. But because of his reputation, the mention of Wang Wu was particularly valuable and useful on the road. However, he got into trouble from time to time because of his cordial relationship with the bandits. One such time involved dozens of robberies and burglaries that occurred in succession around the town, primarily targeting corrupt officials. The Ministry of Justice put pressure on Prefect Pu Wenxuan to apprehend the perpetrators. Prefect Pu sent in a troop of a few hundred soldiers to surround the residence of Wang Wu outside Xuanwu Gate. But they didn't dare forcibly enter when Wang Wu and about twenty people inside resisted arrest. The stalemate lasted well into the night, when the government troops temporarily withdrew. Wang Wu, disguised in a solder's uniform, escaped into the crowd. The next day, however, he turned himself in.

Prefect Pu wondered, 'You resisted arrest when we came to get you. Why do you turn yourself in now?'

Wang Wu replied, 'I countered force with force. Since you've pulled out, I have turned myself in.'

'I know you are not a bandit. But you have to help me solve some cases. Dozens of cases in a row like this make us look really bad,' said Prefect Pu.

Wang Wu said, 'I'll definitely help. But the question is, do you want the stolen goods back or you want the man responsible? I can help get the loot back, but if you want the man, you'll just have to arrest me.'

Prefect Pu decided to accept the return of the stolen goods, so the problem was solved.

Later on, as a sign of appreciation that Prefect Pu was an honest official, Wang Wu dispatched some of his guards to escort Prefect Pu part of the way when he left for Henan after being dismissed from office.

Wang Wu won the nickname 'The Knight Errant of Beijing' for his chivalry and loyalty to his friends. His achievements in martial arts were also outstanding. Among his students who studied sword-craft under him was a Hunanese, none other than Tan Sitong.

Tan Sitong was introduced to Wang Wu by Hu Qi, nicknamed 'long-armed monkey'. Tan called Wang Wu 'Wu Ye', meaning 'master number five', and Hu Qi 'Qi Ge,' meaning 'older brother number seven'. Wang Wu and Hu Qi called Tan Sitong 'San Ge', meaning 'older brother number three', as did Wang Wu's friends. Tan Sitong was the only intellectual among these people, but he didn't feel in any way superior. Everybody knew that San Ge was knowledgeable, willing to teach them, and affable. They liked to spend time with him, listening to him talk of history and current affairs. They also knew San Ge was the son of a government official and would never join them in their trade. But they were all friends, and he was the sworn brother of Wang Wu and Hu Qi.

In the ten years of their acquaintance, Wang Wu and his gang mentioned on numerous occasions matters regarding their organization. They explicitly expressed their opposition to Manchu traditions. But Tan Sitong seemed to hold back each time the subject of the Manchus was touched on. He rarely made any comment, listening with amusement to their outpouring of curses. Maybe because of his ambiguous attitude, these simple brothers just assumed that San Ge opposed the Manchus.

In 1898 Tan Sitong was summoned by Emperor Guangxu and appointed Secretary to the Grand Council of State. The news spread around the city of Beijing and reached Wang Wu and his gang.

'He went to the Emperor! He went to see the Emperor!' The words were like nails striking in the air. Wang Wu and his gang were flabbergasted. They looked at each other without a word. Some people lowered their heads in dejection.

'Tan Sitong betrayed us!' blurted out Hu Qi suddenly.

'No, Tan Sitong didn't betray you,' a firm voice came from the door. It was Tan Sitong himself standing there.

'San Ge,' yelled Wang Wu. He stood up suddenly with his face flushed red. 'San Ge, why did you go see him? What about our position? What about their position? What is there to talk about between us? If there is anything between us, it's that we chop them, and they chop us.' Wang Wu's right hand made a knife fist, swinging back and forth as though chopping off a head.

'San Ge, you are a learned man, not uneducated like us. You are more sensible than we are. But can you explain why you went to see that Manchu? Why? What should we do? How are we going to look at you?'

'That is why I didn't let you know beforehand. I didn't want to burden you. If I had told you, you would've stopped me from going. I didn't know how it was going to turn out. So I chose to give it a try first. If the outcome wasn't good, it would be a personal error of judgement on my part, and you would not have been implicated. But if the outcome was good and you blocked it, I would have made you become the ones who had made the error in judgement. So I decided not to tell you beforehand, I . . .'

'That's all baloney!' Hu Qi stood up abruptly, rolling up his sleeves. So did some of the others. Wang Wu gestured with the palm of his left hand down and drew it across his left chest, signalling to them to desist. Tan Sitong remained seated and fully composed. 'Wu Ye and all of you here, you should let me finish what I have to say. You can decide what to do afterwards.'

'Shit! You went to see a Manchu, the head of the Manchus. You betrayed us. What more do you have to say? We think so highly of you, but still you betrayed us!' roared Hu Qi.

'Qi Ge,' said Tan Sitong.

'Don't call me Qi Ge. Our friendship is over today. Don't ever call me Qi Ge again.'

'Okay! I won't call you Qi Ge. I just want to ask you, I . . .'

'I don't want to listen to you. We are sworn brothers. Let's get out the incense stick today. Remember, this day next year will be the anniversary of your death!' Shouting these words, Hu Qi sprang across the table towards Tan Sitong. Everybody else rushed forward, and teapots and cups rolled to the floor.

'Stop!' The commanding voice of Wang Wu stopped everyone in their tracks. Tan Sitong still sat there, unfazed, but his nose was bleeding and tea was splattered all over him. He let the blood drip without wiping his nose. He was as stationary as a Buddhist statue, not like the glaring warrior attendants of the Buddha, but like a kind-looking bodhisattva.

Wang Wu suddenly took out the dagger hanging from his waist. Everybody was looking at him, but Tan Sitong was undisturbed. Wang Wu cut a piece of cloth off his clothes with the dagger and covered Tan's bleeding nose with it. With a hand on Tan's shoulder, he said: 'Why don't you lie down for a while?'

Wang Wu helped Tan Sitong to bed and told someone to get some wet towels. He used one to wipe the blood off Tan's face and put the other on his forehead. He then put a blanket over Tan and signalled for everyone to leave. He went out last, closing the door gingerly.

⌒o◆o⌒

The gang squatted on the grass outside the room. Wang Wu was silent. He took out his tobacco pipe and lit it. Everybody followed suit, but not Hu Qi. He squatted there, drawing a cross on the ground with a twig. He retraced the cross over and over as the corner of his mouth twisted with the sketch of each line.

Finally Hu Qi couldn't hold it in any longer. 'Big Brother, I really don't understand how a person like Tan San Ge could have betrayed us.'

Wang Wu smoked his pipe without looking at Hu Qi and replied coldly: 'He didn't betray us. Otherwise he wouldn't have come here.'

Hu Qi thought about it for a second and something seemed to dawn upon him suddenly.

'You are probably right. If he had betrayed us, he should be aware that coming here would only get him killed. He should know that we would not spare him. He told us last time that the fourth boss of the Ma Fuyi Gang in Hunan broke the rules. His brothers decided to make him jump off the mountain as punishment. In the end, as the brothers accompanied him up the mountain, Ma himself was still looking after the big brother who had come along, reminding him to watch out for the slippery roads. Ma Fuyi is from the same village and a friend of San Ge. I don't believe that San Ge doesn't know our rules.'

'Maybe he dared to come back here because he didn't think he had broken any rules,' someone suggested.

'Breaking the rules or not, the point is if he has betrayed us, why did he come back? What's his purpose?' another person said.

'The purpose is to pull us down with him, to become the slaves of the Manchus, since he, by himself, is not enough!' yelled Hu Qi, tossing the twig aside.

Wang Wu looked up at the sky with the pipe in his mouth. Finally he turned around.

'Let's not make blind guesses. San Ge must have his reasons that you cannot figure out. I can't figure it out either. He knows so much, and we are uneducated. There are a lot of things we are not sure of. But one thing for sure is that he is not the kind of person who betrays friends. I swear it, on my very own head. I've known so many people in my life and I've never misjudged anyone. I don't believe Tan Sitong is an exception. If he is, I will jump off the mountain before he does. Not only will I jump, I'll gouge my eyes out first!'

'Of course we trust your judgement,' said Hu Qi calmly. 'I don't know why I made the first strike earlier. Maybe because San Ge didn't inform us first, he didn't try to let us understand, and I got mad.'

Everyone looked at Wang Wu, then lowered their heads. So did Hu Qi. Then he looked at Wang Wu and said:

'What should we do now? What do you say, big brother?'

'We should listen to him first,' said Wang Wu as he got up. Everybody did the same and walked into the room.

———◇◆◇———

Tan Sitong was already out of bed washing his face when they walked in. The washbowl was made of porcelain, but looked worn. It had a new base made of an iron sheet welded to it. Welders in the north were masters of salvage. They made use of waste to patch everything up. The impoverished Chinese in their agrarian society kept everything that might have been thrown away. They cherished and took good care of old things. They had a special feeling for well-used goods. They would rather repair something time after time than replace it. This tradition became a law, a custom, and finally a purpose. So the question wasn't the affordability of getting something new;

discarding the old and replacing it with the new was out of the question. It was perfectly all right to keep the old. If not, patching it up would make do. So in Chinese families, articles that had been passed on for decades or even for over a century still remained in use. The poverty of the agrarian society encouraged the Chinese to cherish the old, from an institution down to one washbasin. There were no exceptions.

As Tan Sitong was wiping his face, Wang Wu came in.

'You bled quite a lot. They acted too rashly.'

Tan forced a smile and continued to wash the blood-stained towel.

'Let them do it,' said Wang Wu.

'It's all right. I'll wash it myself. It's not bad to have the chance to wash your own blood. Maybe one day . . . ' He suddenly thought of something, raised his head, and then lowered it back down. 'Maybe one day there will be more bloodshed and I won't have the chance to wash it off myself.'

'Don't mind the impetuousness of the brothers.'

'I don't at all,' said Tan. 'Maybe I am to blame. I never did fully explain this to you all.'

'Then let's clear it up. We've been brothers for over ten years and everybody respects you. But you know where we stand on the Manchus, which is very clear. What you did really hurt our feelings. People in our group will never trust the Manchus. Since things have blown up, let's have it out,' said Wang Wu.

'Maybe it's for the better.' Tan motioned for everyone to sit down.

'Do you remember, San Ge?' said Wang Wu. 'During the reign of Kangxi, the Russians from the north-east harassed China. The Manchus couldn't suppress them, because they didn't have soldiers who could swim and fight at the same time. Someone suggested Kangxi use the Fujianese, who had moved to Beijing after the Qing army conquered Taiwan. They were from families of pirates under the leadership of Zheng Chenggong. Consequently, these people were recruited to fight the Russians.'

'I seem to remember, now that you mention it.' Tan Sitong scratched his head. 'Didn't the one hundred and twenty-eight monks from the Shaolin Temple in Putian, Fujian also help fight that battle?'

'You are truly well informed. That's right, Kangxi forced these descendants of pirates from Taiwan to relocate to Beijing after he conquered Taiwan. When he recruited five hundred of them to fight the Russians, they were reluctant to do so. At this time, one hundred and twenty-eight Shaolin monks came from Fujian and discussed the matter with them in Fujianese dialect, so the others could not understand what they said.

The monks said, "The Manchus are our enemies. They seized our homes and we'll take revenge. But this is an opportunity. This time they need our help to fight the foreigners. Why don't we cooperate with them this time? For one thing, no matter how bad the Manchus are, at least we are all Chinese. Fighting a war against foreigners is more important than fighting your own people. Furthermore, if we win this battle, the Manchus will owe us a favour and will think better of us. They might even soften their high-pressure policy and we can conserve our strength, waiting for the right time to strike back." So the Fujianese were persuaded to fight a river battle with the Russians in the twenty-fourth year of Kangxi. Each Chinese wore a big plate or shield on his head during the battle . . . '

'Allow me to interrupt. The plate was made of rattan.'

'Ah, how strange! How does San Ge know about it?'

'After winning the battle against the Russians, the Manchus printed a book entitled *The Strategy to Suppress Rakshas, the Malignant Spirit*', which mentions the Fujianese rattan-plated soldiers.'

'You are right. We read too little and you are truly well-read.'

'But I don't know how those soldiers fought.'

'They swam over to the Russian boats using their rattan plates as shields, and drilled holes in the boats. The Russians couldn't figure out what was going on and referred to these soldiers as "big-hat tartars". How funny that these people who had been wanting to kill the tartars when they were in Taiwan now found they were called tartars themselves.'

'Then what happened? I heard Shaolin Temple was later burned down.'

'The battle was won. The Manchus said everybody would be rewarded. But the monks didn't want any reward. They turned it down with the excuse that they were monks who couldn't accept any material reward. But in their hearts, they didn't think the Manchus were worthy of bestowing rewards. After the monks returned to Shaolin Temple, the Manchus sent soldiers to burn down the temple. Only five of the one hundred and twenty-eight monks got out alive. They sought out Zhu Hongzhu, the grandson of Emperor Chongzhen, and formed an alliance with him as sworn brothers. In the initiation ceremony, there was a red light up in the sky. Since the character for 'red', *hong*, is pronounced the same as the *hong* in the name 'Zhu Hongzhu', the Hongmen Society was conceived. When the five monks escaped from Shaolin Temple, they made a vow at Shawanko:

> *As enduring as heaven,*
> *And as permanent as earth,*
> *No matter how long it takes,*
> *We will surely get our revenge.*

So the Hongmen believed in revenge; they opposed the Manchu Qing Dynasty and sought to restore the Ming Dynasty to the Han Chinese. Later on, the Hongmen lost the battle at Wuchan and Zhu Hongzhu disappeared. So the group broke up into several branches and developed separately. In the end, they composed a poem as a password for their future communication:

> *At separation we five write a poem,*
> *That our background is known to nobody;*
> *Pass this message on to our brothers,*
> *Until we reunite.*

So each branch developed on its own in secret. Now there is the Triad Society, Heaven and Earth Society, Three-Point Society, Kelao Society, Qingshui Society, Dagger Society, Double-Sword Society, and so on, that have evolved ever further apart. Nobody seems to have a handle on their origins and interrelationships. You are a learned man who should know more than we do.'

'Not so. Hongmen has always been a clandestine organization. There is hardly any documentation of its history. Everything was passed on orally. What I know is also very limited. It's just that some descriptions in the official records match the stories passed on orally. The rattan-plated soldier you mentioned is an example.'

'You are right.'

'In *The Legal System of the Great Qing Dynasty*, it says any Fujianese who enter into a blood alliance or sworn brotherhood will be prosecuted for the offence of treason. Why did they view it so seriously? It was specifically targeting the Hongmen. The Manchus paid attention to the Hongmen, but couldn't figure out how they passed on things. It took them one hundred and fifty years or more until they found a book during the reign of Xianfeng. The book was *The Annals of the Three Kingdoms*, dating back over fifteen hundred years, which advocated the restoration of the Han and used a sworn brotherhood to achieve that goal. So Emperor Xianfeng banned the book.'

'So that is why. But the development of the Hongmen later on was too complicated to sort out. We only know it was initiated for the cause of opposing the Manchu Qing and restoring the Ming. They couldn't see how some brothers chose to work with the Qing court later on, and how they could possibly think of cooperating with the Manchus after what happened to the monks of Shaolin. So what's going on?'

'Well, it's a long story. We have to start with the question of the Manchus, with respect to race.'

Tan Sitong sipped some water and continued. 'There are three major races in the world—Mongolian, Caucasian, and Negro. The Chinese belong to the Mongolian race, and are divided into the major ethnic groups of Han, Manchu, and Mongol. Among these major ethnic groups, the Han have been dominant in the land of China. In the thousands of years of history, China was ruled completely by other ethnic groups only in the thirteenth century, by the Mongols during the Yuan Dynasty, and from the seventeenth century up to now by the Manchus in the Qing Dynasty. The Mongols are shorter, have dark eyes, and small moustaches. But the branch of Genghis Khan, the ancestor of the Mongols that ruled China, were grey-eyed and taller with moustaches. They might have had Manchu blood.

In the thirteenth century, after the Mongols took over China, they ranked the Manchus as number three, and the Han as number four. In the seventeenth century, after the Manchus occupied China, they similarly ranked the Mongols before the Han. They allowed intermarriage with the Mongols, built temples for their monks, banned the Han people from cultivating Mongol land, and disallowed intermarriage between the Han and the Mongols. The intention of the Manchus was obvious. They united with the Mongols to oppress the Han.

Why did the Manchus want to guard against the Han? Because the Han had been the dominant nationality in China for too long. Its roots were deep, and its population massive. Its culture was so well developed. The Manchus felt the need to restrain the Han's power of influence and assimilation. When the Manchus crossed the Great Wall from the north-east of China, it symbolized the failure of the Han people. The chief commander who guarded the Great Wall at that time was the love-stricken general Wu Sangui. When he heard the capital was under siege by the rebels and that the emperor had hanged himself, he stayed put. But when he heard that his lover, Chen Yuan Yuan, had fallen into the hands of the rebels in Beijing, he chose to collaborate with the enemy so he could rescue his Chen Yuan Yuan.

The outcome was disastrous. The Manchu army marched into Beijing and had no intention of leaving. They gave the last Ming emperor a grand funeral, wiped out the rebels, and set up a Manchu emperor.

The Manchus told the Han people: "Our enemy, the rebels, killed our emperor and our emperor killed our enemy, the rebels." It was a clever substitution. The term "emperor" didn't change and its symbol didn't change. It is like overlapping the film of a photograph of a Han emperor and that of a Manchu emperor, to develop a new photograph with the face of the Han emperor replaced by the Manchu emperor.

The Manchus decided to subjugate the Hans by concrete means. They started from the head, changing the hairstyle of the Han people. Whether you submitted or not could be readily ascertained from your hairstyle. The old hairstyle of the Han was long hair. The Manchus wear their hair in braids. As much as we resent the Manchu rule, we still have to wear our hair in braids.

No matter how much the Han hate the Manchus, it's wrong for the Han to say the Manchus are foreigners, because we are all Chinese. The China of ancient times was small, covering only the areas of Henan and Shanxi. At that time, the Han viewed people outside these areas as foreigners. It was actually nonsensical of our ancestors. Also, the definition and scope of "foreigner" was modified over and over again. At that time, Confucius, from Shandong, as a descendant of the Yin Dynasty, was a typical foreigner in the eyes of the people of the Zhou Dynasty in Shaanxi. But before long, the distinction between Yin and Zhou faded and they became one family. In the late Zhou Dynasty, the Shandong clique and the Shaanxi clique viewed the Hubei clique as foreigners and barbarians. But pretty soon, they came together to develop the south, and viewed people in Sichuan and Guizhou as foreigners.

These interesting variations on the definition of foreigners are endless. We can re-examine the history of China from this perspective. The Chinese nation bears the marks of mixing and homogenization since ancient times. The first wave of mixing ended with the Qin Dynasty after it assimilated its eastern and southern neighbours, and part of Baiyue, what is today Zhejiang, Fujian, and Guangdong, western tribes, and northern tribes. The second wave of mixing occurred during the Han Dynasty up to the Northern and Southern dynasties, by incorporating the nationals of Xiongnu, the Turkic tribe, the Di, tribes in today's Gansu, Qiang tribes in today's Sichuan, the Donghu, the Tungusic tribes, the barbarous tribes in the south, and the Shinanyi, tribes in today's Sichuan, Yunnan, Guizhou, and Myanmar. The third wave lasted from the Sui and Tang dynasties up to the Yuan Dynasty, by incorporating the Turks, Tartars, Khitan Tartars, and the Mongols. The fourth wave was from after the Ming Dynasty, until today.

We tend to forget about the blood of the northern barbarians in the Han people. We forget that the mother of Emperor Tang Taizong was a foreigner, as was the mother of Emperor Chengzu of the Ming Dynasty. In fact, the royal families of the Tang and Ming dynasties all had mixed blood. A funny contradiction is that the martyrs in the late Ming Dynasty died because they were "unwilling to serve foreigners", but they neglected the fact that the emperor they had served so loyally was also a foreigner in a broader sense.

Actually it wasn't just the Emperor. Even those martyrs themselves couldn't guarantee that they were the pure descendants of Huangdi. Nobody dared guarantee that their ancestors were not "disturbed" during the invasion by the northern barbarians, that their blood was one hundred per cent pure.

So strictly speaking, the concept of barbarians passed down from our ancestors was fundamentally wrong. Today, it's hard to say who are the real Chinese. Tracing back China's five thousand years of history, if we only look at the areas of Henan and Shanxi, and leave out other areas like the barbaric regions, we really do a disservice to the Chinese nation. People who lived in Henan and Shanxi in ancient times were Chinese, but people who lived outside the Central Plains, beyond the middle and lower reaches of the Yellow River, were also part of the Chinese nation.

Using this more scientific and broader approach, we have to say that the history of the Chinese nation is a history of infighting. All the historical accounts of expeditions to the east, west, south, or north were not aimed at the real foreigners, but at Chinese. When we read the ancient prose *Mourning an Old Battleground*, we always remember the phrases that describe the military achievements of the Qin and Han dynasties. When we conjure up the miserable scenes where the "Qin built the Great Wall that ended at the Shanhai Pass along the sea, millions of lives were tormented and thousands of miles were tainted with blood," and the outcome when "the Han attacked the Xiongnu and took over Yishan. But with skeletons all over the place, the achievement couldn't match the disaster it brought," how do we feel? We have to question the outstanding achievements of many great emperors in the history of China, from Huangdi down to Qin Shihuang, Han Wudi, Tang Taizong, and Song Taizu, particularly those associated with conquering different races and unifying China. In the five thousand years of Chinese history, the only battle with foreigners was the invasion of British troops during the Opium War in 1840. Otherwise, all the so-called barbarians in other wars were Chinese.

Thus, it's meaningless to differentiate whether you are from the Central Plains or the northern border, if you are Manchu or Han. Everybody got it wrong. We shouldn't be so narrow-minded.

As for the secret societies, their slogan of opposing the Manchu Qing and restoring the Ming actually doesn't make much sense. For example, the Triad Society was conceived after the Shaolin monks were killed during the reign of Kangxi. But the organization at that time was anti-government, not anti-Manchu. The Kelao Society was established during the reign of Qianlong, long after the fall of the Ming Dynasty. Its expansion sped up after Emperor Tongzhi's reign, mainly owing to the fact that a part of the Xian army was disbanded and got mad at the Qing government. So the goal held by the secret societies of opposing the Manchu Qing and restoring the Ming hasn't been as pure as most people think. The Qing Dynasty has ruled China for more than two hundred and twenty-five years. Who, with a straight face, can still talk about restoring the Ming after such a long time?

Besides, what if the Ming Dynasty is restored? Is it worth restoring? People who know a little about history realize that the Qing court has been much better than the Ming government. All of the Qing emperors, with the exception of the Empress Dowager, have been better than the Ming emperors, as are their governmental systems. Today, eunuchs like Li Lianying cannot compare with the eunuchs of Ming Dynasty, who actually governed the country. When rebel General Li Zichen seized the capital in late Ming Dynasty, there were seventy thousand eunuchs in the court, and all together one hundred thousand, counting those outside the court. Each eunuch used on average four servants to illegally control the country. What a world that was!

When officials went to the court during the Ming Dynasty, five hundred military troops lined up under Fengtian Gate to make sure court protocol was observed. If any official breached the rules of courtesy, his hat was removed, his clothes stripped open, and a flogging was carried out right there at the gate. Nowadays, the Emperor won't do more than have a eunuch chastise an official at Wumen. But in the Ming Dynasty officials were punished by public spanking or prolonged kneeling. One time one hundred and seven officials received the punishment of kneeling for five days, followed by a thirty-stroke flogging. There were numerous episodes where the officials were humiliated or tortured to death, or became disabled as a result of their punishment. The Qing court is free of such outrageous, dark politics. There is injustice and a darker side under the reign of the Manchus. But the severity of it, in comparison to the Ming court, makes a big difference to the innocent people. Unless we are capable of driving out the black crows, we should take any opportunity to turn the black crows whiter for the benefit of the people.

The emperor today is a Manchu, but he is a good man, an emperor who wants to do something right. Since he intends to undertake reform and modernization to get out of the mess created by the Empress Dowager, and he gives us this mission, we should help him. Helping him will be good for everybody. You are all wearing braids, and you've been waving the anti-Manchu flag for two hundred and fifty years. It shows that the path you've been taking doesn't work. This is all I have to say today. I hope you can give it some thought. If you concur, you'll still treat me as your brother; if not, you can try to persuade me; persuade me to quit the job as Secretary and join you. How about it?'

Finishing his talk, Tan Sitong stood up valiantly. All eyes were on him, but the room was in total silence. Wang Wu's tobacco pipe had long since gone out. He stared at Tan Sitong and nodded slowly. The eyes of the brothers moved from Tan to him. They had no opinion. Their Big Brother's opinion was good enough for them, and they were waiting for him to speak. Finally, Wang Wu opened his mouth.

'San Ge, we are unrefined people who do not necessarily understand those grand arguments. We only know you are our brother. We'll agree to whatever you agree to, and oppose to whatever you are against. We'll overturn whomever you do. Conversely, whoever takes advantage of you is doing the same thing to us.

Whoever hacks you will receive three stabs from us. We are of one heart. You are our light and we trust you. But, but this time, something just doesn't seem right.'

'Wu Ye, say whatever you feel is not right. Go ahead.'

'Well, I can't spell it out exactly. I only feel that not everything seems smooth.'

'Are you saying I shouldn't follow Kang Youwei?'

'No, not really. How can a learned person like Kang Youwei be wrong? We just don't know if Kang Youwei's decision to work with the Manchus will pan out well. Will it turn out to be a disaster? We don't understand Kang's knowledge. But we are just worried that intelligent people might make a big mistake, with consequences so severe that some people might lose their heads. We count on your judgement. You know Kang Youwei. You know if he is making a big mistake.'

'I understand what you mean,' said Tan Sitong.

'I'll say the same thing again. We are uneducated people. We only believe in you,' said Wang Wu.

'We all believe in San Ge,' said the brothers.

'But if San Ge believes in Kang Youwei, we'll do the same,' said Wang Wu.

'If my guess is right, you don't quite believe in Kang Youwei,' said Tan Sitong.

'It's not really so. We simply can't tell if Kang Youwei is right or not. If not, we can't say why.' Wang Wu paused. 'If he has made a mistake, we can't tell what the mistake is. We are just telling you our feelings that something isn't quite right. We are totally different from you. You grew up with books. We grew up with blood. Our life is on the line everyday. But we are still alive after so many years and there is a reason for it; we take care of each other and we count on our own skills, the merits of our ancestors, the blessing of the Buddha, and luck. But there is another reason, that is, we can rely on a hunch. Not that we have one every time. But when it's there, it really bothers us until we make some adjustment here or there. In retrospect, there are quite a few times in the past many years that our hunches have saved us. It might sound incredible, but you have to believe it.'

'You mean you have a bad feeling about the things Kang Youwei and I are doing?'

'I seem to, a little bit. I hope you won't laugh at me.'

'No, not at all. I can tell you I have the same feeling. But we have no choice. I'll be honest with you. I came to the north to get to know brave men like you. I have also befriended people from all circles in the south, particularly in my home town in Hunan. One of them, named Huang Zheng, is now twenty-five years old. He is both a *xiucai* and good at martial arts. He is closely associated with the Kelao Society. Brothers like Huang Zheng believe that revolution is the only way to save China, that only by chasing out the Manchus can we save China.

Working with the Manchus is a mistake. Their feeling that working with the Manchus is doomed to failure is more intense that yours. Before I came up north this time, they advised me to be extra careful, and even asked me to join their movement. Frankly speaking, if I hadn't been influenced by Kang Youwei and hadn't met Emperor Guangxu, I might have chosen the path of revolution. But Kang Youwei has spelled out the reasons for reform so clearly, so convincingly, and the Emperor has shown so much sincerity and eagerness in undertaking reform and in seeking people who can help him, that I have to admit that this is a rare opportunity. Perhaps we can save China with the support of the Emperor, without shedding blood.

I told Huang Zheng and others my ideas and they had to admit that this is indeed an opportunity. Only the chances of success are low. I also believe that there will be numerous obstacles. I have the same hunch as you that things won't go smoothly. But since this is an opportunity of a lifetime, I have to give it a try. If we succeed, the credit goes to everybody; if we fail, I'll sacrifice myself.

When I came here to tell you my news today, I didn't mean to drag you in with me. I just want you to know that whether a civilian or an official, I am the same, I am still your brother. If you give me your understanding, I am here to give you this notice; if you don't, I am here to say goodbye. Maybe we'll meet again someday. I have no idea whether I am going to make it this time. I'll never come back if I fail. Take care of yourselves, brothers.' Tan Sitong cupped his hands to salute everybody, and then fell to his knees in front of Wang Wu and Hu Qi, saying: 'Please, accept my bow.'

Tan Sitong got up, turned around, and disappeared into the darkness.

CHAPTER NINE

The Reform Movement of 1898

Almost as quickly as reforms are officially enacted by imperial decree, the forces opposed to reform counter-attack. The Emperor sends official messages to the reformers seeking a plan to save the desperate situation, and then advising them to flee. The reformers valiantly, but in vain, seek military support from Yuan Shikai, the new military commander. However, Yuan Shikai quickly proves to be on the side of the Empress Dowager's faction by revealing to her the reformers' desperate attempts at military intervention. The Empress Dowager wastes no time. The Emperor is placed under house arrest, and warrants for the arrest of the reformers are issued.

Tan Sitong visits Liang Qichao, who has fled to the Japanese legation. Liang tries to persuade Tan Sitong to flee also, since the Japanese diplomats are anxious to assist the reformers in claiming asylum in Japan. Kang Youwei succeeds in escaping undetected to Shanghai through the assistance of British diplomats. But Tan Sitong is committed to staying and waiting for his arrest and execution, in order to become a martyr for the cause for reform. They speak at some length about his intentions and Liang is unable to dissuade him. He finally leaves the legation, leaving Liang Qichao behind.

Darkness prevailed in the city of Beijing at night, even in the Forbidden City where the tall walls dwarfed the clusters of low houses between them.

Qianqing Gate was smaller in scale than Wumen and Taihe Gates. But it still looked grand as the front gate of the inner court. After dark, the dim light flickered from the gate and illuminated the backs of the pair of bronze lions in front of the steps, giving the place a sense of ghastly stillness. The bronze lions squatting on the low-lying, exquisitely carved stone platform appeared to be protecting the emperor. But they too had fallen into a sound sleep in the dead silence.

There was also an emperor's throne at Qianqing Gate, where the emperor sometimes held court. When the emperor received officials, the eunuchs would carry the emperor's throne to the middle of Qianqing Gate and put a desk in front of it. A pad was placed in front of the desk where the officials knelt. To the left of the imperial gate's marble balustrades was a screen wall with yellow and green glazed tiles protruding from the crimson wall, which was all dark after nightfall. Further to the left of the screen wall and past the right door, there stood three low offices that paled in comparison with the lofty imperial architecture. This was the famous small cabinet— the Grand Council of State. At a right angle to the Grand Council stood Longzong Gate. At a right angle past Longzong Gate appeared three more small rooms. This was where the Secretary to the Grand Council of State worked.

The Grand Council of State was set up by Emperor Yongzheng. At that time, the country was carrying on a long-standing war with the enemy in the north-west. In order to make sure military correspondence reached the emperor once it arrived, and to keep all military information confidential, small offices were erected outside Longzong Gate, where the grand ministers of state were on duty in shifts. This system had been in place for one hundred and eighty years.

The Grand Council of State was an enigmatic and powerful body. The emperor had had to adopt measures to prevent it from getting out of control. For instance, the stamp of the Grand Council was kept in the inner court. When the stamp was needed, the Secretary on duty would go to request it. Central or local government officials were not allowed to reveal the contents of their petitions to the Grand Council. A white wooden sign which read, 'People who enter the Grand Council of State by mistake will be executed', illustrated how strictly guarded this place was. A censor was on duty here every day to ensure strict compliance with these rules.

The grandeur of the imperial place and the shabbiness of the Grand Council offices provided a striking contrast that symbolized the loftiness of the emperor and the lowliness of the officials. Besides office paraphernalia and wooden benches for resting, the office was sparsely outfitted. The only handsome object was the wooden board with the inscription, 'Red Banner of Happy Tidings' that hung high on the wall. Happy tidings were what the emperor hoped to hear from the grand ministers when he saw them. But now, the current Emperor shifted his anticipation to the secretaries of the Grand Council. Owing to the concentration of power in the hands of the Empress Dowager, the Emperor no longer held court at the imperial gate. But this diminished Emperor resolved to make one final attempt at reform.

Under the scheme mapped out by the Emperor and the secretaries of the Grand Council, an epic reform with the collaboration of the Manchus and the Hans was set underway. The Emperor was the only Manchu, and the four secretaries, plus Kang Youwei and Liang Qichao and a few others, were the only Han Chinese involved. All the rest of China, like that pair of bronze lions after nightfall, remained in deep slumber.

—◦◦◦◦◦—

The reform officially began on 11 June. On this day, Emperor Guangxu issued an imperial edict, announcing political reform to the nation. A succession of measures followed. The revocation of old policies and practices included abolition of the eight-part essay in the imperial civil service exam, the academy of classical learning, and non-Manchu military camps, the cutting of excess government offices, officers, soldiers, and banning the practice of foot-binding. The new policies implemented included setting up channels for recommending talent, allowing private schools, establishing agricultural, industrial, and business organizations, encouraging new publications and inventions, allowing academic associations and newspaper publishing, and shifting military exercises and weaponry to the Western style.

As the full-scale modernization movement, led by Emperor Guangxu, was pushed forward in the Forbidden City, the Empress Dowager in the Summer Palace also took action. First she removed the Emperor's tutor, Weng Tonghe, four days after the national reform was announced. Then she arranged for a confidant of hers, Rong Lu, to fill the position of Viceroy directly under the Emperor and Superintendent of Trade for Northern Ports, just to remind the Emperor of the limitations of his power.

With enemy forces pressing in, the Emperor stayed on the course of reform, and remained true to his vow of not becoming an emperor of a conquered nation. He intended to press forward, despite mounting difficulties. During the day, he bypassed the conservative high-ranking officials to promote the affairs of modernization with the help of the four Secretaries of the Grand Council; at night, he consulted with these patriots on overall planning.

But before long, things seemed to be going amiss. Emperor Guangxu finally sensed that a crisis was imminent. Word came secretly that the Empress Dowager would depose the Emperor and quash the actions of the new clique when the Emperor accompanied her to Tianjin for a military review in October. The Emperor was now cornered. On 14 September, the ninth day after the four secretaries had begun working, the Emperor gave Yang Rui a confidential imperial edict; three days later, he asked Lin Xu to deliver two more. The contents of these confidential edicts were:

To Yang Rui,

Recently, I have had the feeling that Her Majesty, the Empress Dowager, has no intention of enforcing the political reforms on a grand scale. Under no circumstances will she be willing to get rid of those corrupt and dull-witted grand ministers. For fear of losing public support, she will never retain the services of more gallant and talented individuals in the administration. In spite of my repeated decrees calling for rectification, her mind is already made up. I am afraid it will be to no avail. For instance, my edict issued on the 19th was thought by the Empress Dowager to be too weighty to carry out. Consequently, I have no recourse but to slow things down. This is the difficulty I am facing.

I know perfectly well that the weakness of our country is attributable to corrupt and dull-witted grand ministers being in power for generations. However, even I, as Emperor, do not have the power to remove those officials overnight with an imperial decree. If I tried to overhaul the system, my position would be immediately in danger. That would not benefit anybody. In view of the circumstances, I now sincerely ask you to recommend a workable solution so that political reform can be implemented, the corrupt and dull-witted grand ministers can be removed en bloc, and more gallant and talented individuals can be recruited to attend to state affairs. We must act quickly to save China from danger and turn its weakness into strength.

In order to fulfil my good intentions, you, along with Lin Xu, Tan Sitong, Liu Guangdi, and the others, should work out a prudent plan at the earliest possible time and submit it to me in confidence in the care of the Grand Minister of the State. Once I have the plan on my desk, I will

*look it over before I decide what to do next. You know this is an urgent
matter and I expect you to treat it accordingly.*

This is for your action.

To Kang Youwei,

*As I see it, we are in a difficult situation; the only way out is to implement
political reform in order to save the country. To enforce the political will,
we must get rid of those corrupt and dull-witted grand ministers and retain
the services of more gallant and talented individuals in the administration.
However, Her Majesty Empress Dowager does not agree. Following my
repeated advice, she became even madder with me. Now that I am myself
in danger, you, along with Yang Rei, Lin Xu, Tan Sitong, and Liu Guangdi
should try to plan a way to save me. You know I am anxious to see that
reform goes through and I know you will not let me down.*

This is for your action.

To Kang Youwei,

*Now I am instructing you to launch an official gazette as soon as possible.
My difficulties are indeed hard to explain in a short note. You should
leave here immediately without delay. I fully understand and appreciate
your loyalty to me and your enthusiasm for the reform campaign. You
should take good care of yourself and build up your strength so that
someday you can take up an even greater task.*

This is what I am hoping of you.

On the morning of 18 September at the Nanhai Association, Kang
Youwei and the others made some urgent decisions after reading the
confidential imperial edicts. First, they had to try every means possible
to save the Emperor. Tan Sitong suggested that they persuade Yuan
Shikai, the commander of the newly established army, to help them.
Yuan was more receptive to new ideas and had donated money to
the Qiangxuehui before. The Emperor also had received him twice
in a row a couple of days ago, indicating that he would play an
important role in the reforms. If they could bring Yuan to their side,
the situation might be turned around. Approaching Yuan was highly
risky, but it was worth a try. Tan Sitong volunteered to go talk to

Yuan by himself. Second, the Emperor urged Kang Youwei to leave Beijing immediately, so some of them would be spared when the unforeseen happened. After the decisions were made, everybody went about their work separately.

On the same evening, Tan Sitong got hold of Yuan Shikai and made an appointment to meet him at Fayuan Temple at ten o'clock that night. Due to his busy schedule, Yuan chose to meet at Fayuan Temple, instead of his own Haiding Villa. As to why, nobody knew. Maybe he was imitating Prince Gong.

In 1860, when the united Anglo-French force occupied Beijing, Emperor Xianfeng fled to Jehol, leaving his younger brother Prince Gong behind to negotiate with the foreigners. At that time, the foreign troops had taken over the Forbidden City and the inner city of Beijing. Unable to stay in his own residence, Prince Gong moved into Fayuan Temple outside the city. As he oversaw the negotiations from Rehe, Emperor Xianfeng told Prince Gong repeatedly never to receive the foreigners in person, because the high and mighty brother of the glorious Chinese Emperor shouldn't condescend to do so.

But in actuality, the Emperor's instructions were irrelevant. As the loser in a battle, with the capital occupied by the enemy, how could China's head of state avoid meeting the victorious enemy to negotiate? Besides, the looting and raping by the Anglo-French force had to be stopped. The negotiations were finally concluded. The enemy agreed to withdraw, willing to live in peace with China, if, in accordance with international etiquette, an ambassador were dispatched to deliver a letter of credence in person to the Emperor.

This final condition bothered Emperor Xianfeng tremendously. He wrote to Prince Gong, 'Although we have entered a treaty with these two foreign countries, there is no guarantee that they won't be back next spring. If we can't remove the clause about delivering the letter of credence in person, disaster might be imminent, even if they agree temporarily to drop the idea. If I return to Tianjin and then Beijing, and have to succumb to their request to meet their ambassador, you'll be held responsible. We have been losing every step of the way in these negotiations. It's a disgrace that you even met with the enemy leader this time. If we give them whatever they ask for, will we have anybody left in the whole country?'

In a vain gesture of protest, Emperor Xianfeng refused to return to Beijing and died in Rehe. His death led to the rise of the Empress Dowager and the downfall of Prince Gong. Thirty-four years after the diplomatic efforts of Prince Gong at Fayuan Temple, Japan defeated China. Four years later, the sixty-seven-year-old Prince died in his attempt to block Emperor Guangxu's reforms. In his youth, he had been an activist in the Tongji restoration movement; in his later years, he became a conservative, opposing Guangxu's reforms. That was his life story. On his way to Fayuan Temple, Tan Sitong recalled the history of Prince Gong's attempt to save the country almost forty years back, and his heart sank as his thoughts turned to Yuan Shikai.

Yuan Shikai greeted this Secretary to the Grand Council of State in court attire. As a seasoned official, Yuan felt the need to show this hot newcomer more respect.

Tan Sitong first indicated that the matter was confidential and asked to talk to Yuan Shikai alone. In Yuan's private bedroom, Tan Sitong showed him Emperor Guangxu's confidential edicts, in an attempt to gain his trust. He told Yuan that this was the only move that could save the Emperor and the country. Tan indicated that the Empress Dowager was the key; only by eliminating her could the problem be solved. He asked Yuan Shikai, first, to kill Rong Lu, and second, to surround the Summer Palace. But Yuan Shikai didn't need to send in the troops to get the Empress Dowager. Tan could find enough help in Beijing to take care of that.

Yuan agreed to the scheme on the surface. But one hour after Tan Sitong left Fayuan Temple, Rong Lu got the news from Yuan Shikai, as did the Empress Dowager the next morning.

After a night of discussions, the reformists walked out of the Nanhai Association the next morning. With the exception of Lin Xu, who totally distrusted Yuan Shikai, the others were merely doubtful. They believed that even if Yuan wouldn't send in the troops, he wouldn't betray them. Tan Sitong concluded that no matter whether Yuan Shikai was trustworthy or not, this was their last chance. To boost the confidence of Yuan, Tan decided to go to see the Emperor today, and ask him to summon Yuan one more time. As for Kang Youwei, he decided to head south the next morning.

On the morning of 20 September, Kang Youwei boarded the train to Tianjin. He was lucky. About ten hours after he left Beijing, troops raided the Nanhai Association and caught Kang Guangren. Missing Kang Youwei, the government ordered the stoppage of trains and closed the city gates to prevent his escape. Steamers in Tianjin were ordered to halt, and searched extensively. But Kang Youwei got away, and with the help of the British, arrived in Shanghai safely.

Acting in similar fashion, the Japanese provided shelter for Liang Qichao at their legation. The date was 21 September. The Empress

Dowager officially presided over court affairs and announced the end of the reform movement that had lasted one hundred and three days. Two days later, the news came that Emperor Guangxu was imprisoned at Yingtai, a small island at the centre of the lake in the imperial palace.

Ignoring the danger, Tan Sitong stayed in town. One day he left the Liuyang Association with a cloth pack and went to the Japanese legation.

———∞◦◦∞———

Tan Sitong had never been to the Japanese legation. When he approached the building, his attention was drawn to the large row of square wooden windows. The windows had a design totally different from Chinese architecture; they were open, square, and allowed large amounts of sunlight in. Tan walked up to the gate and showed his identification, indicating that he wished to see Liang Qichao. The minister, Kensuke Hayashi, wasn't in. A short, sharp-looking Japanese received him.

'I've heard so much about you, Mr Tan. My name is Shu Hirayama. Mr Liang is here. I'll take you to him.'

Liang Qichao dashed forward and grasped the hands of Tan Sitong as Tan walked into his room. 'You are finally here. I've been so worried about you. Sit down and have some tea first.'

Liang took the cloth pack carried by Tan Sitong and left it on the table.

'I was afraid of being followed, so I took a detour and walked here from Yuhe Bridge. If somebody were tailing me, he would've thought I was headed for the British legation. How are you doing? Have you been sleeping well the past two days?'

'I am fine,' said Liang. 'You have still been staying at the Association?'

'Yes, I have been staying there since you left,' replied Tan.

'Is anybody watching the Association?'

'I couldn't tell.'

'Any news from Mr Kang?'

'No.'

'Mr Kang should have arrived in Shanghai. Kensuke Hayashi said he sent a secret telex to their people in Tianjin and Shanghai, asking them to take care of Mr Kang. He was here this morning. So was Hirofumi Ito. But he is out now.'

'Minister Kensuke said he was busy and asked me to take care of you. Hope you don't mind,' added Shu Hirayama.

'How could we? We can't thank him enough,' said Liang.

'It really is a coincidence that Hirofumi Ito is in Beijing. He admires all of you and wants to offer his help. Minister Kensuke thinks the same. So do we. To play it safe, we plan to smuggle you two out of the country in the next three to five days. We can also take other comrades of yours,' said Shu Hirayama excitedly.

'But,' interrupted Tan Sitong coldly, staring at the Japanese and speaking in an unfriendly tone, 'I am not here today to ask for your help. I appreciate your help in this time of danger. But I have no plans to leave China. I am here to give Mr Liang a package.'

'But Fusheng,' Liang Qichao cut in and grabbed Tan Sitong by the shoulders. 'How can you stay behind? Doing so is a meaningless sacrifice and can only lead to death.'

'Of course I realize that,' said Tan Sitong resolutely. 'And I totally agree that you should leave. We each have our job in this joint undertaking. We have only one goal, but the position of each comrade is different. Some are at the front line, some stay behind at the supply depot. Some shell out money, some donate their time, some shed their blood, and some labour. A's job may not suit B, C and D don't have to do a job B alone can achieve. Based on today's circumstances, I think I should stay. But Mr Kang and you must go. You should go abroad and then come back here again to resume our work.'

'Why? Fusheng! Why are you being so stubborn? Is there any advantage to staying behind? What's the use of becoming a victim? No, no, you must come with us. You can't just sacrifice yourself for nothing.'

'Zhuoru, how can you think the sacrifice meaningless? Do you remember the story of Gongsun Chujiu? Those who stayed behind, who sacrificed themselves, were doing something positive; those who left actually sacrificed themselves, over a more extended period. According to the account of Gongsun Chujiu, those who sacrificed themselves first took the easy way out, and those who saved themselves had a more difficult time later. He himself chose the former. I am doing the same today. I want to save the tough work for you and Mr Kang. I am willing to be a martyr and open a way for you. Maybe you can use it as a starting point. If Gongsun Chujiu didn't act as a trailblazer, Cheng Ying's actions later wouldn't be justified. I have thought it over and I have decided to stay.'

Tang Taizong of the Tang Dynasty, a multi-talented emperor with few peers in all of Chinese history.

'Fahaizhenyuan' (The True Source of Law), calligraphy written by Emperor Qianlong of the Qing Dynasty.

The desolate Fayuan Temple, seldom visited by worshippers.

Military Governor Yuan Chonghuan. The truth of his suicide for the sake of the country has never been publicly disclosed.

Shrine of Xie Wenjie: 'It's worth a visit. If you want to gain a better understanding of Xie Fangde's martyrdom, you should go there'.

Prince Gong, a brother of Emperor Xianfeng.

Emperor Xianfeng.

The ruins of the former Summer Palace, Yuanmingyuan, where more than three hundred people were burned to death during the Eight-power Allied Force's invasion of Beijing in 1900.

Kang Youwei, the mastermind of the Reform Movement of 1898 in China.

Weng Tonghe, the emperor's tutor.

The Japanese battleship Yoshino, that defeated the main naval force of imperial China in the 1894 Sino-Japanese War.

The cold, stern, martial-looking face of Empress Dowager, flanked by four eunuchs.

On the throne for twenty-four years, Emperor Guangxu could wait no longer.

Zhengyang Gate in 1900. Imperial wagon convoy in progress.

Qianqinggong, or Palace of Heavenly Purity.

Tan Sitong, who used to say about himself, 'If I don't go to hell, who else will?'

Liuyang Association in Beijing, where Tan Sitong resided. Photo by Chen Zhaoji (1991).

Pearl Concubine, the darling of Emperor Guangxu.

The horrible tiny well, called Pearl Concubine Well.

Troops of the Eight-power Allied Forces inside Beijing.

A Boxer soldier with sword in hand, a product of native culture.

Yuan Shikai, the ambitious one-time president of the Republic of China who aspired to become emperor.

General Cai E at twenty-nine, leader of the revolutionary army in Yunnan province.

Huang Xing, the man who once tried to sneak Tan Sitong out of Beijing before the latter was beheaded.

Henry Yi Pu , the last emperor of imperial China. The good thing about him was that he was a Manchu, which also happened to be a bad thing for him too.

Liang Qichao, the genius scholar who had an almost prophet-like ability to come up with new methods.

Li Dazhao, the communist pioneer who was hanged by warlord Zhang Zuolin.

Minzhong Terrace (photo by Xu Yiqi).

The old residence of the late Kang Youwei in Beijing. photo by Chen Zhaoji (1991).

'How can you? The times of Gongsun Chujiu and Cheng Ying are different from ours. So are the circumstances, the target, and the level of knowledge. You can't draw such a parallel.'

'There is no difference. Like Gongsun Chujiu and Cheng Ying, we face enemies who want to wipe us out. We need some comrades to sacrifice their lives to make a statement to the people and encourage other comrades to continue the struggle.'

'But you forget that the sacrifice of Gongsun Chujiu was part of the ruse to win the confidence of the enemy that he played out with Cheng Ying. We don't have to put on an act. Why do you want to imitate the behaviour of people with that kind of intellectual background? You can't draw an analogy.'

'Yes I can,' replied Tan Sitong firmly. 'I have in this package the manuscripts of my writing on *The Study of the Ideals of Confucius*. I've made a thorough study of the issues we just argued about. Anyway, I am resolved to take some action to prove my conviction. You've read this work before. We've discussed some of its chapters.'

'Yes,' said Liang Qichao. 'The most exciting part of this book is the opposition to blind loyalty, against dying for the emperor without knowing why. I remember that part clearly. But today you want to die as a gesture of appreciation for the Emperor's recognition of you. If you die now, people will mistake your death as dying for the Emperor. As you want to die to carry out the beliefs you advocate in your book, then it only makes sense to die for the cause, not for the Emperor. Is there anything else you intend to die for in addition to the cause you claim?'

'Yes, but those reasons are minor, at least in comparison with the cause.'

'I think they are major reasons as well and I can almost guess what they are.'

'What are your guesses?'

'Don't mind if I guess wrong.'

'I won't.'

'I think besides dying for the cause, another reason why you choose to die is for the Emperor.'

'What?'

'Dying for the Emperor! That's what I am saying. Another important reason why you are resolved to die.'

'I don't blame you for saying that. But you make it sound too serious, almost discrediting the beliefs I advocate in my book. What do you take me for? A person inconsistent in words and deeds?'

'Absolutely not! You are my hero and my good friend. If I think you are inconsistent in words and deeds, that's because I think your deeds are better than your words. It's an honourable kind of inconsistency.'

'But you just said I intend to die for the cause, as well as for the Emperor. That's calling me inconsistent.'

'There is no inconsistency. If you say you want to die for the cause and follow through, that's consistency. If you say you want to die for the cause, but fail to follow through, that's inconsistency.'

'But in my book I advocate dying for the cause, not for the emperor. These two issues are in contradiction. If you say I am dying for the emperor, my words and deeds seem to be in conflict, if not inconsistent.'

'The problem is, you think dying for the cause and dying for the emperor are in contradiction. Actually, there is room for discussion. In the four thousand five hundred years of Chinese history, there have been all together four hundred and twenty-three emperors, including Guangxu. Which of them were tyrants and which were sage kings? Only history can pass judgment. But according to your book, only an emperor's servants and women should die for him, because of the personal intimate relationships between them. Other people have absolutely no reason to die for the emperor. Don't you think such a distinction is too arbitrary?'

'Shouldn't it be that way?'

'Let's recall the story of Yanzi. Duke Qizhuang visited the home of his official Cui Zhu and committed adultery with his wife. Unwilling to be a cuckold, Cui Zhu killed Duke Qizhuang on the spot. Yanzi was a high-ranking official of Qi. When he went to the home of Cui Zhu to mourn the head of the state, his subordinates asked him whether he was going to die for the emperor. Yanzi gave a good answer. He said, "He is not just *my* emperor. Why should I alone die for him?" His subordinates then asked whether he was planning to flee the country of Qi. Yanzi gave another good answer, saying, "It's not my fault that he died. Why should I run away?" His subordinates then asked whether he would go home. Yanzi replied, "The emperor died. Where can I go back to?"

Yanzi was truly a first-rate statesman. His responses, to reject death, flee, and return home were rational, passionate, and justified. When he went to mourn his emperor, everybody thought Cui Zhu would kill him as well. But he went anyway and poured out his sorrow in front of Cui Zhu, who had a sword in his hand. Yanzi was wise, charitable, and brave. I think he truly comprehended the principles of dying for the emperor and dying for a cause. His theory was that an emperor is not above the people, but an administrator of the state. An official is not a person just making a living, but someone who should uphold the state. So when the emperor dies for the state, the official should do the same. But if the emperor dies for himself, then only his cronies and confidants should die with him, not a respectable official.

After Duke Qizhuang was killed, Cui Zhu decided to make the son of Duke Qiling, Duke Qijing, the emperor. Qijing was young, so Cui Zhu appointed himself the Right Prime Minister and Qingfeng the Left Prime Minister. They gathered all the high-ranking officials and asked everybody to make a blood vow in the temple: "If I don't work in one heart with Cui Zhu and Qingfeng, I'll be punished by the sun!" When Yanzi came to take the vow, he changed it to: "If all of you are loyal to the emperor and benefit the country, and I am not in one heart with you, I'll be punished by Heaven!" Cui Zhu was about to get angry, when Gaoguo intervened and pointed out, "You two prime ministers have acted today in a way that is loyal to the emperor and beneficial to the country." Given this flattery, Cui Zhu and his collaborators were forced to accept the conditions set by Yanzi.

Let me ask you, from the story of Yanzi, what would you say if your emperor died for the country? Do you still think dying for such an emperor is wrong, that there are no circumstances under which a person should die for his emperor?'

'Naturally, this kind of emperor is an exception.'

'That is to say your theory allows exceptions?'

'If there are exceptions among emperors, then there are exceptions to my theory.'

'Alright, tell me frankly if you think Guangxu is an exceptional emperor.'

'He is.'

'Why?'

'He was an emperor for twenty-four years before he embarked on reform. He is still an emperor if he does nothing. His position is secure with the "old lady" and the Manchus if he chooses to do nothing. He initiated reform not for himself, but for the country.'

'The emperor took a great risk in undertaking reform. It might cost him his life. If he dies, he dies for the country, right?'

'Right!'

'So that's it. My guess is right.'

'What do you mean?'

'That besides dying for the cause, you are also dying for the emperor. There is a human element in your decision, and that element is the emperor.'

'Your deduction makes some sense. At least after the emperor dies and then I die, in the eyes of other people I will have died for the emperor, or at least more so than dying for the cause. In the history of China, officials have mostly died for their emperor, and the notion of dying for a cause is not prevalent. Even if my book is published in the future, only a few intellectuals will read it. So on the surface, I probably won't be acknowledged as "dying for a cause".'

'That's because there is Guangxu. Guangxu is an emperor. That title alone is thundering. You work with him in reform and die with him. Even if you die for another reason, it's hard for people to think otherwise. Your act of dying for the emperor will definitely be established, but your act of dying for the cause might be obscured.'

'And worse still, in the eyes of the revolutionaries, I might be viewed as a traitor because I died for a Manchu emperor.'

'Time will prove if you are a traitor or not. Actually, in the eyes of the Manchus, the emperor might be considered a traitor because he died for the Hans.'

'It's such a painful subject, the Manchus and the Hans. I can die without regret since that's what I've decided. But I am still troubled by the fact that I wasn't able to persuade Wang Wu and his group on this issue.'

'That's just a matter of time. You didn't have enough time to persuade them. Wang Wu and his gang are rough people. The highly educated and the ignorant are the most difficult to sway.'

'I don't think it's a lack of time. But you are right, they are ignorant. You can persuade intellectuals with words, but persuading the ignorant probably takes more than words. I have discussed with them back and forth the issue of the Manchus and the Hans. They just couldn't accept it. I know they had a hard time because they had so much trust in me. But in the end I not only professed that we should work with the Manchus to save China, I also started working with a Manchu emperor. The change has been too drastic for them to accept.'

'What happens now?'

'I decided not to see them for the time being, to spare them the agony. I decided to use other means.'

'Do you want to meet with them when you leave here?'

'I don't think so.'

'What if you still have time?'

'I won't have the opportunity even if there is time. I would be watched and I might implicate them if we met.'

'Apart from proving that all reforms begin with bloodshed and you are willing to shed your own blood, what else do you prove by your self-sacrifice?'

'One's words breathe goodness in the face of death. What is this goodness? It's worthiness and candour. I can tell you something from the bottom of my heart. After I die, my name will be mutilated.'

'Mutilated? You mean . . .'

'My dying for the cause will assume multiple meanings or interpretations. After you go overseas, you can tell the reformists that I am a martyr for modernization, that I took a giant step, a glorious step forward for the movement. The reform has begun and the Chinese people must march on, treading the blood of Tan Sitong.'

'Yes, I'll say that, because it's true.'

'True? But not in the eyes of the revolutionaries. They will say that it was naïve to carry out reform with the Manchu tartars; that you can't have your way even with the support of the Emperor. That you were all toppled with one strike by that "old woman". All the new policies were discarded. Heads were chopped off. Forget it: Tan Sitong has taught us a bloody lesson, proving that revolution is the only way for China to proceed. Stop your vain hope for reform. Zhuoru, have you thought of this possibility—that my death might give the revolutionaries a push? If so, my name will really be mutilated.'

'I don't see it that way. Since you mention it, you should reconsider whether to sacrifice yourself like this.'

'I've given it some thought.'

'You still want to take the road of no return?'

'This is not the road of no return. It is the road to life, to eternity.'

'You prove life with death?'

'There is nothing wrong with that. Zhuoru, I just said that men speak kindly in the face of death. I am not here to bid you an emotional farewell, but to give you the manuscript and tell you my deepest thoughts. I wouldn't have come if I just wanted to say goodbye. That's why I won't go see Wang Wu and the gang before I die. I came here to see you because of the special connection between us. You have great wisdom and you understand me. You also understand things I can't comprehend. You understand Mr Kang, the future of China, and the path it should take.

I tell you, when I die, everybody knows I die for the reform. Yes, I die for the reform. But there is value and reason in my choosing death over life for the reform. I believe in such value and reason. So I think that you should stay alive and leave here. But why do I want to die? Mencius said, "If you have the choice to die or not to die, and you choose death, it's an act that contradicts bravery." Why do I want to die in contradiction of bravery? There is another reason. This reason has been troubling me all these years like a recurring dream. It provokes a conflict in me that I cannot extricate myself from. That is revolution. Many times I have convinced myself that the only way for China is revolution, not reform. Many times the dream emerged, and many times I suppressed it. Before I came to Beijing, my association with friends from all over gave me more confidence in revolution, and less in reform. Only after I read the writings of Mr Kang, heard of your activities, and met you was I converted to the path of reform.

Now the movement has come to this, and I have the impulse to show my revolutionary friends with my death that they were right and I was wrong. From now on, the only way to save China is revolution. I will collapse on the road of reform to tell others that this road leads nowhere.'

'My! Fusheng, what are you talking about? What you just said is simply terrible. Even if you truly deny the line of reform and affirm the line of revolution, you shouldn't prove it with your life. Why don't you go join the revolutionaries and make a contribution? Why do you have to die?'

'Dying is one way to make a contribution. Since I found out that dying is the best way to explain myself after taking into account all the circumstances, I am willing to die.'

'You think this is the right time?'

'Yes. To tell you the truth, before I got to know you, I could have chosen the course of revolution. After I met you, knowing that you and Mr Kang were taking the road of reform, I came to help. I would still have joined you if you had taken the revolutionary path. You've read my articles and long recognized that inherent in them are drastic ideas of revolution. Actually, you and Mr Kang, who want to preserve China, not the Qing Dynasty, are inherently revolutionaries. We are in real agony. We don't know which way will work, which way is the fastest, or which way causes the least damage.

This coup d'état is actually exploratory in nature and we were the scouts who proved that the road of reform is not workable. I decided to lay my body on the road, telling everybody to go back, telling all the idealists and patriots not to harbour any more illusions, to look at the example of Tan Sitong. So my death is a sacrifice and a ruse in a certain sense. I hope you realize that. My action tells the reformists not to take their path, tells the revolutionaries to continue their course, and tells the Chinese people and intellectuals which way to go.'

'You don't need to die if you just want to tell the revolutionaries to continue on their course. You just need to tell them in words.'

'That's true. But some revolutionary friends will know that I am telling them with my death that they were right and I was wrong. On the surface people think I die for the reform. But from a broader perspective, I die for the revolution.'

'Who will think that you die for the revolution? The revolutionaries certainly won't think so.'

'Dying for the revolution means giving a big boost to the revolution with your life, converting the reformists, and recommending to the people that revolution is the right path.'

'The revolutionaries won't recognize or appreciate your action.'

'I don't need their appreciation. Revolutionaries are like the traits of a flower—some are dominant, some recessive. I am concealed and they are active. I don't need their recognition, because I am a revolutionary.'

'Why don't you go abroad and become an activist?'

'If I go abroad to become an activist, people will say I turned to the cause of revolution because I failed at reform. Some might even think I am an opportunist. If I join the revolution, I am but a new member. If I stay a latent revolutionary, things will be totally different. I think the effect produced by death is much greater than that by living. Death is a form of blood recommendation.'

'Who will know if you don't tell other people that you are recommending revolution with your death? Why don't you go abroad first? If you still want to go through with your decision, you can commit suicide after you make a declaration in support of revolution. It's much more effective than this guessing game that you are playing now.'

Tan Sitong smiled. He patted Liang Qichao, stood up and looked out of the windows. 'Not saying a word adds to the effect of the blood recommendation.' He turned around and looked at Liang Qichao. Liang raised his head to stare back.

Tan Sitong laughed: 'Zhuoru, you have been trying hard to persuade me to go abroad and explain everything in favour of leaving China, saying that it's even better to die abroad. You are a wonderful friend. But you know well that the blood recommendation needs to borrow the knife of the "old lady" to make it more effective. It's actually called murder with a borrowed knife. It's not suicide.

Only by being killed by the "old lady" can I show the world how corrupt this government is, that we should go forward with revolution. If I commit suicide, I will absolve the "old woman" of a crime, remove a thorn from her flesh, and my suicide will invite all kinds of outrageous interpretations. For example, some people will say Tan Sitong committed suicide because his reform movement failed, or some such. Then the effect will be totally off track. So if I want to do a blood recommendation, my blood has to be spilled here, at Caishikou. It's the best place to die and the best way to die.'

'If you are so pessimistic about reform, which path do you recommend I take?'

'I really don't know which way you should go. But I know Mr Kang's path is set. If the Emperor dies, Mr Kang will turn to revolution; if the Emperor lives, Mr Kang will never forsake him. He will advocate constitutional monarchy. I don't know how things will evolve given your relationship with Mr Kang. As I said, you have great wisdom and understanding of me, Mr Kang, and the future of China. I am sure you'll make the right choice. People live in agony because they can only fight the enemy, not their friends, or they can fight their friends, but not themselves. But you might be an exception. You have wisdom, courage and an open heart. You can fight against the "you" of yesterday. Well! Time is up. Zhuoru, take care,' Tan Sitong stood up to go.

'But Fusheng . . . '

'Zhuoru, don't think I am gone. I am not. I am in you. I am the "you" who is dead, and you are the "me" who is alive. Part of your life is gone with me, and part of me stays alive with you. Remember my *Four Poems of Reflection*? The fourth poem reads:

> *What's wrong with the fluttering willow leaves?*
> *Drifting hither and thither without a fixed abode.*

Separated today after having dropped into the water;
They may only meet someday when the leaves become ashes.
How can I bear to see the way life has been treating me, and die the way
*   the willow leaves do?*
Even the Eternal Buddha encountered obstacles put up by Maras and
*   his relatives;*
That's only part of what one must encounter in the course of one's life,
*   and eventually death.*

'We are transient in this life. But the Buddha, Maras, and China, no matter if it's under the Hans, the Manchus, the Mongols, or the Hui, are permanent. We only depart temporarily in eternity and will meet again in the course of life. Goodbye, Zhuoru, goodbye.'

'But Fusheng . . .'

Tan Sitong gave Liang Qichao the cloth pack. 'A man leaves his name behind. I don't really care what kind of name I leave behind. I hope you'll take these manuscripts with you and publish them with other works of mine. I hope you'll use your pen to publicize the results of my life's efforts. I feel I have accomplished much in my thirty-three years, particularly in the past three years since meeting you and Mr Kang. These have been the last days of the blossoming of my life. Of course, the Lotus Sutra says, "The Buddha told Upatisya that even such a wonderful truth exists as briefly as the broad-leaved epiphyllum." I hope in the end life itself is transient, but the wonderful truth is lasting. I am willing to end my life in the midst of its blooming, but I leave some wonderful truth behind as evidenced by my blood. Goodbye, Zhuoru. Don't see me out. Take care.'

Tan Sitong let go of Liang Qichao's hands and walked out of the living room. Shu Hirayama closed the door and followed behind him.

Liang Qichao stared at the door in a stupor. He moved to the window and saw Tan Sitong walking towards the corner of the street with Shu Hirayama at his side. He saw the back of a person moving away, the back of a great comrade who, after working together on an earth-shattering undertaking, had decided to let go for eternity.

After they left the legation, Shu Hirayama asked if he could accompany Tan Sitong to his destination. The streets were quiet and clean. They passed the Spanish Legation, British concession, Russian military camp, Dutch Legation, American Legation, and the American military camp, and then turned south towards Zhengyang Gate. The Chinese atmosphere prevailed beyond the walls of the diplomatic mission compound. The area around Zhengyang Gate was the busiest section of the city. Zhengyang Gate was also called Qian Gate, or 'Front' Gate. The word 'Qian' said everything; in front of it was the diplomatic mission district and the gate itself fell on the centre line of the Forbidden City. Standing about forty metres high, Zhengyang Gate was the grandest structure of its kind in the city. To the south, there was a semi-circular city wall. In the middle of the half-circle stood an embrasured watchtower, which guarded Zhengyang Gate.

Beyond the watchtower stood a city moat spanned by a bridge. Passing the bridge, the street running towards the east was called Dongheyan, and the street running west was called Xiheyan. At the end of the bridge stood five adjoining archways, called Wupailou. So there were actually two structures outside Zhengyang Gate—the watchtower and Wupailou. Outside Wupailou, the big road leading south was called Qian Gate Street; it headed straight to the Tianqiao, or Bridge of Heaven, Tiantan, or the Temple of Heaven, and Xiannong Temple, until it reached the gate to the outer city, Yongding Gate.

Turning left out of Wupailou, one entered the entertainment district of Beijing, the Big Railing. A circuitous street proceeding out of the back of the Big Railing was called Li Tie Guai Xie Street. Beijing was an ancient city filled with history, legends, fairy tales, and anecdotes. Li Tien Guai was one of the eight immortals on an iron stick in Chinese legend.

As they walked, Tan Sitong and Shu Hirayama talked about the places and anecdotes along the way. Tan wondered why this Japanese knew so much about China. Considering his alert expression and broad knowledge, Tan wondered if he was really a diplomat. Tan had heard that many members of the Japanese secret societies, such as Kokuryu Group, were China experts. Maybe this Shu Hirayama was one of them.

Seeing Tan's alert expression, Shu Hirayama tacitly acknowledged that he was in the company of a very knowledgeable person. Finally, in front of the Liuyang Association, Shu Hirayama bowed and turned back, after giving Tan Sitong a heartfelt look.

CHAPTER TEN

The Rescue

A number of Japanese citizens have come to China as 'freedom fighters' to aid the Chinese people. These Japanese citizens, unattached to but in cooperation with the Japanese embassy in Beijing, go to look for Tan Sitong to persuade him not to remain in China and be killed, but to flee to Japan with Liang Qichao. They discuss several Chinese historical figures, and even Socrates, who sacrificed their lives for a cause. They discuss the differing motivations of the different characters, and which had loftier motivations than the others. In their discussions with Tan Sitong, he mentions several Japanese historical figures.

After failing in their attempts to persuade Mr Tan to flee, they part company with him and return to the Japanese Legation. They are impressed with Tan Sitong's wide knowledge of Japanese history. They express their great esteem for Tan Sitong, who exhibits the spirit of the Japanese bushido *(code of the Samurai) swordsmen who live according to high principles of loyalty. They greatly admire his determination to sacrifice his own life for his ideals.*

Five hours later, Shu Hirayama returned to the Japanese Legation and told Liang Qichao that there had been several suspicious men hanging about the neighbourhood as he walked Tan Sitong to the Association. Shu Hirayama thought he must try again to persuade Tan Sitong to change his mind. He walked out of the room to look for Kensuke Hayashi.

'I just accompanied Tan Sitong back to the Association. He has made up his mind to sacrifice his life for the cause.' Shu Hirayama said to the minister. 'However, according to the conversation I just heard between him and Liang Qichao, I can tell there are some hidden thoughts there.

Take his relationship with Big Sword Wang Wu, for example. He seemed unwilling to discuss it further. In addition, in their conversation he skilfully emphasized the importance of activists and martyrs. He reiterated his stance that Liang Qichao should escape out of the imperial city of Beijing. It is my view that one of his purposes in saying so is to assuage Liang Qichao's feelings of guilt, uneasiness, or embarrassment. Tan Sitong is really a man of righteousness and deep feeling. He's brave, thoughtful, and unflappable. It's a pity to have such a great Chinese talent die for no reason! It's really a great pity!'

'We've got to map out a plan,' said Kensuke Hayashi, nodding and looking out the window. He put the five fingers of his right hand against his left hand and tapped his index fingers together, and said, 'The key point is to prove that there's no reason for Tan Sitong to die. This is the best way to persuade him to flee. According to what you say, you feel that there were some hidden thoughts in the conversation between Tan Sitong and Liang Qichao. I guess that's the key point. Maybe that's the reason why Tan Sitong is unwilling to escape. If we can explain this to him, there's a possibility that he may change his mind.'

Shu Hirayama nodded.

'What reasons did he give to Liang Qichao as to why he would not flee?' asked Kensuke Hayashi.

'He gave two reasons. One is that there's always bloodshed in the country when political reform is being initiated. He's willing to shed his blood for the cause. To use his blood to enlighten the Chinese population, in order to publicize the need for political reform. The other is quite odd. He said that at the start he couldn't decide which course was better—to save China through a bloody revolution or through peaceful reform. He was inclined to revolution until he met Kang Youwei and Liang Qichao. He then determined to take the course of reform and to join them in implementing political reforms. He's willing to sacrifice his life to prove that peaceful reform can go nowhere, that the Chinese people have no alternative to a bloody revolution.'

'That's strange. I've heard the saying that only the living can be undecided, but never the dead.' Kensuke Hayashi grinned like a wicked Japanese politician.

'Tan Sitong is a hero and also a great man. Could he be a political opportunist? Nevertheless, one must be alive in order to take advantage of someone or something. If a man is dead, what can he take advantage of? In the case of being forced to die, a man, before dying and having no other option, would probably, as you said, grab a number of wonderful reasons for dying and potentially become a political opportunist. But Tan Sitong is obviously entitled to have an option. Undoubtedly, he doesn't have to die. However, he's determined to sacrifice his life and there are clearly some good reasons behind his firm belief to do so.'

'I really want to know what they are. The Chinese are hard to understand. In our country, they say we're the experts on Chinese affairs. But to understand a Chinese like Tan Sitong is beyond me.'

'Generally speaking, those who are willing to die for a cause are the people with uncomplicated minds, whose beliefs are comparatively simple. Because of the simplicity of their minds and beliefs, they readily become brave and determined. But Tan Sitong is an entirely different person. He's complicated. So complicated that most people find it very difficult to understand him completely. His ability to choose such a complicated way to die for his cause is beyond my imagination, and shows the superiority of his capacities.'

'Let's do what we can,' sighed Kensuke Hayashi. 'Hirofumi Ito has said these Chinese youths are the Spirit of China. We must save them. Ito's point of view can't be overemphasized. Ito has an in-depth viewpoint. From the sheer stance of the government of imperial Japan, I'm merely an acting minister. I really wouldn't dare make any major decision. Fortunately, Ito is now in Beijing. He has said he's definitely going to save them. This lessens my worries considerably.

Now you must gather your comrades and go to the Association to give Tan Sitong some friendly advice. Technically, you can go there in Ito's name, tell him that I act on Ito's behalf, and sincerely hope that Mr Tan will reconsider the vital impact of the current situation, go to Japan first, and carry out the projected political reform at a later date. From an official stance, the Japanese Government cannot actively invite Mr Tan to visit Japan. The only thing they can do is convey Ito's kind hospitality to Mr Tan and ask him to think the matter over again. However, it is you, as an ordinary Japanese citizen, who should pay a visit to the Association and invite him to go to Japan. This is quite different to approaching Japan and asking for political asylum. Tan is a man of strong self-respect. To adopt the aforesaid measures, I think, may be more effective.

In short, we must do what we can, and we're willing to do so. But, as a diplomat, I'm not allowed to clearly and actively expose the official Japanese position to the public. And it would be unacceptable to Tan Sitong, anyway. Personally, these Chinese youths have my sympathy and admiration. I'm more than happy to help them. As its official position, the Japanese Government cannot afford to give up the chance to heat up a cold stove. As long as it does not violate normal diplomatic practice, the Japanese Government will secretly support the second and third wave in China. That's the superiority of Chinese diplomacy over that of the Westerners. They know how to heat up a cold stove. We Japanese should learn from them. But the practical British and Americans are not capable of learning how to do this. Okay, that's all. What do you say?'

'Good idea. My comrades will be here shortly and I'll ask them to accompany me there. Politics is one thing that I have no idea about at all. We only know that we must help these Chinese who have such great ideas and such peerless courage,' said Shu Hirayama.

'I think I know your background,' said Kensuke Hayashi, staring at Shu Hirayama. 'There are not many Japanese people like you who come to China with a relatively simple purpose. Since you are here, I've no choice but to let you know that, in the eyes of other people, all of you must have a strong backer behind the scene. Who is it? Is it Genyo Sha? The Kokuryu Group? Army Headquarters? Or the Capitalists? I guess everybody knows this in their hearts, as do the Chinese.'

'That's not the case.'

'I guess I know you are not what people think you are. However, they don't know the true story and neither do the Chinese. Generally speaking, men of your kind, rather than stay in Japan and lead a happy life, come to China and intend to do what? There are two schools of thought about this.

One is that you are extremists favouring Japanese nationalism. In name, you guys belong to the syndicate, and behind the syndicate is the Japanese Army Headquarters. Therefore, you are the vanguards of the Japanese Army here to carry out their policy of extending Japanese territory. You act like ordinary people and try to lay the foundations by trying to get the Chinese opposition parties on your side. It is possible that you are rightists following the Japanese Doctrine of People's Rights. The backers behind the scenes are the new rising Japanese industrial capitalists, who aim to widen their power, strengthen the system of representative government, and dissolve the dictatorship of the feudal government in Japan. So you have come to China to build up your stronghold here, and, just in case, some day you may use the "China card" to seize the China market.'

'As I just said, we are not what they think we are,' denied Shu Hirayama.

'Like I said, I think I know that. I understand you people. That's why I said there are not many Japanese people like you who come to China with a relatively simple purpose.'

'Then what do you know about us?'

'Do you want to hear? Will you be upset, if I'm just trying to kid you?'

'Yes, I do. And I won't be mad.'

'You are a sort of fanatic. You can't stay home; you love to go out. Always helping others make waves. You enjoy causing a disturbance. You try to overthrow the people and things in authority over you. The Japanese government is too stable for you to overthrow. That's why you come to China to cause a disturbance.'

'You representatives of the Japanese Government are also here to make waves in China, aren't you?'

'Entirely different. When you make waves, at least externally, you're talking about ideas, chivalry, conscience, relationships, and friendship. You help the powerless to fight against the powerful.

But we aren't so stupid. We outwardly help the powerful, and we secretly help the powerless. We can have a stand to bargain with the powerful. One day, if the price is right, we'll sell the powerless to the powerful. If the price isn't right, we'll help the powerless to overthrow the powerful, or help the powerless occupy a slice of territory. In the course of doing so, we aren't talking about ideas, chivalry, conscience, relationships, and friendship; we're talking only about the interests of imperial Japan. What we have been doing is really beneficial to Japan. What you're doing is a nuisance. You hope that China will become powerful. However, once China becomes powerful then Japan gains nothing.'

'According to your plan, then, as long as Japan is powerful, it doesn't matter how powerless China is. From a long-term point of view, China's powerlessness does mean Japan's powerlessness. Don't forget the fact that we are all Asians and yellow-skinned people! This will be the trend in tomorrow's world.'

'I'm a Japanese diplomat, not a Japanese prophet or a Japanese moralist. I've no interest in matters of a hundred years from today. What I'm interested in is different from what you're interested in.'

'But now, both you and I have the same interest—to help the powerless in China. You even try to help us.'

'Help you? Or you help us? Is that so hard for you to tell? You have already done something on behalf of the Japanese Government that the Government is not allowed to do and is also unable to do.'

'We aren't going to be used by the government for its own selfish ends.'

'That is your naive way of thinking. It's really a pity that you can't escape the fate of being used. Perhaps you don't know that. However, it is a fact that you're being invisibly utilized by the the Japanese Government, or by the Army Headquarters, the extremists of nationalism, or by the financial magnates, the rightists of Japanese Doctrine of People's Rights and even by the Chinese, which is even worse.'

'You think we are nuts. Are we so easily used by someone else?'

'Whether you're nuts or not depends on how you view it. At least externally, you're talking about ideas, chivalry, conscience, relationships, and friendship, and want to help the powerless fight against the powerful. On the surface, it seems that you are following a course of stupidity. That's why you are destined to be used. From this point of view, you've tried and succeeded. But your achievements will be enjoyed by someone else. If you fail, you alone will be held accountable. Other people, after visiting and sweeping your tomb, will laugh at you and call you crazy.'

'You mean we are on the wrong track?'

'It depends on your point of view. Generally speaking, the way you have chosen is the way of the swordsman. From this point of view, the judgement of your success or failure is different from that of ordinary people. Other people think you've been used, but you'll just ignore them. Why? Your philosophy on life is to disburse money in the public interest and to settle disputes. You're not really eager to take credit for that achievement, to gain power and authority, fame and wealth, as ordinary people are. So, when you haven't gained these things as other people have, they will think you are nuts, but you'll just ignore them. They'll think you have suffered a loss, but you won't think so.

Therefore, from your swordsman's point of view, you're on the right track. But, who on earth will understand that? The philosophy of a swordsman and his life. The Tang Dynasty novels brought these philosophies to the land of Japan in the ninth century. Now it is the nineteenth century. You're too steeped in the classics.'

'Are you laughing at us as old-fashioned?'

'Not exactly. The classics can be transformed into the future, but never into the present. Your behaviour will become either the past or the future, but never the present.'

'Perhaps you're right. We aren't the present. Neither can we become friends of Tan Sitong. They aren't the present, either. They're like the classical *bushido* of China. They utilize the classical approach to create a future for China.'

'You're right. The classical *bushido* of China. *Bushido* is the Nippon Spirit. Hirofumi Ito has said that they are the Spirit of China. The Spirit of China is virtually the classical *bushido* of China. It isn't true that China has no *bushido*. However, the *bushido* of China has developed in the direction of personal or family favours and hatred, or an individual favour and hatred in an area or in a syndicate. They're too narrow-minded about their objective of being chivalrous and willing to give up their lives. They seldom shed their blood for lofty ideals such as serving their nation. They engage in private readily, but shy away from public welfare.

That's the greatest weakness of the Chinese. Chinese *bushido* can be classified into two categories . . .'

At this moment, somebody knocked on the door. Kensuke Hayashi answered the door. Three Japanese walked in. They were Shu Hirayama's men, Momotaro, Toten, and Kakicho. Shu Hirayama stood up and walked towards them and said, 'I've just talked to the Minister and he instructs us to go together to the Association and persuade Tan Sitong to flee. Let's go.'

The three nodded. Shu Hirayama then said to Kensuke Hayashi, 'Let's hurry. We can't take the carriage in order to avoid being too obvious. We must get out of here right away.'

'I'll walk you downstairs,' Kensuke Hayashi said as he closed the door behind them, and accompanied the four downstairs. 'Let me finish my point. As I said, there are two categories of Chinese *bushido*. One type is that of Zhuan Zhu. The other is the type of Jing Ke. The Zhuan Zhu type will sacrifice his life for a personal feud, but the Jing Ke type will give up his life only for his country. These two chivalrous men were mentioned by Sima Qian in his well-known book, *Records of the Historian*. He put them in the chapter on assassins. Sima Qian was the best at appreciating the deeds of the swordsmen. Unfortunately, he failed to point out the meaningful difference between the lofty objective and the common objective in sacrificing one's own life that exists between these two types of swordsmen.

The Chinese haven't paid any attention to the difference. That's why the Chinese *bushido* has developed into an increasingly narrow niche. This is really a misfortune for China. You four now have the opportunity to encounter the Spirit of China. Should you see the classical Chinese *bushido* and the lofty objective of these Chinese, you're sure to accomplish your life's greatest achievement and attain the open-heartedness of intimate friends!'

At the front gate, Shu Hirayama said, 'Thank you, Mr Minister, for your kind lecture. Please go back upstairs and tell Liang Qichao that we're on the way to the Association to persuade Tan Sitong to come back with us.'

Kensuke Hayashi said, 'Naturally, I'll let him know. Liang Qichao is a Cantonese and he's not used to northern Chinese food. I've already told my cook to make a pot of beef stew for him. While he's here, I'll take excellent care. Please do not worry.'

On the way to the Association, Shu Hirayama told his company about his talk with Kensude Hayashi in detail. Kakicho asked about Zhuan Zhu and Jing Ke and who they were. Shu Hirayama said, 'They were famous swordsmen in ancient China, about two thousand years ago. Zhuan Zhu was a man of filial piety in the small kingdom of Wu. He loved to fight for a righteous cause. Once he started a fist fight with someone, nobody could stop him. However, when his mother stepped out and shouted, "Stop it!" he didn't dare to carry on fighting.

At that time, in the Kingdom of Wu, there was a Prince Guang, who was engaged in a power struggle with his cousin Wang Liao. He wanted to hire an assassin to kill his cousin. Through the recommendation of Wu Zixu, he met Zhuan Zhu. Prince Guang often went to the house of Zhuan Zhu and paid social visits to his mother. He frequently brought her rice, wine, and gifts over a period of about four years. One day, Zhuan Zhu said to Prince Guang, "I'm just an ordinary, uneducated man, but you have never looked down on me. You have treated me so well. It is said that a gentleman is willing to die for his friend, so please be frank and let me know if there is anything you want me to do for you." Prince Guang told him that he wanted him to assassinate his cousin, Wang Liao. Zhuan Zhu said it could eventually be done, but not while his mother was still alive.

Prince Guang said to Zhuan Zhu, "I knew you would have this kind of difficulty. But I'm unable to find a man who is more suitable for the job. In case you fail in the assassination, your mother will be my mother, and your son will be my son." Then Zhuan Zhu said, "In that case, it is all right with me. But you know Wang Liao is kept under very tight security. How can I get close enough to carry out the assassination?" Prince Guang said, "My cousin has a weak point. He is crazy about gourmet broiled-fish. If you can cook a fantastic broiled fish, you'll get the chance to kill him."

Thus, Zhuan Zhu went to the shores of Lake Tai, to learn how to cook an out-of-this-world broiled fish. Finally, he had perfected the skill of cooking this dish. After waiting for a long time, Prince Guang thought his golden opportunity was around the corner. Without saying a word, Prince Guang gave Zhuan Zhu a well known type of tiny dagger called a fish-gutting dagger. Zhuan Zhu knew very well what it meant. He said to the Prince, "At this critical moment, I dare not make such a serious decision by myself. I have to confer with my mother. After that I'll give you a definite reply."

Back at home, when he saw his mother, he burst into tears. His mother realized what the matter was and said to him, "Since Prince Guang has been so kind to us, you should be willing to sacrifice your life for him. You don't have to worry about me. I'm quite thirsty. Go to the riverside and get me some water." Zhuan Zhu went to the riverside and fetched some water. When he got back from the river with some water, he found his mother had hung herself up from a beam and died.

Zhuan Zhu then concentrated on sacrificing his life for Prince Guang. Prince Guang sent him to cook the best broiled fish for Wang Liao. Wang Liao's bodyguards asked him to strip off for the sake of strict security. They ordered him to serve the fish half-naked. Zhuan Zhu hid the tiny dagger inside the broiled fish and successfully assassinated Wang Liao. Of course, he was killed instantly by the bodyguards right on the spot. This is a tragic story. Just as Kensuke Hayashi said moments ago, the sacrifice of one's own life for a common objective by the Zhuan Zhu type of Chinese *bushido* has no significance at all.'

'After hearing that story of yours, I have a feeling that Zhuan Zhu's mother was even more faithful to the spirit of *bushido* than he himself was. Her death was of far more significance than Zhuan Zhu's. Zhuan Zhu gave up his life in direct return for the great favour that Prince Guang, his bosom friend, granted to him. So, he had just fulfilled a common objective. But his mother completed not only a common objective, but a far loftier objective as well.'

'Your so-called far loftier objective is?'

'First, to enable her son to freely fulfil his objective, she adopted a dramatic means of giving up her life—to die ahead of her son, in order to free him from suffering over his dilemma and worrying, so that he could be determined to fulfil his objective. Second, she was not allowed to jointly fulfil the objective with her son, which would have been unnecessary. Once she had died in advance for the sake of the objective, even though she didn't actually participate in the action, in effect, she did. She gave her son in the understanding that he was not doing the job alone, and that she was fully supportive of his action. She didn't just tell her son to do it, she gave up her life first, to show her approval.

Finally, there was a possibility that her son might not be killed in the course of the assassination. Who knew whether the assassination would be a success or not, and whether or not her son would be killed? There was also a possibility that her son might walk out alive. Nevertheless, this mother pushed herself into a dead-end lane with no way out. That clearly revealed her superior lofty spirit.'

Kakicho finished speaking and turned to Momotaro for his opinion.

Momotaro thought for a couple of seconds and then said, 'What you've said, I think, is right. Besides, the subject that draws all my attention is the way the mother died. She said very little. The three points you've just mentioned are all facts, which were left to be explained by the people concerned. She herself didn't bother to explain. She told Zhuan Zhu that he should sacrifice his life for Prince Guang. That's the key point. She had to make it clear. If she didn't, and then killed herself, her son would wonder why. After making her key point clear, she used the simplest way to bid her son farewell. She killed herself of her own free will, which is really remarkable. I think she was a great swordswoman, a person of great substance.'

'There's another lofty character,' Shu Hirayama cut in. 'She belongs to the other type of Chinese *bushido*, the Jing Ke type, as Kensuke Hayashi just explained. Jing Ke lived in a later period than Zhuan Zhu. It was just before the Kingdom of Qin conquered all of the other six kingdoms. Crown Prince Dan of the Kingdom of Yan wanted to use the same means of threatening or assassinating Qin Shi Huang, the First Emperor of the Qin Dynasty, to save his kingdom from being conquered. He therefore paid a visit to an elderly swordsman named Tian Guang and asked him to carry out the assassination. Tian Guang said, "In youth, a good thoroughbred can run a thousand miles a day. In old age, it can easily be surpassed by an ordinary horse in a race. Crown Prince, the 'Tian Guang' you've heard of and admired is the 'Tian Guang' of his youth. Now, I'm an elderly man, unable to carry out your plan. But I have a friend named Jing Ke, who has the ability to help you."

Crown Prince Dan then asked Tian Guang to locate Jing Ke and keep the plan secret. Tian Guang met Jing Ke and won his consent. He asked Jing Ke to see the Crown Prince directly and then took his own life. The death of Tian Guang was just like the death of Zhuan Zhu's mother. What a lofty way to die!

First, a gentleman is willing to die for his friends. Crown Prince Dan asked him a big favour. He was more than happy to sacrifice his life for his country, but he was too old to do the job. Since he accepted the plan for assassination, he was the man who was naturally going to be sacrificed. Theoretically, he should be sacrificed.

Second, he asked Jing Ke to do the job on his behalf. Therefore he was asking Jing Ke to put his life on the line. He thought it unfair to send a friend to the Kingdom of Qin to risk his life while he himself stayed in the Kingdom of Yan. In terms of friendship, he should die for the job.

Finally, it was uncertain whether Jing Ke would be killed during the assassination attempt or not. However, Tian Guang proved his determination to Jing Ke to not wait for any chance of him staying alive in order to stimulate Jing Ke's peerless courage. In fact, he became the first one to die for the job.

According to these three points, his method of fulfilling the task was identical to that of Zhuan Zhu's mother. The only difference was that he told Jing Ke he was going to kill himself. He purposely emphasized that the reason for his committing suicide was that he was the senior. The behaviour of a senior was not open to question. Crown Prince Dan had asked him to keep the plan secret, and he was willing to die to keep it secret. That freed Jing Ke from any embarrassment. Jing Ke outsmarted him. He didn't ask Tian Guang not to kill himself, nor did he try to stop him. He knew full well that it was natural for a man like Tian Guang, having a strong character, to mark a prelude to the plan of assassination by committing suicide in advance. A close friend was not supposed to persuade or ask Tian Guang not to commit suicide. That would sound too familiar and old-fashioned.

Later on, Jing Ke tried to carry out the planned assassination but failed. When he got killed during the assassination attempt, he died smiling. Before his departure from the Kingdom of Yan, Jing Ke was seen off at the bank of the River of Yi by Crown Prince Dan and those who knew of the secret plan. Everyone was well aware that the chances for success were very slim. All of them wore white mourning caps and clothes to bid Jing Ke farewell. They sang a song that went like this: "Over the icy waters of the rolling River of Yi, blowing is the gusty wind! About to start on a distant journey of no return, there goes our respected hero!" Their feeling was clearly reflected by this sorrowful song.

The most touching part of these two stories of assassination is not at all in the drama of the assassination itself, but in the description of suicide committed by these two elders. They had an identical characteristic. Momotaro, can you see what it is?'

'The elderliness.'

'Elderliness is a common scenario. It cannot be considered a characteristic.'

'It's the suicide.'

'Committing suicide is the consequence of a characteristic, which cannot be regarded as a characteristic either.'

'Then what is it?'

'The identical characteristic is that it was unnecessary to die, but they both wanted to die. Their superior lofty character was revealed right there. Did you notice that? If they did not die, they would not be faulted, but if they died, they were dead right.

If they didn't die, there was nothing lost. But, if they did die, they were dead ahead. I really don't know whether I can make my point clear by saying it this way or not.

It even seems that there's a contradiction in what I say. Actually, I have a feeling that if they didn't do it, they weren't inferior; if they did do it, they were far superior. Furthermore, if they didn't do so, they weren't insignificant either; if they actually did so, they were surely far, far more superior and magnificent.'

'I can actually understand how you feel.'

'The boundary line between a hero and an ordinary person is right here. What you've felt is the fundamental difference between a hero and an ordinary person.'

'This is not merely a fundamental issue about being a hero or an ordinary person. This is not merely about being a hero either. This is about being a saint of heroic spirit. Actually, this is being a saintly hero.'

'Speaking of saints, that reminds me of Socrates. According to the law of his time, Socrates didn't have to die at all. For, in accordance with the law, the plaintiff and the defendant would each suggest a penalty and the judge would choose between the two. At that time, the plaintiff was the general public in support of the new authority in the government, and it suggested that the penalty be capital punishment. If Socrates requested mercy, they would duly pardon him. But he felt nothing but contempt for such a request, and was willing to die. Thus, as the defendant, he suggested that the penalty be a fine of thirty coins of small change. This paltry fine really upset the judge. The judge's verdict was to make him take poison.

Later on, a friend of his bribed every single prison guard to let him escape from prison. But, he didn't want to because he intended to die. Finally, he died happily. He took the poison and told his weeping disciples around him to keep quiet, because a real man preferred to pass away in tranquillity.'

'Socrates was a saint and he died as a hero. He was a saintly hero. I have a feeling that Zhuan Zhu's mother and Tian Guang actually were a saintly heroine and a saintly hero, too.'

'Zhuan Zhu's mother was an ordinary elderly woman. According to what you have said, ordinary people can also become saintly heroines or saintly heroes?'

'Of course, it is very rare for ordinary people to become saintly heroines or heroes. Take Zhuan Zhu's mother, for example. We know nothing about the history of her life. What we know of is her death. She died a glorious death. Her whole life was nothing but an ordinary one. All she had was revealed plainly in her death—dying to fulfil her son's wish. She was an ordinary woman and left no honourable name for posterity. Her name was linked with her son's. She was called "the great Mother of Zhuan Zhu".'

⸺∘⊰⊹⊱∘⸺

When they arrived at the Association, Tan Sitong wasn't there. The doorman said Mr Tan had stepped out an hour ago, by himself, and didn't say where he was going or when he would return. He took nothing with him. After waiting for quite a while, they left a note, which read, 'Urgent. Please contact us when you return.' Upon leaving the Association, they decided not to leave anyone there to wait for him. There was an advantage to that. When Tan Sitong got back he could leave the Association right away and go and look for them. This would shorten their wait at the Association—too dangerous a place to stay for long.

It was very late at night when the four got back to the Japanese Legation. Kensuke Hayashi wasn't there, so they went to see Liang Qichao. While they were talking, a Japanese employee walked in and brought them a message from the British Embassy. It said about a dozen people had gone to the residence of Zhang Yinhuan to arrest Kang Youwei. But they had actually caught the wrong person, named Qi, which indicated that the situation was extremely precarious.

Zhang Yinhuan and Kang Youwei were natives of the same town. Zhang favoured political reform, but he wasn't a member of the school of Kang Youwei. He himself was a grand minister, equivalent to the minister of foreign affairs of today. He had been a top-ranking official for a long time and had no need to align himself with these people newly appointed to high posts. For years, he had been appointed as an imperial emissary with the rank of grand minister, to the United States, then Spain, and Peru. He had also headed the Chinese delegation to the Grand Ceremony in Celebration of the Sixtieth Birthday of Her Majesty Queen Victoria of Great Britain. He did not support Li Hongzhang's overzealous pro-Russia policy, which made Li Hongzhang very unhappy.

He was quite close to Emperor Guangxu. His audiences with the Emperor always lasted longer than prescribed by imperial law, which aroused the Empress Dowager's envy and suspicion. At that time, he was the most knowledgeable government official regarding foreign affairs. He had lived in several foreign countries and was aware of the culture and customs of those countries. He also knew China must be modernized in order to have a prosperous future.

The year before Kang Youwei initiated political reform, he had gathered a group of scholars to make a compilation of more than eighty books called the *Series of Western Books to Bolster a Country's Strength*, in the expectation that these books would draw the attention of the general public in China. In the spring of the very year political reform began, a royal prince from Germany visited China.

To comply with Western etiquette, he suggested that the imperial court of the Qing Dynasty accept the international courtesy of shaking hands with the guest of honour as the proper way to receive a Western royal prince. The conservative top-ranking officials opposed his suggestion, but Emperor Guangxu supported him. This made some people think that his behaviour was exactly the same as the political reform initiated by Liang Qichao. On the fifth day of August, he accompanied Hirofumi Ito on an official visit to Emperor Guangxu in the imperial palace. According to Western etiquette, he shook hands with Hirofumi Ito and then, hand in hand, they walked toward the main hall of the imperial palace. Unfortunately, the Empress Dowager saw them through the bamboo curtain hanging from the beam at the back of the main hall of the imperial palace, just behind the grand seat of Emperor Guangxu. On the basis of their intimate gesture she thought he had been in close contact with Hirofumi Ito. That's why he was considered to have been involved in this crisis of political reform.

It was very late at night. There was no word from the Liuyang Association. All four agreed that they'd go there the next morning and see what was going on.

On the ninth day of August by the Chinese lunar calendar, which happened to fall on the twenty-fourth day of September 1898, it was a cloudy day in Beijing. Shu Hirayama hadn't slept well the night before, and he got up earlier than usual. At five o'clock in the morning, he woke the other three and asked them to get dressed to leave the city. As they went through the living room, they saw Liang Qichao. It was obvious that he had been up all night just by looking at his face. Liang Qichao took out three letters he had written from his inner vest pocket, put them into an envelope, and handed it to Shu Hirayama.

'As I can't go in person to persuade him to come here, I wrote this letter to him to try to give him my last bit of advice. In this letter, I reiterated the fact that it's very hard for me to accept his explanation, based on the well known sad story of the Zhao family orphan of ancient Chinese history, as the reason why he won't flee. Please take your time to read it through and then forward it to him. Tan Sitong is a native of Hunan. The nickname for the Hunanese is "donkey". They have the temperament of a donkey and are very stubborn. In working with a Hunanese, you'd better provide them with all the relevant data, and give them time to consider everything carefully. After that, they'll decide on their own, not through your persuasion.'

Shu Hirayama took the letter and read it through together with the other three. And then Shu Hirayama put the letter into his pocket and said:

'Mr Liang, you did a good job. We'll do our best to persuade him to come over here.'

'If persuasion fails, we'll kidnap him to get him here,' interrupted Momotaro, a tough guy.

Everybody burst into laughter. The serious atmosphere in the living room lightened somewhat.

When the four arrived at the Liuyang Association, Tan Sitong was there. At first, Tan Sitong asked them to accept his apologies for not having replied to them. He read through the letter from Liang Qichao and then burned it right in front of them.

'I don't want to leave any trace of this letter, which will give people an idea that Mr Liang is in the Japanese Legation,' explained Tan Sitong. 'Please extend my apologies to Mr Liang for not replying to his letter due to my tight schedule. I won't leave here. I appreciate Mr Liang's kindness and also thank you for your kindness.'

'Your Excellency, Mr Tan,' Shu Hirayama said, 'Mr Liang instructed us that we must make it clear to you that right now it is absolutely unnecessary for you to sacrifice your invaluable life for no justifiable cause. Mr Liang even told us that, with all due respect, we may force Your Excellency to go to our place.'

Tan Sitong laughed, 'How can you force me to go? I don't believe Mr Liang said that. You probably misunderstood him.'

'The so-called forcing you to go,' interrupted Momotaro, 'really just means that we four will escort Your Excellency to our place.'

Tan Sitong laughed. 'That's why I don't believe Mr Liang said that. He's well aware how good Tan Sitong's martial arts skills are, that is, Chinese *gong fu*. He knows that if I don't cooperate, you four Japanese won't be able to get close to my body at all. Furthermore, you want to play at kidnapping in China? That sounds very much like an act of imperialism. To kidnap a person and take him to your Legation is an act in violation of international law!'

'As for the government of the Qing Dynasty, we don't have to abide by international law. Weren't they the ones who kidnapped Dr Sun Yat-sen in London?' said Kakicho.

'That incident has turned into a great joke in the international community, hasn't it? You can't afford to have this kind of embarrassment. That incident involved the Chinese kidnapping a Chinese. But now, you are suggesting the Japanese kidnap a Chinese. How dare you?'

'Oh, we're Japanese! I forgot we are Japanese.' Kakicho rubbed his head.

'Let me remind you that you'd better always remember you're Japanese. In China, it is dangerous to forget you're Japanese,' laughed Tan Sitong.

'Dangerous? Why?'

'Japanese are Japanese. If you forget you're Japanese, the Japanese will forget you. When that time comes, the Japanese will think you're Chinese and the Chinese still think you're Japanese. Then, what are you?'

Shu Hirayama suddenly turned and looked at Kakecho. A trace of suspicion was in his eyes. Shu Hirayama turned back and said to Tan Sitong:

'At that time we will still be Japanese reform fighters in China to help her to win independence and freedom in a time of adversity. The Japanese won't deny us, and neither will the Chinese.'

'They won't? You're too optimistic!' Tan Sitong grinned. 'By saying so you show how little you know about Japanese and Chinese history. Historically, when China was in trouble, Japan never came to help her. The best examples are when Japan didn't help China and was even rude to China first at the end of the Song Dynasty, and then at the end of the Ming Dynasty. A Chinese named Zhu Shunsui went to Japan to ask for assistance. In Japan, he was received and honoured by the Mito Governor. He helped Japan improve its education, politics, and economy. He was regarded as the master teacher of the nation. But, later on, when his grandson came from China to visit him in Japan, the Japanese didn't even allow him to meet his grandfather. The mother of Koxinga (1624–1662) or "Zheng Chenggong"—the leader of an anti-Manchu resistance army, who ousted the Dutch from Taiwan—was Japanese. Koxinga was a mixture of Chinese and Japanese. But when he was in trouble, Japan didn't give him a hand.

On the other hand, China did help Japan. At the end of the Song Dynasty, Japan, through the assistance of a Chinese named Li Zhuying and a Chinese monk named Zhu Yuan, had the strength and spirit to fight against the Mongolians. At the end of the Ming Dynasty, Japan, through the help of a Chinese named Zhu Shunshui, obtained the source of the spirit to rebuild the ancient empire of Japan in the Meiji Restoration. As between nation and nation, Japan owes a debt to China. Japan lacks the tradition of offering its assistance to China. Nevertheless, your coming to China is no simple matter. I advise you then that you'll be better off to remember you're Japanese.'

'According to you, what did we come to China for? And why did we come to the Liuyang Association, in the early hours of the morning?'

'What for? You came here to help the Chinese!' laughed Tan Sitong.

'You did just say, didn't you, that Japan has no tradition of giving China a hand?'

'Yes, I did. You came here to help the Chinese, not China. The Chinese you're going to help are just a small number, not all of the Chinese.'

'What kind of a theory is that? Does it make any sense?'

'It does make some sense. As a matter of fact, there is no moral obligation between nations. To talk about the moral obligation between nations is actually senseless. But between individuals it's a different story. The Japanese aren't people who refuse to honour their moral obligations, but they do so only in matters between individuals. At most, your coming here to help the Chinese is on the force of moral obligation between individuals.'

'Is that really so?' Shu Hirayama thought otherwise.

'In case your assistance clashes with the stance between nations, what then?' asked Tan Sitong.

'At the present time, there is no such clash,' answered Shu Hirayama.

'What about if there is such a clash?'

'An individual is going to be sacrificed, of course.'

'What if such a sacrifice causes damage to moral obligation? And if Japan were to blame?'

'Just let it cause some damage to moral obligation. The boundary of a nation counts. Not the right or the wrong of it.'

'That's why you sacrifice your personal moral obligations for the interests of the country.'

'Exactly.'

'Then you'll sell out any friends of yours for the sake of the interests of the country?' Tan Sitong asked seriously.

'True. But, your use of the word "sell out" is not acceptable to me.' Shu Hirayama pursed his lips.

'It isn't? Now you have come to China to make friends. You are going to sell them out one day, aren't you?'

'I make friends not in order to sell them out some day to save my own skin. I really come here to help them. But I just can't guarantee what I'll do in the future.'

'Then the person who makes friends with you is gaining a potential foe?'

'Don't look at things from such a pessimistic point of view! We came to China neither to make enemies, nor to have a sightseeing tour at Zhenyangmen, but to advance the interests of Japan.'

'Would you do it, if it is against the interests of Japan?'

'Of course not.'

'What are you doing now?'

'What we're doing now is benefiting both China and Japan.'

'I think the other way around is also acceptable—what is beneficial to Japan is also beneficial to China,' interrupted Kakicho.

'This is quite a significant understanding. Didn't we come to Beijing and get up so early this morning to come here, with this in mind?' said Shu Hirayama.

'Absolutely, we did! After hearing what you have just said, I have the feeling that you're not a man of simplicity. You sound like a member of the Kokuryu Group,' said Tan Sitong.

'Do I look like one of them?'

'That's hard to say. A lot of the members of the Kokuryu Group look like nice people. Once they become your friends, they're open-hearted and very faithful. But, when dealing with matters concerning China, they become mean and wicked and very rough. They have a different set of standards. They show no respect for the status of China,' laughed Tan Sitong. 'Although we have some suspicion and disagreement between us, I'm willing to tell you my feelings from the bottom of my heart. I appreciate your kindness. Also, from the point of view of personal chivalry, I trust that your kind act is indeed one of personal chivalry.

Okay. I have a lot of things to do today. Gentlemen, please recall the stories of Gessho and Takamori Saigo in Japan. At the time when a dilemma presents itself, there'll always be someone to die and someone to not die. Please tell Mr Liang that, as for these two Japanese gentlemen—Gessho and Takamori Saigo—he and I shall each choose one of them, and follow in their footsteps.

By the way, please think about the freedom fighters during the Meiji Restoration in Japan. Who was the most meritorious statesman during the Meiji Restoration? Was it Takamori Saigo? Kido? Okubo? Hirofumi Ito? Owaki? Inoue? Goto? Itagaki?

I think it was none of these. The most meritorious statesman was Sonyin Yoshida. He never rendered an outstanding service to his country during his lifetime. He wanted to flee the country but failed; he wanted to gather a group of reform fighters to assist the emperor but failed; and he wanted to send the reform fighters to deter the evil power but failed. Finally, at the age of thirty-something, he was beheaded in a public execution. But after his death, the Japanese population was enlightened by his spirit of loving and wanting to save his country. They all gathered together and strove to reform the government of Japan and made the Meiji Restoration a reality. That's proof that Sonyin didn't die in vain. Though he failed, he actually succeeded. His failure eventually turned into success. Let me leave this story of a Japanese reform fighter with you as a farewell souvenir!'

As they left the Liuyang Association, the four Japanese murmured among themselves.

'I thought that we were the experts on Chinese affairs,' sighed Shu Hirayama. 'I can't believe that His Excellency Mr Tan is an expert on Japanese affairs! When he talks about the history and political situation of Japan, he knows it like the back of his hand. He's fantastic! He's magnificent!'

'Really fantastic and magnificent!' everybody agreed.

'It seems to me that I have heard of some of the names mentioned by His Excellency Mr Tan. But when he talked about Gessho and Takamori, I really had no idea who they were. The so-called Takamori was Takamori Saigo?' asked Momotaro.

'Takamori was Takamori Saigo,' said Shu Hirayama. 'Gessho was a monk at Saikyo Kiyomizu Temple, who was chivalrous and righteous. After returning from abroad, he promoted a campaign supporting the emperor under the pressure of the Western powers and the feudal government in Japan. Later on, as the situation turned grave, he fled to Satsuma through arrangements made by Ko Konoe and was received by Takamori Saigo.'

'In the end, Takamori was considered to be involved in the campaign. Gessho didn't want Ko Konoe and Takamori to be implicated in the campaign and asked Takamori to kill him, because he wanted to be killed at the hand of a comrade. But Takamori just nonchalantly invited Gessho to a dinner party on a boat, for drinking and singing. However, at the end of the party, the two of them embraced and jumped over the boat into the sea together. People came to rescue them. They picked up Takamori, but unfortunately Gessho was drowned. Later on, Takamori made the reform and restoration a success and fulfilled Gessho's will.'

Moments ago, His Excellency Mr Tan asked us to convey to Mr Liang the story of Gessho and Takamori that he told us. His purpose is to advise Mr Liang that he should strive to accomplish their goal, under the encouragement of the death of his comrade. His Excellency Mr Tan is really a man of great spirit. He has our sincerest admiration. While China has such a great man as this, it will be a long, long journey before Japan to conquers and dominates it!'

CHAPTER ELEVEN
Self-sacrifice

Tan Sitong will not be swayed from his conviction that he must become a martyr for his country. He goes to see Big Sword Wang Wu to tell him and his gang of his intentions, and to say goodbye. He also asks Wang Wu and his gang to rescue the Emperor. He advises them that he cannot participate in their rescue attempts. The gang members are incredulous. Not only has Tan Sitong previously come and convinced them of the merit of him cooperating with the Manchu regime—contrary to their secret society's long-held beliefs—but now he goes so far as to ask them to rescue the Manchu emperor! However, he carefully explains his position and tells them that he will sacrifice his life, in part to encourage them to go forward with this risky task. With such unparalleled bravery and fidelity to themselves, his friends, to his cause, and to saving China from its corrupt rulers, the gang members are hard-pressed to dismiss his drastic request.

After leaving Wang Wu and his gang to contemplate what he has said, Tan returns to his room to make preparations for his impending death. Wang Wu comes to see him to report that the group has decided to take up the rescue of the Emperor and to try once again to persuade Tan to flee the area to avoid arrest. But his words are to no avail. Yet, because Tan is touched by Wang Wu's sentiments, he agrees to reconsider. At last, Tan puts his affairs in order and writes farewell letters to his father, his wife, to Wang Wu, to his former teacher, and to a former classmate. He is now fully prepared to leave this world.

After Shu Hirayama and his company had left, Tan Sitong accelerated his activities at the Liuyang Association. He locked the door, checked over the slips of papers left in the room, set some of them on fire and put some of them away. He worked secretly the whole morning and then left in a hurry. Cautiously, he looked around the neighbourhood and then hurried into a small lane. He walked in the direction of the armed escort services company of Big Sword Wang Wu.

When he showed up at the armed escort services company, all the chiefs and guards were waiting there.

'I am here today to say goodbye. The development of the reform movement has gone from bad to worse. Last night, the Emperor was detained under house arrest by the "old lady" at Yingtai. A warrant for mass arrest is soon to be issued. It seems our efforts of the past hundred days or so to enforce political reform are doomed to failure. Since I am the principal, I must bear the responsibility, and I am willing to be executed to settle the score. But the Emperor is still too young. His involvement in the plot may get him poisoned by the Empress Dowager. I simply can't allow that to happen. While I am here to bid you farewell, I must ask you, brothers, to save the Emperor in the name of righteousness.'

Having finished, Tan, bowing, fixed each and every one of them in the room with his eagle-like eyes.

'But San Ge, what's happened to you?' said Hu Qi. 'Since I've known you, we have always taken your word without question. When you say go east, we go east. When you say go west, we go west. But how can you throw us this sort of problem today? Ask us to rescue the Manchus? Last time you said that we should cooperate with the Manchus and help them carry out political reform. At first, we didn't understand that. And we still don't quite understand it now. But we've kept our mouths shut. You're really going too far today by asking us not only to cooperate with the Manchus, but also to rescue the Emperor. San Ge, you know all of us have been united together up to now, for two or three hundred years, just by our deeply rooted hatred of the Manchus. But now it seems that the direction you ask us to take is getting too far away from the goal we have been struggling so long and so hard to reach. That's not quite right, is it?'

'You can't say that,' explained Tan Sitong. 'Frankly speaking, when I came up north from the south, I originally thought that the Emperor wanted political reform, despite the "old lady" over his head. However, the Emperor is an emperor. And he has every right to make some major decisions.

But when I got into the imperial palace, I discovered that he doesn't have a free hand to do anything. In reality, the Emperor has no power or authority at all. Though he lacks real power and authority, he has committed an act of greatness—to try to reform China. For this he has won my admiration. Just as the Chinese sage said, "Do what one knows perfectly well one won't be able to do." But, for the sake of the Manchus and the Hans, he's determined to fight for the implementation of political reform in China, even despite his lack of power and authority. This is the spirit of greatness. Since the Emperor is such a great man, we should do every thing we can to help him. It doesn't matter whether he is a Manchu or not. He first acted to help us, the Hans, without regard for his own throne. As the situation now is so critical, how can we still want to bicker about who's a Manchu and who's a Han? So long as the Emperor is in danger, I can't leave him and run away in order to save myself. Therefore I offer my own life, to ask you to rescue the Emperor when I'm gone.'

'You want us to rescue the Emperor,' said Wang Wu, 'without your participation, my dear San Ge?'

'I'm not going to participate in the rescue. What I have to do is what I ought to do. That is to sacrifice my life first to augment the strength needed to rescue the Emperor.'

'To sacrifice your life?' asked Wang Wu.

'To die in advance.' said Tan Sitong, calmly. 'Allow me to tell you a story to explain this matter. You all know Liu Bang, the First Emperor of the Han Dynasty. Liu Bang was the roughest rascal emperor. He appointed his son-in-law ruler of the small kingdom of Zhao. One day, he visited the small kingdom of Zhao and scolded the ruler, pointing at his nose and yelling at him right in front of his subjects. The ruler of Zhao was so frightened that he didn't utter a word. But his subjects couldn't swallow their anger. A man named Guan Gao acted as a leader in mapping out a scheme to assassinate Liu Bang. He decided to get rid of Liu Bang in a place called Boren. When Liu Bang arrived in Boren, he couldn't sleep that night. Feeling quite jumpy, he got up and asked his lieutenants the name of the place where they were staying. They told him the place was called Boren. Liu Bang said, "Boren means 'being persecuted.' That means someone is going to be in trouble. This name is a bad omen. We can't stay here. Everybody must get out of here right away!" So all of them left the place and hurried onto the road.

At midnight, Guan Gao arrived at Boren with a group of warriors to kill Liu Bang, but he had already left. Later on, when Liu Bang was told about the event, he ordered the mass arrest of the plotters. The assassins knew that they wouldn't live long, so they committed suicide one after the other. All except one—Guan Gao. Guan Gao didn't kill himself and criticized those who did. He said that the ruler of Zhao was unaware of the assassination scheme. But Liu Bang had the ruler of Zhao arrested, too. If all of those involved in the assassination attempt were dead, who could step forward to prove the innocence of the ruler of Zhao?

So Guan Gao was willing to be arrested by Liu Bang's men. They tortured him mercilessly. There were wounds all over his body, but he refused to confess. With his teeth clenched together and blood running down his face and body, he said that the ruler of Zhao was innocent of the assassination plot. His courage made Liu Bang wonder.

Liu Bang sent an old friend of Guan Gao's to bribe the prison guards and ask them to let him bring some fruit to Guan Gao. The man asked Guan Gao whether the ruler of Zhao really knew about the assassination scheme or not. Guan Gao said, "Who on earth doesn't love his parents and wife? But they will be killed because of my assassination plot! If I confess that the ruler of Zhao is behind the assassination attempt, my parents and wife will be spared. I love my parents and wife much more than I do the ruler of Zhao. But I can't make up a story to frame an innocent man out of selfishness. I intend to be a good man and take all the responsibility for what I have done."

As soon he left the prison, Guan Gao's friend reported to Liu Bang that the ruler of Zhao hadn't taken part in the assassination scheme and that Guan Gao was a true friend, faithful, with a strong sense of honour. Liu Bang was deeply touched by the report and decided to set the ruler of Zhao free, and also pardon Guan Gao. When Guan Gao heard the news and thought about the death of his friends who had assisted him in the attempted assassination, he felt that it was meaningless to live, and committed suicide.

This story shows that a good man should take full responsibility for what he has done. Today, we have all participated in the course of political reform in China, but it has gone sour. It is said that the Emperor has been confined to his quarters and nobody knows whether he is dead or alive. If we, the trailblazers, all run away and no one is willing to sacrifice his life, then how can we face our friends? Therefore, I, Tan Sitong, have no choice but to die, and I must die first. Sacrificing my life is the only way to return the kindness and loving care of the Emperor, and of my beloved friends. If I stay alive, I'll be a loser. If I sacrifice my life, I may be a winner.'

'If that's the case,' said Wang Wu, 'my dear San Ge, your coming up north from the south to implement political reform was done without careful consideration. You and your close friends are rare scholars and peerless in China. It's not quite right to let you all sacrifice your lives in vain. You are just like chefs, and chefs should know the right way to prepare food. They're well aware that only a stove at the right temperature will make a tasty dish.

Take stir-fried shredded lamb's stomach, for example. It is one of the most famous dishes in Hunan cuisine. Shredded lamb's stomach is a wonderful Chinese dish, but if it isn't cooked right, it tastes terrible. It is the way it is cooked that counts. It is absolutely necessary to first wash the lamb's stomach clean and shred it into short strings. Second, put some vegetable oil in the wok and heat it up, add some sliced scallions and red peppers, and stir-fry them. Third, put in the shredded lamb's stomach and quickly stir-fry it all again. Fourth, add some leeks and sesame oil, vinegar and salt, as well as a little chicken broth. Finally, stir-fry it all one more time and pour everything out onto a plate and serve immediately. If they are stir-fried too long, the leeks will turn watery and won't be crispy, and the whole dish will be entirely spoiled.

To cook a Chinese dish requires knowledge of preparation and stove temperature. As to your implementation of political reform, if the preparation time is not sufficient and the temperature of the stove is not right, all the ingredients will be spoiled and the serving time will be delayed. What's more, the appetite of the diners will undoubtedly wane.

If political reform is like the cooking of a Chinese dish, you are right. It requires careful preparation and the right stove temperature. However, the current situation is too complicated. So complicated that it seems everything has been tangled together. The whole situation is tightly tangled beyond extrication. At this point, our goal is to unravel this tangled situation. We can't afford to let the current situation remain as it is.

To take action is to seek an opportunity and to make a start. To take no action is to let everything remain the same. We have tolerated the existing situation so long, that we can't tolerate it any longer. So we have to take action now. We don't have the time to be concerned about whether the preparation is sufficient or the temperature of the stove is right or not. What kind of preparation is sufficient and what temperature is just right? Since the current situation is so complicated and it's very hard for us to make a judgement, we must simply take action to make a new situation happen in order to make the right judgement.'

'In other words, you don't care whether the preparation in sufficient and the temperature is right or not?'

'That's not exactly so. At least we can take a look at it based on the trends and from a wide-angled perspective. We are not acting entirely without preparation, nor do we necessarily lack the right temperature. We have prepared ourselves for a couple of decades. My personal preparation is also quite sufficient.

As to the temperature of the stove, although at the moment the general public in China hasn't been enlightened, they seem to expect that it's better for China to have some changes take place. Even though the existing stove temperature is not quite right, we can't afford to wait any longer. Mr Kang is in his forties, and I'm over thirty. We are all middle-aged and have been waiting for a couple of decades. How can we keep waiting like this? If the temperature of the stove is right at some point thirty years from now, we'll all have become decrepit if we aren't already dead.'

'Have you ever thought about why you must be the ones to save the country? If the temperature of the stove is right thirty years from now, why not let the thirty-year-old heroes and heroines of the time save the country?' asked Hu Qi.

'You can't think about it like that. Actually, it isn't impossible for us to succeed. But doing it or not doing it will give a different result. My dear Qi Ge, you weigh the factors of success or failure and maturity or immaturity too highly in considering whether or not to do something.'

'How can he be wrong? It takes a man of steadiness to ensure that everything goes right,' said Hu Qi.

'Yes, that's what a man of steadiness would do. The more steady a man becomes, the less action he takes. Finally, his hair goes grey, and he has made no achievements at all. And his hair also goes grey if he has made all the achievements. Therefore, a man of steadiness will gradually lose his attitude toward doing things and eventually have excuses for not doing them.'

'But you can't always make a careful estimate before starting something. If you foresee the possibility of being a loser, how can you have the faith to start? If, at the very start, you have no idea of the chances of your success or failure, perhaps you're more likely to give it a try. However, if at the start you know that there is no way of succeeding, why would you insist on going forward?'

'To implement political reform in China we must appeal to the general public. Just as Qi Ge said, we already knew that political reform was likely to go nowhere when we started. Qi Ge, what you have just said does make some sense. But, you don't quite understand that to have political reform in China is our appeal, or let me put this way, that the bargaining price is political reform, but our bottom line is publicity for political reform in China. We consider it a success if we can enlighten the Chinese population on the issue that so they can see that China needs political reform. So, we know what the bottom line is. We have no intention of asking too much. Since our bottom line was no higher than this, we didn't feel like potential losers when we started out.'

'Why can't you tell everybody your bottom line? Why have you made the implementation of political reform so hair-raising? If your bottom line is publicity for political reform, perhaps the people in power will have a certain understanding of what you're actually doing and tolerate you and then spare your lives?' said Hu Qi.

'How can we do that? To publicize the implementation of political reform is not the final goal of our campaign, it is merely the first phase of our campaign. After publicizing it, the implementation of political reform is bound to be realized sooner or later. Our spirit is such that it is not necessary for us to be the winners. But this won't constitute a reason not to proceed. According to the process, there is an inseparable and continuous relationship. Technically, we have to utilize the slogan of implementation of political reform as a means of publicizing our ideology. The methodology is that we target the highest goal, so that in case we miss it we can hit the next highest goal; and in case we miss that one, we can probably hit the next one down. We will be far better off this way.'

'You mean that you've utilized your goal—to implement political reform—as your means, which is the very means to publicize the implementation of political reform, to reach your goal, which is your bottom line. Originally, to publicize the implementation of political reform was the means of implementing political reform. Actually, it is your goal. At least, it is your bottom line goal, isn't it?' Wang Wu followed.

'It sounds ridiculous, doesn't it?'

'To utilize the goal as the means and the means as the goal.'

'As for us, we utilize the goal as the means. But, as for the Chinese population, we have combined the means and the goal into one objective. The means is to implement political reform and the goal is also to implement political reform.'

'Is there no such a thing as phase one, being the process of publicizing the implementation of political reform?'

'Right, there is no such phase. As for the Chinese population, there is no first phase of the implementation of political reform. There is only the stage of its success or failure. If we fail, we will naturally reach phase one. We absolutely won't fail at phase one. Now, what we want to see is how successful phase one can be, and to what extent it can lead on to further goals.'

'From what I can see, what you have done so far is too superficial, that is, merely publicizing the implementation of political reform, not the actual implementation of political reform.'

'I fully understand what you mean. I also admit that what you say does make some sense. But, perhaps you won't believe that our goal was originally to publicize. Is that strange? Think it over again. Do you really believe the implementation of a political reform could be a success? Under the pressure of such an evil power and authority, it is very, very difficult for us to make the implementation of political reform a success. In fact, I'm already aware of the critical nature of the situation and its crushing difficulty.'

'Since you already know it and have a bad feeling about the matter, why do you still devote your time to the fulfilment of the task that is obviously bound to fail?' sighed Wang Wu.

'Do what one knows perfectly well one won't be able to do.'

'Do you have a good reason for doing so?' asked Hu Qi, earnestly.

'My reason is that the Chinese population has to be informed of the fact that the time for reform has already arrived. A political reform is vitally needed. This is the first voice of appeal for political reform in China. This is probably the only voice that we can make the general public hear. Actually, we can change nothing here in China. As long as it is a voice of appeal, we'd better make it as loud as possible. So, as you can see, our task has indeed been involved with play-acting. I won't deny that. But, this is not a drama for fun. This is a drama in which real life is on the line. When a man puts his life on the line to publicize a risky task, there will be no question of his sincerity. Nor will there be a problem of putting the goal before the means. Everything will be drowned out by the matter of life and death. The matter of life and death will melt the problems of worry and wonder. My dear Qi Ge, if a person is willing to die for their goal, how can anyone have any reason to criticize? What on earth can they pick on them for?'

'However,' continued Tan Sitong, 'optimistically, to implement political reform is not really a matter of success or not. A so-called failure is but the first step to success. Maybe a success needs two steps, so a failure is half of a success. Perhaps, a success needs ten steps, so a failure is ten per cent of a success. So don't regard a failure as an isolated matter. Regard a failure as a phase toward becoming a success. Regard a failure and a success as the continuation of a matter.

Looking at it from a different angle, you say that I'm devoting my time to a task which is bound to fail. That's right. From its outward appearance it seems to be a failure. But, according to our bottom line, we can still make it a partial success. There are two kinds of failure: one is a complete failure; the other is a failure that lays the foundation for success, or a failure that contains a certain percentage of success. Success needs time and the right climate.

It happens to be my fate that I'm to fulfil the first part of the task. I'm destined to be a martyr, not to be an elder statesman. Since a man like me, at the age of thirty-something, is destined to be a martyr, I have no choice but to be so. As a matter of fact, even at the age of forty-something, fifty-something, sixty-something, or seventy-something, I would still have no other choice.

Do you recall Hou Ying, an elderly man in his seventies? Hou Ying was just a city gate watchman in the Kingdom of Wei. But he was also a swordsman. Xin Lingjun, one of the four princes during the time of the Warring States in China, showed great respect for him and invited him to a dinner party. Dressed in ragged clothes, Hou Ying sat proudly in a luxurious carriage driven by Xin Lingjun. At dinner, he sat in the guest of honour's place and enjoyed the food in a very dignified manner.

Later on, the Kingdom of Zhao was besieged by the Kingdom of Qin. The Kingdom of Zhao asked the Kingdom of Wei to assist them. But the ruler of the Kingdom of Wei refused. Hou Ying then gave Xin Lingjun the idea of asking the concubine of the ruler of the Kingdom of Wei to help him steal the general's seal and stamp it on a military order to instruct the soldiers of the Kingdom of Wei stationed at the border to go to rescue the Kingdom of Zhao. Xin Lingjun took his advice and got the general's seal.

When Xin Lingjun departed for the front, Hou Ying recommended that a butcher, Zhu Haiyi, a friend of his, accompany him, and said to him, "I should go with you two to the front, but I'm too old. What I can do now is to see you two off. However, to show that our hearts are one and that I am not a coward, I'm determined to turn my face towards the north and commit suicide at the time of your arrival at the front, as proof of our lasting friendship." Later on, when Xin Lingjun arrived at the front, Hou Ying actually did commit suicide as he had said.

Poet Wang Wei of the Tang Dynasty wrote in the *Song of Yimen* of the incident: "Not only generous with a marvellous strategy, but also unstinting enough to sacrifice his life; looking in the direction to see the troops off, what more can one expect of a seventy-year-old?"

According to my understanding of Hou Ying, I think it is obvious that this elderly man was determined to sacrifice his life to show that he had no intention of staying alive while his friends took all the risks. On the other hand, though his friends accepted his idea and went to take the risk, they still had a chance of surviving. Hou Ying was determined to sacrifice his own life and gave up all chance of survival.

I came here today, on the one hand, to let you know that I can't split myself in two and let one go to rescue the Emperor; and, on the other hand, to ask you to take the risk of rescuing the Emperor. As a close friend of yours, I've really asked too much. To give the effect of a bloody political reform, I can't commit suicide by cutting my throat like Hou Ying. But I will let them chop my head off at the public execution ground. My death will show our lasting friendship. It is getting late, now. Farewell, my dearest friends!'

Holding his two hands together and up to his chest as a gesture of courtesy, Tan Sitong stepped out of the hall into the dusk of evening. All his friends seemed to want to walk him out to the front gate. But he opened his two palms and made a gesture of appreciation of their kindness and affection. Understanding his feelings, Wang Wu said simply, 'Let our San Ge go by himself!'

———◇○◈○◇———

Tan Sitong got back to his study. He walked into the room and lit the oil lamp. Under the lamplight, three men were sitting in the corner.

All three were dressed the same. Each wore a small black vest. Underneath the black vest there was a white shirt. The first button of the white shirt was unbuttoned and a white collar stuck out. The sleeves of the white shirt were rolled up.

All three stood up and the leader of three said 'Hello' to Tan Sitong. 'Are you Mr Tan?'

Tan Sitong nodded and said, 'Gentlemen, you are?'

'We came here to invite Mr Tan to go with us.'

'Oh.' Tan Sitong smiled, and said calmly, 'I've been waiting for you gentlemen for a long time. You have come here on official business.'

The leader smiled and said, 'Mr Tan, you've mistaken us. We are not from the government. We come from the south.'

'From the south?' Tan Sitong was stunned for a couple of seconds.

'We have brought you a letter, Mr Tan. Please read it through.' The leader took a letter out from the inner pocket of his shirt. On the envelope was written:

Special Delivery To Beijing
To: Mr Tan Fusheng
From: Huang Zhen

Tan Sitong looked at the letter and understood immediately what it meant. He opened the letter, which read:

Dear Brother Fusheng,

It has been quite some time since we last met. Nonetheless, whatever you have planned to do, we all know about it through our network of informants. I sincerely hope that you do not feel offended.

I have dispatched four comrades to escort you to the south. It is terribly important that you consider the whole situation in choosing your course of action and not try to sacrifice yourself for the cause. Mencius once said, 'If the dying is not appropriate, then one's bravery is impaired.' Your immeasurable bravery is well known to us and we all admire that. Furthermore, your talent, rare among all of us, is unparalleled. Now that developments are at a critical juncture, you must move and start anew on a new battleground and work together with us. It goes without saying that with your talent, you must be able to tell which carries more weight than the other. In short, your staying alive is tantamount to our escape from death. Since our friendship is bound with a life and death vow, I sincerely hope you take my advice.

Sincerely,
Huang Zhen

After reading the letter, Tan Sitong set it on the top of the flame of the oil lamp, letting it burn a little at a time, just like a silkworm nipping on the leaf of a mulberry tree.

Tan Sitong didn't ask them to sit down, and said right away: 'Dear brothers, the current situation is very critical. Allow me to make a long story short. I appreciate your kindness and that of Mr Huang Zhen very much. But I can't leave Beijing and have no intention of doing so. I came to Beijing with sufficient psychological preparation. I was going to sacrifice my life if I failed to fulfil my task. Now, as it's going to be so, I'll be more than happy to die here for the cause. I, Tan Sitong, won't leave Beijing as a loser. I can't leave for the sake of saving of my own skin. I want to die in Beijing and let everybody see that happen.'

'Mr Tan, we all understand your intention.' said the visitor. 'Before sending us here, Mr Huang Zhen explained everything to us. At that time he opposed you coming north and suggested that you go east to visit Japan and join the course of their revolution. But you thought that China was too weak and physically too feeble. To have a revolution in China is like asking a sick person to take a heavy dose of medicine, which will definitely do no good to China and maybe will not work either. If there is a moderate approach, it is advisable to give it a try. Since there was a chance in Beijing, we shouldn't let it slip away. Therefore, Mr Tan, you yourself were willing to enter the tiger's den or to jump into the frying pan to give it a try.

Mr Huang Zhen said that he understood perfectly well that Mr Tan and he, though taking differing routes, would eventually reach the same destination. No matter what route you take, Mr Tan, and no matter what means you adopt, we are all comrades. However, today we have found that you coming north has reached a dead end. Mr Huang Zhen is afraid that you will die in vain, and has sent us here to accompany you to the south. Since you have got nowhere to stay in Beijing, it is meaningless for us to let you stay here. Mr Tan, please understand the kindness of Mr Huang Zhen and the purpose of us coming to Beijing. Let us take you away!'

Smiling bitterly, Tan Sitong said, 'It's meaningless for me to stay alive in Beijing. But, it is meaningful for me to die in Beijing. Your great kindness and that of Mr Huang Zhen will always be in my heart. However, I'm already determined to sacrifice my life in Beijing. I'm really sorry that I can't accept your thoughtful kindness.'

Tan Sitong held his two hands together and up and then made a bow. 'The situation is extremely critical out there. I'm not going to show you my hospitality. Would you please hurry back to your place!'

Suddenly, the other two exchanged a glance. One stepped forward to the leader and whispered a few words in his ear. The leader raised his hand and waved it a little bit, signalling his disapproval, and then said, 'We admire Mr Tan's determination to sacrifice his life for the cause of virtue. But, well, Mr Tan, it seems that your determination will compel us to go back to our place empty-handed. We're unable to shoulder the burden of failing to fulfil the mission assigned by our comrades in the south. We therefore ask for your forgiveness if we force you to leave here with us.' While he was speaking, the three approached Tan Sitong.

Tan Sitong burst into a laugh, which contained dignity and appreciation. 'Gentlemen, wait a moment. I've something to say. If I must leave, please do give me a little time to prepare myself.'

'That's right. Give Mr Tan a little time to prepare himself.' A sonorous voice came out from the corner at the back of the house. All three turned their heads and saw a tall, sturdy man standing at the door. In a flash, there appeared four toughs behind the tall man.

Tan Sitong took a step forward and extended his greeting to the tall man, 'Master Wang Wu, these three gentlemen are not from the other side. They have been sent here by our brothers in the south, to escort me to their place.'

'We all know that,' said Wang Wu. 'We overheard your conversation. There aren't just three of them. There's a lookout outside who has been taken care of by my boys.'

'Is he okay?' asked Tan Sitong worriedly.

'Nothing serious. He just passed out. These revolutionaries are only good at revolution, and poor at Chinese martial arts. One punch can knock them down!'

'What do you mean by that?' the leader asked in a harsh voice.

Tan Sitong quickly grabbed his arm and said, 'Allow me to introduce you. This man is one of ours. You'll know him when I mention his name. He is the knight errant of Guangdong—Big Sword Wang Wu!'

The anger on the leader's face immediately melted away. Tan Sitong turned his head to Wang Wu: 'This man is our brother from the south.'

'Great! How are you?' Wang Wu held his two hands together and up to his chest as a gesture of greeting. The other man did the same.

'Let's make a long story short. My dear brothers, I am grateful for your kindness. However, I really can't leave Beijing. You know, political reform in all the foreign countries always began with bloodshed. I sincerely hope that China's political reform will start with the spilling of my blood.'

The leader shook his head. 'Mr Tan, Mr Huang Zhen told us that Mr Tan actually supports the revolution, and opposes reform, and, of course, opposes political reform in favour of modernization.

Mr Tan, you know perfectly well that that is the right course to take. Why do you refuse to take that right way? Why don't you try to be a reform fighter to terminate them, rather than insisting on being a martyr to be terminated by them? Why? Why? Is there any personal obligation, emotional obligation, or anything else? No matter what it is, Mr Tan, those obligations are trifling, as compared to the pursuit of our goal of striving to save the country. Taking those trivial obligations into consideration and overlooking the important issues is unseemly for a man.

Mr Tan, you are our big brother. You are a great hero and teacher in our eyes. We all look up to you. You don't want to leave here. What's happened to you? We really don't get it. Is there anything that is of more significance than you leaving here? You leaving here is not running away, nor is it a journey of no return. You may return triumphant to Beijing as a reborn freedom fighter. What is it, if you don't leave here? What we want is to fly our army flag on the top of the city gate, not to see your head hung up there. Your failure to leave will see your head hanging at the tip of a pole at the top of the city gate. Does that make any sense to you?'

The pitch of the leader's voice was getting higher and higher. He raised his right hand, linking his thumb and index finger in a circle signifying a hanging, and then suddenly dropped his hand on the table, making a very loud sound. The candlelight wavered with the shaking of the table. In the flickering light, the shadows of the men were wavering.

Tan Sitong sat calmly in the armchair. The back of the armchair was vertical. He sat with his back straight, closely paralleling the back of the armchair. The candlelight shone on his face. He didn't look well. Nonetheless, his facial expression was calm and serious, just like the face of a wax rendering of a brave religious martyr. A variety of expressions can be seen on the faces of the religious martyrs. The most attractive one is an expression of calm and seriousness, more of ease than generosity. That sacrifice is more one of peacefulness than excitedness. It is obvious that such great strength comes from the inner heart. Look at the calm and tranquil face of a person that has died a terrible death. They could have such a facial expression in death only because they had that identical facial expression in life.

The face of Tan Sitong showed the leader the shadow of death. In the head and the neck of Tan Sitong, he felt he could visualise that head being chopped off from that neck. He also felt that when the time came, the expression on this calm and serious man's face would not change in the least.

In this solemn atmosphere, Tan Sitong opened his mouth to speak: 'I'm deeply touched by your attempts to persuade me that I should try to be a reform fighter to terminate them, and not be a martyr to be terminated by them. That does make sense. The reason I don't want to leave is that, in addition to reform fighters, someone also needs to be a martyr. There are many projects on this planet, which require different types of people to complete, or to jointly accomplish.

Take Gongsun Chujiu, for example. Without Gongsun Chujiu's first becoming a martyr, Cheng Ying wouldn't have been able to be a humanitarian fighter. That great plan of saving the orphan of the Zhao family wouldn't have been fulfilled. Of course, our situation today is quite different from that of the Zhao family orphan. However, I always think that in the course of completion of a great project, there must be someone to make some sacrifice. We should not fear the sacrifice. As long as sacrifice is necessary, I believe I'm well qualified to be the person to sacrifice his life. To try to be that kind of man is what I have to do.'

'Mr Tan, please stop saying that!' interrupted the leader. 'Tan Sitong, you are such a great talent. How could we allow you to make such a sacrifice. If we must make a sacrifice, it should absolutely not be you!'

'Not me? Then who is the right person?' laughed Tan Sitong. Then he said calmly, 'I think it must be me. I'm the right person to do it. I took a leading role in the course of political reform. Now that this path seems to be the wrong one, and leads to a dead end, shouldn't I, Tan Sitong, be held accountable? If so, shouldn't I take some action in response?

I'm the person who took the lead in the course of political reform. I had to stay alive for that course and I also have to die for that course. Since the this path goes nowhere, I should not take a new course, but sacrifice my life for that cause, to prove that that cause leads to a dead end. This will warn its followers to find another course.'

'Even if we agree that what you say makes sense, is it necessary for you to take such a dramatic way to prove it, or to warn other people?'

'Besides sacrificing my life, is there a better way available? If the best way is to die, why shouldn't I? Please let Mr Huang Zhen know that I was mistaken, my course was the wrong one. Tan Sitong's way of thinking was wrong. I admit that it's all my fault. I not only admit my mistake, but I also take responsibility for it. I'm willing to die to show my personal will. To sacrifice my life is to prove that I'm wrong and you are right. To sacrifice my life is to warn the world and the Chinese people. To talk about reform with a corrupt regime that is fatally diseased is like "talking with a tiger to ask for its skin". It is absolutely impossible. I'm willing to use my dead body to prove how cruel the corrupt regime in China is. I'm willing to sacrifice my life to warn the people that this course goes nowhere.

From now on, everyone in China should be determined to take the course of revolution and never imagine that we can talk about political reform with a corrupt regime. I'm determined to sacrifice my life to prove what I say.'

Apart from the sad and thrilling voice of Tan Sitong there was dead silence in the room. At last, Wang Wu said, 'So long as Mr Tan is determined to stay in Beijing, will our friends from the south please honour his decision.'

———◦◦◦◦◦———

After the departure of the southern contingent, Wang Wu said, 'San Ge, as soon as you left the armed escort services company, we all agreed to follow your request. In addition to sending a man to investigate the confinement of the Emperor and survey the terrain over there, we've decided to protect you, San Ge. Therefore, we secretly followed you here and couldn't believe our eyes when we saw our friends from the south at the Association. So we came out to meet them. I came here to let you know that we've all agreed to try to rescue the Emperor, and the code name for the action is "Project Kun Lun". You needn't worry about the details. Our problem is that if we succeed, the Emperor resumes the throne and political reform is enacted, San Ge will have died unnecessarily, which will surely spoil our whole project. Therefore, we still advise you to leave the area for your own safety. Though it is unnecessary for you to go to a foreign legation for protection, at least you don't have to stay at the Association and wait for them to arrest you. San Ge, would you please not insist on your decided course for all of our sakes?'

That voice coming out from underneath Wang Wu's large beard and thick lips sounded so heavy, it doubled the effect of its sincerity and strength on the other people in the room. It made Tan Sitong's expression become very serious. However, he had already made up his mind. In order not to disappoint his beloved brothers on the spot, he slowly nodded and said: 'Give me a little time and I'll carefully rethink what Master Wang Wu has said. Would you please go to rescue the Emperor first? I must take care of a few trivial matters here. As soon as I am done, I'll come to your place to look for you.'

'How long will it take?' asked Hu Qi.

'About three to four hours.'

'How about you come over to our place no later than five o'clock tomorrow morning?' asked Hu Qi, eagerly.

'Okay, no later than five o'clock tomorrow morning,' Tan Sitong answered, but without sincerity.

'Do we have your word?'

'You have my word.'

───◦◦✧◦◦───

After Wang Wu and his men had departed, Tan Sitong instructed his old butler to go to bed first and started to take care of the things he had not finished earlier in the morning. He burned some things and put others away. Then he sat at the desk and wrote five letters.

The first letter was addressed to Wang Wu, Hu Qi, and their brothers.

> *Master Wu, Qi Ge and fellow brethren,*
>
> *The political reform movement wasn't expected to be a success. The objective of my participation was only to wake up my fellow countrymen. The only one who may enjoy success is perhaps Mr Kang. The Emperor is the only one among the Manchus who is not complacent with what they enjoy. Instead, under the influence of the Han race, he attempted to save the country. Nonetheless, he himself is now in danger and I simply can't sit idly by. Your plan to rescue the Emperor with Operation Kun Lun is a risky mission endangering your lives, and because of that I can't stay alive. I must die first. I therefore hope we can be brothers again in our next incarnation.*
>
> *Cordially,*
> *Sitong*
> *Dated: 9 August 1898*

The second letter was to his father.

Dear Father,

For my failure to follow your instructions, I deserve what I get today. Your beloved son is to die. I certainly hope you will forgive me. At the thought of this farewell, my feeling of reluctance lingers. Indeed, nothing can describe what I feel now.

Your beloved son,
Dated: 9 August 1898

The third letter was to his wife, Li Run.

My dearest wife,

Fifteen years ago we took our wedding vows and pledged to stay together. But now I must break my promise! As I write this letter, I am still alive; but by the time you read this letter, I will have gone to another world. The separation in life and death is indeed difficult. However, despite the departure of my body, my mind remains with you, and I will love you always. The tiny self is gone, but the lofty ideal lives on. We should both reside in the Buddhist Paradise generation after generation like love birds! We could even tease each other and laugh together. What I hope you realize is that the lavishness of life is only but a moment of a dream; it is not real! And death is a routine matter that should bring no joy or sorrow. I shall wait for you in paradise with our deceased son. We will meet again and stay together. My soul and our deceased son's will not be far away; together we shall meet you in your dreams. Please take good care of yourself.

Affectionately,
Sitong
Dated: 9 August 1898

The fourth letter was to his religious teacher, Yang Wenhui.

Dear Teacher Wenhui,

I had the opportunity to hear your lectures at the Jinling Auditorium, and thus am grateful to have learned from you. As the saying by Liang Zhuyu goes, 'In Buddhism, there are two ways to live: the finite impermanent world and the infinite permanent world. In the infinite permanent world, people prefer to live in the jungles, where they make their living by cutting wood and carrying water and eating very little. They use their labour and cultivate a good cause in order to save all beings after reincarnation. If this sort of suffering is intolerable, the alternative is to take the finite impermanent world route where the five relationships of prince to minister, father to son, husband to wife, brother to brother, and friend to friend, and the five constant virtues of benevolence, righteousness, propriety, knowledge, and sincerity, should be observed to the fullest extent. Regardless of how tedious or trivial or laborious the job is, it must be done graciously. There is nothing in between. If there is, it must be hell.' This is what he learned from his teacher.

While I fully understand the meaning of the two worlds, I feel neither of them belongs to me. It is the Buddha's Earth-treasury where I should go. One Buddha pledged that as soon as he reached the supreme perfect Bodhi, he would save all beings without any reservation. Another pledged, 'Unless I can save all beings from suffering and live in happiness leading to the world of Bodhi, I don't want to be a Buddha.' Yet another one pledged, 'To save all beings, even if I can't reach the supreme perfect Bodhi, I would settle for the Buddha's Earth-treasury.' '

I have often quoted from the sutras. Among the tens of thousands of words in the sutras, I have noticed that what the sutra really wants to convey is always one of two wishes. Now that I have engaged in the political reform movement, what I really have in mind is to reach the supreme perfect Bodhi so that I can save all beings. As the matter stands now, I am bound to fail in the political reform movement, that is, 'I can't fulfil my wish to become a Buddha'. Such being the case, 'If I don't go to hell, who else will?' I figure I should not be left behind and, speaking of death, I would rather be the first. If I make up my mind on the basis of the two-world concept, I will never be confused. I wonder if you approve of my plan.

Respectfully,
Student Sitong
Dated: 9 August 1898

The fifth letter was to his old classmate, Tang Caichang.

Dear Brother Chang,

I have broken the old taboo and have finished writing The Study of the Ideals of Confucius. *Having learned in the morning, I am happy to die in the evening.* The Study of the Ideals of Confucius *uses the pseudonym of 'written by a Taiwanese', as I wanted to vent my anger in the name of the Taiwanese. So, even though Taiwan has been ceded to a foreign country, the nationals there should not forget their parent country. In my previous letter, I reminded you that 'What we have been trying to do is to save the people despite the country's demise, since after the country has become history, its people are still there'. Now, on second thoughts, 'Even after I die, the country remains alive; though I may pass away, China will remain'. After my death, the political reform movement may be gone with me. I plead with you to accompany Huang Zhen to Japan to plan the course of revolution. How admirable is the course you are to take.*

Sincerely
Sitong at the study
Dated: 9 August 1898

Having written the letters, he put them into separate envelopes. It was very late at night. Tan Sitong woke up his old butler, Hu Lichen, and said to him, 'Keep the letters to my father, to my wife, and to my teacher, Mr Yang, with you for the time being, and then forward them separately to the right addressees. I entrust the letter my father sent to me, the gifts to my wife, and the souvenirs I have wrapped up here to your care. Please take them to our home town. Those large belongings are left here for you to handle. Now, send the letter to Master Wang Wu to the armed escort service company right away, take the letter to Mr Tang along with you, and ask Master Wang Wu to forward it to Mr Tang. These two letters can't be left at the Association and have to be sent right away. Go to the armed escort services company and tell him that I won't be able to go there, and tell him not to come over here to see me, because I will probably be gone.'

'My Master! Gone? Where are you going?'

'Where am I going?' Tan Sitong put a smile on his face and patted the shoulder of the old butler. 'I'll let you know, for sure. You just go ahead with what I asked you to do!'

CHAPTER TWELVE

From Imprisonment to Execution Ground

Early in the morning of 28 September 1898, Tan Sitong is prepared. The guests he had been expecting, officials from the government, arrive at his residence, where he awaits them. The officials escort their charge to the Ministry of Justice where he is formally placed under arrest and sent to prison.

The arrest warrant is issued in the name of the Guangxu Emperor, despite the fact that the Emperor himself is a prisoner on Yingtai Islet. Eight are arrested that day, including Tan Sitong. Among these is a prominent official, Zhang Yinhuan. The others wonder why Zhang Yinhuan has been implicated in the reform plot. The only apparent connection is that he comes from the same province as Kang Youwei. Zhang Yinhuan wonders about this as well. He finally realizes that the Empress Dowager must be seeking revenge for an indiscretion on his part committed long ago. He once gave her an emerald and the Emperor a ruby, instead of vice versa. He did not consider the palace tradition that dictates that red is worn by legitimate wives and green by concubines. The Empress Dowager was still sensitive about her past, and thus felt slighted, and even though Zhang Yinhuan had apologized profusely, she returned the gift. Ultimately, however, Zhang Yinhuan is spared from execution this time.

High officials are given special treatment in prison. Ordinary prisoners are subject to an elaborate system of bribes to avoid torture, pain, and a prolonged death, whether during their stay in prison or at the execution site. Without money or connections, a prisoner is bound to die from disease, torture, or other effects of the horrible prison conditions.

Tan Sitong is also exempt from the system, since he has many supporters who endeavour to make life in prison easier for him. In his solitary cell, he considers that this very cell has previously held other honourable men who died for a righteous cause. In the dark, his spirit communes with those of the departed, as the cells are unlit and pitch black at night.

As Tan Sitong is bound and led to the execution ground, he is calm and composed. He hails his executioner before the deed is done, and is accorded great respect. He dies unflinchingly, as he has long planned.

Meanwhile, Liang Qichao escapes to Japan, through the assistance of several Japanese citizens not officially connected to, but in sympathy with, the Japanese Government.

⋘◆◎⋙

Despite the fact that the ghost month (the seventh month of the lunar calendar) had just passed, on the twenty-fifth day of September 1898 (or the tenth day of the eighth month by Chinese lunar reckoning), Beijing was still under an atmosphere of gloom. As the light of dawn began to break, the gate of the Japanese Embassy slowly opened and there emerged eight Japanese, dressed in their national attire. With hats worn low over their eyes, they stepped into a waiting carriage. As they reached the railway station, just before embarking on the platform they were intercepted by a dozen or so Chinese officials. Politely, the officials asked to see their travel documents. Their passports showed the names Shu Hirayama, Yoshimasa Yamada, Shunzaburo Komura, Tauchi Noguchi, Momotaro, Toten Miyazaki, Kakicho, and Gessho. Aided by a fluent translator, the Qing officials initiated small talk in Japanese; however, when Gessho was addressed, Shu Hirayama hastened to cut in, speaking in Mandarin, 'I regret that Mr Gessho suffers from muteness and is unable to reply himself.'

The Qing officials suspiciously scrutinized Gessho and Shu Hirayama in turn. In a low, stern tone, Shu Hirayama added, in Japanese, to the translator, 'We demand that proper protocol be accorded to the diplomats of the Japanese Empire by your honourable country. It is hoped that no misunderstanding will ensue. Surely, it would not be pleasant for either side of the matter to be blown out of proportion!'

The translator duly whispered this to the officials. More words were exchanged among the officials, and then their ranks parted to allow passage to the travellers. Under the doubtful gaze of the officials, Gessho boarded the train.

A week later, the military vessel Oshima brought the eight Japanese back to their homeland. The local newspaper headlines trumpeted, 'Prime Minister Owaki formally announced the safe arrival of Qing Dynasty reform activist Liang Qichao through the upstanding assistance of Japanese citizens.'

As the Japanese Embassy's gate opened, so did the gate of the Liuyang Association. It was opened by a man attired in official court dress. He placidly secured both door panels to hold the gate wide open; then he paced in the courtyard for a while before returning to the house. He brewed himself tea in a lidded bowl.

Early tea was a habit he had acquired from the natives of Beijing. The residents of the city were fastidious about their tea. The tea leaves came in a wide variety ranging from Choice Buds, Sparrow Tongues, Fresh Spring, Pearl Orchid, to Jasmine. Jasmine was the most common brew, served with a tea service including a fine china teapot and six matching cups on a yellow copper tray. For the powerful and the wealthy, however, the preferred ware was the lidded bowl, which endowed the ritual with greater elegance and formality.

Sitting in an armchair, he turned sideways to look at the Western clock, which read half past six, still early in the morning. Suddenly, he heard a noise far off, which gradually came nearer; soon five or six armed officers rushed in.

Once inside the house, they were startled. The master of the house observed their panic calmly. Quietly he held up his tea bowl, removed the lid, and gracefully took a sip.

As they regained composure, their leader, the Nine-gate Commander-in-Chief, bowed courteously and respectfully announced, 'Lord Tan, your presence is officially requested.'

'Yes.' The master of the house smiled knowingly. 'I have been expecting you and had already opened the door in anticipation of your arrival.'

Calmly he lay down his tea bowl and stood up.

'I am alone in these quarters,' he said with a smile. 'My old servant will be returning shortly; please inform him of my whereabouts when he returns.'

With that, he put on his court hat, set it square, and walked out with his head held high. The officials scrambled to make way and escorted him to the waiting carriage.

The carriage stopped in front of the Ministry of Justice; Tan Sitong was duly ushered into the building. The clerk on duty produced the registry and requested the prisoner's identity and signature. Here, the touch of the debonair so ingrained in his nature revealed itself. Uttering not a word, he picked up the bamboo brush and wrote his name—'Tan Sitong'.

He was brought to the first cell of the prison's south wing. The room was gloomy and dirty, scantily furnished with a bed, a desk, and a chair, posing quite a sharp contrast to the prisoner's grand court attire.

When the irony dawned on him, he chuckled and spoke to himself the lines by Gong Ding'an:

> *Wearing formal court attire as I am driven to the execution ground, I feel*
> *   as happy as ever;*
> *My only regret is that my body can't be saved for my love, my beautiful*
> *   darling.*

As he finished the poem, he smiled with amusement; it reminded him of how, two thousand years ago, the prominent dignitary of the Han Dynasty had wagered all for the good of the empire's future. Prominent or not, this official had enraged the emperor; no leniency was given, off went his head immediately in the palace's east square. He was still in official court dress, and he was even denied his last words. Gong Ding'an, whose talent was much praised in the early Qing Dynasty, wrote the poem *The Path of Ease*, which stated that dying for a greater cause may be honourable, yet it is still a shame to never again be able to enjoy the pleasure of love. *C'est la vie*: one cannot have it all. Take what honour dictates, forsake what morality loathes, and for what cannot be obtained, have no regrets. Yet, by its very nature, loss is coupled with sorrow.

He thought of his final farewell letter to his wife: 'We should both reside in the Paradise of Buddhists generation after generation like love birds!' Despite these hopes for the next life, the uncertainty of his present life was a blatant fact. He was getting what he had set out to obtain; he had no regrets. But emotionally, he was unhappy about the permanent separation from his wife. By taking on the role of martyr, one can hardly escape criticism for being selfish. He alone had made the decision to separate from his wife. What about her? He sat on the bed with his thoughts running rampant, and became somewhat confused.

Fortunately, this trace of confusion was soon vanquished. This was life; though the world is filled with men of various types, one can only be one type, one can only choose one type; while at the same time one is obliged to turn down the other possibilities despite their fascinating, enticing elements. He could not be a martyr and expect to live to a gracious old age, nor be a reformer and a recluse at the same time, nor be angel and demon both in one, and certainly he could not both sacrifice himself for the nation and spare his wife widowhood. Two opposing forces pulled at him—to choose what was right and to reject the other; for the former, he must be instilled with foresight, for the latter, he must sever any means of return.

Having recognized that choosing is essential in life, and that life is also so very transitory, it becomes clear that one should not grieve over things that are forsaken or be ambivalent about one's choices. Life is so very short, there is not even enough time to exert oneself to the fullest in one's chosen course. To reserve something for any other pursuit, be it in the past, present, or future, is sheer wastefulness; moreover, it diminishes the efficacy of the role one has chosen. Nonetheless, today, being here, was quite different. There was no future ahead. Life could no longer be wasted—today's calendar was blank, today was a holiday, the beginning of a perpetual holiday.

Oddly, once such thoughts were unleashed, he thought of his lonely, helpless wife in their home town of Liuyang. They had been married for fifteen years, with only one little boy, whom death had torn from her bosom in tender youth. He owed the wretched woman so much. How would she bear the sorrow and the long nights when the news of his death reached home and the casket bearing his body was brought to her? It was unimaginable.

Then there was his father. His stepmother's scheming and abuse had led to a long period of acrimony with his father. It was not until the past few years, after he had grown up, that the relationship between them had taken a turn for the better. His father was the governor of Hubei Province, an official of prominence. But he had not wanted to implicate his father; so, yesterday morning, he burned some of the letters his father had written to encourage him to pursue reform.

He then made up some new letters containing reprimands; forging his father's calligraphy with great skill, these letters conveyed a concerned father's vehement objection to his son's involvement with revolt, and to add a finishing touch, he declared their father-son relationship forever severed. At the thought of this, he could not help but feel a certain mirth, thinking to himself, 'These bogus letters will invariably be found when they search the Association; they are sure to be fooled. Then Father will not be incriminated because of the path I have chosen for myself!'

Thus, Tan Sitong's thoughts wandered until interrupted by the so-called lunch shoved through under the prison bars, a miserable fare of one mixed grain bun and a bowl of soup. The jailer who served the lunch had the bearing of a typical underhanded watchdog, with rat-like eyes, feigning a haughty air. His glance glided past Tan Sitong, then quickly scouted around to be certain of privacy; then he produced a packet from his robe, and threw it into the cell falling just at Tan Sitong's feet. The jailer muttered in a low tone, 'A present for you.' This was followed by a loud, vicious grunt, 'When you're done, be sure to put the bowl back out!' Then he turned and stalked away.

Tan Sitong picked up the packet and retreated to the corner, with his back facing the door. He opened it, to reveal beef cold cuts and some red-hot peppers, a favourite with the natives of Hunan Province. Immediately he understood, thinking, 'There are kind-hearted people here who are concerned about my well-being.' In the darkness, he felt a wave of warmth inside.

The afternoon was spent in random thoughts. Tired of these, he decided to abandon such futile mental activity and to inspect his surroundings. He put the chair on the bed and climbed onto it; the height barely enabled him to look out through the window into the inner court of the ministry. The big elm tree in the courtyard suddenly reminded him, 'Isn't this the famous tree which the imprisoned Yang Jiaoshan, also known as Yang Jisheng, planted with his bare hands during the Ming Dynasty? Wasn't Yang Jisheng jailed in the secret police dungeon some three and a half centuries ago? Weren't the previous dynasty's prison quarters converted to serve as the current prison? Wasn't Yang Jisheng restrained in the same cell as he was in today?'

Realizing this, he nearly shouted aloud. Yang Jisheng, irrefutably a patriot of his time, was given one hundred and forty strokes in the presence of his peers for speaking words of truth to Emperor Shizong, exposing the misdeeds of his majesty's court. The disgrace of the flogging was followed by three years of incarceration, and in the end, this good servant of the empire was put to death while in his prime, aged forty. His wife pleaded with the Emperor to be put to death in his stead, but to no avail.

Yang Jisheng had proved himself to be a solid gentleman of substance. The flogging had caused him to lose consciousness many times, yet he survived. In prison, without flinching, he had sliced off the rotted flesh of his buttocks bit by bit with a fragment of broken pottery; the jailer who held a lantern over him shuddered as he watched. Learning of the caning, someone had offered Yang Jisheng snake gall bile, which reportedly could act as an anaesthetic, to which he replied: 'I have gall of my own—why call for that of a reptile!' Right before his decapitation, he left behind two poems, one of which read:

> The natural greatness of my soul returns to the sky,
> and my sincere heart can shine forever throughout the generations.
> Whatever I have not finished during my lifetime,
> I can leave to my successors to complete.

His prayer was answered. Twenty years after his death, Zuo Guangdou was delivered to this world, and martyred like Yang Jisheng at the age of fifty-one. Wasn't this also the same prison that held Zuo Guangdou? And if it was the first cell, Tan Sitong had the privilege to share the same quarters as his honourable predecessors. In defence of the truth, Zuo Guangdou was imprisoned, flogged, and tortured. The main form of torture used was charring; the flaming red-hot iron had left Zuo Guangdou scorched beyond recognition.

One of his pupils, Shi Kefa, bribed the jailer, and, dressed in ragged clothes and straw sandals, disguised himself as a menial labourer to go and see his teacher. It was a disfigured man leaning against the wall, maimed from the left knee down, that met his sight. The pupil fell on his knees to embrace his master, weeping aloud. Blinded, he still recognized the voice of Shi Kefa, and reprimanded him for the visit.

'The nation is in a desperate state; instead of dedicating your efforts to salvaging the state, here you are risking your life out of sheer sentimentality to see me, and for nothing. Once discovered, do you truly believe that your life will be spared? Off with you, or I shall personally see to your demise!'

So saying, he picked up the iron chain and gestured as though to throw it at his pupil who had no choice but to leave. Shi Kefa later remarked, 'My teacher has a heart of steel!' Zuo Guangdou's life was subsequently taken in prison. Another martyr followed Yang Jisheng! Zuo Guangdou had perished under the reign of Emperor Xizong in the Ming Dynasty, in a flash two hundred and seventy years had gone by, Tan Sitong mused.

From Yang Jisheng three and a half centuries ago, to Zuo Guangdou two hundred and seventy years ago, this prison, this very cell, had absorbed the last breaths of many transients. Their bodies existed no more. Though the physicality may have no mirror reflection, the appearance of form relies upon the element of shadow; the shadows of these martyrs still lingered on. The histories they had created, their passion and suffering, their indignation and woe, their lamentations and sighs, had all been caught in the air, frozen in the walls, seeped deep into the ground. The same prison, the same cell, throughout the rise and fall of various reigns, regardless of the individual fortunes of those incarcerated, delivered by the hands of fate, at long last served as their collective meeting ground.

Perhaps in the small hours, in the darkness of dismay, his predecessors' sought consolation from these apparitions; thus the torch against hardship was passed on, continuously and without end, serving as a constant witness to the cumulative wounds of China. Now it was Tan Sitong's turn.

The sight of the historic elm tree closed in on the cell, bringing forth such sorrows, familiarities, permanent separations, grievances, and tragedies; the descent of darkness only served to etch these sentiments even deeper. The jail cells had no illumination, only the corridors were dimly lit with flickering oil lamps. The cell was nearly pitch black. In such darkness, your own shadow leaves you. You yourself are a mere shadow. A shadow loves darkness, and darkness is its home. Once it has retreated to the darkness, a shadow is the master, since a shadow itself is darkness, made of the same hue.

Believing oneself to be of physical form is actually a false notion—at least in darkness, it is a mistaken perception. The self is not pure form; it is form infused with the shadow; light pushes the shadow out of form, yet the shadow follows close by, relentlessly, until light is exhausted. In darkness, sensations begin to surface: the shadow enters form, couples with form, causes it to disintegrate. Not that the shadow is gone, rather, it is form that is engulfed. What the shadow is to form is as dreams to slumber, blade to knife. The shadow is not incorporated by darkness; only its colour is deepened, and it is at such times that the soul seems to lose its footing. Man has never understood what the soul is; at a time such as this, it becomes even more clear that he knows nothing at all. If there is such a thing, it is the first to betray you in darkness; the soul is the mere shadow of a shadow. Thus in the darkness, the form of Tan Sitong slipped into shadow, interfusing with his forerunners.

And so the first night passed.

◇◈◇

At around five the next morning, Tan Sitong seemed to hear knocking on the wooden bars; composing himself, he saw a jailer beckoning to him, holding an incense stick. The incense was full length; common sense told him that the jailer had just started his shift. He climbed out of bed and walked over.

'Lord Tan?' The jailer whispered. 'I am an admirer of yours; the beef cold cuts and hot peppers at noon yesterday were a mere gesture of respect. Your servant brought letters and asked me to bring you a few necessities, which I will put under the door later.' Thus said, he looked around.

'At daybreak, would your lordship request pen and paper; just say that you wish to instruct your servant to bring some essential articles. When the writing instruments arrive, you might like to include a couple more letters, which may contain confidential information. I will collect them early tomorrow and deliver them for you.' Without waiting for Tan Sitong's response, he turned round and left.

At daybreak, Tan Sitong did exactly as he was told. He turned over the first letter openly to the guard on duty; the two additional ones were also written in a roundabout way for the sake of security.

The First Letter
To Tan's household servants Hu Lichen and Luo Sheng
Liuyang Association
Beibanjie Hutong

Upon receipt of this note, send immediately one thick quilt, one hand towel, one set of clothes, including socks and a foot towel, one cotton vest, one pair of heavy cotton trousers, one pillow, one large woollen hat, one pair of boots, one belt, and one set of articles for study.

Your master, Tan Fusheng

PS I also need one copper washing bowl, one pair of chopsticks, and one rice bowl.

The Second Letter

I have received your letter. Your unreserved loyalty and love have indeed made me happy. You may cancel my order to forward the secret report to Xie De.

Last night everything you delivered was in good order. I am all right here, and am not suffering. But you need not come to see me; if you do want to, you must ask Master Wang Wu to help you bribe your way in. Master Wang should be able to drop in; I will ask him to work out some way to improve my diet here.

We need not bother with the dispatch of the message to Hubei since it has been already sent by Mr Guo. Ge Shi may return to Hubei. I heard the Commander-in-Chief took away three books yesterday. Have they been returned yet?

The Third Letter

Upon receipt of this letter, rush to Yuanshun Armed Escort Service to see Master Wang Wu, telling him I am locked up in the head ward of the southern prison and ask him to do something to smooth things out here.

Further, on the ninth, the Nine-gate Commander-in-Chief' confiscated three of my books. Have they been returned yet? Give me a reply as soon as you can.

Ask Senior Master Guo Ziquan to inform Hubei of my present dilemma. Besides this, if you hear anything, let me know right away.

Your master, Tan Fusheng

It was his third morning of imprisonment when the second and third letters were stealthily taken out for him. The obliging jailer informed him that a total of eight men had been rounded up and were held now in isolation. Other than himself, there were Yang Shenxiu, Yang Rui, Lin Xu, Liu Guangdi, Kang Guangren, Xu Zhijing, and Zhang Yinhuan. Tan Sitong thought to himself, 'Since Xu Zhijing is the official who recommended us to His Majesty, his implication may be justifiable. But Zhang Yinhuan is simply from the same province as Mr Kang Youwei, a sheer coincidence. Moreover, he is one of the most knowledgeable officials when it comes to foreign affairs. Why has he been dragged into this?'

Meanwhile, Zhang Yinhuan was leaning against the wall of the end cell in the south wing sardonically reflecting. 'Accusing me of initiating a conspiracy with Kang Youwei; he and his lot are newly appointed to trivial offices; I had attained a high post long before their names were ever heard of. It would be more appropriate to claim that they sought my services for the intrigue.

The actual cause that led to my arrest lies with my misjudgement of a gift-tribute purchased in England on the occasion of paying tribute to Queen Victoria on the sixtieth anniversary of her coronation. I presented a ruby and an emerald to the Emperor and the Empress Dowager respectively upon my return. My open scorn for that odious head eunuch Li Lianying prompted him to comment, while the 'old lady' was admiring the emerald, 'Just like him to make such a distinction, does not Your Imperial Highness deserve the honour of red?'

'This pricked at the "old lady's" sore spot. In the matter of attire for the rear palace, tradition dictates that only the wives may wear red, while concubines must wear green. The Empress Dowager of the west wing had risen to eminence from the harem of concubines. In resentment for the insinuation, the jewel was returned. I kowtowed and begged for forgiveness; the "old lady" waved it off, but an opportunity for her vengeance has presented itself today.'

He mused on, 'When they came for me four days ago, I had not yet had my meal. I asked the Nine-gate Commander-in-Chief to let me finish, to which he agreed. When we left, they muttered, "Better leave your directions for settling your affairs with the mistress of the household"; it dawned on me then that death was intended as my punishment. So, without a fuss, I said it would not be necessary and I left with them. Killing me is naturally an easy matter, though it might be quite difficult for them to explain my death to the foreigners. Let's see how the "old lady" manages that!' With this, he chuckled craftily.

Being an official of considerable renown with many supporters, Zhang Yinhuan received much more favourable prison treatment than the others. By this time he was already sixty-two; his many years of court service had exposed him to artfulness of a wide variety. Familiar with the dark side of the system and of mankind, he had long learned to ride with the tides and deal with the caprice of politics, and through it all, he could always manage to rationalize and resolve things in his favour.

Yet this time, he felt certain qualms, though his optimism kept him from fretting. Already a member of the Grand Council, and actually holding a post equivalent to that of a minister of foreign affairs, he was still an outcast owing to the fact that he had not risen through the regular examination system. Seniority was strictly observed among those processed through the imperial examination structure. Those who earned their positions in the same year's examination referred to each other as 'old boy' and those preceding them were revered as 'senior learned one'. In offices and public squares alike, the calling of 'old boy' and 'senior learned one' reduced him to forlorn awkwardness. Fighting back with irony, Zhang Yinhuan proved quite capable of ridicule at others' and his own expense. He called in three celebrated actresses: Qin Zhifen, Wang Yaoqing, and Zhu Xiafen, and asked them to call him 'old boy', while he would playfully refer to them as 'senior learned one'. Now that he was imprisoned, the roles had changed. Those who had served prison terms before were now 'senior learned one' to him, while his alleged accomplices were the 'old boys'. He could not help but laugh at this absurdity.

Although he had not gone through the imperial examination system, he had had a solid education, and he was quite capable of reciting scores of the classics at any time. Bored with the tedium of prison, he sought amusement from verses, and as he started reciting Fang Bao's *Notes on Prison*, he was startled to realize that nearly two hundred years ago, when the Qing Dynasty scholar Fang Bao was sentenced to death, he was incarcerated in this exact same room.

Fang Bao, fortunately, was pardoned. His memoirs of his prison days were now available to his successors in misfortune. The old scholar described the haunting darkness of the facility as divided into four quarters with five cells each. The jailer would live in one of them, the one facing east onto a courtyard for light and with small windows for air. The remaining four cells would be walled from floor to ceiling, usually housing two hundred or more inmates altogether. Each day before dusk, all the locks would be secured, and all actions related to the call of nature had to be performed in the crammed quarters, wherein mingled the fumes of food and body odours. Winter was the worst time of year for prisoners. Poor prisoners had to sleep flat on the frozen ground; when spring arrived, none were spared from ailments, and deaths often occurred by the dozens. The rules of this punitive establishment dictated that the doors were not to be opened, without exception, until dawn. Thus, throughout the demonic night, the living would lay pressed against the dead. There was simply no escaping these horrific conditions, which also caused a rampage of infections.

Oddly enough, murderers and other serious offenders, probably due to their formidable nature, often survived, and even if infected, their constitution soon quenched the ailment.

The largest number of deaths were among those who had committed minor offences or were wrongfully imprisoned. Fang Bao asked one of the jailers, surnamed Du, 'In the capital, there is a prison facility directly are under the jurisdiction of Shuntian Prefecture, and the quarters under the command of the five-gate censor. Why is it then that the Ministry of Justice is still holding so many prisoners?'

Du explained, 'In recent years, Shuntian Prefecture and the five-gate censor have tried to avoid deciding cases of gravity; moreover, those under the Nine-gate Commander-in-Chief's jurisdiction also go to the Ministry's quarters. Meanwhile, of the fourteen divisions under the Ministry, the deputies, whether of Manchu or Han origin, the members of the justice department, the warden, and the jailers all profit from the prisoners, so naturally the more the merrier. Anyone who is remotely connected will be imprisoned on all imaginable grounds and means.

Once inside the prison, before questioning, on go the handcuffs and fetters. The accused are thrown into the old cells, tormented into a pitiful state, and just as they reach the limit of their endurance, they are counselled about setting bail.

Once released against bond, they still have to report back upon a summons. Extortion is then skilfully carried out according to the individual's family and their own financial circumstances, with bail determined at pre-arranged rates.

For those of above-average means, no expense is spared to make bail. Even to avoid the constant and excruciating pain caused by the handcuffs and fetters requires a considerable sum. For that miserable lot destitute in both finances and connections, the instruments of pain and degradation are flagrantly employed to serve as a constant intimidation and warning for the remaining prisoners. It is not unusual that of those jailed for the same crime, the ones of some means are let out on bond, while those who have been accused of lesser crimes, or even the innocent, if they have no financial means, suffer to no end. Filled with outrage, deprived of decent food and sleep, sick but without money to obtain a cure, these destitute prisoners generally ended up dead.'

Fang Bao also mentioned in the *Notes* that, 'For those under a death sentence, once the execution was scheduled, the executioner would wait outside the door and send off his people to demand money or valuables.

For prisoners of some wealth, terms and conditions were negotiated with the family; for the poorer inmates, the executioner would negotiate with them directly. If the sentence was dismemberment, they would offer, "Here are the terms, if you agree, a stab to the heart comes first; otherwise, I'll leave it throbbing after all the limbs are ripped off." If the sentence were hanging, the offer would go like, "Agree to these terms and I guarantee a quick death; otherwise, it will require other means to finish you off after three botched attempts." All forms of execution were profitable, except for decapitation which left little to bargain about. Even with decapitation, however, extortion was still feasible through the threat of withholding the ghastly severed head from the family.

Thus, the wealthy willingly turned over large sums, and the penniless sold what little belongings they had to ensure a quick, less painful death. Only those utterly destitute of resources would have to endure the atrocities. Trussing up the prisoners offered another source of extra income for the jailers as well. When their demands were not met, they made sure that some bones and tendons were severed in the process. Each year, during the customary execution season in autumn, though the emperor might demonstrate mercy by sparing six or seven out of ten on death row, all the prisoners still had to be trussed up and paraded to the West Square to await the final word on their destiny. Those injured in this process might take months to recuperate, or they might even be left maimed for life.'

Fang Bao had asked an old orderly: 'I'm sure they have no personal grudge against the prisoners; the object undoubtedly is merely to get a bit of money out of them. If the prisoners truly cannot come up with any, would it not be more humane to be lenient?' The old orderly explained, 'It is simply to assert the strict adherence to the rules, to warn the other prisoners as well as future ones. If the rules are not strictly enforced, some might begin to entertain ideas about the absolute necessity of complying with the rules of the game.'

Those who administered torture employed the same tactics. Among one group arrested together, three were subjected to the torture of wooden rods repeatedly compress-rolled over the limbs. For the cost of twenty taels, one only suffered mild injury to the bones and took only one month to fully recover. If one gave double that amount, there were merely surface wounds which disappeared in twenty days. If one paid six times that sum, a prisoner was up and tottering about the same evening. Someone had asked the same orderly, 'Among the general public, some prisoners are rich, and some aren't; every official involved gets his share, so why is it necessary to dictate different sums, on a sliding fee scale, as it were?' The orderly responded, 'Without any distinctions, who would be willing to pay more?'

Fang Bao wrote further, 'Every senior clerk of the ministry kept a set of forged seals; the official documents, in the course of travelling from the central to the provincial level, were often altered. Critical words could be added or eliminated, and this was generally not discernible to the responsible officer. Such practice was only withheld on documents for presentation up to His Majesty or between departments.

According to the law of the Qing Dynasty, in the case of a robbery where no killing had been committed, or where the number of robbers was high, the one or two masterminds were to be executed at once. The remaining accomplices would be held until the autumn to wait for a ruling on sentence reduction or exile to hard labour. The common practice was that when the Ministry of Justice had presented the ruling to the emperor, where there was a case for execution on sight, the executioner would wait by the door, and upon orders, truss up and deliver the prisoner to the execution site without a moment's delay.

There was one case where a certain pair of brothers were imprisoned for robbing a state granary. By law, they should have been executed promptly; the verdicts were drafted. Then a certain official said to them, "For a payment of one thousand taels, I'll keep you alive." When asked how he would accomplish this, the official answered confidently, "This is not in the least bit difficult. It only calls for producing a different written report to the emperor. The verdict need not be changed, we need only replace the names of these two brothers with any two from the list who have no relatives, and at the time for sealing the memorial, substitute the original with this version. That will do the trick."

One of his colleagues then questioned him, "This can fool the deceased, but our superior is not blind; should he discover and re-petition, it would be the death of us all." The official replied with a smirk, "Re-petitioning would surely cost us our lives, but our superior invariably would lose his job for supervisory incompetence. Naturally, the man would not stake his post on two measly lives; therefore, in the end, there is still no reason to take our lives." And it was thus carried out accordingly. The two scapegoats were executed on the spot. The supervisor was aghast and horrified, but in the end dared not pursue the matter. Fang Bao said that during his incarceration, he had also seen these certain brothers whom the fellow identified as "the two kept alive at the expense of two other heads".'

As Zhang Yinhuan recited the article by Fang Bao, he verified its statements against his actual environment, and found that he was housed in the finest cell. In *Notes on Prison*, it is documented that an official under criminal charges could be accorded the courtesy of better quarters. Since he was now given a cell to himself, not exposed to the darker side of the prison, this might well be considered a courtesy.

At this point, intermittent and frightful shrieking reached him from afar, further confirming his perceptions. He was a seasoned bureaucrat, pickled through and through. He recalled an account illustrating the diversity of the corruption of the wardens at the prisons under the Ministry of Justice. One of these was called the 'full package', which was a means of buying everyone off, at all levels, for optimal treatment. There was also what was known as 'two end-caps', which bought off only the internal and the upper level, without spending on the external and the lower ranks. Another format was called 'case knock', a piecemeal approach, whereby a prisoner paid for each convenience as needed. There was also 'plunge aid', exclusively designed to reduce the extent of physical pain at the time of infliction . . .

As Zhang Yinhuan reflected, he chuckled, and muttered to himself, 'My treatment this time amounts to a "full package", except that it doesn't cost me a penny; the title "vice minister" in itself keeps these greedy wardens in awe. There is a saying, "With court connections, life is infinitely easier." Today, my version is, "With a grand official title, life in prison is made easier." If not for the shield of my title, I dare say I would be obliged to experience the full treatment depicted in *Notes on Prison*.'

—◇◆◇—

Simultaneously, a contrasting scene was taking shape in another prison, that of Yingtai. Yingtai is a small island in Zhongnanhai Lake. Since the Ming Dynasty, the palace halls had been built on this islet; by the Qing Dynasty, a renowned architect transformed it into a fantasy land, based on the legend of China's Penglai Mountain. Then it was further transfigured into luxurious quarters of confinement, where the Emperor Guangxu was detained. Other emperors during their reigns had sought their pleasures there. The scenario displayed a lone, young emperor loitering about the fantastical landscape with no hope of returning to his rightful palace. Despite being held prisoner, orders continued to be issued under his name. First, on 24 September, or the ninth day of the eighth month in the lunar calendar, Emperor Guangxu, the advocate of political reform, all of a sudden ordered the removal of Tan Sitong and five other officials. In the same decree, the Commandant of Gendarmerie in Beijing was ordered to arrest the deposed officials and turn them over to the Ministry of Justice on criminal charges. Two days later, a second decree followed, ordering the Grand Minister of State, in conjunction with the Ministry of Justice and the Court of Censors, to conduct a thorough and strict interrogation. In formality, the 'thorough and strict interrogation' took only one day, because on 28 September, or the thirteenth day of the eighth lunar month, a decree was issued:

> *To the Members of the Grand Council:*
>
> *Kang Guangren, Yang Shenxiu, Yang Rui, Lin Xu, Tan Sitong, and Liu Guangdi are to be executed immediately for the crime of rebellion. The executions will be supervised by Gang Yi; troops from the infantry headquarters will be assigned to prevent disturbances.*

Early in the morning, before this order had even been issued, the Board of Punishments officials were already busy harnessing the carts to take the prisoners to the execution ground.

This task had to be performed before the condemned men could be taken to the execution ground. The carts were harnessed to horses or donkeys and everything made ready for departure; the prison echoed with the noise of the preparations. Zhang Yinxuan called to one of the warders patrolling the corridors, and asked in a soft voice, 'Eight people were brought in here; are one or two going to be left behind in the prison?' The guard replied, 'I heard that Yang Shenxiu and Kang Guangren are to be left behind.' This was followed by the sounds of the six carts being made ready.

Zhang Yinxuan thought to himself, 'The "old lady" is serious about getting her revenge. Oh well, I've lived long enough anyway; if I am to die, so be it.'

Just as Zhang Yinxuan was sitting quietly awaiting his death, the sound of cell doors being opened could be heard far off. The different noises all melded into one, but he did not hear the sound of voices approaching his cell in the southern wing—he had escaped death.

Six doors were opened, those of Tan Sitong, Yang Shenxiu, Yang Rui, Lin Xu, Liu Guangdi, and Kang Guangren.

⟨⟩⟨⟩⟨⟩

The Board of Punishments Prison had evolved from the Imperial Prison of the Ming Dynasty, and it was still popularly referred to as the 'Emperor's Prison'. Over the centuries, the prison had developed its own ways of doing things. The northern and southern wings each had two doors, one each at the east and west corner. When prisoners were released or taken to appear in court, they went out through the east door; when they were taken away for execution, they went out through the west door. When Liu Guangdi had been arrested he had been a senior official in the Board of Punishments; as such, he knew all about the regulations, and he knew that this door led to death. Of the six, he was the most familiar with the procedures for execution; he found it highly incongruous that he was now experiencing them in person.

According to common practice, apart from the main central entrance of a government office, there was also another entrance on the left known as Green Dragon Gate, and another on the right known as White Tiger Gate. White Tiger Gate was normally kept locked; it was only opened when a criminal was being taken out for execution.

The usual practice was for the prisoner to be fooled into thinking that he was being taken to court, or that a member of his family had come to visit him. As soon as the criminal passed through the second door outside their cell, a warder would suddenly give them a shove from behind, while shouting out, 'Take him!' More warders who had been hidden on either side of the door would rush forward. One would grab his queue, another would shackle his feet, two more would grab him by the shoulders. They would then all shout out together, 'Got him!' They would then rush him along as though they were carrying a pig. He would be carried down to the bottom of the steps below the main building and forced to kneel down. The original arresting magistrate would read out a warrant to the prison governor. The governor would check the name, age, and place of birth of the condemned man; once this was completed the prisoner was informed that he had been sentenced to death and that the punishment was to be carried out immediately. The order was then given to truss the prisoner up, and their name was ticked off the list in red ink. The writing brush was then thrown onto the ground in front. According to tradition, a writing brush that had been used for this purpose had the power to cure malaria; people would therefore rush forward to try to seize it.

Trussing up the prisoner was an art in itself. As soon as the order was given, the warders would grasp the prisoner's clothing and rip it. The torn upper garment would be pulled down from his shoulders. The two warders grasping his shoulders would then start to pull his arms back. If the prisoner was a strong man and resisted them, the warders would give him a tap on the shoulder blades with a small hammer they carried with them; the prisoner's arms would then automatically relax and could be bound.

The standard method of tying the prisoner up was the 'five flowers' method. A rope was placed so that it extended down from the prisoner's head, with the two ends on either side; it was then pulled taut. The two ends were then tied around the prisoner's wrists, behind his back; the rope was positioned so that it ran between the thumb and forefinger, and then knotted. This was the most secure method of tying someone up. Once the 'five flower' trussing had been completed, the prisoner was given meat and wine. Three pieces of raw meat were skewered on a stick and rubbed across the prisoner's mouth, to symbolize their having been given food; they were also given a large bowl of wine to drink. Sometimes camphor was mixed into the wine, which could make the condemned man go unconscious so that they felt less pain. Of course, camphor was only available to those who had bribed the guards. Once the prisoner had been given his meat and wine, he was placed in a basket, which was picked up by two warders and carried out through White Tiger Gate.

With the exception of Kang Youwei's brother, Kang Guangren, Liu Guangdi and the others were all high-ranking officials, so they were treated with some courtesy. After they were pushed out through the west gate, each was placed on a donkey cart. On top of the donkey cart was a wooden cage, inside which they were placed with their head sticking out. Viewed from a distance, the head appeared like a round handle on top of the cage.

Amidst the sound of shouting, the donkey carts got under way. Several hundred soldiers accompanied them. All were headed for the same place—Caishikou.

⟨○◆○⟩

Caishikou was one of the busiest districts in Beijing. Most people coming from the south, regardless of rank or station, would have to pass through here after crossing over Lugou Bridge and coming through Guang'an Gate to enter the inner city of Beijing. Caishikou had been famous as a place of execution for six hundred years; it was originally known as Chaishikou. Six hundred years before, a Song minister named Wen Tianxiang, who had been imprisoned by the Yuan for four years and still refused to submit to them, was executed here. On his way from prison to the execution ground, his manner was solemn and dignified. He said to the supervising official, 'Everything I could do for the Song Dynasty, I have done: it is over.'

By executing Wen Tianxiang there at the age of forty-seven, the Yuan regime was actually enabling him to complete the task he had set for himself, because by undergoing public execution it was possible for him to send a message to others. The people of China, even including his enemies, had great respect for this martyr; that was why a temple was subsequently built in his honour.

The most visually striking part of the Caishikou district was the T-junction, from where, looking north along an avenue bordered by two rows of locust trees, one could see the towering Xuanwu Gate, the symbol of imperial power. The emperors had chosen this T-junction as the perfect place for public execution; by executing people at such a busy spot, the death could be made to have maximum effect. Markets and execution grounds were not clearly separated from one another. The Xiheniantang Drugstore to the north of the T-junction was one example of this. The Xiheniantang Drugstore had been in existence for several hundred years. It was rumoured that the calligraphy on the sign above the door was the work of Ming minister Yan Song. Whenever an execution was to be held, an awning would be erected next to the store. Underneath the awning stood a long table and a chair. A tin pen-stand was placed on the table, in which was placed a vermilion writing brush; this was for the use of the supervising official.

The supervising official was generally dressed as if for battle, riding a large horse. He rode to the execution ground preceded by musicians beating gongs to clear the way. He was accompanied by soldiers bearing the character for 'courage' embroidered on their jackets, together with the executioners. The executioners had the most striking appearance. They either wore red coats or went bare-chested. They held long swords, and bore fierce expressions.

Executioners made a good living. Generally speaking, they received 3.6 taels of silver for every person they killed, and the best executioners might kill several dozen people in one day. On top of their regular payment they received bribes from the victim's family, generally around thirty to fifty taels. These bribes were paid so that the executioner would kill the condemned person as quickly and painlessly as possible.

By custom, the executioners used 'demon-head swords', which had the head of a demon carved into the hilt. The end of the sword-blade was broad and heavy; the part nearer the hilt was narrow and light. When executing someone, the executioner would hold the sword so that the back of the blade was parallel with his forearm; it was then lined up with the weakest part of the victim's spine at the neck. The sword would then be brought down with all the executioner's might to chop off the head.

Given the level of skill involved, this was not something you could teach yourself to do; the techniques used were passed down from father to son, or learned by apprenticeship from a master. An apprentice would start to practice 'pushing tofu' every day as soon as it was light. They would practice chopping up tofu into small slices. Once they were skilled at this, they would practice chopping along the line of black threads laid on top of the tofu. Once they had mastered that, copper coins would be placed on top of the tofu; they now had to practice cutting along the line of the threads while leaving the copper coins untouched. After the apprentice had graduated from 'pushing tofu', they then had to learn how to feel a monkey's neck. They had to be able to find the space between the first and second vertebrae, and then deduce from this where the space would be on a human body, so that when executing someone they could cut cleanly between the vertebrae, thereby reducing the pain suffered by the victim.

This was why the condemned man's family had to pay a bribe to the executioner. If the execution was carried out by an inexperienced executioner, or an experienced executioner pretending to be inexperienced, it could be a very painful process.

In addition, because traditionally there was a taboo against dying with one's corpse not whole, if the executioner made the killing stroke precisely so as to just cut the windpipe, it was possible to leave the head so that it was still attached to the body by a strip of flesh; in this case the dead person could be considered to have died with their body whole. An executioner who was skilled enough to do this could be sure of receiving large bribes. Most executioners were not this skilful, but even if the head was separated from the body it was possible to hire an expert to sew it back on, to meet the wishes of the dead person and their family.

So there was no getting round the paying of bribes to the executioners; if the bribes were not paid, there was no telling what they would get up to. And it might not end when the condemned man was dead. For example, to stop the blood from the victim's neck from spurting everywhere, the executioner would give the body a kick immediately after cutting off the head, so that the blood sprayed forward rather than back. People would then rush forward carrying pieces of steamed bread with which they would mop up the blood; according to tradition, this blood-soaked bread could be used to cure tuberculosis. Various parts of the victim's body might also be cut off for use in the production of medicines, including even the intestines.

However, these practices applied only to ordinary criminals. When the condemned man was a high official, he would be treated much more politely. The executioners would not try anything funny, nor would the condemned man be carried to the execution ground in a basket; they would be taken in a donkey cart instead. There had even been cases where the executioner would kneel and pray for the condemned official before the execution, praying that they be granted admission to heaven before cutting off their head. Anyone who had been a high official was still treated with respect even at the moment of execution.

Of course, the showing of respect was a two-way process. It depended partly on the status of the official, but also partly on the official's behaviour. There was some variation in the behaviour displayed by Tan Sitong and the five others after they were placed in the donkey carts: some were nervous; some were downcast; some were defiant; and some were cowardly. Tan Sitong, however, was a model of self-possession.

The awning by the side of the Xiheniantang Drugstore had been hurriedly erected; the table, chair, and writing instruments were all in place. On this occasion, the supervising official was no ordinary official; it was Grand Councillor Gang Yi, a Manchu official of the highest rank. He gave the order for the condemned men to be taken down from the carts. In accordance with regular practice, he inspected the condemned men to confirm their identity, ticked off their names with the vermilion brush, and then threw down the brush.

At this point Tan Sitong called out to him, saying that he wished to speak to him. Gang Yi did not wish to be spoken to by a condemned man. He waved for his subordinates to carry Tan Sitong away, while covering his ears with his hands to indicate that he would not listen.

When Tan Sitong saw how embarrassed he had made the old official, he couldn't help smiling. He smiled, and said no more. He was carried out into the middle of the execution ground, which was muddy despite the bright sunshine. He looked round and saw crowds of people who had come to watch the executions; all were silent. 'This is my country: these are my people,' he thought to himself. 'On a sunny day in a dark age they are here to watch us shed our blood. If we had been successful, they would have applauded us and joined us. Now that we have failed, they are standing by to watch us die. We came to save them, because they could not save themselves. Today, they see that we cannot even save ourselves. In their eyes, we have failed. They don't realize that failure too has its joyful side, because failure is the starting point for future victory. My poor compatriots! They don't know; they will never know.'

As the executioner made his preparations, Tan Sitong looked up at the clouds in the sky above; his thoughts began to fly by like the clouds. He thought of how, before their death, professional criminals would shout out in defiance, 'Twenty years from now I will be a man again!' He had the feeling that he should shout out something similar, but he wanted to avoid saying anything related to reincarnation. He did not believe in reincarnation; to believe that you lived again after your death was a form of cowardice, of egoism. The proper way to live and to die was to have no belief in the possibility of any kind of afterlife. He smiled. Suddenly, like a gap in the clouds, he shouted out, startling everyone present:

> *While I have a plan to annihilate the hostile party,*
> *I am nonetheless powerless to do anything.*
> *What a happy ending,*
> *Now that I am to die for a just cause!*

The astonished executioner nodded his head in approval. Tan Sitong smiled at his compatriot with the demon-head sword. Most condemned men would beg the executioner to give them a quick, painless death, but he would not deign to ask this; he had sought and achieved a righteous end, and was already fully satisfied.

Tan Sitong's body lay still on the ground at Caishikou. His bloody head had rolled to one side. Tan's old family servant, Hu Lichen, rushed forward along with another old family servant, Luo Sheng, and the manager of the Liuyang Association. They had asked the Xiheniantang Drugstore to provide them with a basin of water, which they used to wash off the dirt and bloodstains. Holding back their tears, they looked at their young master. His eyes were staring, and his mouth was open, as though he had not died in peace, but rather had died crying out against an injustice. As the head had been cut off some hours before, it was already starting to change its appearance. At first glance it appeared to be shrinking, but in fact this was just the prelude to it swelling up. In another twenty-four hours it would have swelled up so much as to be almost unrecognizable.

The old servants waited impatiently for the coffin to arrive. In the afternoon, it finally arrived, along with the head-stitcher. He skilfully threaded the head back onto the neck, stitching it up at both the front and the back, so that the corpse could be said to have been made whole again. They placed the body inside the coffin, and then nailed the lid shut. The old servants lit an incense stick and knelt before the coffin, kowtowed, and then raised the coffin overhead and started to carry it westwards. The first crossroads they passed was the entrance to Beibanjie Alley; the Liuyang Association was at the southern end of the alley. The old servant Hu Lichen thought sadly, 'I had no idea the young master's residence was so close to the execution ground!'

They continued in a westerly direction. After passing through a further two crossroads they turned left into an alley. They walked down to the end and turned right; an old temple came into view. They stopped to rest for a moment outside the temple gate. Hu Lichen went inside to make the arrangements, while Luo Sheng looked up at the gate under the setting sun. Over the gate were the words 'Fayuan Temple'.

CHAPTER THIRTEEN

They are all History

Tan Sitong's coffin is removed to Fayuan Temple, where Abbot She and Pu Jing are still residing. In sorrow, the two monks speak of the past. Master She finally relates to Pu Jing the story of his life, the journey that led him to Fayuan Temple. His story also explains his connection to Big Sword Wang Wu. At the same time, Master She tells Pu Jing that the time has come for Pu Jing to leave the temple and go into the world to save people.

Two years later in 1900 the Emperor, still under house arrest, is fetched by several eunuchs and the entire royal household flees the imperial city and the capital of Beijing. The capital is under siege by foreign troops in response to the Boxer Rebellion. The royal entourage, travelling on foot, eventually arrives in Xian over a year later.

The Boxer Rebellion is a time of chaos, anarchy, and anti-foreign sentiment; the Qing Dynasty is in its death throes. During this time, an incident takes place at Fayuan Temple in which both Master She and Big Sword Wang Wu are killed.

In 1908 the Empress Dowager dies, and the Guangxu Emperor dies as well under mysterious circumstances. Her death after forty-seven years of rule, which did nothing to end the degredation of the country, opens the door for the revolution of 1911 and the establishment of the Republic of China that same year.

⟶∘◆∘⟵

The coffin was placed in a room at the rear of Fayuan Temple, supported by two long benches. There was no writing on the front to say whose coffin it was; only a few people knew who was inside. The old retainers were busy arranging the coffin on the benches, sweating with the exertion. Hu Lichen pulled out a handkerchief, but instead of using it to wipe his brow, he used it to wipe the coffin dry, as carefully as he had wiped the bloody face of his young master a few hours before. Finally, they set up the incense burner table, knelt down together and kowtowed, and then burst into tears, railing bitterly against the unfortunate end their young master had come to.

At the entrance to the room where the coffin was placed an old monk stood in silence; it was Master She. At his side stood Pu Jing, now a grown man. They did not say a word, but sorrow was etched all over their faces. After a few minutes they walked away. They walked over to the old steles in front of the Daxiong Hall, where again they stood in silence.

'Pu Jing,' Master She said at last. 'What you have just seen is what happens to those who follow the path of reform! It is ten years now since we met Kang Youwei, standing in front of these old steles here. In those ten years, he refused to give up. When he was defeated, he picked himself up, again and again. In the end he was able to persuade the Emperor to follow the course of action he proposed, joining up with Tan Sitong and the others to launch a reform movement. But although he appeared to have been successful, in fact it was a defeat. Kang Youwei's ten years of effort proved only one thing, the thing which Tan Sitong has demonstrated with his blood—that the path of reform does not work. Their defeat has proved that it does not work.

The conclusion we must draw from this is that a revolution will be necessary to save China. Tan Sitong could have escaped, but he chose to die; the main reason that he did so was to demonstrate this fact. I am old, and there is nothing I can do. But I think that you should prepare to leave the temple; you should travel around the country and become a revolutionary.

For a true Buddhist, the temple is only a starting point or a finishing point. When the temple has aroused Buddhist compassion in you, one should leave the temple to go out and save the world. Perhaps one day, when you have played your part in saving the world, you can come back to the temple to die. Or perhaps, if you have tried to save the world and failed, your body will find its resting place in this temple, like Tan Sitong. Either way, this would be more meaningful than spending the whole of your life here doing nothing but eating vegetarian food and chanting the sutras. I believe the time has come for you to go; you are already twenty-six. Do as I say, and get ready to leave.'

As Master She spoke, he gently patted Pu Jing's head. Pu Jing looked solemnly at his master. He lowered his head, then raised it again, and said, biting his lip: 'Ever since I came to this temple at the age of eight, I have been worrying that one day you would tell me to leave. Eighteen years have gone by, and you have finally said those words to me. Of course, I know that it's not because you want to get rid of me, but because you want me to go out and do the things I should do. So I will do as you say; I will go out and travel the country. My only regret is that I won't be here to look after you.'

Master She smiled, and again patted Pu Jing on the head. 'Just think, Pu Jing. Mr Tan has died leaving a father and wife behind him. He didn't spend all his time taking care of them. He ignored his own private emotional ties and dedicated himself to the welfare of his four hundred million compatriots. This is the kind of spirit a monk should have. The Confucians say you should "treat other people's parents as you would your own parents". But for a Buddhist, the proper course of action is to "Care for other people's parents and ignore your own". People who are concerned for humanity do not worry about their own personal feelings.'

'In that case, Master, why did you not become a monk until you were in your thirties?' Pu Jing asked. 'Why did you take the temple as your finishing point at such a young age, rather than as your starting point?'

Master She was taken aback. However, he soon recovered his composure. He turned around to face the temple gate; he did not look at Pu Jing.

'You asked me this question ten years ago. I didn't answer it, saying only that you would know one day. That day has not yet come. All I can tell you is that ever since I became a monk at the age of thirty, I have had the feeling that Fayuan Temple was not to be my finishing point. Although I am sixty-two, I still have the feeling that there is something left for me to do, something I have to complete. I am still not entirely sure what that task is, but I know what it is not; it is not to stay in this temple until I die. Fayuan Temple is not my finishing point. Pu Jing, we met here in Fayuan Temple, and we will die here. Let us say goodbye with a light heart . . . '

As Master She was speaking, two fierce-looking men walked in through the temple gate. As they approached, one of them, whose face was covered with whiskers, directed a piercing gaze at Master She; he stared at him in a very unfriendly way. Master She became aware of this, and his expression changed at once; he frowned and stopped speaking. The two men brushed past them and went into the temple without speaking to them. Pu Jing found it very strange.

'Master, you seem to know who they are, but they seem to be hostile to you.'

Master She looked at him, then looked up at the sky and sighed softly.

'Pu Jing, you are very observant. I do indeed know who they are. The man with the long beard is none other than Big Sword Wang Wu.'

'Big Sword Wang Wu?' said Pu Jing, surprised.

'That is correct,' Master She said simply. 'He must be fifty-two now; he was ten years younger than me. When I knew him, he was only seventeen; that's thirty-five years ago now.'

'You've known him for that long?'

'Yes.'

'He obviously recognized you. How long is it since you last saw each other?'

'More than thirty years,' said Master She. 'I suppose I might as well tell you. I never told you the reason why I became a monk; now that we are about to part, I will tell you.

Big Sword Wang Wu and I lived through the same experience, an experience which neither of us has ever been willing to reveal; we were both once "long-haired rebels". "Long-haired rebels" is the term the Manchus used to describe the Taiping army. During the Taiping Rebellion, the Taipings called for people to abandon the custom imposed by the Manchu government of wearing the hair in a queue, and go back to the traditional Chinese practice of allowing the hair to grow long. That is why we were called long-haired rebels.

At the time of the Jintian uprising, nearly fifty years ago now, the Heavenly King Hong Xiuchuan was thirty-seven, and the other Taiping Kings were all aged around thirty; the Yi King, Shi Dakai, was only twenty. Initially, they were unified, idealistic, and revolutionary, but after they took Nanjing and had half of China under their control, they started to become corrupt and fight among themselves.

Only Shi Dakai remained true to their original ideals. While he was near Wuhan he heard that his comrades were fighting among themselves in the capital, Nanjing. The Eastern King, Yang Xiuqing, had been killed. Shi Dakai rushed back to try to prevent the revolutionary army from breaking up; while he was advancing on Nanjing, his whole family was murdered. In the end, he was unable to win the trust of Hong Xiuquan, and he was forced to leave. He took over one hundred thousand men with him. He led his army through Jiangxi, Zhejiang, Fujian, Hunan, Guangxi, Hubei, and Sichuan. In the end, he was forced to retreat to Yunnan; by this time he had only forty thousand men left.

He failed in his attempt to cross the Dadu River in Xikang, and found himself in desperate straits. Not only was his army in the middle of a wilderness, they were surrounded by Qing troops and local tribesmen. At that time, Big Sword Wang Wu and I were among his subordinates. We had nothing to eat; we were reduced to eating wild grasses. When those were finished, we killed our horses and ate them. By then there were only seven thousand of us left. We broke through the encircling Qing troops and fled to a place called Laoyaxuan, where we again encountered the enemy, and could go no further. Two days later, Shi Dakai disappeared.

They say that he gave himself up to the Qing army in an attempt to save the lives of his remaining seven thousand troops. However, when we put down our weapons and surrendered to them en masse, they started to massacre us. Several thousand of us were killed, and the remainder fled in all directions. Shi Dakai's family had been killed by his own side in Nanjing long before; only his fourteen-year-old daughter, Shi Qixiang, escaped. She was beautiful, and a skilled writer. She had accompanied the army on its long march for six years.

Because I was well educated, Shi Dakai had made me his secretary, which meant that I saw a lot of Qixiang. As time passed, we fell in love with one another, and Shi Dakai planned to make me his son-in-law. But with the army constantly on the move it was impossible to arrange a marriage. After Shi Dakai's disappearance at Laoyaxuan, there was a rumour that the man who had gone to surrender to the Qing army was in fact one of Shi's subordinates who looked like him, who had gone in Shi's place and allowed himself to be killed so that Shi could escape.

When the Qing troops started to massacre us, I fled into the mountains with Qixiang, Big Sword Wang Wu, and about a hundred others. We hid in the mountains and waited to see how things would turn out. There were many among us who favoured trying to slip across the Dadu River. Before we made the attempt, we sent out scouts, who came back with a strange piece of news. They said that a boatman had ferried an old man across the river one evening. They started talking; the boatman, who was very perceptive, got the feeling that there was something strange about the old man, but he didn't like to ask too many questions.

When the old man got out of the boat, he looked back towards the high mountains and sighed, saying, "The earth is still the same, but where has our power gone?" He then walked off at a brisk pace and disappeared. As the boatman described it, he walked with the gait of a young man.

At dawn, the boatman discovered that there was an umbrella in the boat. The umbrella shaft was of iron, with four characters inscribed on it: 'Yu Yi Wang Fu'. The boatman suddenly realized that the umbrella must belong to the Yi King, Shi Dakai. When we heard this news, everyone became very excited, because we knew that Shi Dakai had an umbrella just like the one the boatman had described. Qixiang was most excited of all; she insisted that we go to find the boatman and try to catch up with her father. So we all set out together.

However, when we reached the riverbank, we were ambushed. As the Qing troops charged us, we fled in all directions. As we fled, I heard Qixiang call out as though she was in trouble, but I ignored her cries and kept running. It was a dark night, there was a strong wind blowing and I was sick. It all happened so suddenly that my courage evaporated; I didn't dare to go back to try and save Qixiang. Afterwards we heard that she had been captured and raped to death. I tried to justify my conduct to myself by saying that even if I had gone back to try to save her, I would probably have failed. Nevertheless, given the relationship between us, it was inexcusable of me to run away as I did. I could not forgive myself, and I was too ashamed to see any of the people I knew. So I came back to Beijing, back to this Fayuan Temple with which my family had ties, and became a monk. Thirty years have passed since then; when I think back on that night, I still can't understand how I could have behaved in such a cowardly way. Why did my courage suddenly desert me?'

'Did Big Sword Wang Wu know that you had become a monk here at Fayuan Temple?'

'I think they knew. All of us have been in the north for so long, including people of reputation, I am sure that everyone knows what everyone else is doing. But we haven't had any contact with each other. They felt that I should have died with Qixiang; they despise me for having been concerned only with saving my own skin.'

'So with you becoming a monk and Big Sword Wang Wu starting an armed escort service, none of you have been active as revolutionaries. Is that so?'

'That's right,' said Master She simply. He continued to stare out through the temple gate. He walked forward slowly until he stood next to a lilac bush. Dufu's poem about the lilac, which Kang Youwei had written ten years earlier, came unbidden into his mind. The sun was setting, but suddenly black clouds appeared; changes in the weather do not wait for the sunset.

⸺◦◈◦◦⸺

Two years later, in 1900, late in the evening of the twentieth day of the seventh lunar month, a man sat by the edge of a lake on a deserted island. He was not waiting to view the sunset. He was still young, but looked ill. What was the sunset to him? He himself was in the sunset of his life. He thought to himself that once again it was the twentieth day of the seventh month. Exactly two years had passed since the day on which he promoted four low-ranking officials to the status of Secretary of the Grand Council and permitted them to undertake reforms. All of that had disappeared like smoke. The four of them had been in office less than twenty-four days before they were executed, along with the other two. He himself had become a puppet emperor.

What angered him most was that the imperial edict ordering their execution had been written in his name. He could still remember its bureaucratic prose. The edict said that the six men were to be 'Removed from their posts and handed over to the Board of Punishments for interrogation', and that 'as delays might have unfortunate consequences, after careful deliberation and in light of the seriousness of their crimes, an order was issued yesterday for their immediate execution. This is an extraordinary measure intended to demonstrate the consequences of rebellion'.

So they had been executed immediately so as not to waste time and in case anything unforeseen happened. This order showed that there was no need to follow the laws laid down by the emperor himself. In accordance with Qing law, a person could only be executed if the Suspension of Execution or Immediate Execution procedures had been followed.

With Suspension of Execution, the criminal was kept in prison until the autumn, when a further memorial was sent to the court. If there were no grounds for clemency, authorization was given to execute the prisoner; if there were grounds for clemency, then the prisoner might be spared, or the decision might be put off until autumn the following year.

With Immediate Execution, there was no need to wait until the autumn; the prisoner could be executed as soon as confirmation was received from the Court of Judicial Review. The Board of Punishments was responsible for imprisonment and execution; the Censorate was responsible for investigation of the case; the Court of Judicial Review was responsible for issuing confirmation that execution should take place. If the legal procedures were followed, therefore, there was no way that anyone could be executed so quickly; it was impossible for the trial to be held one day and the prisoner to be executed the next. Now the Emperor had issued an edict saying that there was no need to wait for confirmation before execution. What kind of emperor did that make him?

He thought back to the four orders that had been given in six days; all of them were issued in the Emperor's name. On the face of it, the Emperor had had killed the people who only a week earlier had been implementing reform with him. Fate was mocking him, mocking him as a twilight emperor!

He sat by the water's edge, the thoughts floating on the surface of his mind just as the duckweed floated on the surface of the water. But how could he compare himself to duckweed? Duckweed at least had roots, whereas he as Emperor was stuck here alone on this island, uprooted.

Suddenly, he heard the sound of distant gunfire. 'Why gunfire?' he thought to himself. He didn't bother to ask the eunuchs who guarded him, because he knew they would tell him nothing; they were all loyal servants of the Empress Dowager, and had been ordered to keep their mouths shut. Just as he was wondering what the reason for the gunfire was, he became aware that there were four people standing behind him. As he turned around, the four men, all dressed in commoners' garb, knelt down before him. Their leader was Li Lianying.

'Greetings, Your Majesty,' said Li Lianying in his high-pitched, nasal voice. 'Please forgive me for not coming to see you for so long.' As he spoke, he kowtowed, and the other three kowtowed with him.

'Get up. Why are you all wearing commoners' clothing?' asked the Emperor.

'I have to tell you, Your Majesty,' said Li Lianying, 'that there has been some trouble. Last year, there was a popular uprising by the Society of Righteous and Harmonious Fists. They perform ceremonies in which they become possessed by spirits; they chant

incantations that protect them from swords and bullets. They refuse
to wear foreign cloth or use foreign matches; their slogan is to "protect
the Qing and destroy foreign religion". They have been killing
foreigners and Christians everywhere, burning churches and trains.
Gang Yi and other Manchu officials believe in them, and so does the
Empress Dowager. Eight foreign nations have allied to combat them,
and they have already fought their way into Beijing. The Society
can't stop them. The Empress Dowager has ordered that we flee the
capital, and take Your Majesty with us. That's why we are here, to
collect you. Please change into these clothes! If we dress as refugees
we can still escape; if we delay any longer we will be too late!'

The Guangxu Emperor took off his dragon robe and put on a
black jacket and blue trousers. He fled with them outside the palace
gates, where they got into a donkey-cart. Amidst the chaos, the
Emperor kept asking, 'Where is the Pearl Concubine? Where is she?'

'Her cart is over there.' Li Lianying pointed. 'The women are all
with the Empress Dowager; they will follow behind us. Wait here,
Your Majesty; I will go and find them!' Saying this, he rushed off.

'I'll go with you! I want to pay my respects to the Empress
Dowager,' the Emperor shouted. He climbed down from the donkey
cart, and rushed back into the palace with Li Lianying and the other
eunuchs. When they reached the Zhenshun Gate, they saw a crowd
of people pushing someone, and heard a woman screaming. As they
came closer, they saw the Pearl Concubine being pushed by eunuchs
into a well. The Emperor cried out, and rushed over to stop them,
but he was too late. The screams faded, and there was a sound of
something hitting the water deep inside the well. The eunuchs
grabbed the Emperor when he was still ten paces away from the
well, and pushed him down onto the ground.

An old woman dressed as a countrywoman was standing by
Zhenshun Gate. A group of men and woman, also in disguise,
clustered round her; they were all too stunned to speak. The old
woman was completely casual about the whole business. She clapped
her hands and said coldly, 'Help His Majesty up; let us go.'

They all set off. They had not had time to take anything with
them, and would not have dared take anything with them even if
they had had time.

When they had gone about a hundred miles, they found
themselves in country that was completely deserted. When they
found a well, there was either no bucket to raise the water or else
there were human heads floating in the water. It was not until they

reached Huailai in Chahar that they were able to secure supplies of food. They travelled on from Chahar into Shanxi, into Henan, and then into Shaanxi; after two months on the road, they finally reached Xian.

Seventeen months after they had left, the situation calmed down. China made a formal apology to the eight foreign nations that had joined up to relieve the legations in Beijing. Those held responsible for the uprising were punished, and an indemnity was paid. The indemnity came to four hundred and fifty million taels of silver—at that time China had a population of four hundred and fifty million people, so it worked out to one tael for every man, woman, and child in the country.

This was an amount equivalent to the total national income for five years. Once again, the ordinary people of China had to bear a burden imposed on them by the cruel Empress Dowager, and the burden was not limited to the indemnity imposed by the foreigners. When the Empress Dowager had left Beijing seventeen months before, she left almost empty-handed; when she returned from Xian to Beijing her baggage train included three thousand carriages, and stretched for two hundred and fifty miles. She returned in high spirits, as though she were going on a pilgrimage rather than returning from a defeat. For the last leg of the journey, from Zhending to Beijing, she rode in a train; the Empress Dowager had finally accepted an aspect of western culture. She rode into Beijing in a train of twenty-one cars.

Six years later, on 15 November 1908 (the thirty-fourth year of the Guangxu Emperor's reign), the Empress Dowager finally died, at the age of seventy-three. On the day before her death, the thirty-eight-year-old Guangxu Emperor also died under mysterious circumstances. As to whether he was poisoned, or whether it was just a coincidence that he died when he did, only the Empress Dowager, buried in her magnificent tomb, would know.

Her splendid tomb was known as the Eastern Tomb; it was constructed ninety miles outside Beijing, and cost eight million taels of silver to build. The funeral itself cost another 1.5 million taels, so the total expense came to nearly ten million taels. Of the enormous sums of money the people of China had been obliged to pay for her over the forty-seven years of her reign, this last ten million was probably the only part they paid gladly. When her golden coffin was being carried out through the city gates of Beijing, there was not enough room for the one hundred and twenty coffin-bearers to all squeeze through at once, so the number had to be reduced to eighty-four before they could get through. With her passing, the sun set on Beijing too.

The Qing Dynasty's empire had been bled dry. Three years later the revolution of 1911 was successful, and the Republic of China was established.

With the passing of the Empress Dowager, some other people 'came back to life'. Another of the Guangxu Emperor's concubines, the Jade Concubine (the Pearl Concubine's sister) had a memorial tablet erected to her sister, who had been so brutally murdered. The well became known as the 'Pearl Concubine's Well'. It was blocked up with a stone pillar and wooden lid; even today, there is still something gloomy and depressing about it.

Another person who 'came back to life' was Zhang Yinhuan. After his arrest, because of his many years of diplomatic service in which he had served as ambassador to the United States, Spain, and Peru, and had attended the Diamond Jubilee celebrations of Queen Victoria, the British and Japanese ambassadors interceded on his behalf. Influenced by this, the Empress Dowager issued an edict in the Guangxu Emperor's name in which she said that Zhang Yinhuan 'had a very bad reputation, but was not one of Kang Youwei's party'. Nevertheless, as he was 'crafty, secretive, fawning, and untrustworthy,' he was to be sent to Xinjiang, and kept under close confinement by the provincial governor.

Having escaped death in this theatrical manner, he was handed over by the Board of Punishments to the Board of War to be posted for garrison duty to the frontier. He took the whole thing in good heart, and was very relaxed on the journey to Xinjiang.

He said to those with him, 'The "old lady" is playing a joke on me, sending me on a vacation to the frontier.' However, his good fortune did not last. Two years later, when the Boxer Uprising began, the Empress Dowager was no longer concerned about foreign opinion. She sent a telegram to Xinjiang, ordering that Zhang Yinhuan be executed immediately. When the provincial governor told him the news, he displayed no trace of emotion. Prior to the execution, he produced a fan painting to be given to his nephew. When it was finished, he tidied his clothing and walked to the execution ground, where he told the nervous executioners to relax. One year later, when the Qing government was making peace with the foreign powers, the foreigners claimed that Zhang Yinhuan had been unjustly executed. Once again, the Empress Dowager was influenced by this; she again issued an edict in the Guangxu Emperor's name, stating that Zhang Yinhuan was to be posthumously restored to his official post. Having to rehabilitate Zhang in this way for diplomatic considerations was a serious loss of face for her.

∞∘❖∘∞

The Empress Dowager's conversion from being anti-foreign to grovelling before them was a sudden one; it led to the deaths of many innocent people.

On the surface, during the forty-seven years in which she ruled China the Empress Dowager defeated all her enemies. However, what she was really good at was dealing with internal enemies, with other Chinese. In dealing with foreigners, she showed herself to be ignorant and childish. Just how marked the difference was between her ability to deal with internal enemies as opposed to external enemies was shown by the way she used the Society of Righteous and Harmonious Fists (or the 'Boxers', as they were known to the foreigners).

The Boxers were a product of native, rural culture. They were derived from a particularly lowly form of folk religion, gradually evolving from a cult into a secret organization, and eventually into a popular militia. They wore red or yellow turbans, with matching waistbands, short jackets, leggings tied at the ankles, and boots on their feet. On the upper part of their body they wore a truncated waistcoat with one of the hexagrams from the *Book of Changes* (also known as the 'I Ching') sewn onto it. Their religious faith derived from a wide variety of sources, but all were native Chinese, and most were highly debased. They believed that by chanting slogans they could ward off bullets, and that they could defeat Western guns with swords and spears. They made extensive use of special banners, fans, and other magical tokens. They worshipped the Jade Emperor, Hong Jun Laozu, the Old Mother of Lishan, Jiutian Xuannu, Erlang Shen, Nazha, Tang Xuanzhuang, Sun Wukong, Zhu Bajie, Sha Heshang, Jiang Taigong, Guan Gong, Zhang Yide, Zhao Zilong, Tuota Tianwang, Wei Xigong, Qin Shubao, Huang Santai, Huang Tianba, Yang Xiangwu, and other characters from folk operas and popular novels. The only deity in their pantheon with any real stature was Li Taibo.

The ceremonies that an initiate had to undergo to join the Society were similar to those used by spirit mediums, with the same martial arts movements and frothing at the mouth, the same fainting and speaking in tongues. Their slogans were mostly variations on: 'On the left is the Green Tiger; on the right is the White Tiger; Yun Liang Fo is before us; the Fire God is behind us; we call upon the Heavenly Generals, and upon the Black Spirits.' These slogans were passed on by word of mouth; an adept person could call down heavenly fire to destroy the house of a foreigner merely by pointing with a finger.

The ignorant, superstitious Empress Dowager believed in their powers. They moved into Beijing, and, following the directions of the Empress Dowager, began killing and burning in a frenzy of xenophobia that could be seen as a forerunner to the Cultural Revolution. They burned down any shop found to be selling Western medicine. The fires spread and destroyed four thousand houses and shops, but they would not allow anyone to put the fires out. All they were really good for was killing other Chinese; they were not up to dealing with foreigners. Their slogan was:

Heaven help my fists,
The Boxers,
Foreign devils have invaded my motherland.
They have converted people to their religion.
In reality, they have deceived Heaven!
They don't respect Heaven or the Buddha,
Their women are not chaste, their men not intelligent.
The foreign devils are not the offspring of human beings,
If you don't believe this, look at them closer.
They have blue eyes . . .
God is mad, Buddha is infuriated;
Therefore I was sent down from the mountain to preach our religion.
I am not from the evil White Lotus, whose doctrines are cursed.

Having raised the Yellow Banner and burned the incense,
I have the Eight Immortals descend upon Earth to help the Great Qing
        Dynasty train us in our martial arts.
There is no need for soldiers, only us, the Boxers.
It is not difficult to kill the foreign devils,
Nor is it hard to burn the railroad tracks, or to remove the electricity poles,
        or to sink the steamships.
The French are scared, and the
British, Americans, Germans, and Russians are begging for mercy.

We will kill every foreign devil.
And the Great Qing Dynasty will unite the whole world.

Slogans apart, when it actually came to dealing with the foreigners in the legation quarter in the eastern part of the city, although there were only four hundred foreign soldiers in the quarter, the Boxers were still unable to break through after attacking the legations for two months. As soon as the foreign relief army arrived, numbering over ten thousand men, their true worth became clear.

Nevertheless, although they were ineffective against foreigners, they performed impressively enough against fellow Chinese. They destroyed everything foreign. Anyone seen smoking a cigarette was killed; anyone seen holding a foreign umbrella was killed; anyone seen wearing Western stockings was killed. A family of eight who were discovered to have a match in their home were all killed; six students, one of whom was carrying a Western fountain pen, were all killed. Anyone believed to be an adherent of the 'foreign religions' (mainly Catholics) was sure to be killed.

They called foreigners '*damaozi* hairy men', Chinese who believed in foreign religions '*dermaozi* hairy men', and Chinese who had any kind of indirect relationship with the foreigners '*sanmaozi* hairy men'. While they were unable to kill the primary hairy men, there was no shortage of secondary and tertiary hairy men. Anyone determined to be a secondary or tertiary hairy person would be chopped to death, have their limbs cut off, be cut in two at the waist, be boiled to death, or be buried alive.

There was a variation on burying people alive. Some Christian women were buried upside down with their legs sticking out; as a joke, a candle would then be stuck in their private parts and lit. There was no precise definition as to who should be classified as a secondary or tertiary hairy person. Sometimes, in order to inflate their 'score' they would seize a hundred or more innocent farmers, both men and women, and cut off their heads. The farmers would die weeping and wailing, not knowing why they were being killed.

The 'cultural revolution' that the Empress Dowager had ignited with her use of the Boxers led to a catastrophe. The foreigners' ships and guns presented a challenge that demonstrated the weakness of both Chinese culture and the Chinese nation. At the same time, the running rampant of the debased local culture created a further catastrophe that further demonstrated that weakness. Classical Chinese culture had prohibited the murder of innocent civilians and of ambassadors during the course of war between two states. Now, with debased popular culture running out of control, everyone from foreign ambassadors down could be found lying dead in the streets.

The Empress Dowager herself was not a highly cultured person. Although she had risen to the heights of power, there had been no commensurate rise in her cultural level. The result of this was the approval she gave to the Boxers, approval that was imitated by those further down in the hierarchy, and which created a laughable 'cultural revolution'.

In the ensuing chaos, not only were Chinese peasants killed, foreign ambassadors were killed, the more clear-headed ministers of state were killed, and many political figures currently out of government were killed. People died in large numbers all over China, not only in Beijing. And in Beijing itself, it was not only in the main streets that severed heads could be seen; tragedies of various kinds occurred in the back streets also. One such incident occurred at Fayuan Temple in Xizhuan Alley.

One evening, several dozen Boxers were chasing a man wearing a black robe. The man was already wounded; he ran into the temple, and the gates were closed behind him. The Boxers pursuing him did not respect the sanctity of the temple; they forced open the gates and pushed aside the monks who tried to block their path. They saw the man in black lying on the stone steps in front of the Daxiong Hall, rushed up to him and hacked him to death. They then left, yelling and screaming. No one knew who the man in black was, or why the Boxers had been chasing him.

Subsequently, it was said by people living in the vicinity of Fayuan Temple that the man in black was none other than Big Sword Wang Wu. However, it remained unclear why the Boxers had killed him.

Thirteen years later, when a wandering monk from the south, known as the 'Eight-fingered Monk', was staying at Fayuan Temple, he asked what had happened to the previous abbot, Master She. The Eight-fingered Monk was famous throughout the country for having burnt off the tips of two of his fingers making offerings to the Buddha. Because they admired and trusted him, one of the monks, who had witnessed what had taken place that day thirteen years before, told him the truth about the incident.

It transpired that after Tan Sitong's coffin was moved into Fayuan Temple, Master She had told Pu Jing to leave, telling him that he should not remain a monk. After Pu Jing left, Master She's comings and goings became increasingly mysterious. It was said that he had become involved in a plan to rescue the Guangxu Emperor; this was the rescue plan that Tan Sitong had instructed Big Sword Wang Wu to undertake. However, the Qing government had the Emperor too closely guarded, and the plan failed. Nevertheless, Master She remained in close contact with the people at the Armed Escort Service.

Two years later, when the Boxers were creating chaos in Beijing, it was said that Big Sword Wang Wu once again tried to take advantage of the situation to rescue the Emperor, the task that his dead friend Tan Sitong had left him. Why he was chased into the temple by the Boxers no one knew, but once he was in the temple, Master She told the monks to assemble in front of the gate and try to delay the Boxers, while he remained with Big Sword Wang Wu. Once the main gate had been forced open and the monks pushed aside, the Boxers rushed inside; they ran up to the Daxiong Hall and hacked to death the man in the black robe.

It was only after they left that the monks realized that the man in the black robe who had been killed was in fact Master She! Big Sword Wang Wu had been made to change into monk's clothing and spirited out of the way. The monks tried to save him, but it was no use, and three hours later Big Sword Wang Wu also died. Before his death, he said, 'I misjudged Master She for thirty years. If possible, I would like to be buried near him.'

Nobody knew much about the mysterious relationship between Master She and Big Sword Wang Wu. They had heard only that Big Sword Wang Wu despised Master She, considering him to be a coward. It was only when they saw Master She put on Big Sword Wang Wu's black robe in an attempt to save him that they began to understand. The temple did not dare make the details of their death public; they secretly bought two coffins and buried them behind the tomb of Yuan Chonghuan in the Guangdong cemetery inside the Guangju Gate. When they went through the pockets of the black robe, the monks had discovered a piece of paper with the following poem written on it:

> *Staring at the door to decide whether or not I should come in, I think of*
> *Zhang Jian, the fugitive in the Later Han Dynasty;*
> *I must accept my death and remain in anticipation like Du Gen in the*
> *Later Han Dynasty who was ordered killed.*
> *Under the knife, I smile up at the heavens.*

Between life and death, the utmost sincerity remains in the lasting friendship between the two Kunlun Mountains.

A note stated that the poem was written in prison by Tan Sitong. The monks pondered the poem for a while, but could make no sense of it, and eventually forgot about it. The Eight-fingered Monk was also a poet. That night he lit a candle and sat down in the ancient temple to study the poem. He seemed to suddenly realize something. The first line, 'Staring at the door . . . I think of Zhang Jian', was a reference to Zhang Jian in the Eastern Han Dynasty. When he was in flight following an attempt by the government to arrest him, many people tried to help him because he was so widely admired, and got themselves into trouble as a result. Tan Sitong included this reference to Zhang Jian to show that he did not want to put other people in danger, and so was not willing to try and escape.

The second line, 'I must accept my death and remain in anticipation like Du Gen', referred to Du Gen in the Eastern Han Dynasty, who, when the emperor attained his majority, submitted a memorial to the queen mother requesting that she hand over the reins of government to the emperor. The queen mother ordered that he be placed in a sack and shaken to death. Fortunately, the executioners deliberately botched the execution, so that although Du Gen was injured, he escaped death. With this allusion, Tan Sitong was saying that although he had been unable to take power from the Empress Dowager and restore it to the Emperor, he was sure that his goal would be accomplished some other way after his death.

The third line, 'Under the knife, I smile up at the heavens', showed that Tan Sitong had already come to terms with the inevitability of his death, and was ready to die unflinchingly. The Eight-fingered Monk sighed and thought to himself, 'Making the decision to sacrifice one's life while in an emotional state is easy; facing death without fear is hard.'

Making the decision to sacrifice one's life and facing death fearlessly are two different ways of dealing with problems and facing difficulties. Someone who decides to sacrifice their life may be motivated by the desire for justice or some other good reason, but what shows on the surface is emotion, powerful emotion. One example would be Fang Xiaoru. During the Ming Dynasty, Fang Xiaoru opposed the Yongle Emperor's usurpation of the throne.

The Emperor said to him that this was a family matter of no concern to him, and that he should just write out the edict announcing the emperor's ascension to the throne. Fang Xiaoru wept and cursed, saying that the emperor could kill him, but he would not write the edict. The Yongle Emperor said, 'Maybe you are not afraid of death, but it won't be just you that I kill; I will kill nine generations of your family.'

Fang Xiaoru said, 'I don't care if you kill ten generations of my family.'

The Emperor said, 'In that case, I will kill ten generations of your family.'

Traditionally, executing nine generations of someone's family meant the four generations above the person in question and the four generations below. In other words, the person's great-great-grandfather, great-grandfather, grandfather, and father, along with their children, grandchildren, great-grandchildren, and great-great-grandchildren; the members of their wife's family and mother's family would also be killed.

There was no such thing as executing ten generations of someone's family. Fang Xiaoru said that he didn't care if the emperor executed ten generations of his family, so the emperor had to devise a method of doing so; he had Fang's friends and students executed as well. For added effect, he made Fang witness every execution; Fang displayed no emotion as he was forced to watch. In the end, eight hundred and thirty-seven people were killed, and Fang himself died unflinchingly.

The reason that deciding to sacrifice one's life is said to be easy is because when one makes the decision one is usually emotionally worked up. This makes people act impulsively, and they are liable to do something brave or make a great sacrifice; they haven't sat down to coldly and rationally think through the after-effects of their action. There is no fear, grief, pain, or loneliness to make them depressed or weaken them. Because soon after the emotional peak is reached, the person is dead; things don't get dragged out. This is why it is easier to die in this way. Precisely because this is a relatively easy way to die, some people choose not to give the person in question the opportunity to die like this. So they use whatever means they can to soften them up while in prison, in an attempt to make them submit.

But some people just refuse to submit. The best example of this is Wen Tianxiang. This is an even more exalted level of behaviour than that displayed by Fang Xiaoru. Having to spend many years in prison, one relies not on powerful emotion but on calmness and serenity. This was precisely what Wen Tianxiang displayed. In the end, he too was killed. He remained perfectly calm while walking to the execution ground, and died unflinchingly.

This third line of Tan Sitong's poem, 'Under the knife, I smile up at the heavens', struck the monk as being extremely well written, particularly the choice of the word 'smile'. This one word brought across the calmness with which he faced death. At the same time, however, smiling is an emotional action. Tan Sitong's death thus combined the ease of the decision to sacrifice oneself with the difficulty of facing death unflinchingly. In combining these two, the poem and the poet showed themselves well-matched to one another. But what was meant by the fourth line, 'Between life and death, the utmost sincerity remains in the lasting friendship between the two Kunlun Mountains'? This presented a challenge.

'They are all dead,' thought the Eight-fingered Monk as the candle burnt down. 'Who will stand in judgement of their actions? The Qing Dynasty has fallen, and the Republic of China has been established; as time passes, past events will be forgotten. But what did he mean by his reference to the Kunlun Mountains?'

CHAPTER FOURTEEN

When will the Bright Moon Shine Again?

The year is 1915. Cai E and Liang Qichao are reunited in their efforts to prevent the president of the Republic of China, Yuan Shikai, from becoming emperor. They succeed, but their efforts cost Cai E his life, dying from exhaustion at the age of thirty-five. Yuan Shikai dies of humiliation shortly afterwards. Kang Youwei also participated in this effort, although his goals differed from the other two. Liang Qichao and Cai E sought to preserve the republic, while Kang Youwei favours the formation of a constitutional monarchy, using Great Britain as a model.

Kang Youwei later goes on to join a movement to restore the Qing Dynasty. The restoration movement succeeds briefly in returning Henry Puyi, the last Qing emperor, to the throne but he is ousted in a matter of days by rival forces. Kang Youwei is given refuge in the American Consulate. Kang is strangely out of step with the times, but he is a tireless advocate for a government that will better serve the people. He works on, regardless of his lack of support or followers, and always seems to escape punishment. After his failure at the Qing restoration, he is eventually given assurances of his freedom from arrest, through the intervention of United States diplomats.

'Who is it referring to?' Once again, the same question was being asked. It was 1915, two years after the Eight-fingered Monk had died at Fayuan Temple, and the fourth year since the founding of the Republic of China. This was a terrible year for the people of China. Having finally managed to establish a republic, they found themselves staring into the face of disaster. The President of the Republic of China, Yuan Shikai, decided that he was not satisfied with being president, and that he wanted to be emperor instead. Throughout the country, people were urging him to do so.

Liang Qichao felt that this was a shameful course of events. At his house in Tianjin, he met with a mysterious visitor from Beijing. This mysterious visitor was none other than Cai Liangyan, whom Liang had taught eighteen years ago at the Hunan School of Practical Studies when his pupil was only sixteen, and who had now changed his name to Cai E.

Following the failure of the reform movement, Cai E went to study in Japan, where he met up with his former teacher Liang Qichao, also in exile in Japan. However, Cai and Liang had differing views regarding the significance of the death of his other teacher, Tan Sitong. The view taken by Liang Qichao and Kang Youwei was that Tan Sitong had died in the name of reform, and that they should therefore continue working along the path that he had followed, seeking reform and collaborating with the Qing government. However, Cai E took the view that Tan Sitong had died in order to demonstrate that the path of reform was no longer viable, and that the path to follow was that of revolution.

At the age of nineteen, shortly after the Boxer Uprising, Cai E returned secretly to China from Japan with nineteen others, including his teacher, Tang Caichang. They attempted to launch an uprising, but failed. Zhang Zhidong, the official in charge of the investigation, had been Tang Caichang's teacher. While Tang was undergoing questioning, Zhang Zhidong tried to get him off the hook, saying to those with him, 'This man doesn't look like Tang Caichang. Could we have caught the wrong man?'

But Tang Caichang shouted out, 'I have failed, so it is right that I should die. I will not stoop to this kind of pretence to save my life.' So he was executed. Before his death he recited a poem; the last two lines were: 'I will still have a skull to drink with my departed friends, even if I have no face to see the demons of hell.' He died less than two years after his friend Tan Sitong, making a similar sacrifice.

Before he was arrested, Tang Caichang had managed to burn the list of the other people due to take part in the uprising, so that the government was unable to prosecute them. As a result, Cai E and the other small fry were able to escape back to Japan, to prepare to take part in the next wave of revolutionary activity.

Cai E joined a Japanese military academy, where his grades were outstanding. After graduation, he returned to China and joined the Qing army, where he plotted revolution; he was now twenty-three. Seven years later, on 10 October 1911 the revolution took place. Twenty days later Cai E announced the overthrow of Qing rule in Yunnan, where he took over the reins of government; he was now twenty-nine. Two months later, the Republic of China was established.

Although a republic had been proclaimed, the idea of imperial rule was still deeply imbedded in the popular psyche. When the republic was in only its fourth year, a movement to re-establish imperial rule was gradually growing in strength. Yuan Shikai, who had sold out Tan Sitong in the Reform Movement of 1898, tried to exploit public opinion to turn the republic into an empire, with himself as emperor. Liang Qichao and Cai E could stand it no longer. They determined to stir up opposition to Yuan's plans in order to save the republic. This was a difficult task; first of all, they had to escape from Beijing and Tianjin, where Yuan could keep an eye on them. One night, Cai E travelled secretly from Beijing to Tianjin to meet with Liang Qichao and discuss how they could escape.

'Seventeen years ago,' said Liang Qichao, 'you and I and Tan Sitong were in Beijing discussing whether to leave or stay. Seventeen years on, we are faced with the same problem. As I see it, the way things stand now, you should leave first. Go south, and organize opposition to the reimposition of imperial rule. I can't leave now; if I leave, Yuan Shikai will start keeping you under closer watch, and you won't be able to get away. You must go first.'

'But,' said Cai E, worriedly, 'If I go first, suppose you aren't able to escape?'

'That won't affect our plans. Do you remember the poem that Tan Sitong wrote on the wall of his prison cell seventeen years ago?

> *Staring at the door to decide whether or not I should come in, I think of*
> *Zhang Jian, the fugitive in the Later Han Dynasty;*
> *I must accept my death and remain in anticipation like Du Gen in the*
> *Later Han Dynasty who was ordered killed.*
> *Under the knife, I smile up at the heavens.*
> *Between life and death, the utmost sincerity remains in the lasting friendship*
> *between the two Kunlun Mountains.*

In the fourth line, the Kunlun Mountains are the legendary birthplace of China, and the "two Kunlun Mountains" are two upright, noble Chinese, equally noble whether they go or stay.'

'This must be a reference to Tan Sitong and you,' added Cai E.

'Interpreting the "two Kunlun Mountains" as a reference to Tan Sitong and myself would make sense in terms of the "going and staying". However, I subsequently read the following passage in section fifty-six of the "learning" chapter of Tan Sitong's *Shiju Yinglu Bishi*: "In his account of the military campaigns in western China, my friend Zhou Yuanfan says that the Kunlun Mountains are the Himalayas; I believe this to be correct. One piece of evidence supporting this view is the fact that the Himalayas are located to the north of India, and people in the Tang Dynasty referred to Indians as "Kunlun Slaves". This is the only reference to "Kunlun" in any of Tan Sitong's writings.

As I see it, the "two Kunlun Mountains" are his two servants, Hu Lichen and Luo Sheng. After his death, one of them carried the news to his father in Hubei; the other remained in Beijing to sort out his affairs. Hence the reference to going and staying. This may seem too narrow an interpretation, but I think that family factors were one reason why Tan Sitong was so ready to die.

Although he was abused by his stepmother as a child, his relationship with his father was very close. After his arrest, when his correspondence was being searched, there were several letters from his father criticizing him for his involvement in the reform movement or threatening to disown him; this was why the Qing government spared his father. In fact, these letters were forged by Tan Sitong himself to try and protect his father. I think that one of the reasons he refused to leave Beijing was because he needed time to learn to imitate his father's handwriting so he could forge the letters.

After his execution, his family tried to fool his father into believing that he had only been imprisoned, but one of his friends accidentally gave the game away in a letter. When his father read the news of his son's death, his hands fell lifelessly onto the table, and he wept silently without saying a word. There have been various reasons advanced as to why Tan Sitong refused to leave. Some say it was because he felt he owed it to those who had supported the reform movement; others say that it was to show people that they should continue to work for reform; others say that he died in order to demonstrate that reform could not work and that others should follow the path of revolution; others say that it was to save his father . . . a good case can be made for any of these explanations.'

'Which one do you believe?' asked Cai E.

'I believe that there were several reasons why Tan Sitong was willing to die. But in terms of the Buddhist view that life and death are of no importance, I believe that his fundamental reason was to make use of his death to achieve his goals. As far as his main objective is concerned, I think he wanted to show by his death that reform would not work, and that revolution was the only answer to China's problems.

However, he also had a lesser objective; the reason he was so willing to die was to encourage Big Sword Wang Wu and the others to try to save the Emperor. We mustn't forget that Tan Sitong had a great deal of the knight errant about him. He felt guilty that the Guangxu Emperor had been willing to sacrifice everything to try to save China, and so he wanted to save him. He himself was not in a position to do so, so he entrusted that task to Big Sword Wang Wu and the others, but that also made him feel guilty towards them.

His willingness to die for the cause, to show that a true man is willing to take responsibility for his own actions with his life, was very noble. So in terms of this objective it seems more likely that the "two Kunlun Mountains" referred to Big Sword Wang Wu and Hu Qi. Some say that Big Sword Wang Wu and Hu Qi were knights errant of the Kunlun school. Some note that the Tang Dynasty story *The Indian* contains a character called Mole, who is from Kunlun, and that the Song novel *Taiping Guangji* has the character Tao Xian and his companion, Mohe, who is from Kunlun. In both cases, the word Kunlun has connotations of knight errantry. In this case, the reference to the "two Kunlun Mountains" would refer to the business of saving the Guangxu Emperor. The poem ends by saying that he himself is prepared to face death, while leaving the task of saving the Emperor to the knights errant. So, following this line of reasoning, one of the "two Kunlun Mountains" would be Tan Sitong himself, and the other is Big Sword Wang Wu. The relationship between them is that of one who stays and one who goes.

When Gongsun Chujiu asked, "Which is more difficult, raising the orphan or dying to protect him?" Cheng Ying answered, "Dying is easy, raising the orphan will be difficult." Gongsun Chujiu said, "The Zhao family always treated you well; please undertake the difficult task, while I undertake the easy task of dying." I think that

Tan Sitong came to the conclusion that in the situation he was in, it was better for him to play the role of Gongsun Chujiu. So he decided to be the one to remain, leaving the many tasks that had yet to be performed to Big Sword Wang Wu and the others. I think that would be the best explanation of the poem which Tan Sitong wrote on the wall of his prison cell.'

Cai E nodded. However, there was still one thing he was unsure about. 'In Tan Sitong's *The Study of the Ideals of Confucius* which you had printed for him, there is the concept of "breaking free from one's chains". He says that if humanity is to achieve peace and harmony, we must first break free of our chains.

He says, "First, one must break the chains of self interest: next one must break the chains of traditional learning; next one must break the chains of globalism; next one must break the chains of the ruler–minister relationship; next one must break the chains of traditional ethics; next one must break the chains of belief in Heaven; next one must break the chains of religion; and finally, one must break the chains of Buddhism."

He also says, "For two thousand years, the harm caused by the ruler-minister relationship has been immeasurable. And today it is worse than ever!" He also says, "The ruler is also a person, and of less importance than most people. There is no reason for one person to die for another person, and even less reason for the greater to die for the lesser. . . . To die for a cause makes sense, but not to die for a ruler. To die for one's ruler can only be an action based on private emotion . . . this is particularly true given the distinction between Han Chinese and Manchu; why would I die for the emperor?" To judge from these remarks, Tan Sitong was a republican, and even harboured anti-Manchu sentiment.

Despite this, after the brief period in which he had the ruler's confidence and was able to put his plans into action, he came to a tragic end that bears a very strong resemblance to "dying for one's ruler". You said there were probably many reasons why he chose to die; isn't his desire to die for the emperor one of the most important, if not the only real reason? If this is so, then the motivation for his death becomes even more startling. What do you think?'

Sitting at his writing desk, Liang Qichao nodded, and scratched his head lightly with a finger. He had a big head and large eyes; his face shone with a lively intelligence. In the presence of his student Cai E, this intelligence was accompanied by warmth and companionableness.

'As to the question of "dying for a cause" and "dying for one's ruler", I discussed this with Tan Sitong at our last meeting. Fundamentally speaking, Tan Sitong opposed the Qing and the Emperor. This is why his writings contain praise for the Taiping movement, in which he describes Hong Xiuquan and Yang Xiuqing as having suffered harm at the hands of the Emperor and officials, and praises them for having the courage to stand up and face danger. He also praises the French revolution, describing the revolutionaries as "swearing to kill all rulers, so that their blood flows all over the world, to give vent to the hatred felt towards them by the people".

His anti-Manchu and anti-imperial leanings were already visible when he was teaching at the School for Practical Affairs. The fact that having become the valued advisor of a Manchu emperor, he then sacrificed his life, is bound to be explained as "dying for one's ruler".

However, if you study the situation more closely, I believe that in Tan's eyes the Guangxu Emperor was no longer a "ruler" in the narrow sense of the word; he had become a "cause", in the broad sense of the term. What the Guangxu Emperor symbolized was the unification of the Chinese people, both Han and non-Han; the Emperor had come to symbolize an honest desire to overhaul the legal system and reform a corrupt government; he had come to symbolize the Emperor's willingness to sacrifice himself for his people. What the Guangxu Emperor symbolized was not an ordinary emperor, but rather a true patriot, a man of genuine ideals. . . . In Tan Sitong's eyes, he symbolized not a "ruler", but a "cause". He may even have come to seem like a friend engaged in the same great enterprise. They were no longer ruler and minister, but two great Chinese.

As Tan Sitong wrote, "In the beginning there was no distinction between ruler and minister; there were only people." It was because of this that Tan Sitong was prepared to remain in Beijing and await death. In light of his view that "there are only people", he did not want to leave the Guangxu Emperor alone in Beijing. Of course, this was only one of the reasons. As I just said, a case could be made for any of the possible motivations. Your suggestion that he "died for his ruler" is one more possibility. But there is no way that he "died for his ruler" in the narrow sense, since fundamentally speaking he was opposed to the idea of an emperor.

In the thirteen years after his death, you and I have come to develop a thorough understanding of his thinking. The ancients said, "A great sage appeared in the West in response to the needs of the time." It was in just this way, in response to the needs of the time, that Tan Sitong appeared. In his brief lifespan of thirty-three years, he provided us with a compass and map to guide us in our struggle, and gave us a model of what the Chinese should be. We must remember him: that is the karmic relationship that exists between us and him . . .'

Cai E nodded. 'You are right. The idea of Yuan Shikai becoming emperor is ludicrous. The whole world will be laughing at us; it won't do.'

'You and I are here to stop it,' said Liang Qichao. 'You and I together must do our best to prevent it. If we succeed, we will not expect to be given any rank or title in recompense; we will just go back to our research. If we fail, then we can expect to die; we will not flee to the foreign concessions in Shanghai, and we will not flee abroad!'

So it was that Cai E left Liang Qichao's house and travelled to Japan in disguise. From there he travelled on to Yunnan, where he had influence, and where he worked to stir up opposition to Yuan Shikai's plans to make himself emperor. Two weeks later Liang Qichao took the opportunity to slip away to Shanghai, from whence he travelled to Guangxi and Guangdong, where he encouraged people to support Yunnan.

Despite enormous difficulties and against the odds, the republic was saved. However, those who stirred up the revolt against Yuan Shikai paid a heavy price. The 'Hongxian Emperor' Yuan Shikai died of shame and indignation in June at the age of fifty-eight. Cai E died from overwork five months later in a Japanese hospital; he was only thirty-five.

⣿⣿⣿⣿

While Liang Qichao and his former student Cai E were joining up to oppose Yuan Shikai, Liang Qichao's former teacher Kang Youwei was also getting involved. At the time of the rebellion in Yunnan, Kang Youwei wrote secretly to Cai E, telling him that he should attempt to retake Sichuan. Kang also sold off some of his property to provide funding for the revolt. Liang Qichao was pleased that his teacher was participating in their movement, but he was shocked when he discovered that Kang Youwei's ultimate goal in wanting to overthrow Yuan Shikai was to restore the Qing. After Cai E's death, as the teacher of Cai's teacher, Kang Youwei wrote a funeral ode for him. It read:

Without your personal participation in the Yunnan Uprising,
The world today would have become the prey of Yuan Shikai;
Thinking of you, I am now afraid of hearing the sound of war drums.

'Hearing the sound of drums and thinking of one's general.' This was exactly what was in Kang Youwei's heart. The only problem was, he did not have a first-rate general, he had only himself. Despite this, he did not give up hope; he was still busy planning China's future.

Five years previously, China, which had been an empire for thousands of years, had suddenly ceased to have an emperor. 'Republic' was suddenly the word on everyone's lips. Sun Yat-sen was elected provisional president in Nanjing, and began negotiations with the authorities in Beijing. He demanded that the Qing Emperor abdicate; the Xuantong Emperor was made to abdicate. In Beijing, military and administrative power was in the hands of Yuan Shikai.

After secret talks, it was agreed that Sun Yat-sen would give up the presidency, with Yuan Shikai becoming provisional president in Beijing. For the rule of a country China's size to be decided in this way between a revolutionary and a former Qing official was totally unacceptable. While a China ruled by Sun Yat-sen might not have been such a bad thing, for it to be handed over to Yuan Shikai in this way was ludicrous.

On the surface, China made considerable progress following the change from empire to republic. The queues that had been worn for three hundred years were cut off; the lunar calendar that had been in use for thousands of years was replaced by the Western calendar; a five-colour national flag was devised, based on the five-colour official flag of the Qing Dynasty; people were no longer referred to as 'Lord' or 'Master', and were instead called 'Commissioner' or 'Mister'. The old official titles were replaced by new ones.

However, most of these changes were superficial ones. The government was opposed to foot-binding, and yet foot-binding continued to be practised. The government was opposed to opium-smoking, and yet opium continued to be smoked. The government was opposed to the use of torture, and yet people continued to be tortured. The government was opposed to slavery, and yet people continued to be bought and sold. In nominal terms, the republic was already miles away from the empire, and yet it remained too close to the reality of the empire. In many respects, it was still the empire under another guise!

There was one area in which the republic was unquestionably far removed from the empire; that was in terms of the centripetal force binding the country together. For thousands of years the centralizing power of the imperial state had bound the empire together, creating the foundation for a stable national polity. However, now the republic had been established and the emperor had fallen. Those people who held the reins of power had progressed to the point where they no longer wanted someone else to serve as emperor, but not to the point where they did not want to be emperor themselves. The president of the Republic of China, Yuan Shikai, was one of those who wished to become emperor.

Kang Youwei had foreseen this danger long before. During the period when the new was replacing the old, he called loudly for the old to be restored. However, with everyone calling for revolution no one cared to, or dared to, support him. He was now living in Japan, in his early fifties, but already on the scrap heap. His thoughts were gloomy ones. Before the age of fifty, the conservatives had called him a reformer; after the age of fifty, the reformers called him a conservative. They had begun to do so some time ago. The revolution of 1911 occurred when he was in his early fifties; the day the Republic of China was established should have been the day on which he sprang into action. In the days when he had been the reformer, others had supported him.

Now, when others were spouting anti-Manchu sentiments, he wished to protect the Emperor; when others were making revolution, he was a 'counter-revolutionary'; when others were seeking to establish a republic, he was seeking a constitutional monarchy. He seemed to be completely out of step with the times. Other people were interested only in the Kang Youwei of the past, and not the Kang Youwei of the present.

Nevertheless, Kang Youwei refused to give way to despair. As no one else was willing to print his articles, in the year in which the Republic of China was established he started the magazine *Refuse to Endure It*. The entire contents of this magazine, published monthly, were written by Kang Youwei himself; each issue contained approximately seventy to eighty thousand Chinese characters.

Through his solitary efforts, he appealed loudly to others to wake up from their illusions. However, twenty years before, the person he had been trying to awaken was one emperor; now he was trying to awaken millions of people. The real difference was that while he had succeeded in awakening the Emperor, the Emperor had had the will, but not the ability, to save the nation. As for the general public, he could not manage to wake them up at all; they were like millions upon millions of sleepwalkers. In the end, the one with the desire but not the ability to create changes was Kang Youwei himself.

Did he let this stop him? No. He allied himself with others who had similar short-term aims, although different long-term goals, and set about restoring that which had been destroyed. As early as the time of the Wuhan Uprising, while he was in exile in Japan he had written to one of the revolutionary leaders, Huang Xing (this was the Huang Zhen who had sent some of his comrades north to try to save Tan Sitong, and who was also known as Huang Keqiang), warning him that China had been a monarchy for several thousand years, and that there would be trouble if it were to suddenly become a republic; he said that it would be better to imitate the example of Britain or Japan, establishing a constitutional monarchy that would preserve the nation's stability. He suggested that the ideal ruler for this 'paper monarchy' would be one of Confucius's descendants. But who would listen to such an impractical suggestion?

Five years after the Wuhan Uprising, Kang Youwei's prophecy that the revolution would lead to problems for China seemed to have come true. Kang determined to put things back the way they had been before. There was an excellent choice to be his puppet ruler—the deposed last emperor, Puyi. The main disadvantage in using Puyi was that he was a Manchu, but at the same time this was also the chief advantage. Manchus had been ruling China for two hundred and sixty-eight years; this made for great stability.

As the successor of the Guangxu Emperor, Puyi was given the title Xuantong—a title he held for less than three years before the establishment of the republic and his abdication. Puyi's princes and ministers found themselves the servants of someone who was no longer the ruler. Many of these men were still loyal to the Qing ruling house, and wished to restore it to power. However, they lacked the means to do so.

It so happened that Zhang Xun, the commander of the forces stationed in Anhui Province, was also a Qing loyalist. To demonstrate his loyalty to the dynasty, he had the thirty thousand men under his command retain the queue; they were known as the 'Queued Army'. On the anniversary of Yuan Shikai's death, the restoration of the Xuantong Emperor was proclaimed. Kang Youwei was involved in this farce; he was given the post of Vice Director. However, in only thirteen days the Queued Army had been defeated by troops brought up from the south by Duan Qirui. The Xuantong Emperor fled to the British Consulate and sought political asylum; Zhang Xuntao fled to the Dutch Consulate; Kang Youwei fled to the American Consulate.

The United States Minister gave Kang Youwei a cordial welcome. He was installed in the Mason House in the consulate grounds. He spent all of his time there reading or writing, waiting to see how things would turn out. His greatest regret regarding the effort to restore Henry Puyi to the throne was not that the effort had been a failure; he had half-expected that from the start. He had known that it would be no easy task, and he had no very high opinion of the capabilities of the former Qing officials who were behind the plot. He knew that there was a distinct possibility that everything would go wrong.

What he could not accept was the fact that his number one student, Liang Qichao, had 'betrayed' him. The real force behind the army which Duan Qirui had led north was Liang Qichao. In the telegram that he sent urging resistance to the movement to restore Puyi, Liang stated publicly, 'Those behind this plot are a group of corrupt soldiers and boastful scholars.' This was clearly a direct attack on his teacher, Kang Youwei. While in hiding in the American Consulate, Kang Youwei became deeply upset over Liang Qichao's decision to 'not give way to one's teacher when righteousness is at stake'.

He wrote the following poem:

> Like the mother-eating barn owl and the father-eating jing,
> Like the axe-wielding Xingtian stationed at the gate, as ferocious as a
>   tiger,
> Like the champion archer Fengmeng who shot his teacher Houyi,
> All of these have made me disheartened now that the Republic is falling
>   apart.

The poem is full of examples of betrayal and ingratitude. Below the poem, he added a further thirteen characters: 'The defeat of the imperial army was attributable to the actions of the brigand Liang Qichao!' One can see from this just how upset he was. The student he had been fondest of had abandoned him; his world had become so much more lonely.

However, he still had someone to talk to in his loneliness. That someone was the military attaché at the American Legation, a man named Stilwell, who spoke fluent Chinese. Stilwell often came to chat with Kang, and the two men hit it off quite well. On one occasion, Stilwell asked Kang Youwei about the movement to restore Henry Puyi:

'Some people say that the reason why you participated in this restoration movement was because you are enamoured with the trappings of power, and cannot bear to stay out of politics,' Stilwell said casually as they drank tea together.

'Do you really think me that much of a failure, that much of a reactionary? You are wrong.' Kang Youwei started to get excited. 'I have no illusions about monarchical rule. Throughout history, so-called "saintly rulers" have all been villains of one stripe or another, and so-called "virtuous officials" have merely been people who assisted these villains to tyrannize the people. These former Qing officials and Queued Army soldiers have no idea what politics is all about. The reason I joined the movement to restore Henry Puyi was to establish a "republic with a powerless monarch"; it wasn't because I wanted anything to do with their schemes. Don't misjudge me!'

'A republic with a powerless monarch? Was that what you sought during the Reform Movement of 1898?'

'No, at that time that was not my goal. At that time I hoped to turn the Guangxu Emperor into a new Peter the Great; I wanted him to have real power as an enlightened despot. After the Reform Movement, however, I began to think more in terms of a constitutional monarchy that would place limits on the ruler's power. After the revolution of 1911, since a Republic of China had already come into formal existence, I recommended that we adopt the British model of a "republic with a powerless monarch". My political views are progressive. To the casual observer, it may seem as though I am one of those who wish to restore the emperor.

In fact, the emperor I wish to restore is not the same as the one these former officials and the Queued Army wished to restore. I believe we should cherish the foundations that the Qing Dynasty has built up over the last two hundred and sixty-eight years; it is a force for stability, a centripetal force. The emperor can serve as a symbol of this stability and centripetal force. Look at Britain. There has always been a king, from the absolute monarchy of Henry to the situation today where George is a powerless monarch in what is effectively a republic. No matter how much may change, no matter how much the polity may be changed, they have always had the sense to retain a powerless monarch as a symbol of stability and centripetal force.'

'But if you keep preserving the monarchy, and eventually the monarch comes to be a monarch in name only, just an empty shell, then why go to all that trouble to keep it there? Why not just establish a republic and be done with it?'

'No. You mustn't forget, China has been ruled by an emperor for several thousand years; you have to respect this tradition, even if you respect it by manipulating it. I have spent sixteen years abroad— I have visited Britain eight times, France seven times, Switzerland five times, Portugal once; I spent six months in Mexico and three years in the United States. I have visited thirty-one countries, and travelled two hundred thousand miles. I can't claim to know everything, but I have been a careful observer, and my conclusions are based on solid fact, not on thin air. I genuinely believe that China should follow the example of Britain, and become a republic that retains its monarchy.

As to who should be the emperor, anyone will do as long as they can serve as a symbol of tradition. Whether it be Confucius' descendant the Yen Sheng Duke, or the deposed Manchu emperor, I don't mind either way. At the moment the Yen Sheng Duke is too young, so Xuantong would be a better choice. That is why I joined the movement to restore Puyi. I joined it because I hoped everyone would be working to establish a "republic with a powerless monarch". How was I to know the former Qing officials and Queued Army would be so foolish?

I recommended that the nation should be called the Empire of China, established as a republic with a powerless monarch, that a national assembly be convened, that the divisions between Manchu and Han Chinese be eliminated, that members of the imperial family be forbidden to participate in government, that the kowtow be abolished, and that the prohibition on addressing the emperor directly be abolished. They were unwilling to accept any of these democratic ideas; instead, they wanted to establish a "Great Qing Empire", with a "Great Qing Bank" and what have you. They wanted to restore the old regime, but they were too busy fighting for power amongst themselves. Could anyone seriously suggest that that was what I wanted?'

Stilwell nodded, obviously convinced by Kang Youwei's speech. He stood up, and once again toasted Kang Youwei with his teacup.

'You are a man of broad vision and upright character, Mr Kang. We Americans know this; that is why our Legation was willing to step in to protect you. Unfortunately, your own people don't understand you well enough. This is highly regrettable, and a major problem for China.'

Kang Youwei smiled coldly. 'Surely that is not a problem which is limited to China alone? Isn't it just the same in America? Didn't your founding father Thomas Payne leave America for France after he had brought your country into a new era? While he was in France he was thrown into prison for opposing the use of violence in the revolution. Although the United States President was able to arrange for his release and for him to return to the United States, he was more or less ignored by Americans for the rest of his life. It was not until a hundred years later that his real contribution was appreciated. So you see, you Americans treat your own founding fathers in just the same way!'

Stilwell laughed bitterly and said, 'Jesus said that a prophet is never without honour except in his own country. Nevertheless, the Chinese are a great people. Emotionally speaking, they have their own unique structural characteristics. It may be that one day they will come to appreciate you, Mr Kang; you may not have to wait one hundred years.

Consider your current situation. You have quite obviously committed treason, and yet you are able to escape the law. Although people criticize you for being behind the times, they do not harbour a grudge against you. The ability to take this kind of attitude is one of the greatest things about the Chinese people.

The Ambassador is currently holding private talks with the Chinese Government to get them to turn a blind eye while you go south; this is something you would never be able to do in another country! During the French Revolution Thomas Payne was put in prison just for trying to protect the deposed king; you, Mr Kang, tried to restore a deposed emperor, and yet they are willing to let it slide. The Chinese may not understand prophets, but they don't persecute them either.'

'Wait and see!' said Kang Youwei, interrupting him. 'I am old, and I may not live to see it, but you will see a drastic change take place in China. I think that I may be the last prophet in China, the last prophet to be abandoned by the masses, to be abandoned by the revolutionaries, to be abandoned by the politicians. This is because they believe I am behind the times, so they have cast me aside like a living fossil. But just you wait and see! In the future, there will be less and less of this kind of forbearance. The Republic! There are great troubles ahead. If the Qing Dynasty was the sunset, then the Republic will be the dark night after the sunset; there are great calamities ahead.'

Kang raised his head, and looked out of the window.

'In the last forty years, everything that I have predicted has come true; nobody who did not listen to my advice has failed to be defeated. This is the pain of being a prophet. Someone like me was able to foresee forty years ago what China would be like today, and to tell from what China is like today what it was like forty years ago, even though forty years from now I will be long dead. But this pair of old eyes will never die. Do you know the story of Wu Zixu? Before his death, he ordered that his skull be hung over the city gate, so that he could watch the demise of his country.'

'You shouldn't be so pessimistic, Mr Kang!' Stilwell stood up. 'Even if the Republic is the dark night, you, Mr Kang, are a bright moon illuminating it.'

'Is that so?' Kang Youwei smiled, and he also got to his feet. 'I must be on my way; Mutang asked me to write a few characters for him, so I had better go and wield my writing brush. Calligraphy can be very useful; it's the best way to escape from reality.'

'Everyone says that you are the finest calligrapher the Republic has produced. Your calligraphy alone should be enough to bring you immortal fame,' said Stilwell.

'Not just in the Republic, but the finest in China, the finest produced by the Qing Dynasty. But I don't want calligraphy to be my claim to fame in the Republic. At a time of crisis such as this, to achieve fame through one's calligraphy would be shameful. Having said that, perhaps selling samples of my calligraphy would be the best way to support myself for the rest of my life! Ha ha ha! In the Republic of China, my most insignificant talent has become my greatest asset! Mr Stilwell, here is one prophet who no longer has to live a painful existence, as long as he is willing to keep producing calligraphy!'

◇∘✦∘◇

Three days later, the United States Legation reached an agreement with the Chinese Government. Kang Youwei, who had been hiding in the American Consulate for six months, was to be taken by car to

Tianjin. Before leaving, Kang asked Stilwell to take care of some business for him. One scroll he had deliberately left unsealed. Stilwell unrolled it to have a look, and was startled to see five large characters in bold script:

When will the bright moon shine again?

Underneath, he had written in small characters: 'To Mutang'.

Surprised, Stilwell shook his head. After a while, he turned his head to look out of the window. 'Mr Kang arrived in autumn and left in winter,' he thought to himself. 'It was time for him to go; winter in Beijing would be too cold for him.'

CHAPTER FIFTEEN

Reunion at the Old Temple

Kang Youwei pays his last visit to Caishikou and to Fayuan Temple in 1926. At sixty-nine, he is feeling his age. At the execution ground he says his final farewell to his fallen comrades. At the temple, he encounters Pu Jing, who has also come to pay a visit. They have not seen each other since their first meeting at the temple some forty years previously. Pu Jing fills Kang Youwei in on the details of the death of Master She, the former abbot. The two discuss their political theories. Pu Jing himself has become a revolutionary, a communist. Kang, although seen by Pu Jing and others of the newer group of revolutionaries as a relic, still sees himself as a prophet, as someone who can see clearly how the world will evolve.

Pu Jing analyses what went wrong with Kang's attempts at reform, particularly regarding his obstinate and long-lived adversary, the Empress Dowager. Pu Jing also notes that Kang did not take into account a peculiarity of Chinese politics—the power of the group. Pu Jing faults Kang for failing to wrestle with the massive group of power-holders at the time, while only appealing to one person—the Emperor. Pu Jing concludes that the group itself must be changed in order to succeed, hence his involvement in the Communist Revolution. Pu Jing participated in the revolution of 1911, establishing the republic, and now in middle age is involved in a second revolution.

Kang Youwei expresses fear for the outcome of Pu Jing's Communist Revolution. His fear is that it will involve excessive bloodshed and a long, hard, recovery period. Pu Jing finally does acknowledge, however, the importance of Kang Youwei in blazing a trail for the reformers and revolutionaries who followed. They finally part company with great sadness.

Nine years passed.

The seventh lunar month came round again in Beijing. Once again, the Milky Way changed direction, and once again the weather grew colder.

The first day of the seventh lunar month is the first day of autumn, and the day that ushers in the 'Ghost Month'. The Ghost Month always brings a gloomy atmosphere. Every household has to make offerings to get on good terms with the spirits of the dead. The place that has the gloomiest relationship with the dead is Caishikou, which attracts attention for precisely that fact.

This year, the first day of autumn was a particularly gloomy day. The streets around Caishikou were unpaved, like most streets in Beijing. Although it was already 1926, fifteen years since the Qing Dynasty had been overthrown, Caishikou still looked just the same as it did during the Qing. On clear days, the loose soil on the street made the street seem like an incense burner as dust floated up in the air, darkening both the earth and the sky. On rainy days, it was like a vat of syrup; once you stuck your foot in it, it was hard to get it out again.

No matter what the condition of the road was, people still had to walk along it. They were walking it for the sake of their future. But for one old man it was different; he was walking it for the sake of the past.

In the past fifteen years, whenever he came to Beijing, he would come by himself to Caishikou and look at the dust floating above the street. He would look at the old Xiheniantang drug store, lost in thought. The soil on which he was walking was the soil on which he was supposed to have been executed. The spot in front of the Xiheniantang Drugstore was where the official supervising the execution would have sat at his long desk, ticking off the names of the condemned in red ink. And yet, by chance, he had escaped death, escaped the catastrophe.

Except for the old building of the drugstore and his own pair of old eyes, everyone who had witnessed that scene had turned to dust. The Empress Dowager had turned to dust; the official who supervised the executions had turned to dust; and the six martyrs had turned to dust. The whole business of conservative and reform parties, steps backward and steps forward, despair and hope, indolence and effort, all had turned to dust. All that was left was he, himself, now old, walking alone up to the T-junction, between death and life, between old hatreds and new sorrows, staring at the old drugstore and leaving the imprint of his life upon the earth.

On this visit to Beijing, this trip to Caishikou, he was already sixty-nine. China was in chaos once again. In the north, the leadership was constantly changing, while in the south, a new warlord was setting out to conquer the north. What was more, this time he was being openly assisted by the Soviet Union, which had provided rifles, artillery, money, and advisors. It looked as though the campaign might well be successful. It would clearly not be long before China found itself engulfed in another calamity or series of calamities.

The man himself felt that he did not have long to live. He was not popular, and was living in exile. He knew that he had to start making preparations for his end. On this trip to Beijing, he felt differently to how he had on previous trips. In the past, every time he had come here he had expected to be returning here in the future, but not this time. He felt as though his relationship with Beijing had come to an end. This time, he was not here on a temporary visit or out of nostalgia; he was here to say goodbye. Here at the Caishikou he was saying goodbye to the martyrs who had died here twenty-eight years before, and to himself, who should have been executed here twenty-eight years before, to his past self.

He left Caishikou, and walked out onto the main street outside Xuanwu Gate. He walked into Beibanjie Alley, going north to south. At the southern end of the alley, on the west side, was a low, squat building; this was the Liuyang Association, where Tan Sitong had lived for so many years. Thirty years ago, this had been where they planned reform. He, Tan, and the other martyrs had spent so many days and nights here drawing up the blueprints for a new China.

Thirty years had gone by so fast; the old building was still here, but its former resident was dead, the visitor was old, and there was nothing here now but spiders' webs and dust. The only person to be seen about the place was the old servant who acted as caretaker. After the stranger gave him a tip, he obligingly showed him around. The old servant told him a confused tale of how thirty years before, people of importance had lived and visited here. With great effort he recalled the names of the people who used to come here, including a 'Mr Kang'. He could never have guessed that that 'Mr Kang' was the man standing weeping next to him.

The inscribed board was still there, but the scrolls pasted on either side of the door were weathered and hard to decipher. However, he could still remember what had been written on them. Tan Sitong had originally written, 'Living from hand to mouth, but with the strength of character to defeat ten thousand.' Kang Youwei had felt that it sounded too grandiose, and suggested that Tan change it to something more self-effacing.

Thirty years had passed since then. Tan Sitong had died displaying the 'strength of character to defeat ten thousand', while he himself was left living as though in a dream. 'Goodbye to the misty past; goodbye to rebirth.' Their early years were sealed up here; preserved were the joys and sorrows of those who had sought to save the nation. It was as though the moment immediately before Tan Sitong's arrest had been sealed in amber: welcoming those sent to arrest him as though they were his guests. Humans were but brief passengers in life; only this old house still displayed something of its master, while the master himself had gone to his long sleep.

$$\sim\!\!\ggg\!\!\ast\!\!\lll\!\!\sim$$

Under the overcast sky, he turned into the southern entrance of Xizhuan Alley. He followed the mottled red wall, and walked into Fayuan Temple.

Forty years ago, on his first visit to Beijing, he had stayed in Mishi Alley just outside Xuanwu Gate, and had fallen in love with this old temple. Inside the temple, behind the Tianwang Hall there was the Daxiong Hall. Before the broad platform in front of the hall there was a flight of stone steps, on either side of which stood an imposing array of six stone steles. What he enjoyed most was standing in front of the steles, reading the inscriptions and admiring the stone turtles on which the steles rested. The steles took him back in time, allowing him to forget everything to do with the present. There were actually two kinds of past. One kind was one's own past; the other was the past of the ancients. Although one's own past was only a few decades long at most, it could bring you hurt, regret and misery because it was too personal, too close. At the Caishikou and at Tan Sitong's old residence, that pain had been too close, so much so that he could hardly bear it. The past of the ancients did not have this effect: it brought exquisite feelings from thinking back on the past; it brought a cold beauty; and it brought a sense of appropriateness that lifted one's spirits.

The emotions aroused by thinking back on the past were much stronger than those aroused by thinking about the present. Within the confluence of past and present, there was a misty sense of the vicissitudes of life, an overarching feeling that was not limited to the individual ego. If one tried to think about the present, one was always too late. They say that the man of intelligence ponders the past, the righteous man ponders the present. This does not mean that it is impossible to think about both, but if one ponders the past after pondering the present, it can help to lift one's spirits, and give one a broader perspective on the relationship between sorrow and joy. 'The finest jade bracelet and the flying swallow all turn to dust in the end.'

Precisely because everything progresses from the present to the past, and from the past to nothing, if one uses part of one's life to ponder the past, this should increase rather than reduce one's sense of fulfilment. Your own life may be shortened, but once you link it up with the ancients, it becomes drawn out, it becomes a part of the everlasting. Even when your body has turned to dust, you are part of the same dust as the ancients. You need no longer be so lonely, and neither do your dead friends need to be so lonely. You are a part of them, and they are a part of all men who have sought righteousness throughout history.

When that time comes, you will no longer feel sorrow and pain at their martyrdom, just as, standing in Fayuan Temple, you feel no sorrow or grief for the martyred Xie Fangde. You would not take Xie Fangde's enemies for your own enemies. The emotion you feel is only a kind of respect, a kind of clear, bright, pure, and unblemished respect. This elevated emotion broadens your vision, and enhances your sense of the passage of time. It will be as though you were able to see a thousand miles and converse with the men of the past; it opens up new vistas to you. The strange thing is that you can only achieve this state alone, standing in an old temple. As far as he was concerned, the only temple where he could achieve this was Fayuan Temple.

⟨∘─◆─∘⟩

'You have come to Fayuan Temple to look at the old steles again, Mr Kang.' The voice came from behind him. Kang Youwei turned round, and saw a middle-aged man smiling at him.

The man was of medium height. He had a part, but his hair was in rather a mess. He had a round face, and wore round spectacles with hawksbill frames. His eyes were small but lively; his nose was slightly crooked. He had a moustache above his thin lips. His chin was neatly shaven, so one could tell that his hair was a mess not because he was careless about his personal appearance, but rather owing to unconventionality. He wore an old, brown suit and polished leather shoes; he had the neat, clean air of a university professor.

Kang Youwei thrust out his hand to shake hands with the middle-aged man. Out of curiosity, he asked 'How do you know my name is Kang?'

'You are a famous person, Mr Kang; of course I know who you are.' The middle-aged man gave a friendly smile.

'Have we met before? Is that why you recognized me?' asked Kang. 'Just now you said that I had come here "again". Have you seen me here before?'

The middle-aged man laughed, with a mysterious air. He lowered his head, then raised it again. His lively eyes looked Kang Youwei up and down. He said slowly:

'Of course I recognized you; I have seen your photograph in the newspapers so many times. And we have met before, although it was a long time ago, and you probably don't remember it.'

'How long ago?'

'You won't believe it, but it was nearly forty years ago. Thirty-eight years ago to be precise.'

Kang Youwei's eyes widened in surprise. Filled with curiosity, he asked 'Really? You don't look to be any older than forty-five. If it was nearly forty years ago, then you must have been in your early teens. Where did we meet?'

'Here in Beijing.'

'In Beijing?'

'Right here in Beijing.' The middle-aged man pointed to the ground with a finger. 'Right here in Fayuan Temple, in front of these steles here.'

Kang Youwei was taken aback. He held the middle-aged man's hand, and scrutinized him carefully. 'You are?'

'I am—I was a novice under the former abbot of this temple, Master She.'

Kang Youwei was stunned. He stared at the other man. Suddenly, he stepped forward and embraced him. 'I remember you! I remember! You were the young novice who had fled from the famine in Henan and been abandoned outside the temple gate by your brother!'

The middle-aged man stopped being deliberately mysterious. He embraced Kang Youwei, and his eyes filled with tears. After a while, the two men clasped each other's waist, leaned back, and scrutinized one another. The middle-aged man shook his head in admiration. 'You really do have an incredible memory, Mr Kang. Fancy you remembering a young novice after nearly forty years!'

'It's not that my memory is that good; it's just that you made such a strong impression on me.'

Kang Youwei held the middle-aged man's two hands in his, and said 'I forget your name; it was?'

'Pu Jing. I was called Pu Jing.'

'That's it! Pu Jing!'

'Pu Jing was the name I was given after I became a monk. My real name is Li Shili.'

'Li Shili? You are Li Shili?' Once again, Kang Youwei was taken aback. He pointed to the middle-aged man's chest. 'The famous Peking University professor?'

Li Shili smiled and nodded. 'I am a professor, although not a very good one.'

'You are too modest,' said Kang. 'Everyone has heard of the great scholar who has put forward a new version of the theory of consciousness as the first cause. I have been wanting to meet you for a long time now. Fancy it being you, the young monk I met forty years ago! It really is an amazing coincidence that we should meet here again at the exact same spot where we first met forty years ago! Quite remarkable!'

'There is a line in the *Mozi*, "Scenes do not move". In the *Zhuangzi* it says, "The shadows of flying birds do not move". In an abstract sense, the shadows of the past remain in their original place; the form has gone but the shadow remains. For you and I to be here again in the flesh forty years later, we have provided proof of the old theory that shadows do not move.'

Kang Youwei patted Li Shili on the shoulder, and said, smiling, 'That's true enough. This really is an example of the shadow remaining behind! The sad thing is that I am old, and Master She is no longer with us. If Master She were still alive, he would be in his eighties, wouldn't he?'

'He would be exactly eighty years old. And it just so happens that today is his birthday!'

'What a coincidence! All these coincidences coming all at once! If today would have been Master She's birthday, then the temple must be holding some sort of ceremony for him.'

'They have set up a memorial hall, and all the monks have gone to pay their respects. I have been staying here for the last couple of days, partly to help out with the preparations, and partly to have the chance to think some things over for a few days. It must be fate that has brought you here to the temple at the same time as me.'

'It must be. I came here to Beijing from Qingdao to see old friends. The day before yesterday, the fifth of August, I was invited to eat with an old friend, the former Hanlin Academy scholar Yuan Lijun. We were reminiscing about the events of twenty-eight years ago, when I realized that the fifth of August was the day I fled into exile on a steamer. When the ship reached Shanghai, the British sent two warships to rescue Kang Youwei, but none of them knew what he looked like. It just so happened that Yuan Lijun was on the same ship, and he pointed me out to them; that was how my life was saved.

I hadn't seen Yuan Lijun for nearly thirty years. When we met again this time, the distinguished painter Pu Ru produced a painting of a British warship coming to rescue me right then and there. I wrote a few characters on it. Everyone said that we should celebrate seeing each other again for the first time in nearly thirty years; imagine meeting you again for the first time in nearly forty years the very next day! We should celebrate too. How about it? Once I have gone to the memorial hall to pay my respects to Master She, why don't we go and get something to eat?'

'I would be honoured. But they have prepared a vegetarian banquet here in the temple, so we could just eat here. It's nearly noon now; I'll go with you to the memorial hall.'

The memorial hall was in a very unlikely location—the sutra repository right at the back of the temple. The reason was that before his death Master She had said that he had not done enough reading during his lifetime, and that he would like to be in the company of books after his death. In order to fulfil his wish, the monks had placed his memorial tablet in the sutra repository. In front of the repository there was a hundred-year-old gingko tree; its branches spread out so that half of the courtyard was shaded by them. In front of the steps leading up to the repository was a pair of dwarf crab apple trees, which were over two hundred years old. Once when the famous poet Gong Dingan was tidying his effects he found a bag containing some dried petals from these two dwarf crab apples trees. He was moved to write the following poem:

> *Whether it is intentional or by destiny, you have remained in my memory,*
> *Like a dream, like smoke, it has been another decade.*
> *In the past ten years, the country has been wracked with uncertainty,*
> *Don't blame him; have sympathy for him, for his life, just like a fallen*
> *   flower, has ended in tragedy.*

Sixty years after the death of this great poet, Master She was laid to rest in the old temple. Twenty-six years after his death, his former disciple and Kang Youwei, with whom he had once shared a meal, came together to pay their respects to him.

———◦◦✦◦◦———

The refectory looked the same as it had all those years before. The rectangular, red lacquered table was still there, simple and clean. Xie Fangde's last poem still hung on the wall. It was impossible to guess its age merely by looking at the yellowed paper and black ink. Master She had said that it had been painted one hundred years previously by a monk at the temple; the fact that another forty years had passed since then would mean nothing to it. There were antiquities everywhere in this temple; what was a hundred and forty years? The passing of time has meaning only to living beings; once you have become an inanimate object, what is important is no longer how long you have been in existence, but whether you are still in existence at all.

The fact of the poem being hung up there symbolized its existence: the dwarf crab apple existed in a state of vitality; the sutras existed within the light of candles and the smoke of incense; the old steles existed amidst the wind and rain; and the two lotus-leaf shaped bluestone pillar bases, the oldest in the temple, existed within a timespan of one thousand years. None of the buildings of the original Minzhong Temple as it was first constructed had survived, with the exception of these two pillar bases, which prompted one to imagine what the original temple must have looked like. From their immense size and exquisite decoration, one could picture the original temple in all its glory.

Now Master She was no longer here in the flesh, but his spirit was still in the room. Throughout the meal, he was the subject of the conversation between his former disciple and Kang Youwei.

Kang Youwei asked: 'How did Master She die? I heard that he died during the Boxer Uprising, and that he died here in the temple, but I don't know any of the details. You must know more than I do.'

Li Shili nodded. He thought for a minute, and then started to speak:

'My master's death occurred under very strange circumstances. Even today, I am not sure about all the details, but I have been able to piece together a rough idea of what happened.

Thirty-eight years ago, when you met my master for the first time, he was forty-one years old. At that time he had already been a monk for eleven years; he became a monk at the age of thirty. He never spoke about his life before the age of thirty. Whenever I asked him about it, he became gloomy. All he would say was, "One day I will tell you." My master was generally very calm and composed, but whenever anyone asked about his past he would furrow his brow and refuse to say anything; he seemed to lose his usual composure.

Later on, I realized that something terrible must have happened to my master in his youth that had led him to renounce the world and become a monk. Whatever it was, it was something big, because whenever the subject of his past came up it would still make him ill at ease. That event was directly connected with his death. It was only after my master's death that I began to piece together the story. When I did, I was very moved.

Do you remember that day thirty-eight years ago when you ate with my master at this table? During the meal, my master gave all the egg to you and me to eat; he did not eat any himself. When you asked him why, he said that as a monk he was a complete vegetarian, so he did not eat eggs. I interrupted him and said that as I was a monk like him, I also should not eat eggs. My master said that I was still young and needed the protein, so I should eat them. He also said that I was too young to count as a real monk. I asked him when I would become a real monk, and he said that I wouldn't necessarily become one. I asked why, and he said that I wouldn't necessarily be staying in the temple forever.

I became nervous: I was worried that one day my master might tell me to leave. My master said that that was not it; it was just that he felt that a monk's purpose was to do good in this world, and that there were many ways to achieve that; living in a temple was not necessarily the only method or even the best method. At that time I was sixteen years old. Two years later, my master told me to leave the temple to go and undertake an important task, and so I left.

You must be wondering what the task was. It turned out that although my master was a descendant of the She family, he had always been an active youth who liked to associate with people in the underworld. After he became a monk, he used to tell people that he had always lived in Beijing, but that was not strictly true. In reality, when he was fifteen he left Beijing and went south to join the Taiping Rebellion. Because he had received some education, the Long-haired Rebels felt he could be of use to them, and he became one of Shi Dakai's aides. When Shi Dakai was forced to leave Nanjing because of internal disputes among the Taipings, my master went with him. By the time their army reached Sichuan, they were in desperate straits. Shi Dakai was captured, and my master made his way back to Beijing.'

'I would never have pictured Master She as being one of the Long-haired Rebels, or as being that close to Shi Dakai,' broke in Kang Youwei.

'It's even more incredible than that. Apparently he and Shi Dakai's only surviving daughter were in love with one another, but when they were attacked by the Qing troops he abandoned her to her death. As a result, Big Sword Wang Wu and the others looked down on him. Who would have thought that thirty years later, he would have sacrificed his life bravely to try to save Big Sword Wang Wu, allowing himself to be cut to pieces by the Boxers on the steps of Fayuan Temple? He endured humiliation and shame for thirty years, before finally demonstrating through action what a noble character he had.'

'Amazing!' said Kang Youwei, his voice full of admiration. 'What a shame that Master She is no longer with us, otherwise he would probably have followed the same route as you have taken.'

'Do you think so?' Li Shili said, sounding doubtful. 'I think that if my master had followed any road, it would be more likely to have been yours, Mr Kang. After all, you both belong to the same generation.'

'Do you and I belong to different generations, then?'

'I have to say that we do. Your generation has been bound up in the past; I have been able to adjust better to the new era. For example, I have taken part in a revolution; in the revolution of 1911, I took part in the Wuchang Uprising. But after the revolution, I realized that things were still not right in China, that the revolution had not gone far enough. Only a further revolution could save China. That new revolution is the Communist Revolution.

You, Mr Kang, are a friend, and I need keep no secrets from you, but please do not tell anyone else. I have been involved in revolutionary activity as a communist for five years now. Although I was already forty-nine, really too old to be a revolutionary, Li Dazhao said that as I had been in the revolution of 1911, to have me participating in the new revolution too would be a good model for others, so I was allowed to join. I am currently doing underground work here in the north. On the surface I am a university professor, but in fact I am a revolutionary. Nevertheless, whether I am teaching or undertaking underground work, both are things I have to go outside myself to do; both of them deplete my resources. After a while, I have to come back to the temple here to refresh my spirit for a few hours.

Every time I come back to the temple, it is as though I am coming home, coming back to my own world, the world where I lived with my master. I like Fayuan Temple, I like the peaceful, serene life of the temple. I would like to spend the rest of my days here, and not have to go outside its walls again. But once I have spent a few hours here, I feel a force outside pulling me back out, and another force inside the temple pushing me out. That force derives from the Buddhist law, from the urgings of my master, and from my own conscience. It makes me reproach myself for wanting to escape here. Fayuan Temple is not a place of refuge; it is an outpost, a stronghold, an arsenal.

Although I would like to imitate Yang Renshan, I could never confine myself to this temple. If you do not actually participate in helping to save the world, then what good does it do to honour the Buddha's teachings? Sometimes, participation can be the best way of honouring them. If I do not go down into hell, who will? Ten sentences spoken outside the gates of hell are not worth one step inside those gates.

Twenty-eight years ago Tan Sitong became a model for us in this respect. The cause for which he died was the cause of reform, and yet the fact of his death showed us that reform could not work, and that we needed to follow the path of revolution.

Fifteen years ago I took part in the revolution of 1911; in the last five years I have been involved in the Communist Revolution. I was thirty-nine when I took part in the first revolution; now I am fifty-four and participating in the second. Although I am really too old to be a revolutionary, I cannot stop myself. It is as though if I do not work towards a revolution, there will be something left unfinished in my life. I want to make the second revolution succeed as quickly as possible. Once it has succeeded, I can come back to the temple and fulfil my desire to end my days here. However, given the current state of the nation, I think I am probably being too optimistic. Perhaps one day, if I can't come back here to die, I can at least come back here after I am dead, to pass on into the next world from here like Governor General Yuan. That would be enough for me.'

After listening to Li Shili's words, Kang Youwei appeared to be lost in thought. He stood up and walked over to the window, where he looked out at the lilacs blooming in the courtyard. After a while, he turned round, looked Li Shili in the eye, and said:

'It has been nearly thirty years since the Reform Movement of 1898. What I attempted thirty years ago was not the revolution that is so fashionable among you now, but reform. However, in the eyes of the Empress Dowager and the rest of them, there was not much difference between reform and revolution. Revolution is what was referred to then as rebellion. The punishment for rebellion was to have one's head cut off; despite the fact that we had not rebelled, they still wanted to cut our heads off.

After the deaths of Tan Sitong and the others, you all believed that the path of reform was a dead end, that only revolution would work. Now your first revolution hasn't achieved what you expected, so you want to have another.

Will a second revolution be any more successful? I am old, and I won't live to see it. What I do see is that reform failed, but so has revolution. But I still believe in reform, although the foundation for reform—the foundation built up by the Qing Dynasty over two hundred and sixty-eight years—has already been destroyed. I still doubt whether you can save the nation by tearing it apart. At least, the price one has to pay is a terrible one, and more than we can afford.

What is more, the people's beliefs and values were not built up overnight. It took the Qing Dynasty two hundred and sixty-eight years to achieve the little that it did; how can you expect to create paradise on earth in just a few years or a few dozen years? I don't believe that it will work. I am afraid that the only result will be millions of deaths, so many deaths that people will be heartsick. By then, it will be too late for regrets.'

'Mr Kang, I understand,' said Li Shili slowly. 'But what other choice do we have? The situation we are in now is like when I was running away from the famine as a boy; we grasp at anything that will ease the pangs of hunger and thirst. We can't say with certainty that what we believe in will prove to be feasible, but we do know that yesterday's methods will not work. We have to try.'

Kang Youwei interrupted him. 'How can one afford to "try"? Who will take responsibility?'

'We will. Just like you did twenty-eight years ago. Weren't you also "trying" back then?'

'We were "trying", but the only blood that was spilt because of our failure was our own. The common people did not suffer at all.

But the blood that you will be spilling will be the blood of the people. Is it worth it?'

'Spilling blood is unavoidable; as to whether or not it is worth it depends on which angle you view it from. Even if you only spilt your own blood, the blood of martyrs is still blood. Looking back on it now, it seems doubtful whether your attempt twenty-eight years ago was worthwhile. In reality, in terms of the fundamental ideas behind it, your attempt was all wrong. You thought that if you could convince the Emperor then you would be able to implement reform.

In reality though, even if the Guangxu Emperor had wanted to undertake reform, what would that have achieved? In such a huge organization, what good would it have done if just one person had come to their senses? Don't forget that the Qing government was a huge organization, an unfair organization that oppressed others to protect its own interests and benefit itself. Unless you can change the whole organization, having just one person come to their senses can only lead to tragedy.

If a single person leads an organization to do evil, that single person will receive protection, as long as the evil deeds benefit the organization, even though it may be unjust. If a single person leads an organization to do good, they will be opposed, if doing so has disadvantages for the organization, even though they have been acting justly. The Empress Dowager is an example of the former; the Guangxu Emperor is an example of the latter. Look at what happened. The Guangxu Emperor found that he could not dominate the organization—the organization just stood there and ignored him. He did not represent the organization, he just represented himself.

Do you want to be an idealist? Fine, but idealists are the lowest of people, not the highest. The highest people can only continue to compromise, to work for the self-interest of the organization. If they don't do this, then no matter how high up they are, they will eventually find that they are the only people up there, and that the ladder has been taken away so that they cannot get down.

You are an expert on political history, Mr Kang, and yet you have not noticed that the Chinese polity is remarkably lacking in flexibility. It is a peculiar characteristic of Chinese politics that the ruler is not just one individual but a group, whether it be a family, the eunuchs, the literati or the Manchus; it is never just one person. If any one person within the group has a revelation, if it is only that one person, then it is no use, even if that one person is the head of the group. It can only work if the whole group changes together, but how likely is that? Vested interests and conservatism will have destroyed that possibility long ago.

The reason why your method can't work is that you have ignored this group characteristic of Chinese politics, ignored the group characteristic of the Manchus. You made the same mistake as that other reformer Wang Anshi in thinking that as long as you can convince the emperor at the top, and as long as your ideas will benefit the people at the bottom, then reform can be made to work. That's too simple a view to take. You want to leap right over the intermediate layer between the emperor and the people and implement a peaceful transformation. It is very difficult to see how this could work. A peaceful transformation can't be brought about just because one or two people see the light. First you have to change the organization, but organizations aren't that easy to change. This is why the path of reform cannot work.

Wang Anshi managed to convince the emperor at the top, and his reforms were of benefit to the common people, but the officials at court opposed him. The minister Wen Yanbo said to the emperor, "You rule the empire in concert with the literati; you do not rule the empire in concert with the common people." This was a very perceptive remark. If you want to implement reform, you can't leap over the intermediate level to achieve it. Even if the highest officials support your reforms, if the lower-ranking officials oppose them, it won't work.

The best example is the Manchu Daoguang Emperor and his prohibition of opium. The Daoguang Emperor was not a bad emperor. He was frugal; when his robes got torn and tattered he insisted that they be repaired rather than thrown away; he prohibited operatic performances and all other kinds of ostentation. Everyone knew how much harm opium was causing to the Chinese people. When the Daoguang Emperor decided to ban the traffic of opium, the senior government officials did not raise any objections, but the lower-ranking government officials stood to benefit from the opium trade, and so there was no way it could be stamped out.

In the first year of the Daoguang Emperor's reign, less than six thousand cases of opium a year were being imported into China; just over ten years later that figure had grown seven-fold to more than forty thousand cases. Why? Because officials and merchants could benefit from the trade, so they protected each other. For all his prestige and authority, the Emperor could not make his will prevail.'

Kang Youwei was not convinced. 'But if one accepts your argument, then how does one explain Russia? In Peter the Great's time, wasn't Russia being led from above? And yet Russia still managed to achieve greatness.'

'That's true, but then Peter the Great and the Guangxu Emperor were the product of different circumstances. Although Peter the Great also came to the throne as a child, he had to endure only a seven-year regency by his half-sister who was fifteen years older than him, not like the Guangxu Emperor who had to deal with an aunt thirty-six years older than him who was in power for forty-seven years. There is no comparison.

In any case, it all boils down to the fact that China is the most difficult country in the world in which to implement reform; even the greatest hero cannot implement reform in China. If you are concerned about the fate of China, you cannot follow the path of reform: reform will not work. You need a revolution. The Chinese people have to be reminded that when a regime is rotten to the core, it's no good trying to reform it; if you wait for it to be reformed, it will be too late. It's like when somebody is forced into doing a good deed; nine times out of ten, by the time they get round to doing it, it is already too late. We do not believe that this regime can be reformed—we want revolution! Only revolution can solve every problem!'

'You make revolution sound like a cure-all,' said Kang Youwei, placidly. 'According to what you have said, everything that we did was worthless.'

'Not exactly. You were our forerunners. Without you, we would not exist. The failure of reform was actually the starting point for revolution. You showed that the path of reform could not work. Think how fortunate it was that the death of only a few people was able to show that a certain path would not work; think what a valuable function their deaths had! If in the end the deaths of millions prove that our path cannot work either, then we will have to answer to you, to the people, and to China!'

'At the same time,' Li Shili went on, pointing a finger at Kang Youwei, 'you yourself as an individual have special significance for us. Because of your perception and longevity, for nearly thirty years now—although we may have left you behind and viewed you as being behind the times—this doesn't alter the fact that you were once in advance of us. You are our forerunner: you are the first prophet of twentieth-century China. It is just unfortunate that over the last thirty years time has passed too quickly for you to keep up with, so that from being a forerunner you have become a rearguard. Nevertheless, you still constitute a mirror in which we can see ourselves clearly. Your misfortune was to have been born at the wrong time, to have been born too early; your good fortune is to have been so long-lived, so that you are still with us today. Having said that you were born too early, insofar as you encountered the Empress Dowager and her clique, you were born at just the right time.

When discussing the Empress Dowager and her organization, the mistake most people make is to consider only the evil deeds that they committed after she took power, without considering the things that they didn't do and stopped other people from doing. I feel that fundamentally speaking, theirs was a reactionary organization, impotent and incompetent. Nothing they did warrants praise. So from this angle there is not much to talk about.

But if you look at it from another point of view, in terms of what they couldn't do and also prevented other people from doing, and the harm that was caused to China as a result, there is much more to be said. You need to look at it in negative rather than positive terms. Rather than merely considering what actually happened, it doesn't hurt to think in hypothetical terms too. When you do look at it in these terms, surprisingly enough, the root of the problem lies not in what they did for China, but in what they prevented others from doing for China.

The other crime of the Empress Dowager and her organization was that, besides delaying the modernization of China, they created such a cesspit of corruption that those who were working for reform, both during and after their rule, had to spend a great deal of time and effort cleaning it up and sorting it out. That is to say, both the immediate effects and after-effects of their actions were very serious. To put it crudely, you had to wipe their bottoms for them. On the one hand, they blocked the road forward; at the same time, they defecated all over it.

Their real evil lay more in what they did not do than in what they did. They were like a huge stone; the stone itself did not move forward, and it also blocked the path, preventing others from moving forward. You served as a witness to this, and still do, even today. That was what was so hateful about their regime.

Your misfortune was that your whole life has been bound up with that dreadful old woman. It is as though each of you were a different side of the same coin; when she was facing up you were facing down; when she was enjoying good fortune you were out of luck. You have always been the exact opposite of her, and yet you were thrown together with her by fate so that it is hard to separate the two of you. If one accepts the validity of the metaphor of you two being two sides of the same coin, then that coin represented the times in which you lived. Without her side of the coin, the coin would have had no value in the marketplace. If it had no value in the marketplace, it might still have value to museums and antique shops as a curiosity, but that kind of value is precisely the value of museums and antique shops—historical value, not present, practical value.'

Kang Youwei was taken aback; he stared at Li Shili, and listened intently as the latter continued.

'You were thrown together by fate. That is to say, although you were the opposite of one another, you belonged to the same era, symbolized the same era, and constituted the same era. Today, without her side of the coin, your side represents only a breaking off, not a continuation, an ending, not a beginning.

Perhaps it was fate; perhaps you were fated to have this vicious opponent obstructing you. She was autocratic, venomous, skilful, and had a clique of supporters protecting her. She was lucky, she was long-lived and she was only twenty-three years older than you, so she was able to stand in your way for the best part of your life, so that your side of the coin was always face down. Your whole youth was spent in combat with her, but you could never get the better of her. When she finally died, you were already an old man, and others had taken your place. The times had passed you by, and you were left as the last prophet of the nineteenth century. In the twentieth century, you became a living fossil.

It was your fate to sacrifice yourself for the times you lived in, but you could not go beyond those times. Tan Sitong has long since passed away in both body and soul; your body is still alive, but your soul has long since joined Tan Sitong in death; it is just that you yourself don't know it.'

Kang Youwei was silent. He thought for a long time, and then asked: 'So what about Liang Qichao?'

'Liang Qichao is different from you. Liang Qichao cannot be called a prophet. He does not stand for his times, but he is close to being a prophet, so he has been able to keep updating himself. Before the age of sixteen he was a child prodigy, set on the path to becoming a conventional classical scholar.

After he met you, it was as though he awoke from a dream to become a reformer. After that he was one of those seeking to protect the Emperor; then he split with you and sought to protect the republic, becoming the most revolutionary of revolutionaries. He has constantly sought change—there is no way he could be a conservative. His slogan is, "I must be prepared to do battle with my present and past selves" and he has lived up to that. Particularly during the period when you and Zhang Xun were trying to restore Henry Pu Yi, he "refused to give way to his teacher when righteousness was at stake", publicly castigating you as a "self-important scholar". This kind of spirit rivals that of Confucius! He is fundamentally different from you. Strictly speaking, he did not belong to the same generation as the Empress Dowager, whereas you did. He evolved out of that time, whereas you remained stuck in it. It is not so much fate as bad luck.

It is like the legend of Yugong trying to move the mountain. In wanting to move the mountain, Yugong displayed a noble spirit. But at the same time, it was his bad luck that this mountain obstructed his plans. I said that you and the Empress Dowager belonged to the same generation; she was like the mountain that blocked Yugong's way, standing in your path throughout your life. Your whole youth was wasted in seeking a way forward; this was your great misfortune. If it had not been for her standing in the way, if it had not been for this great stone, you could have used your youth and your talents to build the nation; they would not have gone to waste.

Perhaps your misfortune was to have been involved with them from so early on, so that you wasted your whole youth on them. It is like a relay race. The person who starts the race will not finish it; you only get to run a quarter of the distance before you have to hand on the baton. You were not born to be the one who reaches the finishing line.

Fundamentally speaking, there was no way the Reform Movement of 1898 could have succeeded. On the other side, the Empress Dowager knew this, Rong Lu knew this, and Yuan Shikai knew this. On your side, Tan Sitong knew it and so did Big Sword Wang Wu. Only the Guangxu Emperor and you didn't know it. So in theory, failing a miracle, the reform movement was bound to fail. If it failed, you were sure to die. In the end, the Guangxu Emperor knew this; that was why he forced you to leave the capital.

'You survived against all the odds. The fact that you did not die was a miracle, but that doesn't mean you weren't supposed to die.

Your life should have ended at the same time as the Six Martyrs' lives ended. It was your fate to run the first leg in the relay race; the first leg, not the second, third, or fourth. So although in reality you did not die, emotionally speaking and theoretically speaking you are already dead. When people look at you, they are looking at history. You are no more real than your representation on stage. It said in the newspaper that when they were performing a play about the Reform Movement of 1898 down south, you went to see it, and that when you saw yourself on stage, you wept. In reality, it is the representation of you on stage that is the real you; the corporeal you has already become a living fossil.

Mr Kang, you are my friend. We first met here in this temple, and now nearly forty years later we are meeting here once again. We may never see each other again, so I have to say what is in my heart, to define your place in history. According to Buddhist teaching, "Emotion gives birth to seed; the seed grows through being planted in the ground. Without emotion there can be no seed; without essential nature there can be no growth." It is the fact of having met here forty years ago that has caused us to meet here again and to finally say an emotionless farewell. This is a very strange kind of relationship. Perhaps some day in the future you and I will both be buried here at Fayuan Temple, and we will meet again, "Meeting again after our bodies have rotted away," as Tan Sitong put it. What do you think?'

Kang Youwei's face bore a sad expression; he nodded. As he walked out of Fayuan Temple, Tan Sitong's poem was on his lips:

> What's wrong with the fluttering willow leaves?
> Drifting hither and thither without a fixed abode.
> Separated today after having dropped into the water;
> they may only meet someday when the leaves become ashes.

Over the course of his life, most of his comrades had already passed away. Who would have thought that he would meet Pu Jing today after nearly forty years! Pu Jing's words had brought home to him the fact that throughout his life he had been out of step with the times, either ahead of them or behind. Thirty years ago, he had been seen as a radical; now, thirty years on, he was viewed as a museum piece. In reality, in the innermost recesses of his heart, he did not accept that he was behind the times. He firmly believed that with the methods he had used to try to save the nation, 'The only blood that was spilt because of our failure was our own. The common people did not suffer at all.'

But what about Pu Jing and his comrades? Their actions would lead to millions of deaths, and after all those deaths who knew how long it would take China to recover from the chaos? Of course, he wouldn't live to see it, which was probably just as well. Thirty years ago, China's rulers had been doing their best to destroy the nation; now, thirty years on, a new generation of rulers were doing the same thing. And now a new generation of revolutionaries had arisen to try to save the nation, to destroy those who were harming China. A new generation of people like Pu Jing. They were sincere, enthusiastic, hard-working and willing to sacrifice themselves. All this was very admirable.

The problem was, who could guarantee that things would work out the way they planned? Designing the future was easy. As far as designing the future was concerned, he did not accept that the times had passed him by. He was still a prophet. His *Book of the Great Harmony*, running to over two hundred thousand words, was a detailed plan for the future of the world. While seeking reform in nineteenth-century China, he had been producing a blueprint for the whole world in the twenty-first century: this was being a prophet. A prophet has to look far ahead. At a time when others were concerned only about the Qing court, he had been concerned about China; when others were concerned only about China, he was concerned about the world.

He was always moving forwards, but other people were constantly pointing accusing fingers at him. He felt very much alone. People today only appreciated the Kang Youwei of the past; only the people of the future would be able to appreciate the Kang Youwei of today. By that time, he would be long gone. This was the fate of prophets. He had only the future, and yet was forced to live in the present. On this trip to Beijing, before visiting Caishikou, Tan Sitong's former residence and Fayuan Temple, he had gone first to the Guangdong cemetery.

He went to contemplate Yuan Chonghuan's tomb, to show his respects to a fellow Cantonese who had come to Beijing to try to save the nation. He climbed up to the top of Guangju Gate facing north, and looked around him. To the left of Guangju Gate was Yuan Chonghuan's tomb; to the right was the old battlefield where Yuan Chonghuan had fought to protect the emperor and the people of Beijing. Who would have thought that the man who had fought there to protect the Emperor and the people would have been ordered sliced to death by the Emperor eight months later? At the time of his execution, the people mistakenly believed that he was a traitor, and competed with one another to bite his flesh, even buying his flesh so that they could bite it.

The two places were separated only by a wall, and yet what a distance there was between them in terms of right and wrong. He remembered Master She's words: 'Governor General Yuan's misfortune was that he lived during the transitional period between the Ming and Qing dynasties. The Ming said that he was a servant of the Qing; the Qing said that he was a servant of the Ming. . . . When an individual is caught up in a struggle between two groups, it is bad enough having to sacrifice oneself for the group, let alone to sacrifice oneself and not have that sacrifice known.'

Now Kang Youwei was in the same situation. The Qing Dynasty said that he was too much of a radical, the Republic said that he was behind the times. He was caught between them, sacrificing himself for a group without that sacrifice being recognized. The Qing had called him a radical; he accepted that as true. But now the Republic said that he was behind the times. He could not accept this. In the past, when he had led the way forward, the others had been able to keep up with him. Now when he led the way forward again, the distance between him and the others was too great. They could not keep up with him, and yet they mistakenly thought that it was he who was behind the times. This was not a tragedy for him; it was a tragedy for those left behind.

Since the failure of the Reform Movement of 1898, he had spent sixteen years in exile, visited thirty-one different countries and travelled two hundred thousand miles; he was the only person in China who combined such breadth of learning with such extensive travel experience. He firmly believed his own vision was unmatched by anyone else. However, even as his vision became steadily broader, he himself was growing steadily older, and now no one listened to him. Pu Jing was his last audience—and his best—but Pu Jing was not one of his followers. In the end, as Kang Youwei walked in front of the setting sun, even his own shadow was not behind him.

Pu Jing walked with him to the gate. He stood in front of the entrance to Fayuan Temple and turned around to face the old temple. The bright red gate was half open, displaying the solemn dignity of both man and temple.

'Goodbye, Pu Jing. Goodbye, Fayuan Temple.' His voice was slightly hoarse, but he was still able to finish saying what he wanted to say: 'You have seen the dream of my youth, and you have seen that dream broken in middle age, but you may not see the dream of my old age. I am old, I am going, I will not return.'

He turned around and waved goodbye without looking back. Tears came to Pu Jing's eyes as he silently watched Kang Youwei walk away. 'Mr Kang is old, he walks so slowly.' He suddenly realized something. 'But on this last stretch of the road, he is still walking in front of me.'

EPILOGUE

Grave-robbing

On 28 February 1927, seven months after Kang Youwei left Fayuan Temple and twenty-three days after Liang Qichao held seventieth birthday celebrations for him, he died in Qingdao.

On 28 April 1927, twenty-one members of the Communist Party were executed by strangulation in Beijing on the orders of Zhang Zuolin; they included Li Dazhao and Li Shili. Li Shili's coffin was taken to Fayuan Temple. On the execution platform he lifted up his head to look at the sky, and said, with a smile on his face, 'Mr Kang, although no blood flows when someone is executed by strangulation, I am still paying with my blood.' No one who heard about these dying words knew which Mr Kang he referred to.

On 4 July 1928, Sun Dianying broke into the Empress Dowager's tomb outside Beijing to steal the contents. At first, Chiang Kai-shek made it be known that he was going to investigate the matter, but after his new bride Soong Meiling was presented with some of the loot and started wearing the jewels from the Empress Dowager's hat on her shoes, no more was heard about the investigation.

During the ten years of the Cultural Revolution, from 1966 to 1976, as part of the process of 'destroying the four olds', the Red Guards destroyed Kang Youwei's tomb in Shandong as well as Yuan Chonghuan's tomb and the stele above it. As there was a legend that the tomb contained a 'golden head', the local Red Guard commanders were not content with destroying the tomb. They dug down into the soil to find the body. However, after digging down to a depth of eighteen feet and finding nothing, they abandoned the attempt.

During the period 1987 to 1990 there was a spate of grave-robbing undertaken by ordinary people looking for treasure, during which Tan Sitong's tomb in Hunan was dug up.

All the activity above ground has turned to dust and become supine. All that is left is that silent old temple, standing forlornly in the cold winds of northern China. Fayuan Temple. So many tragedies have begun and ended because of you; so many complications, so much blood, so many wounds. Of course, the fact that only a few stone pillar bases remain from the original Minzhong Temple shows that you are not static and unchanging; you too are in a process of decline. You will not stand forever. But compared to the short span of human life, you are permanent, everlasting. You lead us into and out of history; it is from you, as the Source of Law, that we can see how the history of China is built on blood.

Fayuan Temple. It is not for us to say goodbye to you, but rather for you to say goodbye to us, as we follow one another into death, generation after generation, while you remain standing. We are happy to see that you remain standing, because generation after generation, the blood of the Chinese people has been deposited in you. Your life is our life.

Written in Taipei
31 December 1990